THE SILVER LADIES DO LUNCH

JUDY LEIGH

B
Boldwood

First published in Great Britain in 2023 by Boldwood Books Ltd.

Cover Design by Debbie Clement Design

Cover Photography: Shutterstock

A CIP catalogue record for this book is available from the British Library.

Paperback ISBN 978-1-80162-375-9

Large Print ISBN 978-1-80162-374-2

Harback ISBN 978-1-80162-373-5

Ebook ISBN 978-1-80162-377-3

Kindle ISBN 978-1-80162-376-6

Audio CD ISBN 978-1-80162-368-1

MP3 CD ISBN 978-1-80162-369-8

Digital audio download ISBN 978-1-80162-371-1

Boldwood Books Ltd
23 Bowerdean Street
London SW6 3TN
www.boldwoodbooks.com

For my brother Tony...

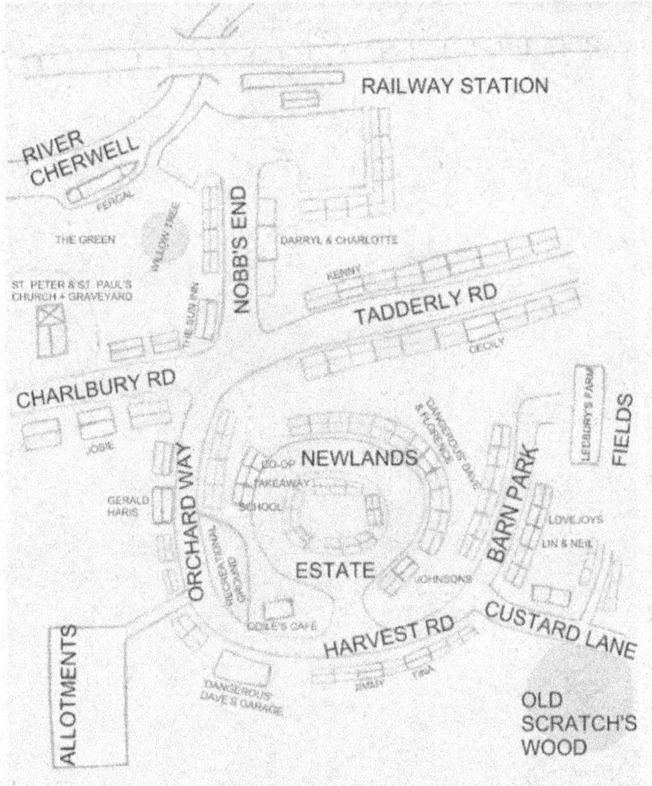

Middleton Ferris

Middleton Ferris, Oxfordshire, present day

1

'Who do you think our new teacher will be?' Josephine Potter fiddled nervously with her long plaits as she stood by the railings of the red brick primary school, beyond the separate entrances marked 'Girls' and 'Boys'. 'Not Terrible Thomas again?'

'He caned me on my hands last year...' Linda Norton cringed at the memory. 'He said my handwriting was like a spider. But my nib broke – the inkwell was full of soggy blotting paper and it splashed everywhere. It really hurt and I couldn't write at all for a whole day. I didn't dare tell Mum, though.'

It was 1959, the beginning of the autumn term. Josephine and Linda huddled in front of the painted wooden sign for Middleton Ferris County Primary School in Oxfordshire. They were wearing grey pinafore dresses, ankle socks, squeaky new shoes. As they linked arms, ten years old, best friends forever, they dreamed of wonderful things, although the dreams weren't fully formed yet.

'It's our last year – we can't have old Thomas again...' Lindy's small face was puckered. 'I hate his guts – he caned Sally Corbyn because she didn't know the seven times table, and she wears callipers.'

'He's horrible.' Josie shuddered. 'I always feel sick on Mondays. I hate

Sing-a-long-a-Monday with that posh woman on the radio with the warbling voice.'

'It's even worse when Terrible Thomas cracks the cane and shouts, "Sing, you buggers, or I'll make you sing."' Lindy sniffed, swishing her glossy ponytail. 'His face goes all red.'

Josie said, 'He's the worst teacher in the school. He's so bossy.'

'He made me dance with Jimmy Baker in country dancing. Jimmy Baker stinks.' Lindy pinched her nose to show how bad the smell was.

'Jimmy is a sweaty stink bomb,' Josie agreed. 'Old Thomas made me dance with George Ledbury and he smells just like the pigs on his dad's farm. Fergal Toomey says he sleeps with the pigs, but I don't believe him.'

'I wish I could dance with a nice boy when we do country dancing...' Lindy said dreamily.

'Who do you think's the handsomest boy in the class?' Josie asked, grasping her friend's hand.

'Neil Timms – he's gorgeous, he has come-to-bed eyes.' Lindy sighed, blushing. 'I don't know what come-to-bed eyes are, but his eyes are really nice... he has curly eyelashes...'

'It's certainly not Dickie Edwards.' A slim girl with long unruly hair joined them, her face bright with mischief. 'I knocked his front tooth out in the rec when he tried to bully our Tina. It hasn't improved his ugly face one bit.'

'I wish I was as brave as you, Minnie,' Josie said, linking her arm through Minnie Moore's.

'Or as clever.' Lindy linked the other arm. 'You'll go off to the grammar next year and leave us behind at the secondary modern.'

'My dad says I can't go.' Minnie spat on the ground and rubbed it into the tarmac with her plimsoll. 'He says it's a waste of money for a girl.' She shrugged. 'I don't care. I'll go anyway.'

'Even Terrible Thomas said you're exceptionally bright.' Josie said.

'I am. But I'm not singing "Shenandoah" again, whether old Thomas is our teacher or not.' Minnie frowned. 'He can cane me all he likes. And I'm going to tell him to stop caning Kenny Hooper and making him cry. It's not fair.'

'Ugh, Kenny...' Lindy pulled a face. 'He's weird.'

'He's not weird, he just sees things differently,' Minnie said, picking at the threads on her second-hand pinafore dress. 'One day, people will say he's a genius.' She sighed. 'I hope they have some new books on the library shelf. I read all the Famous Five books three times last year. Can't they get some Greek myths or some Shakespeare?'

An infants' teacher came out into the playground, a woman in a long skirt, her hair in a roll, to clang a hand bell loudly.

'We'd better go in,' Josie murmured. 'Then we'll find out who our teacher is...'

'I hope it's someone who can teach,' Minnie grumbled. 'Someone who won't keep making us bloody sing – or dance with silly boys. I tell everyone Fergal Toomey's my country dancing partner because he doesn't come to school half the time and I get to sit out and read.'

'I hope we get someone who can keep Dickie Edwards under control...' Lindy cringed at the thought. 'He scares me a bit, to be honest.'

'He doesn't scare me. We stick together.' Minnie pulled a face. 'That's how it's going to be. I don't care about old Thomas and Dickie Edwards and smelly Jimmy Baker. We'll make this the best year yet.'

The three friends walked through the door marked 'Girls'. They crossed the hall that always stank of stewed cabbage, sweet pink custard and sweaty plimsolls. It smelled different today, a sharp whiff of too much polish and disinfectant. They made their way towards the classroom, taking their seats one behind the other. Most children were already there. Minnie went to sit at the front. She twisted round and winked as Lindy and Josie took the desks behind. Kenny Hooper sat down with a thump, looking around nervously. Dickie Edwards flopped behind him and flicked Kenny's ears, causing him to yelp.

Then they heard the clack of heels, and a new teacher walked into the room. The class was quiet, studying the calm woman who stood before them. She wore a fitted blue dress with a swirling skirt and blue shoes with pointed toes. Her hair fell in blonde waves to her shoulders. Her fingernails and lips were painted red. She looked like a film star.

She smiled, and when she spoke, her voice was blanket soft. 'My name is Miss Hamilton. I'm your teacher for this year.'

Someone sighed; it could have been relief that she wasn't Mr Thomas or it could have been love.

Miss Hamilton glanced around the room. 'So, I thought we'd start off today by getting to know each other, and the best way to do that is to sing.'

Minnie groaned. Sally Corbyn visibly shuddered, heaving her callipered legs into a safer position. Miss Hamilton moved behind her desk and reached for a large case, taking out a shiny acoustic guitar. She strummed a chord once, twice, and turned to the class with a smile as Dickie Edwards made a hollow sound from his backside, a low farting noise that rippled against the chair. Jimmy Baker laughed loudly and Kenny Hooper waved a hand in front of his face as he yelled, 'Miss, he stinks – he did that on purpose.'

The class held their breath as one, watching the new teacher. She smiled again, placing the guitar carefully against her seat, and walked towards Dickie, skirt swishing, heels clacking. She leaned over the desk, her red-nailed fingers taking Dickie gently by the ear, and she whispered, 'Do you have a medical problem you'd like to tell me about, young man?'

Dickie's cheeks were burning. He stammered, 'N-no, Miss...'

'Then let's see if you can sing as well as you blow the trumpet, shall we?' Miss Hamilton held his earlobe for a moment longer, sashayed back to her seat and picked up the guitar.

Minnie Moore mouthed across the classroom to Josie and Lindy, 'Not bloody "Shenandoah"...'

Miss Hamilton was already strumming the chords to Buddy Holly's 'That'll Be the Day', and every member of the class sat up straight, then forty-four faces smiled as one and joined in with the teacher, whose strong voice carried to the back of the class. They sang 'Wake Up Little Susie' and 'Peggy Sue'; Miss Hamilton even let them clap their hands in time as they boomed 'Jailhouse Rock' as loud as they could. Georgie Ledbury, the farmer's son, waved an arm in the air. 'Can we sing some Chuck Berry songs, Miss? He's my favourite!'

They sang 'Maybelline' at the top of their voices. Kenny Hooper was louder than everyone. Then Miss Hamilton put her guitar down and smiled. 'Thank you, class. That was delightful.'

Josie gasped and Lindy turned round, wide-eyed. No one had called them delightful before; Mr Thomas never said thank you. Miss Hamilton scanned the room, her eyes falling on an empty desk. 'Who's missing?'

'Fergal Toomey, Miss,' Minnie piped up.

'His family are bargees,' Jimmy called out. 'They live on the barge down on the Cherwell. He'll have gone rabbiting with his dad.'

'They are Irish, Miss,' Dickie added in an attempt to endear himself with new information to the beautiful young teacher. 'He don't come to school much.'

Miss Hamilton faced the class, her eyes bright. 'I see. Right. So now we've warmed up, I'll take the register, then let's do half an hour of arithmetic. We'll get those times tables perfect, and then we'll learn about some of the most incredible countries in the world. After that, we'll all be ready for playtime, and we'll have earned our bottles of milk.'

The day passed in a swirl, and by three o'clock, every member of the class was in love with Miss Hamilton, even Dickie Edwards, who collected the exercise books and put them away. Then Miss Hamilton took out a copy of *The Wind in the Willows*, and said, 'Right, class, make yourselves as comfortable as possible please. It's story time.'

Dickie and Jimmy both laid shorn heads on their arms. Minnie closed her eyes blissfully. Kenny Hooper's crumpled face was suddenly calm. Josie and Lindy leaned against the wall next to the belting radiators that made the room smell warm, the toasting scent of washing powder on their jumpers. Miss Hamilton began to read a story about several animals, a Mole, a Rat, a stubborn, proud Toad, an elusive Badger, and the children dreamed of a land where animals could talk, where they were friends and had adventures.

Miss Hamilton read clearly, her voice comforting, and all around the classroom eyelids grew heavy, faces puckered with smiles as everyone drifted into a wonderful world of imagination and hope, where friendship was everything. The lesson they learned that day would bind them for life.

* * *

The year passed too quickly and, finally, the summer term came. Every pupil, even Fergal Toomey, arrived at school each day, eager to learn.

Minnie Moore passed the eleven plus and Miss Hamilton visited her home, telling her father that his child had an exceptional intellect and the grammar school was the right place for her. Mr Moore grudgingly relented, saying sullenly that his daughter would get ideas above her station, go off to do some highfalutin pointless job, marry a toff and never pay her father a penny back.

On the last day of term, Miss Hamilton accompanied them into the dining hall at lunch to share a feast she'd brought, sandwiches, cake, lemonade. She told them how important it was to give and receive.

'The ancient Greek playwright Euripides told us, "Friends show their love in times of trouble,"' Miss Hamilton said. 'So we share lunch as friends.'

She gave each pupil a notebook inscribed: *A good friend is like a four-leaf clover; hard to find and lucky to have.* Then she said, 'So, before we all go – and I wish you all so much happiness – I want each of you to tell me what you hope for most in the future. What do you want to do with your unique lives?'

Dickie shot his hand up. 'I want to drink beer, Miss.'

'I want to sing like Chuck Berry and have a big tractor like my dad's,' George said with a grin.

'Neil?'

'I want to fix cars, Miss – and I want to drive a brand-new car, like a Frog-Eyed Sprite...'

'That's nice. Fergal?' Miss Hamilton prompted.

'I'll live on our barge...' Fergal shrugged, gazing towards the open door.

'And I wish you happiness. Josephine?'

'I want to own a nice house in Middleton Ferris and travel and see the world.'

'I'm sure you will. Linda?'

'I want to live happily ever after – and be really good at cooking...'

'Lovely.' Miss Hamilton smiled. 'Minnie?

'I'll learn everything there is to know and live in a big house filled with books.'

Miss Hamilton nodded knowingly and Dickie groaned. Sally put up her hand. 'Miss, even though my legs won't go fast, I'm going to travel miles away on an aeroplane.'

'That's an excellent answer, Sally. And Kenny?' Miss Hamilton smiled sweetly. 'What do you hope for?'

Kenny thought for a moment, then he said, 'I want to stay here with you in your class, Miss. I ent bothered about no big school. I'm safe here. My gran says growing old is painful so I'm going to stay eleven forever.'

'How wise, Kenny.' Miss Hamilton's voice was filled with affection. 'If only we could stay as we are. But grow older we must, and we must all move forward with our lives. And on that note, I wish you happiness and friendship. You have been a wonderful class and I'll remember you all, even when I'm an old lady. So, don't forget, laugh together, share lunch together and take care of each other, whatever comes along. Now off you go, class – into the rest of your lives – and good luck.'

2

Josie Sanderson stretched out on the double bed in the cabin of the cruise ship, her eyes closed, thinking about her schooldays. It seemed such a long time ago. So many things had happened, some good, some not so good. As Kenny had said, growing older was definitely painful. Josie was seventy-four years old, and here she was, cruising around the Caribbean: she should be happy. As a child, she'd dreamed of travelling to such places. On board there were shows, dinners, games for single passengers, and now she was going on deck for a cocktail, wearing a swimsuit and sarong against the afternoon heat. As she gazed at her reflection in the mirror, she pulled back her shoulders and smiled, trying to look cheerful. The real problem, the painful bit, was that now she had no Harry to tell her how gorgeous she looked. He would have kissed her shoulder and said that she was lovely. He should be here with her now, sharing the sights and the sounds of the Caribbean islands, especially today. It wasn't the same anniversary celebration on her own.

They'd been talking about the cruise for years: she was determined to enjoy everything promised in the brochure. In the last five days, she'd experienced idyllic Barbados and the rhythms of Jamaica. She'd had cocktails, joined in competitions, karaoke and cookery, shows and gala dinners. Harry would have loved it – it had been his idea.

Josie would be back in Middleton Ferris before long – she was determined to make the most of the holiday. She pushed her sunglasses firmly on her nose, tugged on the floppy sunhat, locked the cabin and sauntered along a corridor. Her sarong swishing, she walked up a small flight of steps. The heat on deck hit her immediately. She paused to fan her face with her hand and bumped into Mr and Mrs Wiesner, a friendly American couple whom she'd met at dinner. Mrs Wiesner smiled warmly. 'Mrs Sanderson. Josie. How nice to see you again.'

Josie liked her married name; she loved sharing everything with Harry. Besides, she hadn't been Josephine Potter for fifty years. Any mention of Harry still gave her a glow of pleasure. 'Nice to see you both.'

'Arnie suggested that we head back to the cabin.' Nancy beamed. 'It's too warm on deck.'

Arnie gave a little cough. 'Nancy loves the sunshine but her skin burns.'

'I used to be able to sit outside all day when I was young but now I just turn the colour of a lobster.' Nancy waved a hand, dismissing the problem. 'Will we see you for dinner again tonight? There's a pianist and a band.'

'And we love to waltz.' Arnie beamed, hooking an arm through his wife's. 'We're going to the cabin for a siesta now, then we'll be raring to go again. It takes it out of you, all that heat and dancing until midnight.'

Nancy agreed. 'My Arnie still cuts a dashing figure on the dance floor.'

Josie peered through the gap between them; she could see the deckchairs, the white rails and beyond, the sea sparkling, almost blinding in the sunlight. She said, 'I'm going up on deck with a cocktail.'

Nancy clasped her hands. 'I recommend the margarita. It's just so refreshing.'

'Margarita it is then,' Josie agreed.

'Enjoy,' Arnie called as he propelled his wife forwards towards the steps. Josie watched them go. They were a sweet couple, still in love, making the most of their later years together. For a moment, she envied them. She found a cluster of loungers away from the others. She'd read a while and enjoy the sunshine and the whisper of the waves.

Josie arranged herself on a deckchair and reached into her bag for a book, a romance set in a cute animal rescue centre: she'd had a fondness for books about animals since her last year at primary school. She opened the page, stretching her legs. It was quiet; there was no one else on deck apart from a man wearing a Panama hat and a colourful shirt who was gazing into the sea. She'd noticed him yesterday and the day before at the singles' games; he'd looked awkward and hadn't joined in.

The sun on her face felt good. Even behind the shades, the glare of the rays filtered through. A voice from above murmured, 'Would you like to order a drink, madam?'

The waiter in dazzling white, a dicky bow at his throat, smiled. Josie wriggled upright. 'A margarita would be nice.'

'Coming up,' he replied easily and walked away. She read half a page and he was back, handing her a glass of pale liquid, a slice of lime perched on the side. She took a sip before smacking her lips. 'Thank you.'

The waiter hovered. 'Will there be anything else?'

Josie held up the glass. 'I might have another later on...'

The waiter inclined his head and moved away. Josie picked up her book again, finding the page, reading the first few lines.

Her eyes drifted to the man in the Panama hat and bright shirt, standing by the railings. He leaned over as if to inspect a fish in the sea. Then he slumped forward, lolling over the railings, flopping like a rag doll. He didn't move.

Josie wondered if he was ill. He didn't look well. She stood up slowly and marched over. 'Are you all right?'

The man didn't seem to hear. He stared into the sea. She laid a hand on his shoulder. 'Can I help?'

He raised his head to blink at her, his hat askew, and she was astonished to see that his face was covered in tears. 'No, I'm sorry, no...' He took a breath. 'I'm fine.'

He clearly wasn't fine; his whole body was trembling. Josie took in the jazzy shirt, the lilt of his voice, Welsh probably. 'Why don't you come and sit down with me for a moment, get your bearings?'

The man pushed himself upright, his knuckles white against the railings. 'I shouldn't have come on this cruise...'

'Well, you're here now.' Josie didn't know what to say but she was blurting the first thing that came into her head. 'Can I get you a margarita?

They are lovely.' The man stared at her for a moment and she said, 'I'm Josie.' She grasped his elbow, leading him to the loungers, guiding him to the seat next to hers.

'Thank you.' He eased himself down, adjusting pale shorts over paler legs. 'I'm so sorry...' He was still shaking. 'I'm David Ellis.' He took off his hat, wiping a hand over his damp forehead. 'Yes, please – I think I might join you in one of those. Margarita, is it?'

Josie nodded. The waiter was hovering and she ordered another cocktail. Then she put a gentle hand on his arm. 'Do you feel better?'

'Yes, no... oh, I don't know...' David muttered. 'I've been so silly, coming here by myself.'

Josie's eyes were full of sympathy. 'It's hard when you're on your own.'

'Are you alone?'

'I am.' Josie smiled bravely. 'I'm here for the glorious sunshine.'

David turned to her, bright blue eyes in a blank face. 'It's too hot for me. I'd be better off on a Baltic cruise...'

'Why did you choose the Caribbean?' Josie frowned behind her sunglasses.

'Research, I'd hoped,' David muttered. 'I'm writing a crime book set on the islands. I thought it would be good for me.'

'But it isn't...' Josie watched his face carefully to check if he was recovering, '...good for you?'

'Ah, a fortnight's a long time by yourself on a boat.' The waiter had arrived with the cocktail. David took it in trembling fingers and sipped eagerly. 'I thought it would help me get over my problems, but it's made them worse.'

Josie attempted to approach the conversation from a different angle. 'You're a writer?'

'I'm not published yet,' David admitted. 'I've been trying to write for years. You don't think seventy is too old to be an author, do you?'

'You can do anything if you set your mind to it.' Josie met his eyes.

'You seem a determined woman.' David nodded. 'I admire your pluck.'

'What makes you say that?' Josie asked.

'You're on a cruise by yourself... you're very sociable.'

She was momentarily taken aback. 'Sociable?'

David was alarmed. 'Oh, no, sorry, I didn't mean to be rude. No, what I mean is… I admire how you have the courage to enjoy your own company. I'm grieving, and I thought it would bring me out of myself being here, but it's made me feel worse.'

Josie touched his hand. 'Do you want to talk about it?'

'My partner died last year. He always wanted to go on a Caribbean cruise but we never got round to it so… I'm here by myself.'

Josie understood too well the effort it took to do things by herself nowadays. For a moment, she was lost in thought.

David brought the drink to his lips again and said, 'Alan and I were together for thirty-five years – we lived in Aberystwyth. We always said we'd take this cruise, but we kept putting it off.'

'I'm sorry.' Josie gave David her full attention. 'So, your ambition is to write a novel?'

'It is.' He smiled and Josie noticed how his eyes shone with tears. 'I'm going to make my hero a gay Welsh detective by the name of Alan. He's going to be a handsome, gallant man with spectacles and a sharp intellect, just like my own Alan was.' He gulped the margarita. 'Tell me about yourself, why you're here.' He grinned. 'We're all looking for something.'

'I'm as fine as I can be.' She noticed David inspecting her wedding ring. 'I promised myself this trip. Tomorrow we're doing…' she recalled the brochure, 'the calypso of Trinidad and the stunning scenery of St Lucia.' She held up her glass. 'I promised myself I'd celebrate.'

'Oh, I agree.' David clinked his glass against Josie's, although his face was sad. 'It's just tough by yourself.'

Josie thought he might cry again; she was tempted to stretch out a hand and squeeze his fingers. Instead, she said, 'Our loved ones would want us to enjoy the rest of our time for their sakes. I'm not a believer in giving up, David, although it would be so easy.'

'It would… I've been feeling like I don't want to try any more. I'm too… tired.'

'But we won't give up, will we?' Josie clutched the stem of her glass. 'We owe it to them. You write your book, make your hero the best you can based on your beloved Alan and have a glorious time on the cruise, for him, for yourself.'

David nodded. 'I will try. Thank you, Josie. You really are an inspiration.'

She shook her head. 'I'm doing my best. It hasn't always been easy.'

'Why?' David met her eyes. 'You've lost someone special too, have you?'

'I have.'

'I'm sorry.'

Josie felt the familiar mist of tears cloud her vision and she blinked hard. 'My husband, Harry. This is our anniversary cruise.' She drained her glass. 'He died a year ago. I'm here because he wanted it so much. I won't let him down. I'm celebrating for us both.'

'That's wonderful.' David sighed. 'It's a lovely thing to do.'

'I think so.' Josie composed her face. 'And I'm determined to have the best time. I'm thanking him in each moment for the precious years we had together.' She swallowed. 'This cruise is mine and Harry's. It's just that – there's only me here.'

'Oh, that's so true,' David agreed. 'And I'm here for Alan, the love of my life.' He was thoughtful, gazing at his almost empty glass, then he said, 'Josie – I don't suppose...?'

She adjusted her sunglasses. 'Suppose what?'

He took a breath. 'Would you have dinner at the same table as me tonight, and we can order a bottle of champagne, and you can tell me all about Harry and the best times you shared...'

Josie smiled. 'I don't see why not.'

'And you wouldn't mind if I told a few tales about my Alan and the larks we had over the years?'

'I'd love to hear about them,' Josie said.

'That way we can bring both of them here with us on the cruise.'

Josie smiled. 'I always keep Harry with me. He's in my thoughts every moment.'

'Alan loved to dance.' David's eyes gleamed. 'I wonder – do you like dancing?'

'I've had two left feet since country dancing at primary school.' Josie was suddenly enthusiastic. 'But Harry was a fabulous dancer. He could put a few moves together.'

'Then we'll dance tonight after dinner, for them,' David suggested.

'And for ourselves,' Josie added. 'Do you know, today is our fiftieth anniversary, mine and Harry's.'

David leaned forward. 'That's awesome. So, Josie, tonight...' He took a breath. 'You put on your glad rags, I'll put on my best bib and tucker and we'll celebrate with champagne.'

'We will.' Josie reached out and patted his arm. 'We'll have a real party.'

'Thanks so much, Josie, really. You've no idea how much I need a friend right now.' David's eyes shone. 'I've just spent the last hour staring into the deep water, wondering what my life was all about, thinking I'd never write that novel, not with Alan gone. But now...'

'Now...' Josie met his eyes. 'The sun is shining. Let's make the most of this. That's what they'd want for us, I know it.'

'You're totally right.' David looked around for the waiter, calling out, 'Excuse me – could I have two more margaritas, please? Life's too short to settle for just the one...'

3

Smoke billowed from the oven, filling the kitchen with the stench of burned cheese. The lasagne was charcoal black. Lin's reading glasses steamed up as she stared at the recipe book and she saw nothing but fog for a few moments. She placed the porcelain dish on top of the cooker and stared at her hands, small inside the oven gloves. 'Oh, dear.'

Her vision cleared a little: the burned topping had leaked over the side of the dish and stuck, brittle. She took a pace back, stared at the lasagne, and said it again. 'Oh, dear.' For a while, she didn't know what to do except to inhale the harsh smell of spoiled food. She put the oven gloves down next to the burned lasagne. 'It's ruined.'

She grabbed a handful of her hair and sniffed it. Burned cheese. Her clothes smelled of it too. Blue smoke hung in the light from the window. Lin took her glasses off and glanced at the wall clock. It was five to seven. Neil would be home at seven on the dot – he was Mr Reliable and she'd promised him a birthday meal to remember.

This year, Lin had been determined to cook something nice. Her exact words were, 'I'll make you a meal to remember...' Her friend Josie was on a cruise trip to the Caribbean – she was a widow now – and it reminded Lin that her husband was special; he deserved spoiling. 'I'll cook Italian and we'll have a romantic evening together,' she'd promised. 'You go and have a nice stroll in the woods, stretch your legs and I'll make you the genuine taste of Italy. That's what it says in the cookery book.'

The tiramisu was a disaster: she'd tried her best to follow the recipe but she added too much coffee. She couldn't offer it for dessert – it was like mud. A raspberry yogurt from the fridge would have to do. The starter was supposed to be antipasti, boiled eggs and slices of meat, but she forgot to buy sourdough bread for the bruschetta, so she'd buttered thick triangles of white sliced loaf and they didn't look right. The eggs were undercooked, all jellied whites and runny yolks, and she'd fried the prosciutto ham by mistake. It looked like toenail clippings.

The problem had always been the same: Lin couldn't cook. She had no talent for it. Long before the arthritis in her fingers kept her awake at night, she'd never been able to make a decent meal from scratch. It was a standing joke since she and Neil married, he'd either have to live off ready meals or learn to cook himself. He was a good cook now, but forty-nine years of marriage hadn't improved Lin's skills at all.

Neil was the best of husbands – he never complained. He told her every day that he loved her. Their marriage was perfect except for the fact that she was the worst cook in the world, and in the grand scale of things, he said, that wasn't important.

Lin left the smelly kitchen behind her and drifted to the lounge, peering through the window. Neil was parking the Sharan in the drive. He glanced towards the window, grinning, waving. Lin waved back. Her eyes fell upon the two wedding photos that had been on the window ledge for many years. In one photo, Lin wore a cream dress, her hair loose beneath a veil, and Neil was smiling in a smart suit as they cut a two-tiered cake. The second picture showed them both holding hands in front of their beloved sports car, a green Frog-Eyed Sprite, while colourful confetti floated in the air above them. Lin smiled. She'd married the most handsome boy in primary school forty-nine years ago, and they'd been happy ever since. He was her soulmate, her best friend.

Neil stood in the doorway, pulling off his jacket and cap. His hair was paler now, but he had the same easy smile, twinkling eyes, long curly lashes. He wrapped his arms around her. 'What's that gorgeous smell? Is it my dinner?'

Lin pecked his lips then pushed him away. 'You're teasing me – it's burned to a cinder.'

He shrugged. 'I like my food well done.'

'Charred!' Lin was horrified. 'I've ruined your birthday meal.'

Neil took her hand, tugging her towards the kitchen. 'It'll be all right – with ketchup.'

'It won't be...' Lin wailed. They had reached the kitchen and were both staring at the incinerated lasagne.

Neil joked, 'I've had worse.'

'I promised you a taste of Italy and all you have is a taste of something really disgusting. I'll have to throw it in the bin.'

'It doesn't matter. Life's been good to us.' Neil wrapped an arm around her shoulders. 'When we were first married, we were poor as church mice – we had burned toast and stew three times a week.'

'And my stew was like sludge...' Lin smiled, remembering. 'You'd just started working in the garage and we were so poor. I'll never forget our tenth anniversary – you sold the Frog-Eyed Sprite and bought me this... It was such a nice surprise.' She held out a finger, showing a small eternity ring. Lin sighed; her fingers had been tapered and elegant then. Now the arthritis had twisted them a little.

'I thought you'd guessed.' Neil brought her fingers to his lips. 'I've always been rubbish at keeping secrets.'

'You have an honest face.' Lin pecked his cheek. 'But what are we going to eat? It's your birthday and I've ruined dinner.'

'I have an idea...' His arms were around her. 'Let's go down The Sun, shall we? They'll have a carvery.'

'But it's *your* birthday...' Lin gasped.

'And I'll have an evening out with the most wonderful wife in the whole of Oxfordshire.'

'I so wish I could cook.'

Neil kissed her nose. 'Come on, Lindy, let's live a little. It's not every day that a man is seventy-four...'

Lin sighed again. 'Poor Harry was only in his early seventies. And now Josie's taken herself off on a Caribbean cruise for one – I don't know how she can do it.'

'She'll be back soon. She'll tell you all about the fun she had.'

'I worry about her,' Lin said. 'I worry about everything.'

He stopped her words with a kiss. 'Don't worry today – it's my birthday... Now go and put on something nice – and that perfume that makes me want to chase you around the sofa...' Neil winked, his face mischievous. 'Let's have a nice roast dinner and a sticky toffee pudding.'

'Well...' Lin was unsure.

'Lindy.' He stared into her eyes. 'I'm the luckiest man in the world. I remind myself of that every day. Go on, get yourself ready and I'll give Dickie Junior a ring and reserve the table near the window.'

Lin remembered the lasagne. 'What about the spoiled food?'

'There's a vixen with cubs in the field beyond the garden. I'm sure they'd all love a taste of Italy.' Neil winked. 'And what they can't eat, the blue tits will finish.'

'If the blackened cheese doesn't stick their beaks together...' Lin hesitated, then she grinned. 'A night out with my handsome husband would be great, though.'

'There's no accounting for taste.' Neil laughed. 'I always thought Jimmy Baker was the one the girls liked.'

'Poor Jimmy, he was so smelly and we treated him so badly. He's widowed now. And Sally Corbyn's moved to Australia. Kenny Hooper's always been on his own...' Lin was suddenly sad. 'There aren't many of us from Miss Hamilton's class left.'

Neil agreed. 'I like Kenny. He helped me out at the garage when I needed another pair of hands. He's genius with fixing clutches. And he's a good lad – Jimmy too.'

'Mmm...' Lin was still thinking: it seemed so long since she and Josie were at school; everyone was so much older now, yet time had passed so quickly and she felt no different. It didn't make sense.

Neil guessed her thoughts. 'Don't worry about us, Lindy – your cooking keeps us strong. We have the constitutions of oxen.' He winked again. 'Unless we die of starvation. Come on – let's get going.'

Lin was about to move, then she paused, threw her arms around Neil and kissed his lips.

He was momentarily taken aback. 'What was that for? Not that I'm complaining.'

'Because you're the best.' She gave a little shrug. 'And because it's your birthday and I'm so lucky…' A sob caught in her throat. She was far too emotional nowadays. She blamed it on the tablets she took for the arthritis.

Neil was grinning. 'The black dress is my favourite. The one with the neckline…' He squeezed her arm. 'Go on, get changed. I'll book a table for eight o'clock.'

Lin mouthed, 'Love you,' then she was on her way upstairs, to the shower. There was some spicy shower gel and a coconut shampoo. It might just get rid of the smell of burned lasagne.

***

Josie had chosen her favourite black dress. She sat across the table from David Ellis, who was dapper in a dinner jacket, and Arnie and Nancy Wiesner, clad in matching white. A band played swing music, although the dance floor was currently empty. Arnie poured from a bottle of champagne as the group talked and laughed.

Nancy leaned towards David. 'So, you guys only met just this afternoon?'

'We did, yes,' David replied. 'We shared cocktails on deck. Josie and I had a great time talking about… life and… things…' He glanced in Josie's direction, a little nervous about what to say.

Josie helped him out. 'David is a writer – he's researching a detective novel.'

'I have a title…' David proclaimed. 'What do you think of *Murder in Sweet St Lucia*?'

Arnie pulled a face. 'Is it a horror?'

'More of a mystery,' David replied.

'You might make the title about Alan, his role as a detective…' Josie suggested.

'Oh, I just love thrillers and crime novels.' Nancy fanned herself with her hand. 'As long as they aren't about real-life crime, which scares me witless. And I adore novels set in the Caribbean.'

'May I make a toast?' Josie raised her glass. 'It's a special occasion for me – my husband and I are celebrating our fiftieth wedding anniversary.'

'Oh, that's so nice...' Nancy was puzzled. 'But where is he?'

Josie's face was calm. 'He died not long ago. This was our dream trip. I wanted to come here for him.'

'Oh, Josie, that's so brave of you,' Nancy breathed.

'Then of course we must remember him,' Arnie added. He raised his glass. 'To Josie and...'

'Harry,' Josie said, her voice strong.

'Harry...' came a chorus of three voices.

Then Josie added, 'And to Alan, David's partner who is also sadly missed. May they live in our hearts forever.'

'Forever...' David wiped away a tear. The band launched into 'Ain't Misbehavin''. Several couples sauntered to the centre of the room and began to dance.

Then Josie stood up. 'We should dance too.' She held a hand out towards David.

'I'd love to.' David was on his feet, sweeping Josie into his arms. As they swirled across the dance floor, he whispered, 'Thanks for this evening, Josie. I think you might just have saved my life.'

Nancy was in Arnie's arms and they were gazing into each other's eyes as they swayed. Then Nancy leaned across to Josie and murmured, 'This is quite a workout.' Her voice was a conspiratorial whisper. 'Tonight, it's champagne and dancing with new friends until gone midnight. Let's show all the youngsters around here that we golden oldies still have what it takes, eh?'

4

Josie arrived at The Willows, in Middleton Ferris, well past one o'clock, falling into the welcome warmth of her own bed, the one she'd shared with Harry until not so long ago. The Caribbean cruise had been relaxing, but the journey home was exhausting. She closed her eyes: sleep wouldn't come easily. Images of the holiday flashed back like snapshots; the white sands and crystal seas of Jamaica, the green tapered mountains of St Lucia, the honey sunsets and the shared evenings with David and the Wiesners. She'd had a fabulous time, returning bronzed, with a phone camera full of memories. Josie rolled over in the familiar bed, feeling troubled. The holiday was over now: there was nothing left to cling to but the certainty that she was a widow for the rest of her days. At seventy-four, her life wasn't over. She'd told David as much as he'd whispered to her on the dance floor that his loneliness had been bone-deep and he'd thought of hurling himself in the ocean.

Josie understood loneliness. She couldn't allow it to define her life, but she had no intention of replacing Harry; she'd never love anyone else. Now she needed to find herself all over again, the newly single Josie Sanderson. But after a glorious marriage and years of shared love, the rest of her life was going to need some thought.

Josie woke after eleven o'clock to gaze into Harry's eyes. The photo smiled back at her from the bedside table and her heart was warmed by the familiar grin. 'Good morning, gorgeous.' She kissed her fingers and placed them tenderly on Harry's lips. Then she paused – someone was banging at the door downstairs. She struggled into a dressing gown and shuffled towards the stairs, bleary eyed and barefooted. The door opened to a blindingly bright April morning and Lin Timms was standing on the step with her arms out for a hug, clutching a packet of chocolate chip cookies. 'Welcome back.'

'Come in.' Josie tugged her friend inside, towards the kitchen. 'I'll put the kettle on...'

'You look fabulous...' They were both speaking at once.

'It was wonderful,' Josie said just as Lin asked, 'How was the cruise?'

They stopped, both laughing, and Josie said, 'How was Neil's birthday?'

'A total success – we ate out at The Sun. The sticky toffee pudding was to die for.' Lin pulled a face. 'I incinerated the lasagne. How on earth does Nigella do it, every meal's so sexy and delicious?' She shook her head. 'So – the cruise... Josie, tell me everything.'

Josie was pouring tea into cups. 'It was fantastic. The Caribbean is incredible.'

'The sunshine, the beaches – it must have been stunning...' Lin was imagining herself there. 'Weren't you lonely, Josie?'

'I met a fantastic American couple, Arnie and Nancy – I promised we'd stay in touch – and a lovely man called David from Wales.'

Lin caught her breath. 'You met a man?'

'He's a writer, my age, widowed, gay.' Josie picked up her cup. 'He was good company and he could dance.' Lin nodded, as if she understood, then Josie clapped her hands excitedly. 'I bought you something...' She placed a bag in front of her friend. 'The stuff in tissue paper is yours – the Angostura bitters are for Neil.'

Lin dived in, unwrapping a silver bracelet. 'Oh, I love it.' She tore the paper from a book and her face betrayed her terror. 'A recipe book... *Tastes of the Caribbean*?'

'We'll have some Caribbean nights in the summer... it'll be fun.'

'Not if I'm cooking, Josie.' Lin threw her arms around her friend. 'But thanks so much. Yes, we'll cook up a storm and dance in the garden. Oh, I can't wait to hear all about your holiday.'

Josie reached out a hand, patting Lin's. 'I adopted a turtle while I was out there. And I've brought enough rum back to last us ages. Not that Harry liked rum much...' She paused, closing her eyes.

Lin hesitated. 'Are you all right?'

'I'm fine.' Josie took a breath. 'More than fine. When are we next doing lunch with Minnie?'

'The Silver Ladies' lunch? I came round so that we could double check the dates. I think it's this Saturday, at Odile's café. Neil's going for a hike in Old Scratch's woods.'

'I love that you call us Silver Ladies,' Josie said. 'It makes me feel like we're a special group.'

'We're strong women of a certain age... there's a dignity to the name. I hate getting older... there's so much prejudice about ageing – and so many problems.' Lin looked at her fingers. They were stiff and sore this morning.

'I don't mind getting older – I just miss Harry.' Josie exhaled. 'Minnie couldn't care less about how old she is. If anyone says anything to her, she tears into them.'

'I remember her telling a kid off who called her a crone in the street. What did she say? "Crone means witchlike woman, so I'm going to curse you..." Then she shouted something in Latin that sounded like it had come from Harry Potter.'

'It will be nice to see Minnie again.' Josie cupped her hands around the mug of tea. 'I wonder what she's been up to?'

'Last time we did lunch, we had all the terrible weather - we went to the pub outside Charlbury. She almost started a fight.'

Josie smiled. 'The man in the bar was making racist comments at the football on the TV screen. Minnie was amazing.'

Lin put on an aristocratic voice. 'She said, "If you insist on using outdated language, young man, then I'd appreciate it if you'd take it outside in the rain. Such terminology belongs in the gutter..." Then she told the publican to throw him out.'

'Everyone in the bar was on her side, though.' Josie sighed. 'I wish I had Minnie's courage.'

'And her beautiful house in Oxford. She's done so well.'

'She has, Lin.' Josie pulled a face. 'Is she still dating the maths professor?'

'Didn't she dump him for the archaeologist last year?'

'I can't keep track of Minnie's love life. No one can.' Josie lifted her cup. 'Another cup?'

'Oh, yes, please.' Lin picked up the packet of cookies from the table. 'And let's make a start on these.'

* * *

An hour later, Lin was strolling home from Josie's house back to Barn Park. She wondered if she should stop in the Co-op and buy a pizza for Neil's tea, then she recalled he'd promised to cook. She passed Chandos, Gerald Harris's large bungalow not far from the recreation ground. He was outside pruning roses in his immaculate garden. He waved and called out, all strangled vowels, 'Good morning, Linda.'

'Morning, Gerald.' Lin pressed her lips together – she'd almost said, 'Morning, Bomber,' by mistake. His local nickname was predictably Bomber Harris – he'd been in the RAF and had retired to Middleton Ferris as a widower three years ago. There was a lot of gossip about him in the village. Locals often commented on his tendency to grumble about others. What did Jimmy Baker once say about him in The Sun Inn? 'He'd sell his own mother for a glass of Scotch – he's the sort of bloke you'd turn your back on and expect to be stabbed in it...'

Lin knew he was just lonely, but people in Middleton Ferris liked to gossip, especially Jimmy and Dickie when they got together in the pub. She continued her walk past the recreation ground. The sun was out and the swings and roundabouts gleamed. A lone woman was there with a child in a pushchair. The rec hadn't changed much in sixty years, although the rides had been replaced by safer, smarter ones. She'd spent so much time on a swing as a toddler in the early 1950s.

She recalled the old slide with the hump halfway down, an iron monster with the words *Kettering* forged in metal on the steps. She, Josie, Minnie and Tina had been playing on it one day when they'd been eight years old, sliding down at speed, pretending they were Alice in Wonderland disappearing down the rabbit hole. Lin had been thin then; she'd come down over the hump too fast, shot off the end and landed on her backside in a muddy puddle. She'd burst into tears and Dickie Edwards had been riding his bike with friends and he'd laughed at her, calling her Skinny Linny, telling everyone she'd pooed her pants. Josie had shouted at him to shut his cakehole and Minnie had waved her fist, causing him to ride off, the girls' shouts of derision ringing in his ears. Lin smiled. They were good days, a lifetime ago.

She arrived at Odile's café feeling the cold. The chilly March wind had filtered through her anorak and her arthritis had started to play up. She pushed the door open; the immediate warmth comforted her like a hug. Odile looked up from wiping tables and grinned. Dangerous Dave Dawson from the garage was hunched over a plate of sausage and chips. He called out, 'Hello, Lin – how's Neil?'

'Fine – he's upstairs on the laptop in the box room, staring at pictures of old cars.'

Dangerous Dave continued chewing the sausage. He had egg yolk around his mouth. 'Tell him to call in to the garage soon. I bet he misses the old place.'

'I think he does sometimes.' Lin sat down at a clean table. Dangerous Dave had been called Dangerous long before he'd taken over Neil Timms's Garage because he was always having accidents. She smiled: he'd probably been called Dangerous since childhood. 'We were glad to sell you the garage, though. It's our time now.'

'As long as Neil's enjoying himself,' Dangerous Dave said. 'Business is good.' He licked his lips. 'I'm on my lunch break...' He winked as if making an excuse for not being at work.

Then Odile was at Lin's shoulder, her round face smiling. 'Hello, Lin. Chilly day today, isn't it? What will you have?'

'A nice hot cuppa.' Lin rubbed her hands in anticipation.

'Coming up... Florence will be with you straight away.' Odile's rolling hips swayed towards the entrance to the kitchen, the doorway festooned with colourful plastic strips, and she disappeared into the back of the café.

Dangerous Dave winked. 'Florence loves working here. Best move she made. She wasn't cut out to be my assistant at the garage.' He shovelled fried bread into his mouth. 'It's too quiet in the village, though – no life for a twenty-two-year-old. I keep telling her she should move somewhere else, have a bit of life, but she loves being here with her old dad...'

On cue, Florence Dawson arrived with a tray. She moved easily, a slim girl with brown hair tied in a ponytail, a dimpled smile, a flowery dress beneath an apron. She placed a cup of tea in front of Dave. 'Here, Dad, get that down you, and then you ought to get back to work.'

'She bosses me, my princess.' Dangerous Dave said to Lin, his face shining with pride.

'Someone has to, Dad.' Florence was at Lin's side, placing milky tea and a cream horn in front of her. 'Nice hot cuppa for you, Lin.'

'Thanks, Florence.' Lin cupped her stiff hands around the mug and felt immediately comforted. 'But I didn't order a pastry...'

Florence winked, the same kind expression as her father. 'Odile says it's on the house – she likes to look after you.'

'Oh, tell her thanks.' Lin breathed in the steam from her tea and settled back in her seat.

Florence hovered by her side. 'When are you and Josie and Minnie coming here for lunch again?' She raised her eyebrows. 'You three are my favourite guests. You always seem to have so much fun.'

'The Silver Ladies are catching up next week.' Lin inspected the cream horn and wondered which end to bite to stop the cream shooting out.

'Is Josie back from the cruise yet?' Florence asked. She put a finger to her ear and touched the pretty silver hoop. She had lost the other – they'd been her favourite pair.

'Yes, she's just come back...' Lin turned the cream horn around. 'Fancy going to the Caribbean!'

'By herself, though. It was a shame about Harry...' Dangerous Dave's plate was almost clean and he was wiping it with a slice of bread. 'He was a nice fella, Harry. She must miss him.'

'Oh, she does,' Lin agreed, and felt a moment's sadness. She knew how hard it had been for Josie to go on the cruise. She turned the cream horn round again.

'And I love Minnie – she's such a character,' Florence added. 'She told me her real name is Araminta. Is that true?'

'Her mother called the girls Araminta and Albertina. She hoped it would give them the best start in life.' Lin put the cream horn on her plate and licked her fingers. 'They were a poor family and their father was incredibly strict.'

'I like Minnie. She always says exactly what she thinks.' Florence picked up her father's plate. 'Are you done, Dad?'

'How about a free cake for me, princess?' Dave quipped, almost knocking over his mug of tea. Florence put out a hand and steadied it, then she moved it away from his huge hands to a place of safety.

'I'll see what we have out back,' Florence said, then she was gone.

Lin sipped tea, thinking about Minnie as she bit into her cream horn. The cream shot out and landed on her knee. It would have made Minnie laugh. Most things made Minnie laugh. Lin closed her eyes dreamily; it would be nice to be together again. She'd text her as soon as she was home.

5

Dr Araminta Moore cycled along Botley Road in Oxford in a long grey army coat and red Doc Martens boots. A St Hilda's woollen scarf was wrapped tightly around her neck, a ruffle of blue and white, the crest edged in gold. It had been a gift from a student when she retired from teaching classics at the university eight years ago, replacing her original, threadbare one. She peered over half-moon glasses as she wove between traffic; strands from the unruly grey hair she had stuffed beneath a beret came loose, waving above her head in the wind. She pushed the pedals harder, grunting as she left the publishing house behind her, inhaling the smells from the fish market and the coffee roastery. She leaned forward urgently, passing ancient stone buildings, the towers and spires that gleamed in the springtime sunshine: she wanted to get to the bookshop as soon as possible. The bicycle whizzed past the station and the modern Saïd Business School with its tall green pyramid tower, and Minnie dodged between two cars and three young men on bicycles and turned into George Street.

She reached the glass-fronted bookshop, secured her bicycle, adjusted her beret and went inside. She was hungry; she'd forgotten to eat breakfast. Minnie decided she'd buy books and take them to The Slug and

Lettuce, have a halloumi and avocado wrap and half a pint of best bitter before cycling home.

Immediately, Minnie inhaled the smell of books. It was a fragrance she adored, almost too light for some people to notice, but Minnie had a trained nose – books had a distinctive smell all of their own. It took her back to her first year at university, fresh from school and completely overawed by the way people spoke and their confidence in their own right to learn. The first scent of dusty pages and old tomes or the inhalation of a crisp new book made her heart race, and she was ready to delve inside and fill her head with the knowledge stuffed between the pages.

She'd loved being at St Hilda's; all her free time in the first term was spent in the Sackler and Bodleian Libraries, and the Ashmolean Museum. She treasured the stillness, the way time seemed to hold its breath while she opened books and traced the words with her fingertips as if the pages could transfer their knowledge through touch. Besides, she preferred her own company in those early days. An unfriendly student had laughed at her accent: she'd been asked if she'd bought a certain book and she'd replied, 'I ent gunnu – it's too expensive.' Some other students had found it hilarious.

Minnie had worked so hard. Classics had not been easy at the beginning, but she loved the way her brain ached with the effort of it all. Once she had been accepted by more of the students in her classes, it was suddenly difficult to be accepted at home by her own family. During the first Christmas holiday, at the end of the Michaelmas term, her mother had asked her if she wanted jam on her toast and she'd spoken without thinking. 'I don't like jam, actually.' Her father had slapped her as she sat at the breakfast table, whack! Out of nowhere. Then he'd said, 'We ent having no nobby talk in this 'ouse.' Her lip had bled, her mother had turned away and Tina had cried. Minnie had stared her father down and jam was never mentioned again. But the experience had made her stronger.

Minnie rummaged through the women's contemporary literature section. Her fingers caressed several paperbacks – novels that Josie and Lin would read from cover to cover without wanting to put them down. Minnie often took books to Middleton Ferris on their Silver Ladies lunch dates, chosen specially. Josie and Lin were always pleased with her choices – books they'd never have heard of. Minnie glanced up at a high shelf – there was one she hadn't read yet, and she plucked it free and held it to her nose. Fresh, unread books, ahhh! She took her treasured pile like a captured secret to the cashier.

Once the books were bought and wrapped, Minnie slipped them into her backpack and made for the door. A drink in the pub was uppermost in her mind. She was almost outside when she collided with a broad-shouldered man with a white beard. She muttered 'Umm...' and stood back to let him through. Then she noticed the white hair, the craggy face, the green velvet jacket, and her heart sank. 'Felix...'

'Minnie... oh, how fortuitous.' Felix waved a hand as if he was Gandalf commanding attention. 'It's been too long. I've called you on the telephone countless times.'

'And I haven't answered,' Minnie said firmly. 'Now if you don't mind.'

Felix clearly minded a lot; he was refusing to budge and Minnie was stuck where she was, just inside the bookshop. He took a deep breath. 'Look, we need to talk.'

'We don't.'

'I have things I need to say to you.'

'I don't want to hear them,' Minnie said. 'Felix, if you would just move out of the way.'

His expression changed; he was distraught. 'But you can't leave me like this, not with so much unsaid.'

'I'm afraid I have no choice,' Minnie replied simply. It was best to be honest, not lead him on. She had never done that.

'But I have feelings for you.'

'A romance takes two people, Felix, and you are just one.'

'You felt for me once.'

'I went to the theatre with you once. That's not the same thing.' Minnie gave him a determined look. 'Now, may I pass?'

Felix reached out a hand and placed it on her arm. 'Let's talk it over in The Slug and Lettuce?'

'I have somewhere I need to be,' Minnie said. She didn't want to hurt him.

'I beg you, Minnie.' He tried once more. 'I'm a passionate man and a man of passion needs his woman. You are she, believe me.'

'Felix.' Minnie breathed out sharply. 'You and I met up how many times – three?' Her face was kind. 'We aren't compatible, you know that. It simply wouldn't work.'

'We'd make it work.' He grasped her hand and bent his knees. 'I'm begging you...'

'I never led you to believe there would be any romance.' Minnie felt his lips against her hand, a wet slobbering kiss, and she tugged it away. Several young people had arrived at the bookshop and were queueing to get in.

An impatient voice muttered, 'Would you excuse me, please?'

Minnie saw her opportunity. She pushed past Felix and the small group of students who were waiting to come in, rushing to her bicycle, unlocking it, shoving her backpack in the little basket, perching on the saddle. Her foot found the pedal and Felix was beside her again, grasping the handlebars. 'Just give me one chance, Minnie. Love between two such as we must be watered like a precious flower...'

'I don't think so,' Minnie began, launching herself and the bicycle forwards. She stood hard on the pedals and made for the road, hearing Felix's sharp breath behind her, panting. He was in hot pursuit.

'Minnie, Minnie...'

She could hear him running. She called over her shoulder. 'I'm sorry, Felix.'

'One... more... chance...'

Then she was away, cycling down High Street towards Magdalen College. She glanced back to where he was running, his face red as he seemed to recede into the distance. She passed the ancient buildings of Magdalen, cycling on towards St Hilda's, and she felt something in her heart cry out: the stone walls, the big square windows and the high gables, the spires and the tall tower, it was all as familiar as her own skin. Over the years, she had become a part of the fabric, the tradition: she'd loved strolling round the beautiful gardens, a book in her hand. The cloisters, the chapel and medieval bell tower had been beloved companions. She'd had a boyfriend or two from Magdalen, conveniently just down the road from St Hilda's – women were not allowed to be students there in those days, but she'd visited the grounds many times. Oxford had held her in its safe hands, quenched her thirst for knowledge and offered her even more. She'd spent years researching; she'd joined in with the choral singing; she'd gazed at roaming deer in the park; she had fallen in love countless times sitting on the banks of the Thames. Oxford had moulded her into the person she was now, a respected authority on classics who had lectured for thirty years at St Hilda's, whose life was framed by the dreaming spires, whose knowledge unfolded like the pages of books. She was no longer skinny Minnie Moore, she was a confident adult, maturing and improving with each changing season.

Felix was far behind her now. Minnie had always had this effect on men; they fell in love with her easily. Poor Felix was a friend of a friend she'd accompanied to the theatre, to a party. She hadn't intended to have a relationship with him, let alone break his heart. But she knew the reason, it was always the same: the more she distanced herself, the more men pursued her. There was no space for a significant other in her life. She preferred the company of a good book. It fulfilled her thirst for knowledge and it never interrupted her concentration.

Minnie pushed her feet on the pedals; the Doc Martens boots felt heavy now. She wanted to put them up on a comfortable bar stool and drink half a pint of best. The Slug and Lettuce was in the other direction, and she'd promised herself lunch. Minnie never broke promises that she made to herself. She'd turn around and head for the pub, sit amongst the young students, listen to the chatter, order a wrap and half a pint and start reading the new novel.

She'd grab a bite to eat and text her friends from the pub. It would be April soon; a time of daffodils and swallows, sunshine and long afternoons. She'd take the train to Middleton Ferris next week and meet the gang for lunch. They'd laugh and remember the best old times. It was just what she needed.

* * *

Florence washed her hands, shrugged a light jacket over her floral dress and called out a cheery goodbye. Odile rushed over, pressing a brown paper bag into her hand. Her cheeks puffed out in a smile. 'This is for you to take home, Florence – just some burgers, some bread, a bit of ginger cake for your dad.'

'Thanks, Odile.' Florence was tempted to hug her but Odile was gone; she hugged you when she wanted. Florence hugged the bag of food instead. 'I'll see you tomorrow.'

'Bright and early,' Odile called back, then the door chimed behind her and Florence was on her way home. Odile was kind; she'd given the food because her mother had left seven years ago and she felt sorry for Dangerous Dave, working all day in the garage, and Florence, tired from being on her feet all day. Odile would always say, 'What did your father eat for his dinner last night?' and 'How are you both managing nowadays?' Florence knew what she really meant was, 'How are you both doing, now you've been abandoned by your-mother-the-hussy who left you for the man who came round to fix the boiler?'

Florence hadn't heard from her mother for well over a year when she'd had a birthday card, a cheque for Christmas – no one gave cheques any more. The letter had come from Northampton, so that's presumably where her mother was now. Florence was too thoughtful to ask her father about it; he rarely mentioned her, keeping a jolly smile on his face, so Florence knew his heart was broken.

But that wasn't what was troubling her right now. As she went home past the primary school, past the Co-op, she glanced towards the playing fields where some kids were kicking a ball; someone was walking a dog. She increased her pace: it was past five and the wind was chilly. There was a rumbling engine behind her and Florence looked to see if she knew the driver. It was Bobby Ledbury, the farmer's grandson, on his motorbike, and she waved a hand, but he didn't wave back. Perhaps he hadn't seen her.

As she walked through the estate of 1960s houses, Florence considered her plans for the evening ahead: she could wander down to the rec in case there was anyone there she recognised. Her best friend from up the road, Malia Johnson, was home from Warwick uni. Florence was desperate to see her, to explain what was troubling her – a problem shared was a problem halved. Malia would hug her and understand. But Malia's brother would be home and Florence wasn't sure she wanted to see Adam Johnson. But she needed to talk to someone, and urgently.

There was Natalie Ledbury from up at the farm, Bobby's sister. Florence could give her a ring, but she wasn't sure it was a good idea: Natalie was with Brandon, her fiancé from Tadderly, most evenings. She and Florence had always been close, but wasn't that the way of it sometimes? A boyfriend came on the scene and that was the end of the girl-bond. Florence thought she'd probably sit in her room and message her friends instead. Or she'd watch TV with her dad.

She was constantly nervous. The problem wasn't going away. She ought to confide in her dad; he'd be supportive, but after her mother leaving, she wasn't sure how much more bad news he could take. No, she'd get home, cook the burgers, and they'd sit across the table and eat and smile and talk about their day. She'd say nothing and the problem would be as bad as ever.

The thought made Florence feel sick.

6

Josie had always loved Sunday mornings, the way the day stretched out like a sleepy cat with nothing to do but laze. She walked down the path of her detached house, past the apple trees, recalling how much Harry had adored apple pie made from their Bramleys. At the gate, she gazed towards the village green, the weeping willow and the church, St Peter and St Paul's, where Harry was buried. Later she'd take flowers down to the graveyard and stroll towards the river Cherwell where she and Harry used to sit on a grassy bank in the evenings waving to the Toomey family on their barge, watching the occasional train shuffle past and the world go by. They'd hold hands and Harry would whistle a silly tune – what was it? 'Don't Worry, Be Happy'. Josie used to tell him off good humouredly. 'Oh, no, not that old song again!' she'd say.

What she'd give to hear that whistle now.

Josie walked briskly along Orchard Way. The sun gleamed on the pavements and she examined her feelings, asking herself how she felt at this precise moment. She had grown used to being numb. She was in that place where the yo-yo was neither up nor down. Besides, she was on her way to Lin's for a late morning coffee and being with Lin always cheered her up. Thank goodness for friends.

'Bomber' Harris, Gerald, was in the front garden of Chandos wearing a wide-brimmed hat, clipping roses. His garden was perfect; he did nothing all day but trim the lawn and prune the flowers. She suspected he was lonely too. He stood up straight as a rod when he saw her and called out, 'Good morning, Mrs Sanderson.'

Josie thought he was going to salute. She smiled. 'Hello, Gerald. Lovely day, isn't it?'

Gerald tipped his hat. 'It is. And how are you this fine morning?'

He took up a position, one leg bent, which meant he wanted a chat. Josie hated the question, 'How are you?' It had another meaning – it meant how are you now your husband has passed away? How are you coping with the loneliness? She put on her standard brave smile. 'I'm very well, thank you.'

'I was wondering...' Gerald moved closer to the neatly manicured hedge, '...if you'd like some daffodils? I have so many and I thought they'd cheer you up... in a vase of water...'

Josie extended her smile; he meant well. 'Thank you,' she said. 'That would be lovely.'

She had plenty of daffodils in her own garden – Harry could grow anything, flowers, vegetables – but Gerald was being kind.

'I'll have some cut and waiting for you. What time will you be passing?'

'In a couple of hours – I'm going to Barn Park for coffee.'

'Ah, good. I'll have a nice bunch ready. And...' Gerald clearly wanted to keep her talking. 'How is Mrs Timms?' He knew perfectly well how Lin was; he'd seen her a couple of days ago.

'She's fine, thanks.'

'And her husband? I used to like taking the BMW to him for a service when he had the garage. I'm not so keen on Dave Dawson. I find he's a bit ham-fisted.'

Josie shrugged. 'I think Neil's enjoying retirement.'

'Well...' Gerald changed his weight from one foot to another, getting comfortable. 'I must say, you're looking rather well. Have you been away?'

'I've been on a cruise. The Caribbean.' Josie wondered if he'd forgotten. She'd mentioned it to him before she'd left.

'Ah, the Caribbean,' Gerald repeated, as if he knew it well. He frowned for a moment. 'I don't think I'd like it there. All that heat...'

'I really loved it,' Josie smiled. Harry would have loved it too.

'I'm not sure I'd want to go on a cruise by myself.' Gerald took off his hat to scratch his scalp.

'I had a great time, Gerald. Anyway, I'm on my way to Lin's now. I'll see you later.' Josie made a polite excuse. She didn't want to be late. 'I'll look forward to the daffodils.'

'Anything I can do to be of service, Mrs Sanderson,' Gerald replied with a little bow.

She felt him watching her walk away and Josie wondered why he was so formal. It was easy to use her Christian name, they were almost neighbours. Perhaps he'd had a strict childhood – she remembered something about him having been brought up by a military father. She walked on past the recreation ground where some children were kicking a football. Dangerous Dave's garage, and Odile's café, were closed.

There was a rush of light air and something whizzed past her. Josie almost fell off the kerb. She heard a faint humming of wheels as a vehicle tried to pass her in an unswerving line. The purple mobility scooter and its occupant, a woman who could easily have been a hundred years old wearing a huge faux-fur coat brushed Josie's shoulder, almost knocking her into the road. Josie gaped as the vehicle and its driver shuddered down the road like an oversized furry insect. She was pleased that the old lady was out for a Sunday morning constitutional, but she wondered who the rider was: she hadn't seen her in the village before.

Once Josie arrived at Lin's, she'd forgotten about the flying bumblebee on the scooter. Neil stood in the kitchen wearing red overalls, holding out a plate containing a lemon drizzle cake that smelled heavenly.

'I made this earlier – I knew you were coming round, Josie.'

Lin hugged her husband proudly. 'Neil makes gorgeous cakes. I'll put the kettle on.'

'Not for me, love.' Neil tugged a cap on his head. 'I'm just out the back, putting spuds in the garden. I thought some new potatoes would be nice in a few months' time.' He kissed her cheek and disappeared through the back door.

'He's a treasure.' Josie's eyes shone.

'He is...' Lin busied herself with the kettle and water from the tap. 'I feel really awful, though...'

Josie sat down at the table. 'Why?'

'We were talking over breakfast and Neil asked if I'd like to go on a nice boat trip somewhere and I said it was too much of an expense. He wants to do something special for our fiftieth anniversary in October, especially since my seventieth birthday bash was such a flop.'

'Why was it a flop?' Josie asked. 'We had a great time at The Sun, me and you and Harry and Neil.'

Lin shook her head sadly. 'I know, but Debbie couldn't come – she was too busy with the kids, she said, and Neil felt that she should have made time for my birthday lunch. It's odd, not seeing much of her and the grandchildren... Debbie's almost a stranger now.'

'That's tough,' Josie agreed, accepting the mug of coffee. 'When did you last see her?'

'Almost a year ago. I offered to go to Peterborough last month, but she had something on. She sends the odd text, and when we do chat on the phone, it's often cut short because she's so busy.' Lin shook her head. 'Oh, I don't know.'

'She's missing out,' Josie observed, then she leaned across the table and patted Lin's arm. 'It's such a shame.' She sighed. 'Now Harry's gone, I often wonder if it would've been a comfort to have a son or daughter.'

'Comfort's not guaranteed...' Lin shook her head. 'Debbie was my world when she was little, but I don't think she has time for me now. If I... if I lost Neil, I don't think I'd see much of her.'

'I'm sure she's there for you. You're a great mum. You did everything for Debbie,' Josie conceded.

Lin was surprised to feel tears stinging her eyes. She sniffed. 'I'm sorry, Josie, I shouldn't feel sorry for myself... It's these tablets – they make me all weepy...'

Josie was up from her seat, wrapping her arms around her friend. 'Lin – we've been best friends since we were kids. We share everything, the good and the bad.'

'That's true. Since primary school...' Lin took a deep breath, her eyes wet.

'That seems so long ago.'

'It does. They were happy times, though.'

'We are still best friends – these are happy times too,' Josie soothed. She sat down again and reached for the mug of coffee. 'We have to make these days count. Right – so – when are we meeting Minnie for lunch?'

'Next Saturday at Odile's.'

'I love our Silver Ladies' lunches.'

'I'm looking forward to it.' Lin cupped her hands around her mug. It eased the ache in her fingers. 'You know, Josie, I get so tearful nowadays but I shouldn't. I have Neil and we have the best life. He loves me... and I have you and Minnie...' She picked up a knife and hacked two hunks of cake, easing them onto plates. 'But I often worry about losing Neil. It scares me. I shouldn't say it but now you're all on your own, the thought's always in my mind. I'll be frank, I don't know how you do it.'

Josie smiled. She knew there was no malice in Lin's easy honesty; she recognised the concern shining in her friend's eyes – there was nothing there but love.

'It certainly is tough,' Josie admitted. 'But life goes on.' She accepted a giant slice of cake. 'I make the best of things. It's what Harry would have wanted and it's the least I can do after fifty wonderful years.'

Lin put a hand to her face; it was covered with tears. 'Oh, what's the matter with me? You're such an inspiration. I'm sure I wouldn't be half as brave as you are if...'

'You're made of strong stuff, Lin.' Josie bit into the cake. 'You and Neil have many more years of happiness. And we have each other – and Minnie.' She was thoughtful for a moment. 'I wonder what that mad girl is up to right now? She's full of surprises, that one.'

'I expect she's still in bed, eating croissants with some academic hunk...' Lin smiled through new tears.

'Or cycling through the streets on her way to a library to seduce the librarian?' Josie suggested.

'Or down the pub drinking Scotch, smoking rollups and chatting to students about the Greeks and the Romans...' Lin grinned.

'In Latin... and Greek.' Josie countered. She lifted her mug. 'To our friendship, Lin. Me, you and Minnie. May it be everlasting.'

'To friendship.' Lin almost spilled coffee as she clanged her mug against Josie's. 'You're right. I have you and Minnie and Neil – I don't realise how lucky I am.' She thought about her words again and took a deep breath. 'Let's live a bit, shall we? How about another slice of my delicious husband's delicious lemon drizzle cake?'

'You're on,' Josie agreed. 'I wish Minnie was here now. She'd love this cake.'

* * *

Minnie was sitting in the secluded back garden of her four-bedroomed bay-fronted Victorian mid-terrace in Newton Road, wearing cut-off shorts and a skimpy vest, sipping the last of the jasmine tea in a china cup and eating Victoria sponge cake. The house was far too big for one person, but she'd bought it forty years ago as a young lecturer at St Hilda's with the intention of filling it with friends, parties, soirées and good times. When she wasn't having fun, it was her place of solitude, to read, to think, to be alone. She loved the house; it was a short cycle ride from all the colleges and bookshops. Stuffed with books everywhere, in each room, and photos, crammed with knick-knacks, it probably needed a good dusting, and a good clear-out. But it was her home, her sanctuary, and she felt at peace within its brick walls.

She picked up her book, *SPQR: A History of Ancient Rome* by Mary Beard. It was one of her favourites. The sun bathed the small garden with light, illuminating the lawn. Daffodils bent lean stalks in the light breeze and Minnie stretched out her bare feet, wriggled her toes and started to read.

She heard a banging on the front door, and stiffened, listening. There was another sharp knock, a third. She wasn't expecting visitors.

Instinct took over and Minnie knew who was there. She collected her book and scuttled indoors, sidling into the lounge, falling on her stomach like a spy, wriggling towards the bay window. As she'd guessed, *he* was at the door, anxious, pacing around: Felix.

Minnie's sharp mind worked quickly. He must have asked one of their mutual friends where she lived; they'd have passed on Minnie's address without a thought. She crouched beneath the bay window, popping up her head to look at him as he strode up and down clutching a bunch of flowers like a sword. She ducked down again, considering how to answer his persistent knock.

Minnie edged to the front door, knelt up on the welcome mat and pushed open the letter box, calling out, 'Felix.'

'Minnie.' He knelt down, his mouth close to her ear, the door between them. 'I need to talk...'

'Felix – I won't open the door because I won't go out with you. But I will tell you that you're a fascinating man.'

'Does that mean...?'

'Fascinating for someone else, not for me. I think you should go away and do something for yourself, something fulfilling that you'll enjoy.'

'Enjoy?'

'Absolutely. Put yourself first.' Minnie shifted position to make herself more comfortable. 'Take up Tai Chi. Join a life drawing class. Learn conversational Japanese.'

'Japanese?'

'Feed your mind, Felix,' Minnie suggested. 'That's what I want you to do.'

Then she let the letter box go with a clack and crawled back to the kitchen. She felt better now, her conscience eased. She'd go back into the sunny garden with her book, and have another cup of tea by way of a reward, and a slice of sponge cake.

7

Josie and Lin took their tea and cake into the back garden. The space was full of neat flowers, pots of herbs, and the vegetable patch had been freshly rotovated. Neil was leaning on a spade, grinning as he surveyed the planted potatoes: he had done a good job.

Josie gazed beyond the garden to the sprawling farm fields edged with trees. George Ledbury's farmhouse was just visible dipping below the hill. The field beyond the Timmses' hedge was tilled red-brown earth, the beginnings of something green growing in tufts. Often George would put cattle or sheep in there to graze. Josie thought about her own neat garden. Not so long ago, Harry had made it beautiful, filled it with flowers and plants. Now it was too much for her to keep up; she paid the Toomey boys to keep it tidy, but it wasn't the same.

Neil shook soil from his hands and walked over. His lips brushed Lin's cheek. 'Do you mind if I pop down The Sun for a swift half with Dangerous Dave? I expect Jimmy and Kenny will be there. It would be nice to catch up with the lads...'

'You go and enjoy yourself,' Lin beamed. 'Josie and I have this delicious cake.'

Neil's cheeks crinkled in an affectionate smile. 'I thought we'd make a spag bol tonight.'

'Neil thinks if we cook together, I'll pick up some of his brilliant skills.' Lin turned to Josie. 'Last time, I burned the spaghetti – I was trying to put it in water and I left a lot of it sticking over the gas flame and it got scorched...'

'I like my food well done.' Neil hugged her. 'I'll just go grab a jacket and I'll be off, love.'

He wandered inside, and Lin turned to Josie. 'He deserves a pint with the boys.'

'Of course. The boys from primary school are still thick as thieves.' Josie inhaled the spring air. 'It's lovely out here.' Her phone pinged and she tugged it from her pocket. 'Oh, it's Minnie – she's confirming lunch next Saturday at Odile's.'

'I must have left my phone inside...' Lin checked her pockets. 'It'll be good to see her. I expect she'll pop in and see Tina first. Maybe she'll bring her along.'

'Tina's always busy with her allotment. I don't know how she manages that big piece of land by herself,' Josie observed, then she paused as music wafted from the upstairs bedroom in the house next door. It was an acoustic guitar, then a plaintive male voice began to sing.

'Jack's awake then...' Lin grinned. 'What's he got for us today?' She listened hard. 'It's a Leonard Cohen song. He must be feeling a bit moody...'

'He's very talented,' Josie observed. 'Lovely voice.'

'Oh, I hope Jack's not disturbing you.' A head popped over the fence, a dark-haired woman with coral lipstick. 'Hello, Josie. How are you?'

That question again. Josie smiled. 'Fine thanks, Janice. How are you and Geoff?'

'All fine, touch wood,' Janice Lovejoy said, patting the top of her head. 'I brought you some fresh eggs, Lin.' She handed a box across the fence. 'Susan is laying like there's no tomorrow. Jane is still chucking them out despite her age and Mrs B'Gurk, our newest addition, is a regular little egg factory, so there will be plenty more where they came from.'

Lin accepted the box gratefully. 'That's so kind.'

'Would you like a few eggs, Josie?' Janice offered. Josie heard the pity in her tone.

'Only if you have some to spare…'

'I'll go and get some directly. Oh, I could make meringues every night for Geoff and still have lots of eggs left over.' Janice waved an arm to show how many eggs she had. 'Do you make meringues for your Neil?' she asked Lin.

'All the time,' Lin lied, with a wink to Josie. Jack's voice drifted from his room again. This time he was singing 'Take Me Home, Country Roads'.

'He's cheered up a bit,' Lin noted.

'He still hasn't found any proper work.' Janice pushed her hands deep into her jacket pockets. 'He thinks he can make it as a musician. He goes busking in Tadderly or Charlbury most days in that old banger of his. Geoff keeps nagging him to get a nine-to-five job but he's only twenty-two. I think he should follow his dreams for a while. It's not as if he has any responsibilities.'

'Absolutely,' Josie agreed. 'He's still young.'

'That's what I keep telling Geoff.' Janice was about to go, then she remembered something. 'Oh, Lin – have you met Nadine yet?'

'Nadine?' Lin was puzzled, racking her brain. 'I don't think so…'

'George Ledbury has a new sow, a Hampshire pig. He's called her Nadine – after a Chuck Berry song. Penny Ledbury was telling me in the Co-op yesterday. Apparently, the pig wanders everywhere, into the village – she's even been inside the farmhouse. She sits in the kitchen in George's big armchair next to the Aga. George lets her do whatever she likes. He's besotted – goodness knows what will happen when it's time for the slaughterhouse. I told Penny he should have called the pig Houdini, not Nadine, but Penny said that Houdini is a man's name.'

'He was Harry Houdini.' Josie said and felt suddenly sad.

'Oh, Harry – yes, Josie, I'm so sorry for you – I heard about the cruise, all by yourself…' Janice began.

'Houdini was an escapologist… of course – just like the pig.' Lin changed the subject neatly.

Janice took up the conversation. 'Nadine, yes. Well, watch out for her. She's a little thief too. Don't be surprised if she doesn't eat all the lovely daffs you have growing here.' She gave a laugh and was gone, heading towards the hen house where several chickens clucked and scuttled behind wire netting.

Lin placed a hand on Josie's arm. 'Are you okay? Janice was a bit heavy with the sympathy.'

Josie nodded, grateful for her friend's sensitivity. She offered her empty mug. 'A refill would be nice.'

'More tea...' Lin grinned. 'It's the answer to everything.'

'It is.' Josie agreed. They both looked up as Jack Lovejoy began to sing again. This time it was R.E.M.'s 'Everybody Hurts'. Lin listened for a while.

'My goodness, that song is depressing.' She shrugged. 'Well, perhaps tea's not the answer to *absolutely* everything...'

* * *

'I think I'll be getting off home now.' Neil Timms finished his pint and placed the empty glass on the bar, nodding to Dickie Edwards Junior, the owner of The Sun Inn since his father retired.

Dickie Junior looked at the wall clock above the bar. 'It's not two yet, Neil. Have another one, eh?'

Dickie Edwards Senior, now large and bald, chimed in, 'Linda's got a tasty lunch ready for you, I suppose?' He barked a laugh; Lin's reputation as a terrible cook was widely known.

Neil shook his head good-naturedly. 'You leave my lovely Lindy alone.'

Dangerous Dave swigged Hooky Bitter. 'Are you sure you haven't got time for one more?'

'Some other time.'

'We'll see you next Sunday then, Neil?' Jimmy Baker leaned against the bar and scratched his armpits. Neil was reminded that he had been teased for his constant sweaty smell as a child. Nowadays, Jimmy smelt overpoweringly of sharp cologne.

'Next Sunday, definitely,' Neil said. 'I might treat Lindy to lunch.'

'I'll see you before then.' Dangerous Dave called out. 'I've got a question for you about a starter motor in a BMW 1 series. Old Bomber Harris's car is on the blink again.'

'I'll call in to the garage tomorrow, Dangerous,' Neil replied as he rushed towards the door. 'But you'll probably need a new starter and solenoid, and they aren't cheap.' Then he was gone.

'Nice fella,' Dave observed.

'Always has been a good bloke, Neil. Reliable, honest.' Jimmy scratched his head.

'The girls loved him in primary school,' Dickie Senior reminded everyone. 'Another Hooky Bitter in there, son.' He held his glass out to Dickie Junior, then he swivelled round. 'Do you want another one, Kenny?'

'Ah, I will, ta.' Kenny Hooper hunched in his old grey jacket, watching the action from a chair near the window. He finished the last mouthful in his glass and stared through the pane into the car park, frowning. Neil Timms was outside now, talking to a woman. Kenny gnawed his thumb as he watched; the woman was blonde, wearing a white blouse and a black skirt. He leaned forward, taking in the details, wondering why she and Neil were having a long conversation. The blonde woman laughed and patted his arm, then Neil reached into his jacket pocket and took out his wallet, handing her a roll of money.

Kenny sniffed, then accepted the pint Dickie Senior placed in front of him. 'Thanking ye, Dickie.'

Kenny's eyes were back to the window, watching nervously. Neil and the blonde woman were still talking in the car park, then he saw them move away together. A deep indentation appeared between his brows: Neil was handsome – Dickie Senior had just said that the girls loved him, and now he was going somewhere with this woman who wasn't his wife. He muttered to himself, 'That ent right. He shouldn't be doing that.'

Dickie Senior called from the bar, 'What's up, Kenny?'

Kenny wondered if he should say something, but his instincts told him that it might mean trouble: he was no gossip, even if his friends liked to tittle-tattle. He reached for his pint and grunted. 'Ah, well, I ent complaining. Nice pint of Hooky. Thanks, Dickie.'

* * *

Florence Dawson sat in her bedroom. It was past midday but she was still in pyjamas. The sun streamed onto the duvet cover where Betty Boop danced in red high heels waving a top hat. She wiped the tears from her face, picking up her phone again, pressing the button, listening to the purring tone. There was a male voice, *his* voice, the one that set her pulse thudding, asking her to leave a message. She took a deep breath and repeated the same words she'd said half an hour ago. 'It's me, Florence – I need to talk to you. Please, ring me. I...'

She wasn't sure what to say next, so she finished the call. He wouldn't reply: he hadn't replied to the last five messages she'd left. Since that evening she'd spent with him, he'd deliberately avoided her.

Florence chewed a broken nail and her hand shook. Her father was out with the boys, drinking beer at The Sun. Sunday was his day off and he wouldn't be back for an hour or so. She wouldn't tell him today. Perhaps she wouldn't tell him at all. Perhaps she'd run away. She wished she could.

Florence swallowed air and it shuddered in her lungs She needed to talk to Malia Johnson. Malia would come straight away; she'd know immediately that something was wrong. She'd hug her and say something kind. But nothing could change the situation.

Florence's hand shook: she was completely alone.

She picked up the pregnancy test kit from the bed and stared at the double lines again. Positive. There was no escaping the truth. It was hard to imagine a new life growing before she could see or feel it. She'd suspected for weeks, but now she knew for sure. This moment led to an inevitable chain of events that she couldn't avoid.

She'd have to explain it to her dad, and he'd cry. Then he'd promise to help her and he'd ask the question that everyone would want to know, the one she didn't want to answer. He'd ask who the father was.

She couldn't tell anyone his name.

8

On Saturday lunchtime, Odile's café was bustling. Josie, Lin and Minnie – wearing a beret and black raincoat – huddled around the table, chatter bubbling as they spoke over each other, catching up with each other's news. Florence brought them a tray of food, squeezing between the other tables. Dangerous Dave, Kenny Hooper and Jimmy Baker were tucking into enormous fry-ups and talking about cars. Linval and Rita Johnson ate pumpkin soup while comparing their two children: Malia had been no trouble as a youngster, whereas Adam had never been anything but.

Linval had tears of laughter in his eyes as he recalled how Adam had got himself lost in Old Scratch's woods, not far from Ledbury's farm, when he was ten years old. He'd been found the next day hiding up a tree, terrified because he'd believed that the devil lived in the woods and came out at night to eat children. Rita flashed her eyes and told Linval it hadn't been funny at the time; she'd been worried witless. Rita was proud of Adam; he was a fine accountant, a sweet-natured young man. It was Malia who concerned her now, because she was undecided about her future.

As Florence passed the table, Rita reached out a hand. 'Florence – Malia's home. Come round tonight? I'm cooking fish. Adam will be there. I know he'd be glad to see you.'

Florence blushed awkwardly. 'Malia's popping round to mine later on

– we haven't had a chance to catch up...'

'Normally we can't keep you kids apart,' Rita said with a glance towards Linval. 'Is everything all right?'

'Fine, great. I can't wait to see Malia and find out what jobs she's applying for.' Florence's smile was breezy.

'I'm trying to persuade her to go into teaching, but I don't think she'll follow me.' Rita held her soup spoon high, thinking.

'She doesn't want to be an accountant, that's for sure. She's far too bohemian,' Linval added.

Rita gave him an affectionate shove. 'Nothing wrong with a bit of bohemian, Linval.' Linval blew her a kiss.

'I'll catch up later.' Florence offered a professional smile. 'Is the food all right?'

'Delicious,' Rita replied as Linval showed his approval by scraping the dish with his spoon.

Florence moved away, weaving between tables, calling back, 'Tell Malia I'm looking forward to seeing her.'

Dangerous Dave waved a hand, 'Teas all round, when you're ready, Florrie, and make them good and hot. Plenty of sugar in mine...'

'Right, Dad, coming up – and don't call me Florrie,' Florence said good-naturedly, twisting between the colourful plastic strips that concealed the entrance to the kitchen. Odile was cooking, the air rich with smells of frying bacon and chips. The forced smile disappeared from Florence's face and she clutched her stomach, propelling herself towards the toilets. She felt nauseous.

Josie, Lin and Minnie had hardly touched their food. They were still too busy talking.

'Tina's allotment is incredible. I went there first thing and she was out in overalls planting row upon row of potatoes...' Minnie began.

'Neil has just done the same. I love new potatoes. At least I can't burn them – except I did once, when I let the pan boil dry...' Lin remembered.

'The Toomey boys do my garden for me now... they keep it nice.' Josie exhaled sadly. 'I often wonder if I should move somewhere smaller but...' She stopped: all her memories of Harry and their life together were at The Willows.

Minnie patted her hand. 'How are the Toomeys? Are they married yet?'

'No.' Josie laughed at the idea. 'Devlin must be getting on for thirty, Finn is a couple of years younger. They like to play the field.'

Minnie toyed with her salad. 'Handsome boys, both of them.'

'Their dad was handsome too. Fergal always had admirers. He didn't settle down until he was almost in middle age.' Lin leaned a hand on her cheek. 'Who'd want to live on a barge with three men? I bet it's chaos on the small boat, all that testosterone...'

'Devlin and Finn have their share of girlfriends; I've seen them on the village green and in The Sun,' Josie agreed. 'But Fergal's heart is still with his wife. There won't be anyone to replace her. I can understand that.'

'Ros Toomey kept those men in order,' Minnie said, then a thought occurred to her. 'Talking of strong women, I bought you some books by two of my favourite writers.'

'Oh, that's lovely.' Lin clapped her hands together as Minnie delved into her bag and pulled out neatly wrapped packages, handing one to Lin and one to Josie.

Josie peeked inside. 'Jeanette Winterson?'

'Sarah Winman? I haven't read anything by her.' Lin unwrapped the paper from the book in one impatient movement. She tugged out the book, turning it over to read the blurb. 'Looks great – thanks, Minnie.'

'I haven't told you about what happened to me while I was trying to leave the bookshop. So, this man, Felix...' Minnie made a humph! sound.

'An admirer?' Josie clapped her hands.

'Another admirer?' Lin leaned forward. 'We can't keep track of all these men, Minnie...'

'Well, Felix is a retired economics lecturer... he's nice enough and we have lots of friends in common. I went to the theatre with him and we went to a party somewhere. He brought flowers to my front door...'

'He's not for you, though?' Lin asked.

'No, I'm happiest sticking with my very good friends.' Minnie took their hands. 'What did Miss Hamilton write in our notebooks when we left primary school? *A good friend is like a four-leaf clover; hard to find and lucky to have.*'

'Isn't that the truth?' Josie murmured.

'Why did you go out with him then?' Lin asked.

'We went to see a play.' Minnie shrugged as if it was obvious. 'I don't mind going to the theatre alone, but sometimes it's nice to have someone to talk to afterwards. You know – "Why do you think the bride rebelled against the constraints of Spanish society?" That sort of thing.'

Lin nodded eagerly; she knew exactly what Minnie meant. 'Sometimes Neil and I have those sorts of conversations about TV, *Happy Valley... Coronation Street.*'

Josie sighed. 'I think it's companionship I miss the most.'

'It *is*,' Minnie insisted. 'That's why we all get on so well. We need the stimulation of others from time to time. I'm fine with a book, but we all need human contact from those we trust.' She squeezed Josie's hand, a gesture of empathy. 'Are you okay, Josie?'

Josie nodded. 'I manage, yes.' She forced a grin. 'Thank goodness for our lunches together.'

'Yes, the Silver Ladies' lunches.' Minnie was suddenly excited. 'We need to plan some more time together now it's virtually summer. You must come to Oxford and I'll take you to The Bookbinders – or we could go to London?'

'Not London!' Lin gasped in mock horror. 'All that way... all those crowds...'

'Normally we don't make it out of Tadderly,' Josie agreed.

Minnie leaned forward. 'Then we should visit somewhere exciting. Paris, Edinburgh. Anywhere.'

'That's not a bad idea,' Josie agreed. 'It certainly took me out of myself for a while, going on the cruise. That reminds me, I must email David Ellis.'

'Who's he?' Minnie was interested.

'A new friend she met on the cruise...' Lin explained.

'He'd just lost his partner, so we teamed up for company.' Josie caught Minnie's expression. 'Don't worry, he won't become obsessed with me as your Felix is with you.'

'He's not *my* Felix...'

'I promised David I'd message him. I want to ask how he was getting on with the novel he's writing in memory of his partner.'

Odile was at the table, arms folded. 'So, can I get you lunching ladies a nice dessert? Florence is taking a break and I said I'd pop out front.'

Lin patted her stomach. 'Do you have anything low in calories?'

'Let's push the boat out. I love puddings.' Minnie was as slim as a wand.

Odile said, 'I have sticky toffee pudding, carrot cake or I have a bit of pineapple and ginger upside-down cake.'

'I'll have some of the sticky toffee pudding when you're ready,' Dangerous Dave called out loudly.

Linval waved a hand. 'I'll have the pineapple upside-down cake, Odile. It's so good.'

'Absolutely,' Rita agreed. 'For me too.'

'Odile's carrot cake is delicious, to die for.' Jimmy slapped Kenny's arm. 'I recommend it, mate.'

'You're joking, ent you?' Kenny looked alarmed. 'Cake with carrots in it? Sounds like summat a rabbit would eat.'

'Looks like everyone's ready for one of your famous desserts, Odile,' Minnie grinned. At that moment, the door clanged open, the little bell tinkling, and a woman in a faux-fur coat leaned against the door jamb, surveying the café. Kenny shouted out, 'Shut that door up, missus – the wind's howling around my legs and I'm bloody cold.'

The woman took a step forward, allowing the door to close behind her. She removed her hat, revealing neatly coiled silver hair, her face lined like the contours of a map. All eyes were on her, completely self-contained, elegant, surrounded by the scent of floral perfume, her lips a film-star red colour as she smiled sweetly. 'Kenny Hooper, you know better than to be so rude. You used to be so well mannered...'

Kenny stared at her and then the penny dropped. The voice had given it away, the smooth cultured tones the class had listened to so many years ago, telling them about the adventures of Moley and Ratty on the river. He hung his head. 'I'm s-sorry, Miss Hamilton.'

Minnie gasped. 'Miss Hamilton! How nice to see you.'

Lin's eyes were wide. 'Miss Hamilton? Oh, it's really you.'

'It was you on the scooter, of course...' Josie added. 'I saw you last week.' She decided it might be better not to mention to her teacher that she had almost bowled her over.

Miss Hamilton looked at each of them in turn. 'Minnie Moore... Linda Norton... Josephine Potter... how delightful to see you all together after so long. I knew you had the sort of friendship that would withstand the changing years.'

'Come and sit down with us, Miss.' Minnie patted the seat next to her, gazing at the teacher as she had done over sixty years ago.

'I'd love to.' Miss Hamilton eased herself slowly towards the table. 'The scooter is parked outside. I don't get around as well as I used to: my arthritis is very annoying, but I have a good doctor and she keeps an eye on me. That's why I've moved here. I've just bought a nice bungalow on Tadderly Road.' She sat down carefully, Minnie pushing out the chair, extending a hand. 'Well, how pleasant. Just like old times.'

'You're most welcome.' Odile offered a wide smile. 'What can I get you?'

'Tea...' Miss Hamilton ignored the menu that Odile offered. 'And did I overhear someone say carrot cake? A slice of that would be wonderful. With a dollop of cream, if you have it.' She turned to the three former pupils who sat at the table looking at her, their eyes shining. 'This is nice, isn't it? It's been quite a while...' She leaned forwards, her voice soft with warmth. 'Well, you must tell me about everything you've been doing over the last sixty years. It will be good to catch up with all the news.' Then she stared across the café and she was suddenly stern. 'Please do close your mouth, Jimmy Baker. You're staring again, and you know it's impolite to stare.'

'Yes, Miss,' Jimmy replied automatically, and Dangerous Dave dug him in the ribs and began to laugh. Jimmy hung his head and Kenny looked around nervously.

Miss Hamilton turned to the three friends at the table. 'So, my girls,' she purred. 'I want to hear all about your lives since we last met. Every detail.' She patted her silver hair. 'Oh, I know so much has changed, but it's good to be back in Middleton Ferris. I can't wait to settle in and become part of the village. I know it's going to be wonderful.'

9

Florence sat on the edge of her bed fiddling with a bracelet, still in the green dress she had worn for work. Malia huddled next to her, legs crossed, shoes off, and Florence noticed how well she looked, all smiles and wild hair and torn jeans, her life open in front of her like an unwritten page. She sighed. 'So, you're going to London?'

'I want to work for a publisher – I'd love a marketing role.' Malia leaned forwards. 'It doesn't take long from here to London by train.'

Florence nodded. 'London's a big place...'

'I'd love the bustle. I don't want to be like Adam, living here, working with my dad. Or teaching forever, like poor Mum.'

Florence wasn't sure what to say, so she took a breath. 'Does Adam like living at home?'

'He's saving for a mortgage; he'll get a flat in Tadderly.' Malia met her friend's eyes. 'He asked about you before I came out. He said to send you his best.'

Florence nodded. 'That's nice.'

'He still likes you,' Malia explained. 'He hasn't got over you finishing with him last summer.'

'I'm sorry about it...' Florence's eyes filled with tears.

Malia noticed, reaching over and grabbing her hand. 'Did I say something?'

'No...' Florence wondered if now was the time to tell Malia her news.

But before she could say anything, Malia was suddenly excited by a new thought. 'Why don't you come to London? You and I could get a flat – you could find a job working somewhere trendy.'

'Me?'

'We could have some fun.' Malia was thoughtful. 'Who are the cool couple who recently moved to the village, the wife commutes to London sometimes, we always see them out running?'

'Darryl and Charlotte Featherstone.'

'Yes, they'd know about working in the city. Maybe they'll know about the best places to live.'

'They might.' Florence shrugged. 'It can't do any harm, I suppose.'

Malia squeezed her hand excitedly. 'Come with me. You must be bored at Odile's, seeing the same faces every day.'

Florence shook her head. 'I don't suppose I'll be there much longer. Today, Odile saw me being...'

A loud voice from downstairs interrupted her words. Dangerous Dave called up 'Everything all right, girls?'

Florence made her voice sound light. 'Fine, thanks.'

'Do you want me to bring you some hot chocolate? Marshmallows? Sprinkles?'

'No, we're good, Dad,' Florence yelled, hoping he wouldn't come any further than the bottom step. Malia laughed into her hand and Florence rolled her eyes. 'He thinks we're fourteen – I'm still his little princess.' Her words brought a large lump into her throat and she burst into tears.

Malia was next to her. 'What is it? Something's wrong, isn't it?' Her voice became suddenly anxious. 'What are you not telling me?'

There was no point dragging it out. Florence blurted, 'I'm pregnant. Odile found out today. She caught me being sick in the loo.' Her expression was desperate. 'No one else knows.'

Then Florence and Malia were in each other's arms, Florence sobbing, making her friend's shoulder damp.

Malia rocked her slightly, then said, 'Are you sure?'

Florence nodded weakly.

'Have you done a test?'

Florence nodded again.

'So how... pregnant?'

'Three months, maybe a bit more...'

Malia asked the question that filled her thoughts. 'Are you... seeing someone?'

'No.' Florence sniffed loudly.

'Does he know? Have you told him, the father?'

Florence sat upright, wiping her face with the back of her hand. 'He hasn't answered my calls.' She swallowed. 'Please don't ask me who he is... Promise me you won't ask?'

'I promise,' Malia said. 'Do I know him?'

Florence nodded once, tears streaking her face again. 'It's such a mess. Dad will be so upset and I'll lose my job and everyone will know.'

Malia snuggled closer and looped an arm around Florence's shoulders. 'Do you want to keep the baby?'

Florence nibbled the end of her finger. 'I think so – yes. I couldn't... you know...'

'So, what about the father? Can he help? Does he love you?'

Florence flinched. 'Can we just not mention him?'

'All right.' Malia took Florence's hands. 'Then we have to make a plan together, you and me. We'll...' She was thoughtful for a moment. 'Let's sleep on it tonight, think things out, then we'll meet up tomorrow and you can decide who you want to tell, who can help, and the first thing on your list is to see the doctor. She'll give you advice...'

'The thing is, I don't want anyone to know.'

'You can tell whoever you want, whenever you're ready. It's about what's best for you.'

Florence muttered, 'Thank you,' and wrapped her arms around Malia. 'I've been so scared.'

'Of course. But I'll help.'

'You're off to London...'

'I'm your best friend.' Malia pressed her lips together. 'I'm here for you. Things will work out, you wait and see.'

Florence felt a little better. Just telling Malia made her feel less isolated, more positive. Then she thought again: Malia would go home soon, and Florence would be left with her thoughts and anxieties. The problem would still be the same.

She exhaled sadly; it was her baby: she'd have to go through the pregnancy and the birth by herself. She was absolutely alone.

Florence felt more miserable than ever.

* * *

'I don't feel so alone now I've moved to Middleton Ferris.' Miss Hamilton ushered Josie and Lin into her bungalow in Tadderly Road. 'It's such a friendly village and with the mobility scooter, I can get around quite well.' She waved towards the flowery sofa. 'Do sit down, please. My old place in Tadderly was huge, at the top of a long hill. Do you know I lived there for sixty years? Can you believe I'm ninety now?'

'You look well on it, Miss Hamilton,' Josie said kindly, looking around. The room was simple but pristine. An acoustic guitar stood on a stand in the corner.

'Please – we're not at school now. Call me Cecily.'

Lin sat down awkwardly, then she stood up. 'Can I make us all some tea, Cecily?'

'Would you?' Cecily eased herself into an armchair. 'That would be so nice, Linda. And you married Neil Timms. Who'd have thought it, that handsome little boy – he was so good-natured.'

'He still is.' Lin moved to the small kitchen, and filled the kettle. 'He's perfect.'

'I did so enjoy sharing lunch with you. I've never forgotten Euripides' words...' Cecily said. '"We share lunch as friends."' She turned to Josie. 'What a pity Minnie couldn't come back with us.'

'She had to get the train to Oxford, Miss – Cecily.' Josie hid a smile beneath her hand – old habits were hard to shake.

'She's done so well. Classics at St Hilda's.' Cecily leaned back in her seat, stretching slim legs. 'I'm so pleased I argued with her father about her education. He was a difficult man.' She frowned. 'What happened to her sister... Tina, wasn't it?'

'She's fine, she lives just down the road. She has an allotment. Years ago, she used to be an ambulance driver. She's very down to earth, a lovely woman.'

'Is she married?'

'Not now.' Josie shook her head. 'I think the ambulance job cost her dearly – her husband was the sort of man who wanted his wife at home. He left years ago.'

'Loyalty is everything in a relationship...' Cecily paused. 'Josephine, I'm sorry to hear about your husband passing.' Her eyes were kind. 'Tell me about him.'

'He was called Harry.' Josie took a breath. 'I met him at a dance when I was twenty-one. I was working as a hotel receptionist and Harry had a job in a bank. We clicked. I knew he was the one straight away. He was lovely – nothing was too much trouble. We were...' Josie put a knuckle to the corner of her eye. 'We were happy.'

Cecily sighed. '"If I had a flower for every time I thought of you... I could walk through my garden forever."'

'That's beautiful,' Josie said sadly.

'Alfred, Lord Tennyson.' Cecily had a faraway expression.

'Did you not ever think of marrying...?' Josie tried to make her voice compassionate; she didn't want to intrude.

'Once,' Cecily whispered, then Lin was in the room carrying a tray.

'At least I can make tea... although I could burn water.' She grinned, placing the teapot and three delicate cups on a low table. 'This is a lovely home you have here, Miss Hamilton.'

'Cecily,' Cecily insisted.

'Do you still play?' Josie indicated the acoustic guitar on the stand.

'I do. My fingers aren't as nimble as they were.'

'Shall I pour then?' Lin asked politely.

'I think you should, dear,' Cecily said, her voice still strong and authoritative. 'Then you can tell me all about everything I've missed over the last few years and what I have to look forward to here in Middleton Ferris. Now, I've seen Kenny Hooper and Jimmy Baker already. So... whatever happened to Dickie Edwards? Is he still alive?'

'He is.' Lin beamed. 'He owns The Sun Inn, not far from here. His son, Dickie Junior, runs it for him now – Neil and I often eat there.'

'That's good news.' Cecily smiled mischievously. 'We shall have to call in on Dickie. I am partial to a gin and tonic on occasion, and I'm sure he'd be glad to buy my silence if I threaten to tell Dickie Junior what a naughty boy his father was when he was ten years old...'

* * *

Minnie arrived back at her Victorian terrace in Newton Road and slumped on the sofa in the lounge. She kicked off her Doc Martens, wriggling her toes, closing her eyes as the sunlight streamed through the window. She basked in the comforting warmth and sighed. It had been good to see Tina at her allotment and to have lunch with Lin and Josie. Meeting Miss Hamilton again had been wonderful too; it was nice to see her looking so healthy: the old teacher certainly hadn't lost her feistiness.

Her thoughts moved to the rest of Saturday; she had nothing planned. An evening in with a glass of red wine and a good book would do fine. She was looking forward to the next Silver Ladies' lunch: the time she spent with her friends was precious. Odile's café was lovely, but it would be nice to change the venue during the summer and encourage her friends to try somewhere different. The problem with living in Middleton Ferris – or anywhere – for too long was that she was soon itching to escape beyond the boundaries. She laughed – wasn't that true of just about everything? Boredom was a big problem for Minnie: she was always looking for a new challenge, a new encounter. She wondered if she could persuade her friends to come to London for their next lunch date; they could throw themselves in at the deep end at The Ritz or find a café with a good pianist or, even better, treat themselves to dinner and a show. Minnie clapped her hands excitedly. It might be fun to go somewhere beyond the village.

Her phone buzzed and she held it against her ear. 'Hello, Araminta Moore... oh, Francine, how are you?'

Minnie listened as an old colleague from St Hilda's chattered, her voice rattling in the earpiece. Then Minnie said, 'Dinner? Of course, yes, I'm free on

Wednesday evening.' She listened again before a low chuckle escaped. 'Oh, so I'm making up numbers, am I? Well, make sure you sit me opposite a good-looking man with an interesting brain.' Then she smiled slowly. 'Francine – I'll see you on Wednesday, around seven... That's lovely, I'll look forward to it.'

Minnie put the phone down and burst out laughing. She'd been offered a last-minute dinner invitation on Wednesday – that could only mean that another single female had just cancelled. Minnie wasn't always the first-choice guest – she had a reputation for speaking her mind and upsetting the applecart. She'd cut conversation dead by responding curtly to people she knew were clearly wrong. Minnie didn't suffer fools gladly. But she'd been invited to dinner and Wednesday evening was ripe with possibilities. Francine Jarvis had been a lecturer with Minnie; they knew each other well and it would be good to catch up with some old faces and talk about interesting subjects. There would always be controversy.

She eased herself to her feet and stretched her arms above her head, twirling once. A dinner party with an old friend and lots of banter. Perfect.

10

On Wednesday morning, Lin was collecting breakfast dishes in the kitchen, listening to a sentimental tune on the radio, singing along with the lyrics. Outside, the lawn was illuminated green and gold in the sunlight. She peered into the back garden through the kitchen window, noticing the neat vegetable patch, clusters of primroses, daffodils swaying. Beyond, in George Ledbury's field, a piece of farm machinery chugged along, throwing out soil. Lin picked up a tea towel and began to dry the breakfast plates. She wondered what Minnie would be doing now; she'd probably be stretched out like a happy cat on the sofa, reading a book. Josie would be doing the same thing, basking in the garden. Lin hadn't started her own book yet; it was still in the torn wrapping paper.

She compared herself to her teacher, Miss Hamilton. Cecily was much older, but she was inspirational – she hadn't lost any of her elegance and zest for life. She'd be in her neat bungalow now in perfect lipstick, enjoying a leisurely breakfast. She might even be playing her guitar. All three women were alone, Minnie, Josie, Cecily – but Lin felt lucky, she had a gorgeous doting husband. Her blessing suddenly became an anxiety: Lin worried about losing him. What if he became bored with her? He was so outgoing; she wasn't sure that she was very interesting nowadays. She rarely had anything new to say; she and Neil had been married for forty-nine years and they knew all there was to know about each other. Perhaps they should spend time together today, to go out for a drive, or a walk in Old Scratch's woods. The bluebells would be out and the birds would be twittering above dappled branches. They could talk; she could tell him that she sometimes felt tearful, a little depressed.

Neil came downstairs, damp from the shower.

'Oh, you've had a shower?' Lin remarked and was immediately annoyed that she had stated the obvious. She felt even more dull.

Neil shifted from one foot to the other. 'Is that a problem?'

'No, of course not.' Lin searched for something interesting to say. The wrong words came out, boring words. 'It's a nice day, sunny...'

'It is...' They stared at each other and then Neil said, 'I thought I'd go out to see Jimmy Baker. He's asked me for some help with something.'

'Oh, what's that?' Lin said sadly. She'd wanted company.

'His bicycle. It needs a bit of a... service.'

'Oh...'

'You don't mind, do you, love?'

'Of course not.' Lin tried to conceal her disappointment with a wide smile. 'You'll be back for lunch?'

'Well, I was thinking I might have lunch round at Jimmy's, just a sandwich... it might be a long job...'

'Oh, all right.'

Neil shuffled his feet. 'Are you sure, love?' He pecked her cheek quickly. 'I'll be back in time to cook dinner.'

'Yes, fine, fine.' Lin heard an edge to her voice, irritation. Neil seemed not to notice. He reached for his jacket, the smart dark one he'd bought a month ago.

Lin frowned. 'Isn't that jacket a bit nice for wearing to fix a bicycle?'

Neil offered a cheeky grin. 'I thought I'd break it in...' He moved towards the door. 'I'll see you later.'

'Yes, fine.'

Lin watched him go then she stared around the empty kitchen. She felt inadequate and annoyed with herself. Josie spent every day alone and yet Lin was tired with her own company after just a few minutes. She wondered again if Neil found her dull. Perhaps that's why he'd gone to Jimmy Baker's, for some interesting conversation.

She gazed through the window and told herself that she was being silly – she just felt a little down today. The arthritis medication made her feel tearful. Outside, the farm machinery was still rumbling along, parallel to the garden, and she could see Bobby Ledbury at the wheel, handsome, moody, in his early twenties. Lin smiled; he reminded her of the actor James Dean. In her childhood days, James Dean had been the symbol of restless youth and Bobby Ledbury was that sort of young man, dangerous and a bit unpredictable. She'd never had a proper conversation with Bobby, but she often spoke to Penny, his grandmother, in the Co-op and she said that he was always out on his motorbike until late.

Lin folded a few tea towels and thought about her daughter Debbie. She wasn't rebellious, but she was difficult to pin down. She and her family lived less than two hours away, but whenever Lin and Neil offered to visit, Debbie had something else to do. She and her husband Jon worked hard at their catering company, so it was understandable; Debbie's children were teenagers now, probably a handful. Lin remembered when she'd last seen them a year ago – Debbie had been welcoming but detached. The grandchildren were lovely – Melissa was fifteen then, doing so well at school, Louis was thirteen and sporty, a bit quiet, but he had eagerly accepted the money Lin had offered him as they'd left.

Lin's shoulders drooped; she felt depressed. It didn't help that Bobby Goldsborough was on the radio singing a song about a tree in the garden, how it had just been a twig the day his beloved planted it. It was a song about time passing and death and it made Lin feel worse.

She'd ring Josie and they'd go for a walk in the woods together: at a time like this, Josie would be there for her. She glanced out of the window again. The farm machinery was creating a deep rut in the earth as Bobby drove along. Lin put her hands to her face and they came away damp – that's how she felt too, in a rut.

* * *

Minnie's cheeks were flushed with delight as she sauntered along Harpsichord Place, just off Cherwell Street, not far from the river. In a velvet cape and daisy print Doc Martens, she strolled past the golden spires and turrets gleaming amber in the light of the setting sun. Bright hanging baskets hung from old buildings as students sailed along the roads on bicycles, elegant in scarves, books heaped in front baskets as they glided languidly, singly or in pairs. Minnie increased her pace. She was looking forward to dinner; her hair twisted on the crown of her head, she felt sophisticated and charming. Tonight, at Francine's, she'd meet some old friends and make some new ones, witty, erudite people who would challenge her views and offer interesting perspectives on the world.

She paused at the bay-fronted terrace, with bricks painted white, and a blue door approached by two white steps, and she knocked once.

The door was answered by a willowy woman wearing an elegant dress. She threw her arms around Minnie in a flourish of enthusiasm. 'You're late. Come in. We're just sitting down. I was about to introduce everyone...'

'I'm fashionably late, Francine.' Minnie kissed her cheek. She knew it was 7.15, she'd just checked her watch. From the doorway, she could smell roasting vegetables, spiced meat. 'Mmm. Something smells divine.'

Minnie followed Francine as she swept through the hall and into a vast dining room with shelves of books on every wall. A woman with a high voice was holding forth on the policies of the Green Party, telling everyone that in her opinion they didn't go far enough. Music was playing, easy sleazy jazz, and Minnie moved to squeeze onto the empty seat as Francine's husband Melvyn greeted her with a twitch of his bushy brows and filled up her glass with red wine. Francine rushed out. 'I'll check the food.'

'Where were we?' Melvyn asked. 'I ought to introduce... ah, Minnie...'

'I know most people...' Minnie gazed around the table; there were several people she knew fairly well, a politics lecturer and her husband, an author of historical tomes and his wife, who were already talking amongst themselves. There was a man she didn't know sitting across from her, the unaccompanied male for whom she'd been invited to make up even numbers. He was tall with unruly white hair that stuck out from his head like a cloud. He wore gold-rimmed spectacles and had an intelligent face.

Minnie watched him slicing bread neatly as Francine rushed in, placing bowls of emerald-coloured soup in front of them.

The other four guests were still chattering about politics and the man opposite Minnie watched, his face perplexed.

'So, introductions...?' Melvyn was about to continue as Francine gestured towards the steaming bowls. 'Ah, yes, my wife's creamy watercress. Get it while it's piping hot. Dig in.'

There was a clanking of spoons, polite sounds of appreciation, then Melvyn said, 'The Tories have been at it again this week. My newspaper has been full of it – I've been inundated all week with letters. Did you hear about the politician who's been suspended pending allegations of misconduct?'

The historical author groaned. 'I expect his solicitor will get him off with a warning – he'll be back in a year or two when everyone's forgotten.'

'I think he's going to find it difficult to wriggle out of this one, mark my words,' the politics lecturer said.

'And your words are seldom wrong, darling,' her husband announced with a furtive glance at the author.

'Oh, politics can be so dreary,' Francine sighed with a smile towards the politics lecturer's husband. 'Has anyone been to see the latest exhibition at the Modern?'

'I haven't been yet,' Minnie said, spoon in hand.

'Oh, you must,' the author's wife gasped. 'The artist uses installation to expose systems of power.'

'She does,' the author leaned forward. 'She demonstrates how governments can be as precarious as mortal bodies...'

Minnie noticed the man with a cloud of hair watching the other guests carefully and he caught her eye, raising an eyebrow. She raised one back. He hadn't been introduced yet – Melvyn had forgotten and Francine had been too busy. Minnie didn't know his name but, when the chance came, she'd ask him. At the moment, everyone else was gushing about art and she and the stranger smiled knowingly.

'My favourite artist is Lowry. I love the political impact of his paintings.' The politics lecturer finished her soup. 'But then I'm from Manchester.'

'I'm not from New York, but if you want a political artist, then Basquiat is your man,' the politics lecturer's husband insisted.

'Oh, no.' The author's wife pulled a sour face. 'Basquiat was just a graffiti artist with no skill.'

'Do you think so? I like his work...' Francine began to collect bowls, her face troubled.

The man sitting opposite Minnie looked bemused and Minnie copied his expression.

'American art often leaves me unimpressed,' the politics lecturer suggested. 'Jackson Pollock – what is that all about?'

'And American playwrights too – I can't name a good one,' the author said bluntly.

'Nor can I...' his wife agreed.

'There's Miller – Tennessee Williams – Kushner—' Minnie began.

'Well, I like them all,' Francine said quickly as she moved from the table and Melvyn began to refill glasses.

Minnie watched the man with the cloud of hair as he observed everyone, his eyes bright behind glasses. She leaned forwards – she could sense a storm coming so, as the Szechuan beef arrived with all the trimmings, she said mischievously, 'I love American plays – I prefer a good Tennessee Williams any day to, say, a mediocre Noel Coward, who was writing around the same time – I like a play I can get my teeth into.'

'Oh, I can't agree.' The politics lecturer was adamant. '*Cat on a Hot Tin Roof* – horrible! – and Albee's *Who's Afraid of Virginia Woolf* – all that shouting.'

'And Eugene O'Neill too, those dead-enders who live in a flop house... just, no.' The author's wife shuddered.

'More wine, everyone?' Melvyn began filling glasses quickly.

Francine took over hurriedly. 'Let's talk about something else – Minnie, have you read anything interesting lately? Minnie is the most cultured of us all—'

'In fact,' the author cut across Francine, 'I don't like American literature. Any of it.'

'Indeed,' the politics lecturer laughed. 'And American politics – oh, my goodness.'

'Ah, we might discuss...' Melvyn began.

Francine interrupted. 'I hope the beef is good.'

'Perfect... you must give me the recipe.' The author's wife smiled. 'Back to America, though – the food – I don't think I've tasted worse.'

The man with the cloud of hair leaned forward. He was openly amused now. Minnie caught his eye and raised both brows.

The author laughed. 'I hate to say it, but nothing good has come out of the USA recently.'

The politics lecturer's husband guffawed. 'Not since Marilyn Monroe.' He was pleased with himself. 'And I always thought our Diana Dors was a better actress...'

Minnie put down her knife and fork deliberately and gave a loud sigh: it had gone far enough. 'This music is really good. What is it?'

Melvyn was relieved to change the subject. 'It's Buddy Bolden...'

'Wasn't he the father of jazz music?' Minnie waved a finger. 'From New Orleans, ragtime, the origins of jazz?' She smiled at each guest in turn. 'I was in the States six years ago for a string of conferences: Boston, New York, San Jose. I had some of the best food, saw some of the best live theatre and musicals and made the acquaintance of some of the most cultured people I have ever had the pleasure of meeting.' She clapped her hands once. 'But then that's just my opinion.'

The man opposite her was grinning. 'Hear, hear,' he said and everyone at the table froze at his first two words and his cultured New York accent.

Francine covered her horror with an effusive smile. 'Jensen, I still haven't introduced you, I'm so sorry – well, I was busy with the food and... everyone, this is Jensen Callahan, from Greenwich Village... New York.'

Time held still for a moment while everyone took a breath, then the gushing began. 'I've been to New York...'

'We saw *Hamilton* on Broadway – we loved it, didn't we, dear?'

'Oh, the breakfasts, those bagels, to die for...'

'Times Square is simply stunning...'

Francine's smile broadened as she offered more vegetables. 'Jensen is a theatre director.'

Jensen shrugged as if it was nothing. 'I've just finished a six-month run of Miller's *Death of a Salesman*.'

'One of my favourite playwrights,' Minnie said mischievously. 'But I love all of them.'

Jensen beamed. The politics lecturer asked, 'What are you doing here in Oxford, Jensen?'

'I'm working at the Playhouse, as a co-director, an advisor really. They are doing a production of *Julius Caesar*.'

'Shakespeare?' The author shook his head. 'Hardly an American play...'

'An American interpretation, all about the politics, with Caesar in a red baseball cap.' Jensen was delighted. 'I met Melvyn at the theatre – he was doing an article on the show, and he invited me to dinner, and here I am.' He leaned back in his seat, stretching his legs, then he grinned in Minnie's direction. 'I have to say, I love everything about Oxford, the beautiful buildings, the culture, the friendly people.' He met Minnie's eyes. 'I do hope you'll all come and see the play. It opens next week.'

The other guests were suddenly full of enthusiasm. 'Oh, we'd be delighted.'

'How wonderful.'

'We'll be there, won't we, darling?'

Francine let out a sigh of relief. 'Well, that's all good. Now, how about I get us all some pudding? So, there's a choice: Eton Mess – or pecan pie with ice cream?'

The guests' voices chorused in unison, 'Oh, the pecan pie.'

Jensen said, 'I'll have Eton Mess.'

'So will I,' Minnie grinned, her expression already complicit.

Then Jensen Callahan caught her eye and he winked. Minnie was sure of it. She raised an eyebrow provocatively and winked back.

11

On Saturday morning, Josie and Lin sat on the bench near the weeping willow tree opposite St Peter and St Paul's church. From this position, they could see the banks of the Cherwell beyond swathes of nodding daffodils. The river shone glass smooth, reflecting the light that dappled the water. The Toomeys' red and black barge was in its usual place by the riverbank. There was no sign of the occupants, but the strong smell of cooking bacon and sausages wafted on the air: Fergal was below deck, making his famous Joe Grey stew. Josie was thoughtful: she'd just visited Harry's grave, holding a conversation with him in her head, before meeting Lin. In her mind, she was still with Harry, crouched on the grass next to the raised earth he lay beneath, a bunch of flowers in her hand.

Lin hadn't stopped talking. Josie was trying to listen; she was clearly troubled about something – she'd been talking about it since she arrived. 'It's been three times this week. Surely Jimmy's bike isn't in such a state of disrepair...'

Josie shook her head. 'I'm sorry... what about Jimmy's bike?'

'Neil's helping him fix it. He was late home on Wednesday – he said they got chatting and forgot the time. Then he went again yesterday, and this morning he said he'd better help him try it out on the roads.' Lin frowned. 'Josie, do you think I'm boring?'

'Not at all.'

'It's just that I've hardly seen Neil – it feels like he's avoiding me.'

'I'm sure he's not.' Josie offered an encouraging grin. 'Has he finished work on Jimmy's bike now?'

'He has.'

'Then have lunch at The Sun tomorrow. Take some quality time.'

'Do you think so?'

'Of course – tell him that's what you need.' Josie patted her arm.

'Thanks, Josie. Yes, I will – I'll talk to him...'

They were quiet for a moment. A couple jogged past, sleek from head to toe in Lycra, a slim woman with a long swishing ponytail and a tall handsome man.

Josie said, 'What a beautiful couple. Eros and Psyche.'

'Beyonce and Jay-Z.' Lin agreed.

'Liz Taylor and Richard Burton.' Josie smiled.

'The Posh and Becks of Middleton Ferris.' Lin stifled a giggle. 'They're called the Featherstones. They recently bought one of the big houses at Nobb's End.'

'I heard she works in London some days...' Josie said.

'And he's a lawyer in Charlbury. He's Darryl and she's Charlotte. I spoke to them briefly in the pub at Christmas time.'

'Are they nice?' Josie asked.

'Darryl's really friendly. Charlotte's a bit quiet. She's probably lovely when you get to know her.'

'Look at them both, so fit.' Josie sighed. 'Oh, to be young again.'

'What do you mean?' Lin gave her friend a quizzical look.

'I don't know – if I had my chance again, I'd do some things very differently.'

'I wouldn't.' Lin shook her head. 'I'd still marry Neil, have Debbie...'

'Oh, I'd never change marrying Harry. I don't mean that. But...' Josie took a breath. 'If you were twenty-one *now*, what would you do?'

Lin watched Darryl and Charlotte Featherstone loping towards the river Cherwell. 'I wouldn't mind a bit of what those two have, the house, the car...'

'I envy their independence; the choices,' Josie agreed. 'I was a receptionist in a hotel when I met Harry. Our first car was a little Mini. But what if I'd made the cars, or designed them or driven them. I could have been a racing driver...'

'Would you like to be like Lewis Hamilton?' Lin was shocked. 'It must be dangerous, going that fast.'

'No, I don't wish I'd been able to race.' Josie folded her arms. 'I'm just saying – we had such modest aspirations. We had a simple view of what we wanted from life – marriage, home. No one ever told us to try something different. Nowadays, kids see something they want and they don't hesitate. I never ever thought there was a life for me outside Middleton Ferris.'

'Aren't you happy here, Josie? With your friends...?'

'Oh yes, of course.' Josie frowned. 'But our horizons were limited. Modern girls have so much more going for them.'

'They have, that's true.' Lin sighed, then she pointed. 'Look...'

Devlin and Finn Toomey were walking up from the riverbank, taking the path towards the pub. They were both handsome in tight jeans and clean shirts. Devlin tipped his trilby as he passed. 'Mornin' to ye, ladies.'

'Morning, Devlin, Finn,' Lin said, then she pressed a hand over her mouth and laughed. 'You're right, Josie, if we were twenty-one again...'

Josie shook her head, amused. 'I think we're done here, Lin. Let's go to Odile's for a cuppa. Perhaps Cecily will be there.'

'Right.' Lin eased herself upright. Her fingers felt stiff and numb. She linked an arm through Josie's and was immediately comforted by the warmth. They began to walk along Orchard Way towards the recreation ground. As they approached Chandos, Gerald Harris's house, Josie whispered, 'Gerald gave me some lovely daffs last week. They are still as fresh in the vase as when he picked them.'

'He has a soft spot for you,' Lin suggested.

'Oh, I hope not,' Josie said anxiously. 'I think he's lonely.'

'He likes you,' Lin insisted.

'I expect he'll be in his garden, manicuring the lawn. He keeps it so nice.'

They reached the house and stopped in their tracks. Gerald was in his front garden, scratching his head beneath his hat. Josie and Lin could see why he was perplexed – his lawn was dug up in patches, soil scattered everywhere. Some plants had been ruined; a few daffodil heads littered the path, but a huge square of grass had been dug up and turned into mud.

'What's happened, Gerald?' Josie called out. 'Have you got moles?'

'Moles? No.' Gerald turned a distraught face towards her. 'I woke up this morning and looked out of my window and – I saw this. I'm furious.'

'Surely it's not children?' Lin began.

'No – I rushed down in my pyjamas and there it was, digging away for all its life – I chased it off.'

'It?' Josie asked.

Gerald took a deep breath. 'A black and white pig, burrowing into all my plants, snuffling at my best daffodils.' He made a deep sound of disgust. 'A pig, I tell you. A big one. Can you believe it?'

'Ah, that would be Nadine,' Lin said, her face a picture of sympathy.

'Nadine?'

'George Ledbury's pig.' Josie shook her head. 'We were warned about her by Lin's neighbour, Janice. Apparently, she likes to go on the rampage through the village – Nadine that is, not Janice.'

'Well, George Ledbury will pay for my plants...' Gerald was furious. 'This garden is my pride and joy.'

Josie nodded sympathetically. 'We're off to Odile's. You could come with us.'

Gerald waved his arms again. 'But just look at the mess. It's like a... a pigsty.'

'Indeed,' Lin said sadly.

'I've no time for drinking tea.'

'I'll have a word with the Toomey boys, if you like,' Josie soothed. 'I'm sure they'll come over and help you sort it all out.' She took Lin's arm. 'And if you need a cuppa to cheer you up, we'll be at Odile's.'

* * *

The following Sunday morning, Florence walked down to the river Cherwell to meet her friends. It was almost lunchtime – Florence could see The Sun Inn car park: Jack Lovejoy had taken up position not far from the entrance, wearing a colourful cap, playing his guitar. The chords were light on the wind. She thought about going over to him, holding her arms out for a hug: she could do with one. Then she saw Neil and Lin Timms arrive for Sunday lunch, pausing to put money in Jack's baked beans collection tin. Her father would be there soon for his regular pint. Florence felt the breeze lift the hem of her dress and she smoothed it flat. In the distance, two figures were approaching from Orchard Way. They waved to her and Florence waved back. It was Malia, with Natalie Ledbury. In minutes, they were beside her. Malia threw an arm around Florence's neck. 'What are you up to?'

'Watching Jack busking.' Florence sighed, gazing towards the pub.

Natalie played with her hair. 'I used to think he was gorgeous when we were at school, but not as gorgeous as Finn Toomey.'

Malia agreed. 'Everyone had the hots for Finn Toomey.'

Florence shook her head sadly. It wasn't a conversation she wanted to join in; talking about boys would eventually lead to secrets she didn't really want Natalie to know, not yet. She cupped her hands over her belly.

'You liked Finn, didn't you, Florence?' Malia smiled. 'You liked Adam once too, and I'm sure he still likes you.'

'Apparently lots of girls like Bobby.' Natalie wrinkled her nose. 'Why anyone would like my moody brother I don't know, but they do.'

Florence stared at her fingers folded in her lap. Malia asked, 'What's Bobby up to nowadays?'

'Apart from working? He's always out late on his bike, goodness knows where. Grandad wants him to start taking more responsibility on the farm. He's getting on a bit and Dad's more interested in managing the accounts.' Natalie waved her left hand, lifting a finger to show a sparkling diamond. 'Brandon wants to work on the admin side. Grandad will let us have one of the little cottages when we're married. Of course, the farmhouse is big enough for Grandad and Grandma and my parents, but Brandon and I want some privacy.'

'When are you getting married?' Malia asked.

'Next summer, after Brandon finishes his farm management course.' Natalie leaned forward, excited. 'I'm choosing a wedding dress already. I love going into Tadderly and Charlbury, looking in the windows of the bridal shops. Hey...' She grabbed her friends' hands. 'Come with me next weekend. It'll be fun.'

'We could...' Malia glanced at Florence, who smiled half-heartedly.

'Brandon and I are going to wait a few years before we have kids, though.' Natalie took a deep breath. 'Brandon wants three or four. I'm not sure. I look at people who were in our class at school who have had kids, and they look so miserable.'

'Not everyone ends up like that,' Malia said quickly. She reached for Florence's hand.

'They do,' Natalie insisted. 'Do you remember Chelsea Phillips in our class who was pregnant at sixteen? Her little one is six now – can you believe it? And she's still on her own. Nobody wants a woman with a kid in tow. She looks so awful – I don't think she even washes her hair. And the kid is so naughty.' Natalie stopped talking: Florence's face was covered with tears. 'What did I say?' Her mind worked quickly. 'Oh – Florence, tell me you're not...' She watched as Florence's eyes squeezed closed and a sob caught in her throat. 'I didn't know... Florence, I'm so sorry. Who's the father? I didn't know you were seeing anyone...'

Florence allowed Malia to wrap her arms around her, then she took a deep breath. 'I'm not.'

'Not pregnant?'

'Not seeing anyone, Nat. But yes, pregnant.'

'Oh, I'm so sorry...' Natalie didn't know what else to say.

'Odile's the only other person who knows,' Florence whispered. 'She promised not to say anything. She told me it's my business and as long as I'm fit to work at the café, I'm welcome to stay as long as I can. She's been very understanding.'

Malia said, 'Shall we go round mine now? Make some hot chocolate, chill out.'

Florence hesitated. 'Who will be in?'

'Mum and Dad have gone for a walk; Adam has a new girlfriend, I think – he went out straight after breakfast.'

'Then yes – thanks.' Florence accepted the hug both girls gave her, then she added, 'I'm going to see Dr Müller after work on Tuesday. Can I tell Dad I'm with you, Malia?'

'Of course...'

'Dr Müller's really nice,' Natalie said gently. 'I went to see her about contraception advice.'

'Will you both come with me?' Florence reached for both their hands. 'I'm terrified.'

'Of course,' Malia muttered.

'You've got your friends around you,' Natalie promised, then she frowned. 'But the father should step up as well...'

Malia shook her head. 'Florence will tell us about him when she's ready. Until then, we don't say anything, right?'

'Oh, definitely,' Natalie agreed.

'Thanks.' Florence closed her eyes. She could hear the birds twittering, and beyond, the light notes of Jack Lovejoy's guitar and his voice, singing. She recognised the song, it was by Ed Sheeran, and she knew the words: 'Small Bump', the song he wrote about his daughter. Florence was filled with so many emotions all at the same time, guilt, shame, fear, the unfairness of it all, and she bit her lip. She would not cry. It was time for her to accept the way things were and to deal with them.

12

The amber lights glimmered in the bar of The Sun Inn. Neil and Lin sat at a wooden table in the corner, finishing dessert. Neil reached across and touched Lin's hand. 'How was your lunch?'

Lin could still taste the chocolate brownie ice cream. 'It was lovely. Thanks so much for persuading me to come out.'

'You deserve it, love.' Neil caressed her fingers with his rough hands. 'How's the arthritis pain?'

'Not too bad – the tablets help a bit.' She sat up straight, offering a cheery grin. 'Shall we treat ourselves to a coffee?'

Neil stood up. 'I'll pop to the bar and ask Dickie for two coffees... and a chocolate mint.'

Lin watched him go, her eyes resting on his smart shirt, the way he moved in jeans. He was still gorgeous: she loved him more than anything else in the world. It came to her again that one day, one of them would pass on, leaving the other one alone, like Harry and Josie. Lin felt tears prick her eyes: those darned tablets again. She looked up as the door opened and, momentarily, she could hear Jack Lovejoy outside playing a sad song. Then she saw Josie walk in, supporting an older lady. She smiled and Cecily waved in recognition. Lin called out, 'Join us.'

They approached the table and Josie said, 'We've come in for a drink – we don't want to disturb your dinner.'

'Not at all – we've finished.' Lin beamed. 'Neil will be delighted to see you again, Cecily, and you know how he loves you, Josie. Sit down, please...'

'In that case,' Cecily eased herself onto a chair. 'It will be wonderful to see young Neil. And I can't wait to see Dickie Edwards and tease him.'

Josie sat down. 'You might see a few old faces that you remember in here.'

'What about the farmer's son, George?' Cecily asked.

'He comes in quite often, all the Ledburys do,' Lin explained. 'He's a grandfather now – they live in the big farmhouse and the cottages behind Barn Park. And Kenny Hooper comes in here most days for a pint of Hooky.' She pointed to the bar. 'That's Jimmy Baker over there.'

'Of course – I saw him in Odile's café.' Cecily was delighted. 'And what about the Irish boy who lived on the barge?'

'Fergal Toomey? He's still on the barge, but he has two sons now.' Josie made herself comfortable at the table. 'They do lots of odd jobs in the village, gardening to DIY. They are very good.'

'I'll bear that in mind when I need work done on my bungalow,' Cecily said just as Neil sat down. She extended a hand. 'I remember you, Neil Timms.'

Neil was amazed. 'Miss Hamilton...'

'Don't tell me I haven't changed – it wouldn't be true... but I'll accept flattery from the handsomest boy in the class.'

He took in the coat, the lipstick. 'You were like a film star. We boys were besotted.'

Cecily laughed and Lin smiled, warm with pride: Neil was so charming. 'I'll get you a drink,' Neil began, but Lin stood up.

'You stay here and catch up on the old times. I'll get them. What do you want, Cecily?'

'Gin and tonic, a large one.'

'Josie?'

'Juice – elderflower or orange.'

'Right.' Lin made her way to the bar where Dickie Junior was washing beer glasses. He looked up with a grin.

'Hello, Lin. How was the roast?'

'Heavenly, and so was dessert,' Lin replied. 'I just want a gin and tonic and an elderflower pressé, please.' She leaned forward confidentially. 'You see the woman opposite Neil?'

Dickie Junior squinted. 'The old dear?'

Lin met his eyes. 'She was your dad's primary school teacher, and mine and Neil's, all those years ago. She's threatening to tell you lots of juicy tales about him.'

'Then these drinks are on the house.' Dickie Junior busied himself with the optics. 'I'll go and tell Dad she's here – he can come over and say hello. He's out the back, watching the football on TV.'

'Thanks.' Lin reached for the glasses and turned to go.

Jimmy Baker was standing next to her, his voice low. 'That's Miss Hamilton over there...'

'It is,' Lin smiled.

Jimmy was staring. 'She's back, after all these years. Who'd have believed she'd still be alive? What's she doing here?'

'She's moved to Tadderly Road.'

'I'll have to go over and say hello properly.' Jimmy grinned. 'She recognised me in Odile's. I don't reckon I look much different – the hair's gone a bit... and I have a bit of a paunch nowadays.'

'I don't think you have a paunch,' Lin said kindly. 'But I'm sure the bicycle riding will improve things.'

Jimmy frowned. 'What bicycle riding?'

'Your bicycle. The one Neil helped you fix up this week.'

For a moment, Jimmy looked completely confused. Then he nodded energetically, as if he had suddenly remembered. 'Oh, yes, *that* bike... silly me, the *bike*.' He took the drinks from her hands. 'I'd forgotten completely. Yes, Neil helped me with the – with my bicycle. Right. Yes. I'll take these to Miss Hamilton for you, shall I, Lin?'

Lin watched him head towards the table, smiling at the woman in the fur coat who reached out to pat his arm. But Lin couldn't move. Her breathing had slowed for a moment – she was paralysed with shock. The sudden realisation that Jimmy was lying floored her. He'd had no idea about the bicycle: Neil had made it up – it was an excuse. He hadn't been at Jimmy's.

Lin was mystified. Neil turned to look at her and their gaze held. She beamed too enthusiastically and waved, and he smiled, a grin that looked like relief, and waved back.

Bravely, Lin took a deep breath and went over to sit down at the table, attempting the widest smile her aching face could muster. But inside, she felt hollow. Neil had deliberately lied. She could hardly believe it. It wasn't like him at all.

* * *

Minnie made her way up the steps of the imposing Ashmolean Museum wearing half-moon spectacles and a cloche hat. It was cool inside. The smell of old artefacts and rediscovered treasures, natural history collected over three millennia, made her pulse quicken. The objects fascinated her; a Greek tragic mask dating from the first century BC; *The Hunt in the Forest*, painted around 1470, by an Italian artist named Paolo Uccello; the Anglo-Saxon Alfred Jewel, made of enamel and quartz enclosed in gold. But this afternoon she wanted to see the Egyptian and Sudanese artefacts, the mummies, the Statue of Sobek the crocodile god, and the Cicero, excavated in Rome in 1614. She'd immerse herself in the ancient times, let history and culture seep into her skin. There was a good reason. She had someone special she intended to impress.

Minnie inspected a coffin containing mummified remains, reading the inscription carefully. 'Her name is Meresamun and her title is *Singer in the Interior of the Temple of Amun*.' She imagined the occupant, a high priestess, performing important rituals. She'd have come from a wealthy family – her vulture headdress indicated her high rank. Minnie calculated numbers quickly – if the priestess had lived in 830–715 BC, she'd have preceded Julius Caesar by quite a long time – he was assassinated in 44 BC, and he had taken over Egypt in the Battle of the Nile before he placed Cleopatra on the throne. Rome, Egypt; she had a timeline.

Minnie closed her eyes, hearing the raging battle of the Nile in 47 BC, clashing armies, Cleopatra sedately watching from her ship while Caesar shouted commands on horseback. She wanted to drink in the atmosphere, hear the sounds and inhale the smells. Then she would think about *Julius Caesar*, the play that was being rehearsed for production at the Playhouse. She needed to know everything about Caesar's background; first Egypt, then ancient Rome. Her knowledge had to be at least as good as Jensen Callahan's: she'd expect equality in a relationship.

She was about to leave the gallery when she saw him walking alone along the corridor, tall with a cloud of white hair, horn-rimmed spectacles. Of course he'd be here – the Playhouse was a stone's throw away. Minnie dodged back into the gallery and held her breath. For some reason she couldn't explain, she didn't want to see Jensen Callahan yet. She liked him; she found him intriguing. When she was ready, with all the right knowledge at her fingertips, she'd make her move.

She peered into the hall again and he had gone. She was relieved: Minnie wanted to meet him on her terms. She didn't want to be caught on the hop, exchange a polite greeting and then leave. He was fascinating, and she intended to be equally fascinating. She'd scintillate with her knowledge of Caesar; she'd bowl him over.

The next three hours slipped away and, by the time Minnie had visited all the artefacts, it was almost five and the museum was closing.

She skipped down the steps of the museum, turning down Magdalen Street towards Waterstones. She wondered if the bookshop would still be open, and if she had time to call in and browse. Then a voice made her shoulders stiffen. 'Minnie – wait a moment – wait for me, Minnie.'

She heard the clattering of feet behind her and she turned sharply, gazing at a man with white hair and a green velvet jacket. 'Felix.'

'Minnie – I wanted to see you.'

'Well, here I am.'

'Minnie...'

'Felix.'

He took a breath. 'You recall we went to the theatre together to see *Blood Wedding*.'

'We did.'

'And you enjoyed it.'

'I did.'

'Then I came to your house with flowers... and you wouldn't let me in.'

Minnie folded her arms. 'Where is this conversation going?'

'You suggested I take up Tai Chi and life drawing and conversational Japanese.'

'I did.'

'I wanted to thank you. I did exactly what you said. The Tai Chi has energised me. I feel so relaxed. I started a life drawing class and the people there are wonderful new friends. I'm meeting them next week – we're going to an opera. Then I started conversational Japanese classes and – guess what – I'm taking the teacher out to lunch tomorrow.'

'That's great news.' Minnie was genuinely pleased.

'And it's all down to your advice.'

'I'm delighted.' Minnie smiled sweetly. 'You're a wonderful person, Felix – you have a fine mind.' She took his hand, pressing it kindly. 'You don't need me now. Go forward and make the absolute most of life. Enjoy every precious moment. Perhaps your Japanese teacher will adore you for the exceptional man you are.'

'I hope she will – and if she doesn't, lunch will be a glorious experience, and I'll learn a new language.' Felix looked pleased with himself. 'Thank you, Minnie.'

Minnie raised a hand in a wave. 'Go and enjoy life – may good fortune accompany you.' She turned to go. '*Bonam fortunam tibi exopto.*' She had just wished him good luck in Latin. '*Kaíre pollá!*' She'd told him to have a nice day in Greek.

'*Arigatōgozaimasu,*' Felix blurted his thanks in Japanese. He was delighted. He shook her hand vigorously before hurrying away. Minnie watched him go before turning into the breeze, heading towards Corpus Christi and Oriel College, her step brisk, a smile on her face. She had a lunch date to organise too, with Josie and Lin. There were plans to hatch and her friends were her priority. She intended to give the Silver Ladies a memorable time. Besides, The Bear would be open for business and there was a pint of best bitter with her name on it.

13

'He thinks the world of that pig,' Penny grunted.

Lin called in to the Co-op on Thursday morning on her way to visit Josie. She was standing in a queue holding onto a packet of chocolate digestive biscuits and a jar of coffee. Penny Ledbury was clutching cleaning products, her face indignant. 'George loves her more than he loves me.'

Lin pulled herself from the thoughts that jumbled together in her head. She was still anxious, remembering Jimmy Baker's words in the pub, but she tried to concentrate. 'He loves who more than you?'

'Nadine.'

'Who?'

'The Hampshire pig he's named after the Chuck Berry song. He takes her out in the tractor with him now. She sits up in the cab and he feeds her chocolate. She's devoted to him. She comes indoors at night-time and sits on the rug by the fireside.'

Lin was confused. 'The pig?'

'Yes. I'm not exaggerating, Lin, he'll have her sleeping in our bed soon.'

'A pig in the bed?' Lin wasn't listening properly – she wasn't sure if Penny was joking.

Penny was still ranting. 'It's so difficult up at the farmhouse. My son

Tom just does the accounts all day, shirking all the hard farm work. His wife's the worst cook in the world; Natalie talks of nothing but wedding dresses; Bobby is out every evening and now George is in love with a pig.'

'No, *I'm* the worst cook in the world,' Lin mumbled sadly.

Penny frowned. 'Goodness knows what will happen when we take Nadine to the slaughterhouse. It's never a good idea to give an animal a name, especially when it will eventually end up on the butcher's slab.'

Lin shook her head. 'You're going to kill Nadine?'

'She's a pig, Lin.'

'Yes, but...' Lin was suddenly full of sympathy. 'That will be so hard for poor George.'

'It will teach him not to get so attached,' Penny announced, then it was her turn to be served at the till. Lin sighed; she was looking forward to seeing Josie. There was a lot she needed to confide in her.

Ten minutes later, she was wandering down Orchard Way, the neat rows of allotments on one side. She could see Tina Gilchrist, Minnie's sister, weeding the soil, her pale hair over her face. Lin called out a cheery hello, but Tina was out of earshot. She passed the recreation ground, where an older man sat on a swing drinking something from a can. Lin was sure it was Kenny Hooper. She raised a hand in a wave, but he didn't see her. She wondered if she was invisible.

Then she arrived level with Gerald Harris's house. Devlin and Finn Toomey were working in the garden, raking and digging, sorting out the mess, while Gerald rushed around flapping his hands anxiously. Devlin raised a hand. 'Mornin', Lin. How are ye?'

Finn looked up and grinned. 'Full of the joys of spring?'

'I'm fine, thanks,' Lin nodded. Both Toomeys were without shirts, their skin glistening as they worked. Gerald was red faced and anxious. He turned to Lin. 'George Ledbury has offered to pay for the garden. I told him it's all very well but that pig ought to be locked up.'

'Nadine,' Lin said.

'I beg your pardon?' Gerald asked, puffing out his cheeks.

'Nadine – after a Chuck Berry song.'

'Ah, we know the one, don't we, Dev?' Finn laughed and he and his brother joined in a jig, miming playing a guitar, kicking out a leg Chuck Berry-style, screaming, 'Na-deeeeen!'

Gerald was perplexed. 'I told George I want the garden just as it was before the pig attacked it.'

'It'll be lovely when the lads have finished,' Lin soothed, then she was on her way.

She was still thinking about George's pig as she knocked at Josie's door. She handed over the coffee and biscuits.

'You didn't need to bring these,' Josie chided.

'I did,' Lin said sadly. 'I need coffee and sympathy.'

Lin wasn't sure where to start, how to tell Josie that Neil had lied to her. Lin knew that Josie would believe there must be a mistake: Lin had a wonderful marriage, a doting husband. Josie would tell her not to bottle up her worries, to ask Neil about it outright – there was bound to be a simple explanation.

Lin sank down on the leather sofa as Josie bustled around making coffee. She'd baked a sponge cake. Lin gazed around the living room, at the pretty chintz curtains, cream walls. The house was too big for one person. The walls were adorned with pictures of Harry, of Josie and Harry together; there was more than fifty years of love, but it had come to an end. No, Lin decided, she wouldn't say anything about Neil and Jimmy's bicycle: she was just being silly.

Twenty minutes later, they were laughing about an incident in Miss Hamilton's class years ago, when Fergal Toomey had proudly laid a dead pheasant on her desk, its feathers glossy and its beady eyes still open. He'd bragged, accompanying his words with perfect mime skills, that he had shot it just for her specially in Old Scratch's woods before the sun rose. Dickie Edwards had laughed loudly and Lin had burst into tears.

Then, at playtime, Neil had given Lin a whole packet of Love Hearts and walked off without a word. When Lin had opened the packet, the first sweet was a pink one inscribed with the motto Be Mine. Lin remembered it and it filled her heart with tenderness for her wonderful husband. She decided to forget about the bicycle episode. It was a lot of fuss about nothing.

Then Josie's phone rang and she held it to her ear, mouthing to Lin,

'It's Minnie.' She tilted her head to one side. 'Lunch, yes, of course. When? The 30th would be fine – Sunday, okay. Yes, Lin's here now – oh, no problem...' Josie looked across at Lin and handed over her phone.

'Hi, Minnie, it's Lin.' Lin opened her eyes wide. 'Oh, well, yes, that would be incredible. I'm sure Neil would have no problem with me taking it on the Sunday.' She sighed. 'He'll probably find plenty to do, go for a hike with the rambling group or see his friends... oh, well, he might come with us – I'll ask him – yes, let's do it. Cecily? Why not? We'll talk to her... great, that's sorted then – we'll ring you back.'

Josie held her hand out for the phone. 'Lunch on the river and then the theatre...'

'Minnie's asked me to drive. I'm sure Neil won't mind me talking the Sharan. In fact, Minnie's going to get five tickets in case he wants to come with us.'

'I haven't been to Stratford for ages. Harry and I went once to see *Much Ado About Nothing*. I can't remember what it was about – nothing much, I suppose.' Josie's face was wistful for a moment. 'What are we going to see at the theatre?'

'Minnie didn't say,' Lin said thoughtfully. 'But we're all going to have a picnic on the river. I'm sure Cecily will be delighted to join the Silver Ladies.'

'Heavenly.' Josie grinned. 'It will give us something to look forward to. Meanwhile, how about another cup of coffee and a slice of cake?'

'Perfect.' Lin held out her cup and tried a smile. Perhaps life wasn't so bad after all.

***

Florence waved goodbye to Odile, closing the door with a tinkle. She had a hefty slice of cake and several pies in her basket: Odile had said she looked a bit peaky and needed to keep her strength up, then she had winked knowingly. Florence had already decided she'd give the pies to her father for his tea. She wasn't hungry.

As she walked towards Newlands, she passed the Johnsons' home. She thought about knocking at the door, stopping for a chat with Malia. Her best friend would be going back to uni in a week or so for the final term. Florence gazed up at the house, a neat semi with a tidy garden. It was past five; the family would all be there. Adam Johnson might be home and Florence didn't really want to see him. There was an intensity in his eyes when he looked at her, there always had been, long before they broke up last summer. And Malia had said he had a new girlfriend – Florence didn't want to meet her, or to intrude if the family were having dinner. She didn't feel much like being sociable.

She walked on, gazing at her feet. Malia had been so supportive during the visit to Dr Müller's surgery a few days ago; Natalie too. Dr Müller had talked Florence through the healthcare process and told her that she'd be supported throughout the pregnancy, the birth and afterwards. Dr Müller advised her to tell her father and Florence had shed tears of hopelessness. She welled up again at she thought of it. Her dad's heart had been broken by her mother. He did his best for Florence; he always called her his princess: this would shatter his trust. She could imagine his face when she told him, he'd be so disappointed, so hurt. Then he'd ask who the father was and become protective. He wouldn't understand that she couldn't tell him.

Florence could see their house at the bottom of the hill. Her dad would be sitting in his armchair with a cup of tea watching Sky Sports. She ought to tell him about the baby. It was only fair – he deserved to know.

Jack Lovejoy drove past in his old car. He'd probably been busking in Tadderly. She didn't wave and he didn't notice her. Florence sighed: soon, everyone in the village would know about the baby. They'd see it for themselves.

She'd almost reached the front door, the key in her hand, when she decided she'd tell her father straight away, before they made tea. It made sense; otherwise, he might hear it from someone else, and that would be worse. What if Natalie mentioned it to her mother, who'd tell her gran, and Penny Ledbury was bound to say something in the Co-op. Or Natalie would let it slip to George and he'd say something to one of the men in the pub who'd blurt it out to her father. Soon, people would be bound to notice: Florence was slim, the bump didn't really show yet. But it wouldn't take long before prying eyes stared at her middle and someone would ask,

'Are you putting on weight?' Her dad couldn't find out that way, she wouldn't allow it.

Florence closed the door behind her, feeling the immediate warmth from the radiators. She could hear the TV rattling. If she told her father tonight, the hardest part would be over. Then she could look forward: she could start to believe things would be all right, she could accept the rush of love for the baby that already filled her heart.

Her voice was deliberately breezy as she rushed into the lounge. 'Hi, Dad...'

Then she stopped dead in her tracks. He had a cup of tea in front of him, holding it precariously with his left hand. His right hand was swathed in bandages. She gasped. 'What have you done? Dad?'

Dangerous Dave forced a laugh from his chair. 'Ah, it's not so bad...'

'What happened?'

'Nothing to worry about, love. Just a small burn. A lad brought a motorcycle in and I burned my hand on the exhaust.'

'It's not serious?'

'I had it dressed at the General in Tadderly. I rang Neil and he took me in. It was a bit of a wait in A & E.'

'Dad?'

'Ah, it'll heal. I just wasn't thinking properly at the time...' Dave laughed and raised his bandaged hand. 'The doc said it'll be right as rain – I'll be back to work soon. I've been a silly sausage. Talking of sausages – how about some bangers for tea?'

Florence lifted the basket. 'Odile sent some pies.'

'Bless her.' Dave eased himself up from the armchair, wincing a little as he brushed his sore hand against the chair arm. 'And bless you, my princess – you'll have to cook by yourself tonight. Your old dad's crocked.' He wrapped his arms around Florence in a hug. 'Ah, you're a good girl, the best. What would I do without you, eh?'

'I don't know, Dad.' Florence took a deep breath. She wouldn't tell him about the baby tonight, or tomorrow. She'd wait until his hand had healed. She'd tell him then.

14

'Are you sure you don't want to come with me, love?' Lin asked as she shrugged on her jacket.

'I don't think I will, Lindy.' Neil stood in the kitchen, gazing out of the window. 'It's a nice day and the rambling group are going for a hike in Old Scratch's woods. I might go with them. You take the Sharan, have a lovely time.'

'There's a spare ticket...'

'Minnie might be able to sell it back to the theatre – someone will be glad of it.'

'Are you sure?' Lin reached for her handbag, wishing he'd change his mind.

Neil looked up at the sky. 'It's a lovely day. Stratford will be beautiful.'

'Minnie's bringing a picnic.'

'What are you going to see?' Neil asked.

'I've no idea, Minnie didn't say.'

'Oh, I don't believe it,' Neil exclaimed and rushed out into the back garden.

'What is it?' Lin followed him through the back door, before standing next to him, staring into the farmer's field. George Ledbury waved as he passed, a grin on his face. His cap was firmly pulled down over his eyebrows and, next to him in the cab, a black and white pig sat proudly. Lin almost expected it to wave a trotter.

Neil gasped. 'He's got a pig in there with him.'

'Nadine – she's named after a Chuck Berry song,' Lin explained.

A voice came from beyond the hedge. 'Penny Ledbury is sick of it. She told me in the Co-op.' Janice Lovejoy's head came into view. 'Penny says the pig goes everywhere with George. He feeds it biscuits, you know.'

'And chocolate,' Lin replied.

Janice sniffed. 'Did you know the pig snaffled Bomber Harris's prize daffs?'

'Penny told me George would be upset when it was time for the pig to be taken to...' Lin made a face, 'you know where. Poor George.'

'It's only a pig,' Janice remarked. 'And everyone loves bacon.'

'I think it's really sweet,' Neil observed. 'Some people have dogs and cats; George has his pig.'

Janice shook her head. 'Kenny Hooper saw her in the rec the other day, just strolling home. I expect she was coming back from her raid on Bomber's daffodils.'

'She'll be popping into Odile's for a coffee next,' Lin joked.

'Or a ham sandwich?' Janice barked a laugh. 'Do you want some eggs? Susan has given me a beautiful brown one this morning.'

'Thanks, the last ones were lovely,' Neil said, watching the tractor chug towards the horizon. Janice disappeared into the house and Lin was still thinking about the village gossip; everyone seemed to know everything that as going on, and she suddenly felt cold. She imagined people talking about her, about Neil pretending to mend Jimmy's bicycle. She wondered again where her husband had been.

'I'd best be off,' Lin said and Neil kissed her cheek.

'Have a great day, Lindy.'

'Will you be here when I get back?' she asked hesitantly.

'Where else would I be?' Neil's eyes twinkled. 'I'll get something organised for supper, shall I?'

* * *

Lin was still thinking about village gossip as she drove to Josie's, then they picked up Cecily, making her comfortable in the front seat, and drove past the village green to the railway station. Josie pointed out Florence Dawson, who was sitting on the bench talking to Devlin Toomey, deep in conversation. At the station, Minnie was waiting outside wearing a Che Guevara sweatshirt and beret, a picnic basket in her arms. She clambered on board, snuggling into the back seat.

'Well, this is very luxurious, Lin. I can't imagine why Neil needs such a big car, but I'm very glad he has it.'

'We bought it ten years ago. We hoped we'd be able to use it to take the grandchildren out and about, Debbie too, but it never really happened.'

'So where is Neil now?' Minnie asked.

'He's gone hiking,' Lin replied awkwardly.

'So, we have a spare ticket?' Josie observed.

'We might be able to return it and get the money back,' Lin suggested as she manoeuvred the car past the village green.

'Stop,' Cecily commanded. 'Stop at once.'

Lin pulled in by the kerb, wondering if Cecily needed the toilet. 'Is everything all right?'

'Do you know that young person?' Cecily asked, pointing to Florence. She was by herself now, seated beneath the weeping willow, gazing at her fingers.

'It's Florence,' Josie said. 'She works at Odile's café.'

'Call her over,' Cecily commanded. 'We have a spare ticket for the theatre and there's a young person who seems to have nothing to do.'

Josie wound down the window. 'Florence? Have you got a moment?'

Florence walked obediently towards the car. Her movements were slow. 'Hello, Josie...'

Cecily called through the open window. 'What are you doing with yourself today? Would you like to come to Stratford?'

Florence shook her head. 'I don't know... why would I?'

'We have a spare ticket for the theatre,' Cecily said simply.

'It would only go to waste,' Josie said.

Florence glanced towards The Sun Inn. Her father would be there soon for his Sunday pint. Jack Lovejoy was already opening his guitar case, tuning up. She could see him, wearing his colourful cap.

Josie continued, 'We're having a picnic, watching a play and then we're coming home.'

Lin called over, 'You can message your dad. I'm sure he won't mind.'

Florence hesitated. Malia was working on an essay today; Natalie was out with Brandon. She'd made no plans. She glanced to the left; Darryl and Charlotte Featherstone emerged in Lycra from their house at Nobb's End, off for a jog.

'I could come.'

'It would be an adventure,' Cecily smiled. 'Hop in.'

'Give Dave a call,' Josie urged. 'Tell him where you're going.'

'Seize the day,' Minnie teased. 'We'll have you back home before the witching hour.'

Florence shrugged. She may as well go to see a play – she knew Josie, Lin and Minnie well and they were always cheerful. She'd feel depressed if she was by herself – she still hadn't told her father about the baby, and the bandage had been off his hand for days.

She forced a smile. 'I'd love to – thanks.'

Minnie held the car door open. 'In you get.'

Florence got in the car, pulled on the seatbelt, adjusted her dress, and they were off. Minnie cheered. 'Stratford, here we come – the Silver Ladies do lunch...'

Florence stared through the window throughout the journey. She'd only been to Stratford twice, although it wasn't very far from Middleton Ferris, but she'd been too young to remember anything except the boats on the river. As they chugged along in traffic into the town, there was a row of houses, a roundabout, a school. She wasn't sure what all the fuss was about.

Then they reached the town centre, and Florence gasped. There were so many Tudor houses clustered together, layered row upon row, just like in the time of Queen Elizabeth I. She marvelled at the crowded buildings with the classic black and white frontages, the thatched roofs and overhanging upper storeys. Several of them were taverns, and Florence imagined men in tunics inside noisy pubs, the rooms smoky as they drank from frothy tankards served by women in frilly caps. She gazed at the hotchpotch of houses with zebra stripes and patterns. Then they turned a corner and she saw the theatre beyond the river, a beautiful modern building crafted from bricks with a tall tower and huge glass windows.

She whispered, 'Is that where we're going?'

'It is,' Minnie smiled. 'We're going to see *Coriolanus*.'

'What's that?' Lin asked. 'Is she a romantic heroine?'

'He's a Roman soldier,' Cecily explained. 'I love that play!'

'The Romans?' Lin wrinkled her nose. 'I hope it's not boring.'

'I'm going through a bit of a Roman phase at the moment.' Minnie smiled to herself, fully aware of her motives. 'It's a play about pride and the power of the plebeians. What could be more relevant today?'

'Isn't there any romance in it?' Josie asked.

'Most romance is overrated,' Minnie replied with a tight smile.

Twenty minutes later, Lin had found a space for the Sharan outside the park, and the group traipsed across the grass to sit on blankets by the riverbank. Josie helped Cecily as she took small steps, creeping forward slowly, her face creased in a smile. Lin flopped down, stretched her aching legs and sighed. 'This is idyllic, isn't it?' She gazed at two men who passed by in a small rowing boat, oars dipping in the river making a gentle lapping sound. Two swans slid by, their long necks turning like periscopes.

The river was a surface of rippled glass, and trees hung over the banks, trailing low leaves in the water. Beyond, the sky was filled with curled lamb's tail clouds. Minnie placed plates on a mat, and arranged dishes of food.

'What are we eating?' Lin asked. 'It smells good.'

Minnie was delighted. 'I've brought salmon sandwiches, courgette mini-quiches, prawn and avocado Vietnamese summer rolls, chicken katsu, beetroot and chickpea dip, guacamole, mint and basil griddled peach salad, bread…'

Florence stared. 'I've no idea what any of those things are, apart from the bread.'

'It sounds heavenly. I'm delighted to have been asked to join your little group,' Cecily said. 'Did you make it all?'

'Some of it.' Minnie winked. 'Euripides said, "Friends show their love in times of trouble" – our lovely Miss Hamilton told us – "so we share lunch as friends."'

'I wish I could cook though.' Lin pulled a face. 'I can't even make toast.'

'I can cook sausages, but not much else,' Florence said hesitantly. It occurred to her that she might have to prepare food for the baby. She had no idea what to feed a child.

Minnie offered a smile. 'Just try it and see what you think, Florence.' She was thoughtful for a moment. 'The first time I tried smoked salmon, I was not much younger than you are now. I was at a banquet at St Hilda's, a fish out of water. I'd never had food like it – someone gave me crème brûlée and I asked if it was cold scrambled eggs and everyone laughed at me.' Minnie pressed her lips together, remembering. '*Per ardua ad astra.*'

'What does that mean?' Josie asked.

Cecily smiled. '*Through adversity to the stars*... It must have been difficult, Minnie, going to Oxford straight from a small village like Middleton Ferris.'

'At first.' Minnie nodded. 'If only I had a coin for every time someone laughed at me for being a yokel. But I had many supportive friends too. They got me through.' She flourished a salmon sandwich. 'And here I am now. I've brought chilled champagne for a light Buck's Fizz each and a bottle of Blood Orange and Bitter Lemon Shrub for the driver and those who don't want alcohol.'

'That's me, please,' Florence said quietly. 'I don't drink...'

'Well, that's refreshing,' Lin grinned. 'Most youngsters can't get alcohol down their throats quick enough. I remember when Debbie was your age, Florence, she guzzled cider every weekend. She'd come home so tipsy...'

'Oh, we all drank it when we were teenagers in the rec, didn't we?' Josie remembered. 'Dickie Edwards used to pilfer it from his dad's pub.'

'Those were the days,' Minnie said as she filled glasses. 'But today, we'll enjoy some of the finer things. We deserve it once in a while.'

'We do,' Cecily agreed. 'We'll eat this delicious lunch, stretch out for a while on the grass to let the food digest, and then we'll pop over to the theatre and watch Coriolanus meet his fate.'

They sat in the glorious sunshine, listening to the gentle lapping of the river. Then Florence asked, 'What happens if I don't understand any of the play because it's by Shakespeare?'

'The story's quite straightforward.' Minnie sipped Buck's Fizz. 'Coriolanus is a brilliant soldier and a proud man, but he's foolish. He ignores the smelly rabble, makes a bad choice. One mistake costs him dearly... and there's no turning back after that.'

'Oh, that's so true, one mistake...' Florence was surprised to realise she had tears in her eyes. She watched a boat glide past on the river, filled with tourists. 'It's the same as it is now – if you make a mistake, you have to live with it for ever.'

Lin sat upright. 'Things can be spoiled by one single thoughtless slip-up. It can ruin trust, marriage, friendship.'

Josie added. 'But you can't change what's happened in the past, once it's done. You have to go forwards.'

There was stillness for a moment. Then Minnie forced a short laugh. 'Well, the food is all gone, and time has flown, as it always does.' She put a hand on Florence's shoulder, exchanging a glance with Lin and Josie. 'Let's pack up shall we, and put these things in the car? Then we can stroll across the bridge to the theatre. It's time to get our teeth into some good old-fashioned tragedy.'

15

Minnie spent a great deal of the time not watching *Coriolanus* on stage. She knew the play well, and she could hear the actors' voices booming in her ears. Instead, she watched the faces of her four companions. It was fascinating.

Lin's mouth was open, observing every movement as if she had never seen anything like it. She was caught up in the emotion, betrayal, deceit, her hands pressed together, holding her breath. Josie was sitting next to her, her head turned to one side, frowning. Minnie could tell she was following every word each actor spoke, puzzling out the meaning. Cecily was smiling like a child with candy floss, her face illuminated. But it was Florence's expression that captivated Minnie most. She clearly hadn't expected to enjoy the play, but it seemed to have pulled her into its centre as if it was real and held her there as she watched the story unfold. Minnie noticed her fingering her one solitary silver hoop earring, and how the skin between her eyes puckered as she thought about the characters and their actions.

Minnie reflected upon her own life; she'd started with a thirst for knowledge in a home where learning was scorned. It had made her determined to emerge from the drought and drink up every drop. She thought of Tina, held back from an education by their blustering father. Minnie's liberty had forged the bars that kept her younger sister a prisoner. Tina trod her own path, married Les Gilchrist, become an ambulance driver, divorced and then she'd immersed herself in her organic vegetables. Minnie marvelled at her sister's strength and resilience, but she blamed herself for the route Tina's life had taken; she'd escaped, and as a result, Tina had been made to stay.

Before she knew it, the play was over, Coriolanus was dead, and the audience were applauding the actors, standing in appreciation. Minnie watched her friends clapping and smiling. Josie and Lin helped Cecily to her feet. She was stiff and moved slowly, despite being cushioned by everyone's jackets.

Florence turned to Minnie. 'That was amazing – I loved it.'

'I'm glad.' Minnie studied Florence and decided the play had struck a chord.

The friends followed the queues outside into the fresh air. Lin said, 'Poor Coriolanus. Fancy having a mother like Volumnia. She was harsh.'

Cecily agreed. 'Isn't she meant to represent Queen Elizabeth I, strong and powerful?'

'Imagine having a mum like that, though,' Josie breathed. 'She was so pushy, it was horrible.'

They began to walk back to the car slowly. 'It's not easy being a mother,' Lin admitted. 'Not that I was pushy with Debbie. Perhaps I should have been. Perhaps she'd have had more time for me if I'd been like Volumnia.'

Minnie agreed. 'Strong women were completely responsible for my education – my mother argued with my father and Miss Hamilton came round the house and read the riot act.' She patted Cecily's arm. 'I'll always be grateful for that.'

'My grandmother believed that women's education was just as important as men's, and so do I.' Cecily smiled. 'My grandmother was a suffragette. She was called Cecily too.'

Lin sighed. 'I'm not sure mothers are appreciated, even now.' They were almost back at the car, walking slowly for Cecily. 'It's still a man's world. Men do as they like.'

'I won't take a back seat on things I believe in,' Cecily replied grimly.

'I'm ninety years old. I haven't got time to play second fiddle. I'm going to make my last few years count...'

Josie said, 'Volumnia was a bad mother, though.'

'She was,' Minnie agreed. 'Thou shalt no sooner march to assault thy country than to tread... on thy mother's womb, that brought thee to this world.'

'Everyone blames mothers when things go wrong, though,' Lin insisted. 'Never the father. Men get away with all sorts.'

Florence stopped walking. Her face was covered with tears. 'I'm so frightened...'

Lin was concerned. 'Did the play upset you?' She wrapped warm arms around her. 'Florence, it was just a play...'

'No.' Sobs shook Florence's shoulders. 'It's not that – it's... being a mother is going to be so hard.'

It took seconds for the women to understand. They exchanged glances, then they moved towards Florence as one. Josie said, 'You're pregnant...'

Florence nodded, wiping her face on her sleeve.

'When is the baby due?' Minnie asked, ever practical.

'Early October, the doctor thinks.' Florence sniffed.

'Was it planned?' Lin asked gently and Minnie rolled her eyes. 'I mean, what does your boyfriend think?'

'There is no boyfriend,' Minnie whispered. 'Am I right?'

Florence swallowed. 'I don't want to say who he is.'

'That's absolutely up to you,' Minnie agreed.

'Won't he support you?' Josie asked. 'He ought to.'

'I don't want that...' Florence shook her head, new tears springing up. 'I haven't told him. I can't...'

'Doesn't he love you?' Lin asked and Florence shook her head.

'Men like that disgust me.' Cecily made a low noise. 'What about your mother? She'll support you, surely.'

'My mother left us ages ago.'

Cecily's face was horrified. 'You have no mother to turn to? Oh, Florence, that's just not fair.'

'No, you're right, it isn't...' Florence took a breath. 'Odile knows about the baby, and Malia and Natalie, and Dr Müller, but no one else knows.'

'Not Dave?' Lin asked.

'He'll be upset,' Florence said quietly. 'I can't bring myself to tell him.'

The four women closed in tighter, a circle of hugs, and Lin muttered, 'He'll be there for you.'

'I can't tell Dad... He's been so supportive since Mum left...'

'You don't have to tell him yet,' Josie said. 'It's your choice.'

'But he'll notice soon enough,' Lin offered.

'How can we help?' Cecily asked. 'What can we do?'

'Why don't we drive you home?' Minnie suggested. 'We can talk about it in the car. You tell us what you need, and we'll do whatever it takes.'

'Thank you,' Florence whispered. 'I'm so grateful for your help...'

They had arrived at the Sharan. Josie eased Cecily into the front seat and said, 'Anything, just ask.'

Lin started the engine. 'We'll be Team Florence.'

Florence clicked her seatbelt. 'Thank you.'

'It makes my blood boil that your mum isn't there for you,' Cecily said irritably. 'And as for the father... it's just ridiculous, a man makes a woman pregnant, he gets off scot-free and she's left to fend for herself. It's so wrong. A man should show some backbone.'

Four faces turned to look at her, surprised by her sudden vehemence. Cecily folded her arms firmly. 'I'm just saying. It's absurd. And appalling.'

'It is,' Minnie agreed. 'I don't know much about babies, though.'

'Nor me,' Josie added. 'But we'll support you, Florence.'

'Too right we will,' Lin promised.

'And if you do decide that you want the shameful man who's left you in the lurch to step up, dear,' Cecily clenched her hands, 'I'd be glad to go round to his house in place of your absent mother and explain a few things to him. And I won't be very refined about it.'

Florence smiled, imagining Cecily going to visit the man who had fathered her baby, knocking on his door, expressing her views to his embarrassed face, grabbing him by the collar, a ninety-year-old woman making threats. The image was too much, and Florence's smile became a grin.

Then she couldn't help it, laughter came tumbling out, and she was in fits of giggles for the first time in ages.

* * *

Florence stepped into the warmth of her home, and hung her coat in the hall. Lin had dropped Cecily off first, then she'd deposited Minnie at the station before leaving her outside her door. Lin had been relieved to receive a text from Neil who said he'd come back from rambling and made shepherd's pie, opened a bottle of wine and he was waiting for her at home. Florence couldn't imagine going home to a man who loved her enough to make dinner; she'd probably still be cooking sausages for her father's tea and looking after her young one for years to come.

Dangerous Dave was in the lounge; Florence could hear the TV chattering, the chant of a football crowd. She called out, 'Dad, I'm home.' She took a deep breath: she was ready.

'In here, princess,' he called. She plastered a smile on her face and walked into the lounge. The gas fire was blazing. She scanned the TV; Chelsea were drawing 1-1, so it probably wasn't the best time to chat. Dave sipped from a beer can. 'I made a sandwich for my tea. I made you one too – cheese and pickle. It's in the kitchen.'

'Thanks, Dad.' Florence was standing in the doorway; she didn't move.

'How was Stratford?' Her father grinned. 'Imagine my princess going to the theatre and watching Shakespeare. Did you have a good time?'

'I did.' Florence heard the surprise in her voice. 'The women I went with were lovely.'

'I like Lin and Josie...' Dave muttered before taking another swig. 'They are proper old school – and Neil's a good bloke.'

'He is... he's made her dinner.'

'Oh, right – he's a good cook.'

'Have you had a nice day, Dad?'

'Oh, ah, yes – I had a couple of drinks in The Sun at lunchtime. I met the rambling group coming back from their Sunday hike. I felt sorry for them – there were only three of them, the vicar and two women... not the best turnout. I expect there will be more when the weather gets warmer.'

'Ah...' Florence paused. 'Dad?' She took a breath.

'Florence.' He twisted round, giving her his full attention, a smile ready on his face.

'I have something to tell you.'

'Oh?' Dave raised his brows.

'It's really difficult...' She fidgeted, moving from one foot to the other, chewing a nail. Suddenly she wondered if she should tell him at all. It would be easy to say something else, to talk about the picnic, the river, the play. She didn't need to tell him about the baby, not yet. It was too hard; she didn't want to see his face crumble.

There was cheering on the TV. The commentator was yelling. Someone had scored, but Dave's eyes were on his daughter. 'It's not difficult, love. I know.'

'What do you know?' Florence froze. The room spun a little bit.

'I found the thingy – the testing stick – in your bin when I was emptying the rubbish... I wasn't sure at first, then it occurred to me what it was.' Dave offered a weak smile. 'So, I'm going to be a grandad?'

'Oh, Dad – I'm sorry...' Florence fought back tears. She didn't want to cry. She wanted to be strong.

Then he was up from his seat, taking her in sturdy arms. 'Do you want to tell me about it?'

Florence sniffed. Her face was wet, dampening his T-shirt. 'What do you want to know?'

'How are you feeling? Are you over the moon? Do you have morning sickness? I remember your mum did...'

Then they were both crying. Florence tried to catch her breath. 'Are you angry, Dad?'

'Why would I be?'

'Disappointed?'

'Not at all.'

'I've been to see Dr Müller.'

'That's good.' Dave raised his head. The commentator on the TV was shouting excitedly. Chelsea had the ball again. 'Shall we go in the kitchen and make a nice cuppa? You can tell me all about the baby, whether you want a boy or a girl, and we can discuss what colour we're going to paint the spare room. Sunshine yellow, that's cheery...'

'You're not going to ask me about the father? Dad, it was a mistake, I don't really talk to him now, and I don't want people to think...'

'Who cares what people think? It's your baby and it's what you want that counts.' Dave pressed his rough face against the top of her head, feeling the smoothness of her hair. He'd stroked it so many times when she was a teenager, after his wife left, as she sobbed into the pillow. He'd been there for her then and he wasn't going to let her down now.

Florence gazed up into his eyes and saw so much kindness there. 'Thanks, Dad.'

'Nothing to thank me for. I'm your dad, you're my princess and I couldn't be prouder.'

16

Josie woke to a fine May Day Monday morning, a broad sunbeam illuminating the duvet. Harry's smile met her eyes as it always did first thing, grinning from the bedside photo. She pressed kissed fingers to his lips and thought again of his happy whistle, how she'd give anything to hear it now. She stretched her limbs, pulled on comfortable clothes, and rushed down to the village green. It was early, not yet nine; preparations were already in progress for the festivities. A maypole was in the centre, with colourful pieces of cloth hanging down, ready for the dancing. There was a selection of stalls; loudspeakers were being tested. The willow tree was decorated with bunting and multicoloured lights. She sidled quietly into the churchyard, her feet treading on familiar grass as she approached Harry's grave.

As she always did, Josie spoke to Harry in her head. 'We went to the theatre in Stratford, love... You'd have enjoyed it, but you'd have liked the picnic more, the calmness of the river, the Avon... George Ledbury has a pig now, Nadine – he loves her more than Penny...' She smiled. 'It was good to see Minnie – she looks so well... Lin too, although her meds make her tearful. Neil is devoted to her as ever... I wish you could have met Miss Hamilton, Cecily – I've told you how she used to read to us and play the guitar, oh, and we took young Florence Dawson with us –

remember her, Dangerous Dave's lovely daughter – poor thing, she's struggling—'

Josie was pulled from her thoughts by a deep voice from behind. 'Ah, I see you're conversing with the dead too...'

Josie turned to gaze into the twinkling eyes of Fergal Toomey. She stood slowly. 'Fergal – it's a bit early...'

'I come here to talk to Ros most mornings.' He shrugged. 'Not that she's here, she was cremated. But it's a quiet place and I like to think about her here. We have conversations with each other in my head.'

'Do you?'

'I do. I'm a bit of an eejit that way...'

'So am I.' Josie sighed. 'It helps.'

'It does. Your man hasn't been gone that long?'

'Over a year.'

'Is it a year now?' Fergal shook his head. 'Ros died twelve years ago. Finn was only fourteen.' He wiped a hand across his brow.

Josie met his eyes. 'Does it get any better?'

'It does, slowly.' Fergal placed a fist over his heart. 'There's a big hole where she was, and it's still tender, but it doesn't ache so bad now. At first, I thought I was having a heart attack, it was that hard to breathe – but I guess a broken heart feels just the same as angina.' He grinned. 'How's yourself, Josie? How are you keeping up?'

'Some days are better than others,' she said honestly.

'I hear you've been on a cruise. That took some balls to go all that way by yourself.'

'It did.'

'And someone told me Miss Hamilton is back in the village. Ah, we all liked her. She looked like a film star.'

'She still does.'

'I saw them all setting up for the May Day hoolie on the green.'

'Yes. I'm going to watch.'

'Devlin and Finn will be there, drinking and dancing. I used to be the one for it myself but I've not got the heart for it any more. I can hear it all from the barge.'

'We could watch it together,' Josie suggested.

'Ah, yes, we could do that.' Fergal rubbed his chin. 'Have you eaten breakfast?'

Josie shook her head. She had forgotten. It wasn't the first time; breakfast had always been a shared experience, coffee, laughter, conversation.

'Come to the barge – the lads will have a pan of Joe Grey on the stove.' He grinned. 'We barge boatmen like to have ourselves a good breakfast. If we have nothing else for the rest of the day, our bellies are still full.'

'Thanks,' Josie smiled. 'I'd love to.'

They sat on the deck of the red and black barge, eating a stew of sausages, bacon, beans. Devlin and Finn were below deck. Josie could hear their rumbling voices, Finn's light laughter. She licked her lips. 'This is good, Fergal. Is it your own recipe?'

He shook his head. 'Ros used to make it every morning. I can't do it like she did. I use stock cubes but she had the proper stock.'

'Where did you meet her?'

Fergal's eyes twinkled. 'I'd had my share of being footloose and fancy free. I was just in my forties and I decided I wanted a wife, so I went up to Appleby Fair. Most people come back with a horse but I came back with Ros Crocker. She had the longest hair I'd ever seen and she was twenty-four and she only had eyes for me. I was smitten.' He shrugged his shoulders. 'Finn and Devlin are just like I was at their age – their heads are all over the place, they don't want to be tied down. They meet one girl, then they move on to another, but I've told them, one morning they'll wake up just like I did and they'll want a wife for keeps.'

Josie was thoughtful. 'Do they date local girls?'

'Sometimes – ah, they've broken a few hearts, my two boys. But they'll live and learn.'

'Like you did with Ros?'

'I never looked back once I'd met her.' He sighed. 'I just wish we'd had longer. Her illness was a cruel thing to see – watching my love fade away was so hard to take, for us both.'

'It must have been.' Josie reached out, touching Fergal's hand.

He met her eyes, his own misty. 'Harry went quickly, didn't he?'

Josie nodded. 'We'd spent the morning walking on the riverbank, not far from here. We loved being by the Cherwell. We went back home and

Harry said he had a bit of indigestion. He told me he wanted a rest before lunch and he took himself off to his armchair in the conservatory. He liked it there, looking out onto the garden. I took him a cup of tea half an hour later. I thought he was asleep.' She sighed. 'He never drank the tea...'

Fergal nodded. 'And now we're here, the pair of us left behind.' He raised his eyebrows. 'Making the most of it all, for them.' He was thoughtful for a moment. 'Will we go to the May Day later, Josie? I'd like a bit of company.'

'So would I,' Josie agreed. 'Lin and Neil will be there, and Cecily.'

Fergal laughed. 'Miss Hamilton. Oh, I liked her. She was nice to me.' He scratched his head. 'Do you know she came down to the barge to talk with my da, to tell him I needed to go to school? She had a proper ding-dong with him. Da said all I needed was to learn to shoot a gun and kill a rabbit. She told him I'd need to add up any money I earned and to spell the word rabbit. He listened to her, my da did, and after that he sent me to school. Well, I think it was probably Ma who told him straight that I had to go. I took Miss Hamilton a pheasant by way of a thank you.'

'I remember it well,' Josie said with a smile. Lin's shrieks had filled the classroom before she burst into tears. Lin had always been sentimental and kind-hearted. Her relationship with Neil had probably started then with the packet of Love Hearts, the sweet that proclaimed: *Be Mine*.

They walked along the riverside for an hour or two, Fergal telling stories of Ros, their courtship, and the larks they'd had with their boys when they were younger. Josie smiled fondly at the memories. They made their way to the village green where the activities were just beginning. A huge crowd of people were watching the Morris dancers who were dressed in bright yellows, greens and reds, clacking sticks and skipping around each other. Josie recognised a few of the dancers. Jack Lovejoy and Bobby Ledbury were among them, twirling and leaping energetically. Fergal pointed to Devlin and Finn, who were helping Dickie at the drinks stall, wearing floral hats. He pressed her arm. 'Can I get you something to wet your whistle? There's fruit punch.'

'That would be lovely,' Josie answered.

Fergal shuffled towards the stall while Josie gazed around. The Morris dancers were jigging to the accordion, pipe and tabor. Gerald Harris was standing, hands in his pockets, face glum, watching. Penny Ledbury was selling jams and chutneys; there were craft stalls and face painting. A hog was roasting on a spit; there was a cake stall, pies.

Josie felt a gentle pressure on her arm and found Lin next to her with Neil.

'It's a nice day for it, Josie,' Lin said cheerily. 'The whole village has turned out. Oh, hi...' She waved to Florence, who had arrived with Dangerous Dave. 'I think Cecily's coming too.'

Neil grinned. 'Lin told me about the Shakespeare and the picnic. You must have had a great time.'

Josie nodded. 'It's a shame Minnie couldn't have stayed on. She was May Queen once...'

'We all were,' Lin recalled. 'I was Miss Middleton Ferris 1964.'

'I remember.' Neil pecked her cheek. 'You're still as lovely.'

Lin flushed with pleasure. Fergal arrived with two glasses of fruit punch for Lin and Josie. 'Here you are, ladies.' He turned to Neil. 'I'm getting myself a cider – do you want one, Neil?'

'Oh, I'm not staying.'

Josie frowned. 'Not staying to watch the fun?'

'Neil's doing a lot of walking at the moment – his cholesterol is a bit high,' Lin explained uncomfortably.

'The weather is perfect for a walk,' Neil added. He pecked Lin's cheek. 'I'll see you this evening, love. I'll make us an omelette with Janice's hens' eggs, and a salad.'

He walked away from the village green, and Josie said, 'It's good he's keeping himself fit. Didn't you want to go walking with him, Lin?'

'I ought to – I worry that he might stumble and fall in Old Scratch's woods. The phone reception is not good from there...'

'Ah, he'll be fine.' Fergal had arrived back with a glass of cider, and took a deep draught. 'That's good stuff.'

Dangerous Dave wandered over towards them, glass in hand. 'Lin, good to see you. Where's Neil? He was here a moment ago...'

'He's off for a walk.' Lin sighed. 'How's Florence?'

Dave gazed at his daughter, who was watching the dancers. 'She's fine.' He turned to Josie. 'She told me everything when she got in last night. I wanted to say thanks to you – and to you, Lin – for taking her under your wing.'

'She's a lovely girl,' Josie said.

'Oh, I'm proud of her – she's all I have.' Dave shook his head. 'And a baby on the way. That's two of them to take care of now.'

'A babby is it, Dangerous?' Fergal sipped cider thoughtfully. 'That's the one thing about having boys – you don't worry about them bringing a kiddie back to the house.'

Dangerous Dave sipped from his glass. 'I keep wondering who put her in the family way – I bet he's here today.' He gazed around, his eyes falling on Jack Lovejoy and Bobby Ledbury, who were dancing with the Morris men. Beyond, the Johnson family had assembled, Rita and Linval and Adam. His eyes swivelled to the Toomey boys at the makeshift bar, laughing and joking.

'Hello.' A polite cough came from behind Josie and she turned to find the vicar wearing clip-on sunglasses and a Panama hat. 'Are we all having a lovely time?'

'Hello, Andrew. It's a great turn out, isn't it?' Josie beamed.

'It is.' Andrew Cooper waved a hand to indicate the growing throng. 'A perfect sunny day for the celebrations. It was Lin I wanted to see – well, Neil, really.'

'Oh?' Lin offered a warm smile. 'Neil's gone for a walk in the woods.'

'Ah, I know he likes rambling – I wanted to ask if he'd join us in the ramblers' group next Sunday? Only we are a bit low on numbers.'

'You should have asked him yesterday, Andrew, when he was out with you.'

'Oh, no. It was just myself and the Turvey sisters yesterday, but I hoped Neil would come and support next week.'

'I thought he...' Lin felt her cheeks warming with embarrassment. 'Didn't he...?'

'Tell him I've asked.' Andrew turned to go. 'Well, enjoy the festivities.'

As Lin watched him stroll away, she put a hand to her face as if she'd been slapped. 'Neil said he'd been out with the rambling group yesterday...'

Dangerous Dave frowned. 'He was probably walking by himself – maybe they left a bit early.'

'Oh.' Lin was confused. 'Perhaps I got it wrong.'

'You were all having a good time in Stratford, and he just fancied a stroll around the village to stretch his legs,' Dave suggested.

'I like Stratford. The river is beautiful, lovely barges there,' Fergal added and Lin wondered if the men were trying to change the subject.

Lin stared around. Florence was deep in conversation with Natalie Ledbury, Natalie's hand through the arm of Brandon Dyer, her fiancé, a broad-shouldered young man with cropped hair who seemed to hold himself apart from the conversation. Lin watched him detach his hand from hers and move towards the makeshift bar to talk to the Toomey boys.

The dancing was in full force. Bobby Ledbury was in the centre of a clapping group, flipping over in a somersault. Lin's eyes suddenly filled with tears; Neil had lied to her about being with the rambling group and about Jimmy's bicycle. He'd lied twice now. And his friends had just covered for him. She wasn't sure what to think.

In the distance, a figure on a mobility scooter was heading towards them. Cecily waved a merry greeting. Adam Johnson had detached himself from his parents and was watching the Morris dancers. Darryl and Charlotte Featherstone were talking to Andrew the vicar, no doubt discussing the merits of the rambling group.

Lin shook her head, willing the tears back – Neil had deliberately deceived her again. There could be no other explanation. Josie was laughing now at something Dave had said, Fergal too. No one had any idea how awful she was feeling, so close to tears. Lin was racking her brain for an explanation – she was sure Neil had told her he'd been with the rambling group. She'd double check when she arrived home later – he'd never lied to her before. She wiped her eyes on the back of her hand and took a deep breath. She was all right.

Just at that moment, a loud cry went up, and everyone turned to stare. George Ledbury, in wellingtons and a heavy tweed jacket, a trilby hat perched on his head, was strolling across the green. Someone cheered, someone else clapped. There was more applause as George sauntered into the crowd, a black and white pig trotting happily at his side.

'Hello, George, I see you've brought Nadine with you.' It was Devlin Toomey.

His brother Finn laughed. 'Inseparable, that's George and Nadine.'

George strode along proudly, lifting a hand in greeting, Nadine trotting happily, keeping up with him. Then there was a shriek from behind the jam stall. Penny Ledbury rushed forwards, her hands on her hips, her chin jutting out. 'George!'

George put out a protective hand towards the pig. 'Hello there, Penny.'

'You've brought that pig,' Penny growled.

Devlin Toomey called out, 'It's his new girlfriend, Penny.'

Penny gritted her teeth. 'It's not right, George—'

'Well, Nadine wanted to come.'

'You think more of that pig than you do of me.'

George stooped to pat the pig protectively. 'Nadine and I were just watching the Morris dancers.'

Penny folded her arms, furious. 'Just get rid of her. If she isn't gone soon…' Penny's gaze fell upon the spit where a pig was rotating over a low flame. 'I'll personally make sure she ends up as the next hog roast!'

George knelt down again and put an arm around the pig. 'You'll do no such thing.'

The pipe and tabor music started up again, lifting on the air, and the Morris dancers began twirling long scarves and skipping. Nadine twisted round, her snout twitching, and then she scuttled off, excited to join in, weaving through the dancers' legs. The crowd cheered and clapped as Nadine rushed into the centre of the Morris dancers, a bright ribbon caught around her neck, and she sat stubbornly down in the centre just as a somersaulting Bobby Ledbury leaped into the air and fell across the pig to land flat on his face.

Lin gazed at the dancers who tumbled on top of Bobby like a shuffling pack of cards, sprawling across the grass: she was sure Nadine was smiling.

17

As Florence watched Natalie rush off to join her fiancé at the beer stall, she noticed her father scrutinising all the eligible men at the May Day celebrations. She knew him so well, how his mind worked, how protective he was, and it troubled her. He was examining every face for a shadow of guilt – a sudden shifty glance would prove certain paternity. She hoped he wouldn't accost random young men and start asking questions. He clutched his glass of cider furiously; he'd had one too many and might feel prompted to find things out for himself.

Florence was suddenly shaking: *he* was here now, inches from her. She recognised the scent of him first, and it took her straight back to their brief encounter. He'd just walked past and ignored her – he hadn't even made eye contact. After everything that happened between them, he'd pretended she wasn't there. She caught her breath; what could she say to him now? She looked away, embarrassed. Soon the pregnancy would be noticeable and people would ask questions. She glanced back to her father, who was talking to Fergal Toomey, to Lin and Josie.

Then she felt a movement next to her and there was Cecily, pursing her red lips ready for conversation. 'Florence, I'm glad to see you,' she said happily. 'Why aren't you May Queen?'

'I was May Queen two years ago.' Florence smiled shyly, then she added, 'Pregnant women don't make good May queens.'

'You look a million dollars,' Cecily retorted. 'Besides which, the baby doesn't show yet and when he or she does, you'll be positively glorious.'

'I don't feel very glorious.' Florence gazed down at her feet.

'Are you looking forward to bringing the little one into the world?' Cecily didn't hesitate to ask the question uppermost in her mind.

'To tell the truth, I'm terrified.'

'Of what exactly?' Cecily's eyes were small and inquisitive.

'Take your pick...' Florence breathed in raggedly. 'Childbirth. Coping with feeding, sleepless nights. And that's before we get to the wagging tongues and village gossip.'

'That's quite a list,' Cecily agreed. 'Yet you still want the baby?'

'I do.'

'Then make your mind up to enjoy every moment. It's your party – you own it. Besides, your father will help. Have you told him the good news yet?'

'I told him last night, when I got in. He was wonderful,' Florence said.

'Florence, don't you think the baby's father should take some responsibility?' Cecily's voice was low. 'He should at least offer you money. Doesn't he want to be in the baby's life?'

'No.' Florence shook her head. 'It's just me and the baby.'

'It's ridiculous – some men need to think beyond the end of their genitals,' Cecily snorted. Florence opened her mouth but wasn't sure how to reply: Cecily was ninety years old, but she was impressively bold and outspoken.

Cecily met her eyes. 'Can't you talk to him, at least?'

'I don't want to.' Florence thought briefly of the single evening she had spent with the baby's father. She'd trusted him; she'd fallen for his persuasive words, the smell of him, the huskiness in his voice as he'd taken her hand and led her to his room. It had been a whirlwind of passion; she hadn't thought about what would happen afterwards, but it had taken her by surprise that he had ignored her at the May Day revels.

Cecily reached out a gloved hand. 'My offer still stands.' Florence was puzzled, so Cecily added, 'I'll go with you – we'll pay this young man a visit. I'm not afraid to tell him exactly what I think. A man who disrespects a young girl and leaves her in the lurch should make amends – it's his duty. Oh, it makes me so furious.' Cecily clenched her fist.

'Thanks, Cecily, but – I'd rather not.'

'So,' Cecily looked around the village green, narrowing her eyes. 'That young man over there, I've heard he's a very good guitarist.'

'Jack Lovejoy, yes, he is,' Florence replied, her voice deliberately light.

Cecily examined Florence's tone, the movement of her face, to see if there was affection there, or sadness – anything that might give the game away. She wasn't sure. She tried again. 'And who is the young man who dances so well, the one with the feathers in his hat? He's very muscular.'

'Bobby Ledbury. He works on his grandad's farm.' Florence sighed. She knew what Cecily was up to: she'd ask about every man on the village green unless Florence stopped her.

'Shall we get a drink, Cecily? I think there's some fruit punch at one of the stalls...'

'Let's,' Cecily said. 'But don't think you've heard the last of it from me, young lady. I know it's not my business, but I can't abide injustice. The idea of you being taken advantage of by some village slimeball who's not worth the mud off your shoes makes my blood boil. Right, come along then, Florence, fruit punch it is. I'm buying.'

* * *

May Morning in Oxford began at sunrise as it did each year for Minnie, with the refrains of a Latin hymn swelling from the top of Magdalen College. Bells clanged across the city, beyond colleges, steeples and spires. At ten o'clock, she stood beneath Magdalen's Great Tower in a large crowd of revellers wearing floral straw hats and colourful costumes. Minnie was wearing a grey raincoat, purple beret and her St Hilda's scarf; you never knew if the weather would change. But for now, the sun was bright, although she could feel the chilly snuffle of the wind around her knees.

Minnie watched the processions, Morris Men in top hats, lifting their knees rhythmically, bells jingling. A young woman wearing garlands of creamy flowers rode a white stallion festooned with fresh greenery. Several figures lurched from the procession, dressed in forest green from head to toe, wearing emerald masks, wild wigs and antlers. The parade of musicians followed wearing bright hats, leafy garlands, playing violins, accordions, percussion. A band with trumpets and saxophones sauntered past, each musician in checked clothing, then a choral group in Elizabethan costume walked along sedately, singing madrigals. They were followed by yet more jangling music as revellers leaped and twisted, waving bells and scarves to the squashy breath of an accordion.

Minnie smiled. The little carnival in Middleton Ferris, where she'd been May Queen in 1965, was a small affair compared to this packed celebration of tradition and ceremony. Right now, Lin and Josie would be enjoying the fun on the village green. When Minnie first arrived in Oxford, students would hurl themselves from Magdalen Bridge parapets into the Cherwell below. Some students still performed the traditional May Day leap, although the police always advised against it, especially when river levels were low. Minnie had jumped once, to prove to a fellow student that she wasn't afraid. She'd been the only female to leap that year, and she'd nursed a grazed knee for the next week, but she'd basked in other students' respect for the rest of the Trinity term.

The procession continued, and Minnie decided that the pubs would be packed, so lunch in The Bear or The Slug and Lettuce wouldn't be a good idea – there would be queues and nowhere to sit. She could install herself in the sunshine on the riverbank and watch the spectacle shuffle past from a distance. Or she could go home, sit in the garden and read a book. There was a good one on the coffee table in her living room that she'd just started, called *Et Tu Brute?* about the murder of Julius Caesar and political assassination. Minnie was already extremely knowledgeable about all things Roman, but now she was becoming even better.

A hand squeezed her shoulder and a voice called, 'Minnie.'

She whirled round to see Francine Jarvis, and Minnie offered a smile. 'Francine, nice to see you.' She gazed over her shoulder. 'Is Melvyn with you?' Francine rarely went anywhere without her husband at her elbow.

'He's over there somewhere – talking to someone from his newspaper.' She waved a hand in no particular direction. 'I saw you and I just had to come over and apologise.'

'Whatever for?' Minnie wrinkled her forehead. 'The dinner party was wonderful fun.'

'For what happened with Jensen Callahan, the American. I should have introduced him properly before all the others started to make ghastly comments – they hadn't realised he was a New Yorker. Melvyn told me afterwards that he'd tried to change the subject twice but – oh, I felt so dreadful, all that stuff about artists and playwrights. I apologised to Jensen before he left, but he didn't mind at all. In fact, he found it quite humorous.'

'I bet he did,' Minnie agreed with a smile.

'He was very taken with you too...'

'Oh?' Minnie tried to make her face appear surprised. 'I'm not sure we had much in common...'

'He said he loved talking to you about theatre and literature over dessert. Minnie, he asked if you were single and if I had your phone number. Of course, I didn't give it to him, not without asking you first.'

'Quite right too,' Minnie said, a cat-with-the-cream expression on her face. If Jensen Callahan wanted to meet her again, he'd have to try harder than that.

'But we must have another dinner party soon and, of course, you'll be invited...'

'Thank you – that would be lovely.' Minnie inclined her head graciously. 'And now summer is coming, I might have a soirée in the garden.'

'Melvyn and I will be there – and we could ask Jensen.'

'I'll look at my diary.' Minnie was being deliberately enigmatic. 'Oh, is that Melvyn waving?'

'It is – I must go.' Francine kissed the air twice. 'I just wanted to thank you for saving my dinner party – it could have gone so horribly wrong and you said all the right things. We'll meet soon.'

'My pleasure,' Minnie replied, remembering how much she'd enjoyed the Eton Mess, glancing into Jensen's twinkling eyes and bantering with him about the arts.

Minnie turned away from the heaving procession, the jangling bells and trumpeting music, and strolled along the banks of the Cherwell, the grounds of St Hilda's to her left. As they often did, Minnie's thoughts drifted back to her first term as an Oxford student. She'd been eighteen, skinny, all wild hair, second-hand clothes and books, a third-hand bicycle, edgily conscious of every sarcastic comment from those who were affronted by her presence at the university. But there were the others who supported her too, good friends, rebels, admirers, boyfriends, and one particular lecturer who had championed Minnie, reminding her very much of Miss Hamilton, the first person to believe that she had first class brains in her head.

Minnie always marvelled at how far she'd come. As she walked past the gleaming river, ice-blue, dappled in sunlight, daffodils clustered on the banks, she felt thankful. She had won life's lottery ticket: an education that led to independence and more. Most importantly, she had friends, books and an unshakeable confidence in her own mind. She was lucky; she was healthy, happy. She needed nothing more than this beautiful May Day in Oxford.

Then from nowhere Jensen Callahan flickered into her thoughts, and she saw his bright eyes and the fascinating mind that lurked behind them. He was attractive, self-assured, and interested in her; she'd known that before Francine mentioned it. Minnie noticed the sunshine sparkling on the water's surface, the fresh grass, the raucous twittering of kissing birds fluttering on the air, and something strange happened. Her heart expanded. It was a feeling like being topped up with champagne, a new strangely fizzing sensation.

If Minnie had been younger or less wise, she'd have thought it was the beginning of love.

18

Cecily sat in her bedroom, gazing through the window. It was past nine; the light was dimming outside, the sky an expanse of deep grey and pink. The moon was up, a thin paper circle. She could see across the back garden beyond a low line of jagged hedgerows. A blackthorn was in shadow but she could make out the yellow of the tiny primroses below huddled in clusters. Beyond was a stretch of open grassland, tall pylons extending to the sky. In ten years' time, the field would be crammed with leap-frog rows of identical modern houses and patchwork gardens. She hoped it would at least be neighbourly, a friendly community for young people like Florence to bring up their families; she probably wouldn't be here to see it herself.

Two pigeons strutted in the garden, their wings tucked behind their backs, their heads nodding this way and that. Cecily was reminded of a programme she had seen on TV of lawyers in court summing up evidence. She reached for the cup of tea she always took up to bed with her, sipping tentatively. The tea was cold now. Cecily felt cold too; the skin on her arms beneath the nightdress was gooseflesh.

She lifted the photograph album from the duvet. It was a dark blue one embossed with gold, with a tarnished clasp. She gazed at yellowed pages, the edges curled with age. The first picture was faded, an old black and white portrait of a woman with neat sensible hair, wearing a floral dress with a rounded white collar. She had kind eyes, her lips in an almost-smile as if it was forbidden to be too happy. It was her grandmother, Cecily. Then another photo, a blonde woman in the 1930s, holding a baby wrapped in a shawl. Cecily barely recognised her mother. She had been just a few months old then, with dark tufts of hair and a perplexed expression.

She examined her mother's face to see if there was any evidence of affection there, but the woman stared at the camera, her expression disinterested, the baby abandoned on her lap as if she had nowhere else to put her. There was no bond between this mother and her daughter; Cecily had seen modern photos of mothers exchanging adoring smiles with babies, skin against skin, eyes tender with love, but her mother's expression was empty. She had not wanted Cecily, but her grandmother had welcomed her into her life with open arms.

Cecily gazed at the pages, turning them over carefully, seeing herself gawky in smart school uniform, then later in 1952 with pinned hair and nylon stockings. There were three more photos on the page, one of her with a hopeful face, leaning against a gate in the countryside, happy and relaxed; another of her, now a glamorous blonde, and a third with Joyce Perkins, her best friend, an arm lazily resting around the other, grinning. Joyce had loved the old films, she had photos on her wall of all the actors: Gregory Peck, Victor Mature, Humphrey Bogart. Cecily recalled how she and Joyce had been to the cinema together to watch *How to Marry a Millionaire*, and from that day on, Joyce had modelled herself on Lauren Bacall, complete with sultry voice. They were best friends then, inseparable.

In the 1950s, Cecily had been stylish, ambitious and daring. The world was at her feet and she was ready to embrace it, ready to fall in love. She turned the page and there he was, Eddie Blake, looking boldly at the camera, that roguish half smile making a dimple in one cheek. His hair was thick, brushed back, and his dark eyes glimmered beneath strong brows. It was a rugged face, Cecily thought, undeniably handsome in a rollneck jumper. There was another photograph of them together, Eddie in a jacket and casual trousers, his arm draped around her shoulders as if she belonged to him. Cecily frowned; she was gazing up at him in the photo. There it was, in a click, the man she'd loved beyond words, the one who made a big mistake, the one that changed her life, her direction, forever. No, she didn't regret taking up a career in teaching, coming to Middleton Ferris, devoting her life to children and their education. That wasn't the point. Cecily's hands became fists – it had just been so unfair all round. She put the photograph album carefully on the bedside cabinet, next to the cold tea, and curled up in bed. Her feet were cold.

She closed her eyes, but sleep didn't come. It was harder to fall asleep nowadays – she was tired, but she didn't sleep deeply or well. It was the ragged sleep of strange dreams, cobweb hauntings from the past, and she would wake confused and weary as if she had been rushing around all night.

Her thoughts were jumbled, tossed in the air, falling randomly. Eddie Blake was still stubbornly there, a smiling image. She'd fallen for him, the self-assured way he pulled out his wallet from inside his coat, the habit of ruffling his hair to draw attention to his good looks. As if it had been yesterday, she recalled the way he looked at her when there were just the two of them, how she filled his eyes, the way he smoked a cigarette as if he'd devour it. Yes, Eddie had been a passionate man. That's what attracted her to him and it had been his downfall. He told her he wanted her more than anything, and she'd believed him; she'd trusted him completely, agreed to marry him, believing that he was her future. She exhaled, a moment of loss and bitterness – she had been so wrong.

She thought of Lin, married to handsome Neil, and Josie, who recently lost the love of her life. Like the May Day maypole, life swung people around in its random dance, partners were exchanged, people danced in pairs, then alone, then they didn't dance at all.

Cecily's thoughts flew to Florence Dawson, that sweet girl living with her big-hearted father. She'd be all right, hopefully. She'd be a good mother. The child would not be short of love. But Cecily wished there was something she could do to make things fairer.

Cecily rolled over in the darkness and an idea came to her. She'd organise a Silver Ladies' lunch with her friends, just as Minnie had, but this time it wouldn't be in Stratford by the riverbank. It would be somewhere quiet, where they could feel calm and surrounded by nature, with simple food, simple pleasures. She'd invite Florence, offering her a network of women to support her. Cecily had been made welcome again in the village and it would be her way of saying thank you.

She closed her eyes and breathed in deeply. A plan had been made. It wouldn't change things dramatically, but it might help. A smile played on her lips briefly as Cecily fell into a happy sleep.

* * *

The next morning, Lin sat in the garden, a mug of coffee in her hand. An email had just pinged on her phone from Cecily, organising a picnic lunch for the following Sunday. Neil was indoors washing up, having warmed breakfast croissants, insisting that Lin go outside to finish her drink and enjoy the sunshine. She gazed across the farmer's field, scrubby brown soil leading towards patchwork greenery and clumps of trees on the horizon where Old Scratch's woods began. The scent of summer was in the air, honey sweet. It was the end of May now. The house martins were back, swooping and diving, building nests beneath roofs.

Lin heard the faint ticking of an engine; on top of the ridge, a piece of farm machinery chugged into view. She frowned sympathetically: poor George Ledbury never had a day off. She wondered if Nadine was sitting up in the cab with him, filing her trotters. There was a scuttling in the hedge and a chicken scampered onto the lawn. Lin watched, mystified, as the ginger hen with a fluffy bottom began to peck at the grass. Then Janice's head appeared over the hedge; she spoke directly to the chicken, ignoring Lin. 'You naughty girl, what are you doing in Lin and Neil's garden? Come back home.'

Lin smiled. 'She's very lively.'

'That's Mrs B'Gurk. They like to roam, my hens. That one thinks she's a dog.' Janice smiled indulgently. 'She's one of the family now, isn't she, Geoff?'

'She is.' A cheerful balding man popped his head over the top of the fence and Lin tried to banish the idea of two cartoon characters in a children's programme as they swivelled and smiled. Geoff held out a handful of grapes. 'Here, Lin – feed her these. Mrs B'Gurk loves grapes.'

Lin was bewildered, but she took three grapes from Geoff and held them out tentatively towards the chicken. It stopped pecking the grass and scurried towards her, its neck jutting forward and back, then it stabbed at the grape with a sharp beak.

'She loves grapes,' Janice repeated.

'The grapes make her lay more eggs,' Geoff said authoritatively. 'She's a proper little egg factory.'

'Can we give you some eggs, Lin?' Janice offered kindly. 'To make Neil some meringues?'

Lin hid a smile. 'I'd love some – thanks. We must start paying you.'

'Oh, not at all,' Geoff insisted. 'Neighbours and all. And Neil's very good when anything here needs fixing – he did a great job changing the air filters on my car. I'm useless with these things.'

'He did,' Janice agreed. 'He's so useful to have around, Lin. You're a lucky woman – he's a keeper.'

Lin bent down and offered another grape to Mrs B'Gurk, smoothing the feathers on her back.

'Pick her up if you like,' Janice offered. She noticed Lin hesitate and added, 'She loves cuddles.'

Lin collected the chicken in her arms, feeling it nestle against her, warm and fluffy. The chicken closed its eyes and began to purr. Lin gasped. 'Is this normal?'

'Oh, yes, she always purrs when she's happy,' Janice cooed. 'It's just like having a baby in the house.'

Lin wasn't sure, but Geoff proved the point by sweeping up a speckled hen in his arms. 'Susan likes cuddles too,' he added as he rocked her. Susan looked less than impressed but lay stiffly in Geoff's arms, her beady eyes unblinking. Lin clutched Mrs B'Gurk and stared across the field. The farm machinery was approaching, engine rumbling. She said, 'Is that George in the cab?'

'With Nadine?' Geoff laughed.

'It might be Bobby,' Janice suggested. 'Although I was talking to Penny the other day and she told me her good-for-nothing grandson stays out all night, then comes back in the morning tired out.'

'Perhaps he's got himself a girlfriend?' Geoff suggested with a wink.

'Penny worries he's out at rave-ups, taking drugs, then he drives home too fast on that motorbike.' Janice sighed and held out her arms as Geoff passed a placid Susan to her for a hug.

Lin felt suddenly uncomfortable – she knew that gossip travelled fast in Middleton Ferris and she wondered who else knew about Neil's lies, if they were lies. She wasn't wholly convinced yet, but she'd bide her time. She lifted Mrs B'Gurk gently towards Geoff. 'You'd better take her back – she's falling asleep.'

At that moment, the sound of a guitar strumming came from the top window, Jack's voice bellowing 'The Sun Ain't Gonna Shine Anymore'. Lin and her neighbours listened to the plaintive song for a moment and Lin thought how powerful music could be, how it could lift the mood or dampen it. The sun slid behind a cloud.

Janice's mood seemed to have hit rock bottom too. 'I'm so worried Jack's music career isn't taking off. He went busking in Tadderly every day last week and he only made twenty-four pounds.'

'He needs a job.' Geoff rotated his head towards Janice at exactly the same time that she looked at him. Then Janice sniffed. 'What's that awful smell?'

The farm machine ploughed a path parallel to the houses, a chute of brown mud flying from the back of it. Geoff nodded sagely. 'That's Bobby Ledbury. He's muck spreading.'

Janice wafted a hand in front of her face. 'On a Sunday morning? Oh, for goodness' sake!'

The stench of rotten eggs and ammonia attacked their nostrils and Lin covered her nose. 'I might just go inside...'

'Oh, the stink fills the whole house... Poo!' Janice protested.

'There should be a law against it...' Geoff added. 'Country smells.'

Jack's voice came from above, crooning 'Blowin' in the Wind'.

Neil approached from the kitchen, oblivious. He took the cup from Lin's hand. 'Have you finished your coffee, love?'

'I have, thanks.'

'Morning, Janice, Geoff. The hens are looking well.' Neil grinned. He gave Lin a small kiss. 'I was just wondering, Lindy – are you busy today?'

She looked at him, her eyes anxious. She dreaded what was coming. 'I was thinking of doing some dusting...'

He was still holding her cold hand in his warm one. 'I might pop out for an hour or two...'

'Oh?' Lin struggled to conceal her disappointment. She was hoping he'd suggest a trip somewhere together. 'It's a nice day...' she began.

'It is. But I promised Dangerous that I'd give him a hand with a car and then he offered me a pint down The Sun. You don't mind, do you?'

'Oh, not really.' Lin knew she sounded unconvinced.

'Great.' Neil pecked her cheek. 'I'll be off then. I'll be back to cook tea...'

Lin watched him go. Beyond the fence, the farm machinery was spewing manure in a wide brown arc. Janice raised her eyebrows inquisitively and muttered, 'Where did Neil say he was off to? Will he be gone all day?'

Then Jack began to sing again and from his bedroom, the plaintive notes of 'Your Cheatin' Heart' filled the air. Lin was rooted to the spot, unsure what to say. She needed someone to talk to; she needed lunch with her friends, Josie and Minnie would know what to do. But she trusted Neil completely, she always had.

Lin wondered if she was too trusting. She'd heard about men going through a mid-life crisis, behaving erratically. She took a deep breath; she was strong, patient. She'd wait, watch, find out the truth. Then she'd have it out with him once and for all.

19

A week later, just as Josie was about to leave for the picnic, her phone pinged. She stared at the email sender, *djellis*. The name confused her for a moment, then she recalled David Ellis, the friendly man she'd met on the Caribbean cruise. She was immediately annoyed with herself; she'd only sent him one short well-wishing message since she'd arrived back from Florida at the end of March and it was now the beginning of June. She opened up the long message and read it quickly; David hoped she was well, then he added that he'd given up writing his detective novel – he was stuck for ideas and didn't know where to go in the story. Or, as he put it, the book had a case of sinking cake syndrome, a soggy middle, underbaked.

Josie smiled and sat down at the table. She'd be a little late calling at Lin's, but she wanted to answer him straight away. An idea came to her as she typed a reply: David needed to introduce a dashing romantic hero, someone like himself, to meet his handsome detective Alain di Angelo. That would add some spice to the story, and he'd involve himself in his tribute to Alan. Then she pressed *send*, reached for her jacket and her basket and stepped out into the warmth of the garden. Cecily had organised the picnic in Old Scratch's woods, Minnie would be there, Lin and Florence. Cecily had sounded excited on the telephone; she had all sorts of ideas for a memorable group celebration. Josie hurried forwards to meet her friends, a spring in her step.

She strolled down Orchard Way, past Chandos. A familiar male voice, all clipped vowels, called to her as she passed. 'Mrs Sanderson, good morning.'

Gerald Harris hurried forwards, keen to chatter, so she paused. 'The garden looks nice now– the Toomey boys did a good job.'

'Humph.' Gerald shook his head. 'I've been meaning to talk to you.'

'About what?'

Gerald approached the subject carefully. 'I meant to ask – did you enjoy the May Day festivities?'

'I did.'

'It was something of a surprise, George bringing that pig.'

'It was.'

'I thought it was well attended this year – quite a success.'

'Indeed.'

'Er, Mrs Sanderson...'

'Josie, please,' Josie tried.

'Mrs – Josie...' Gerald attempted a lopsided smile. 'I did notice – I have to say – at the May Day celebrations, that you were there with Fergal Toomey.'

'With?' Josie wrinkled her brow. 'Fergal bought me a drink.'

'Ah, yes... a drink, indeed.' Gerald shifted his feet uncomfortably. 'I have to say I was a little astonished...'

'Why so?' Josie asked, mystified.

'Well, he's hardly your sort... I mean, the way those people live, on a boat on the Cherwell...'

'Those people? Fergal and I are old friends; we go back to primary school – we've known each other for years.' Josie thrust out her chin. 'Besides, his boys made a great job of your garden.'

'What I mean is – if it's company you need...'

'Company?' Josie shook her head. She was on her way to a picnic with her best friends – she had plenty of company.

'If you needed someone to... I could...' Gerald stared at his feet, his face flustered.

Josie felt immediately sorry for him. She took a breath. 'Gerald – I'm going to a picnic now in Old Scratch's woods with lots of good people. We're all taking food.' She lifted her basket. 'Why don't you come along? You'd enjoy it.' She beamed hopefully.

'I – er – the hedges need clipping.' Gerald took a step backwards.

'Well, another day, maybe?'

'Perhaps...' Gerald watched Josie take a step away, then he called. 'Will *he* be there, Toomey?'

'I'm not expecting to see Fergal today, as it happens.' Josie looked back over her shoulder. 'But he's a lovely man, Gerald – I'm sure you'd get on well. Why don't you come along with me?'

Gerald shook his head vigorously, waving a garden implement, muttering, 'Trowel. Busy – weeds...'

Josie carried on walking. It was sad what loneliness did to people, she thought, as she passed the rec and the allotments, and turned towards the road that led to Lin's house in Barn Park.

She was still troubled, talking about her conversation with Gerald as she and Lin walked down the narrow path towards the woodlands. Lin sniffed. 'How horrible, though, to be talking about Fergal like that. He and the boys are always so polite and nice.'

'They are.' Josie sighed. 'But Gerald is lonely. Loneliness does strange things to people.'

'It does,' Lin agreed. 'I think he's a bit jealous.'

'What do you mean?'

'I mean he fancies you...'

'Oh, I hope he doesn't.' Josie shuddered at the thought. 'I thought I was past all that now.'

'You're an attractive widow,' Lin said, then her face was sad. 'And I'm an abandoned wife.'

'No, you're not.' Josie hugged Lin's arm. 'Where's Neil now?'

'He took the car – he was driving Dangerous to Tadderly. He said he had to buy some bits and pieces for it.'

'On a Sunday?'

'Andy's Motor Mart is open on a Sunday morning.'

'So will he be joining us later?'

Lin shook her head sadly.

'Are you okay, Lin?'

'I think so.' Lin felt the familiar salty rush of tears in her eyes. 'He's just always so busy nowadays. He has no time for me.'

'Why don't you suggest a day out together? Tell him you're feeling a bit neglected.'

'I was thinking about it,' Lin said. 'It's our fiftieth wedding anniversary this year and I wondered if we could maybe manage a romantic weekend somewhere really nice.'

'October is a long way away,' Josie said quietly.

'It is.'

As they approached the woods, the air suddenly became cooler. They stepped beneath a green canopy of leaves surrounded by thick clusters of trees. A squirrel scampered across the path and scrambled up a tall trunk, disappearing along a branch.

In a clearing, a group of people sat on the grass around a large cloth covered with dishes of food. Cecily was perched on a camping chair, looking pleased with herself. Her mobility scooter was parked a little way off. She waved eagerly. 'Here we all are.'

Josie and Lin called out greetings and a chorus of replies echoed back. Minnie was sitting cross-legged on the ground, warm in a military coat, black beret and sunglasses, next to a woman in dungarees with pale hair, hunched awkwardly as if she'd rather be elsewhere. Josie called, 'Minnie, Tina – it's good to see you.'

Florence was next to them on a cushion, wearing a cardigan over a loose dress, and next to her Jack Lovejoy was strumming a guitar, his fringe covering deep-set eyes. Cecily smiled gleefully. 'I asked Jack to come.'

Florence seemed a little uncomfortable, shifting position away from him as Jack launched into 'With a Little Help From My Friends'. Cecily was the queen at the head of the table. She smiled towards Florence. 'Poor Florence couldn't be the only young one with all us Silver Ladies. Jack's a very good musician.'

Jack smiled. 'Cecily has a guitar – she plays a lot.'

'I do,' Cecily admitted.

'She used to sing to us when we were at school,' Minnie added.

'What did you sing?' Jack asked.

'"Wake Up, Little Susie",' Lin recalled.

'"Jail House Rock",' Josie added.

'We loved it – anything but "Shenandoah"...' Minnie agreed.

Tina took a breath. 'When I was in Miss Hamilton's class, we all sang "Itsy Bitsy Teeny Weeny Yellow Polka Dot Bikini".' She laughed. 'We thought it was dead racy.'

'Then let's sing it now,' Jack grinned, playing the chords. Josie was surprised he knew all the old songs – he had an incredible repertoire. They launched into the song together, Minnie swaying from side to side, Cecily conducting. Then, when they had finished, Cecily said, 'We have so much food: lemonade, quiche, sandwiches, cake – dig in.'

'I don't mind if I do,' Jack said, winking at Florence as he reached for a plate of rolls.

There was a rumbling sound in the distance, then a motorbike leaped over a mound on the horizon, racing towards them, a figure in leather passing by in a cloud of smoke. Florence shuddered. Tina pointed a thumb. 'Bobby Ledbury rides that old bike everywhere. Did you hear him revving up?'

'Teenage angst,' Lin suggested.

'He was in the year above me in school,' Jack explained. 'That makes him twenty-three or twenty-four. Florence and I were in the same year.'

'I was.'

'He was a rebel, Bobby Ledbury. So badly behaved at school... the girls loved him.' Jack munched the last morsel of his roll.

'Did they?' Cecily asked craftily as her eyes moved to Florence.

Florence stared at the sausage roll in her hands; she'd eaten very little. Jack said. 'I saw Natalie this afternoon. She was with her fiancé – they were walking in the woods, all loved up.'

'Oh, they are often down here,' Tina explained. 'I expect they must need a break from that big family in the farmhouse. Mind you...' She elbowed Minnie. 'I was always in the woods when I was younger, snogging some lad or another. It's where everyone goes.'

Florence blushed and Minnie added, 'Not everyone – I was always at home studying.'

'You were,' Tina laughed. 'Dad thought that there was something wrong with you, not going down to the woods with boys. At least he never minded when I was out.' She sniffed. 'Fat lot of good it did me.'

Cecily lifted a bottle. 'Pink lemonade, anyone?'

'Yes please.' Jack raised his glass, then he turned to Florence. 'You want some? Singing's thirsty work.' Florence held out her glass and muttered thanks.

'Look who's here,' Cecily exclaimed delightedly as the Toomey brothers emerged from the gloom carrying a brace of rabbits. 'Stop and have a drink with us, boys – you must be hungry too.'

'Well, we could...' Devlin paused, the rabbit swinging from his shoulder. Lin covered her mouth as she stared at the limp animal.

'Ah, no, we should be on our way, Dev,' Finn muttered with a glance at Florence, then at Cecily. 'Another time, maybe. Kind of you, though.'

'We'll be seeing you, then,' Devlin grunted. 'My dad sends you his best, by the way, Josie.'

'Give him mine too.' Josie raised a glass and Cecily eyed her thoughtfully as she offered a plate of biscuits.

Jack began to sing 'Norwegian Wood'. His voice was filled with emotion, and Lin felt tears spring to her eyes. Then Cecily gave a small cough. 'There is a special reason why I invited you all to Old Scratch's woods this afternoon.' She gazed around the group, her eyes resting on Florence, smiling briefly, then to Minnie, Josie and Lin.

Florence held her breath. Cecily's eyes glinted as if she had a secret plan, and Florence knew what it was. Cecily had invited Jack Lovejoy deliberately, mentioned Bobby Ledbury and tried to persuade the Toomey brothers to join them for the picnic. Her keen eyes were on Florence all the time, watching her reactions, hoping to work out who the father of her child was. Florence was almost sure she'd follow through on her threat to tell the baby's father that he was accountable. She couldn't think of anything more embarrassing – she'd been sure at one point that Cecily was going to ask Jack straight out if the baby was his. She took a deep breath – she was stronger now, she was used to the idea of having a baby.

The second scan was already scheduled for June and the bump was visible if you looked for it. Florence set her jaw firmly – although Cecily had her interests at heart, she'd do things her own way, she'd announce her baby to the world on her own terms.

Cecily took out a book from her bag. 'I'm going to read everyone a bit of *Wind in the Willows*, just like I did years ago.' Florence looked relieved.

'Lovely.' Lin closed her eyes with the memory and threaded an arm through Josie's, who leaned her head on Lin's shoulder.

Minnie called out cheekily, 'Can we have the bit about Toad's car, Miss?'

'Of course.' Cecily beamed. 'Now do help yourself to refreshments as I read the chapter. And...' She watched as Jack curled up in a ball. His head was almost on Florence's knee, '...if anyone falls asleep during story time, I really won't mind.'

Cecily read for half an hour and Josie and Lin felt their eyelids growing heavy. Lin thought briefly about Neil, if he'd be back at the house when she returned. Josie wondered about Gerald Harris and Fergal Toomey, if they were both lonely and how they coped. Florence rested her hand on her stomach and felt a flutter, just like a rising gas bubble, and she smiled. Lin and Josie linked arms and snuggled closer, and Minnie reached for the pink lemonade and poured herself a glass, then another for Cecily.

Cecily read on, her voice soothing as an embrace, a hug from a book. It rose and fell with each emotion: Toad stealing a car, Toad in prison, Toad escaping dressed as a washerwoman. The past flooded back, the children leaning forward, their faces shining, small gasps of excitement as Cecily read the thrilling parts. Then she closed the book with a thud. 'There we are.' She raised her face and her eyes shone. 'Did you enjoy that, class?'

'We did,' came the chorus and Minnie shouted, 'Don't forget what Miss Hamilton wrote in our notebooks. *A good friend is like a four-leaf clover; hard to find and lucky to have.*'

'That's what friends are for,' Lin agreed with a glance at Josie.

'Another song, everyone?' Jack began to play 'Jailhouse Rock'. The group wrapped arms around each other and sang along, rocking from side to side, then he launched into 'Rock Around the Clock' followed by 'Blueberry Hill'. Cecily clapped her hands, her face a picture of joy.

A small group emerged from the bushes led by Andrew Cooper, the vicar. The Turvey sisters were there in matching anoraks, one tall and slim in shorts, one slight in jogging bottoms. Behind them were Darryl and Charlotte Featherstone in expensive hiking gear, smart boots and backpacks.

Andrew took a step forward. 'Well, what a jolly pleasant way to spend a Sunday.'

Cecily clasped her hands. 'Vicar, good to see you. There's plenty of spare food. Come and join us...'

'Oh, I don't mind if I do.' Andrew gazed at the food on the picnic rug and patted his stomach. 'Those sausage rolls look moreish.' He turned to the group. 'Do we have time for a quick bite?'

'The lemonade might be refreshing,' Rosemary Turvey said.

'And the cake,' her sister Jill added. They sat down precariously next to Jack, legs sticking out.

Florence lifted a bottle and gazed around the group. 'Lemonade all around, then?'

'Not for us, I'm afraid, although we'd love to join you all.' Darryl Featherstone didn't move, but his smile was charming. 'Charlotte and I need to get home. We have to prepare for work tomorrow. We'll go on ahead, shall we?'

Charlotte looked disappointed. 'I suppose we'd better...'

'Thanks for this afternoon, Andrew,' Darryl offered politely. 'We had a lovely time exploring Old Scratch's woods. Charlotte and I are getting our bearings around the village now.'

'We are,' Charlotte agreed.

'So – thanks for the invitation.' Darryl's eyes rested on Josie, then Cecily. 'I look forward to seeing you all again.'

'Yes, another time,' Charlotte said. The group watched as they walked away into the sunlight.

Andrew the vicar said, 'What a delightful couple.'

'Especially Darryl,' Rosemary Turvey agreed, clearly impressed by his good looks.

'Charlotte is a bit quiet…' Jill Turvey commented.

Jack was ready to sing again. 'Right – so, what's it to be?'

'"Take Me Home, Country Roads"?' Lin suggested.

'"We Are the Champions"?' Josie offered.

'"Losing My Religion"?' Minnie asked mischievously with a glance at Andrew.

'If I could choose,' Andrew said gleefully. 'I'd pick "Oh Happy Day", but Florence, why don't you select a song first.'

'Right,' Florence said decisively as Jack began to strum. She sat up straight. 'My choice then – we're all going to sing "Papa Don't Preach".' She smiled determinedly at the group of faces. 'That's a perfect little song to announce that – in case you didn't know – I'm having a baby.'

Florence exhaled and felt pleased with herself. It was out in the open now and she wouldn't be afraid of anyone's reaction again. Jack didn't show any surprise, he began to strum the first chords, and when Florence yelled the line about keeping her baby, he winked in approval. Lin, Josie, Cecily and Minnie joined in lustily, giving their full support, while Tina seemed baffled, Andrew's face creased with confusion and the Turvey sisters looked completely shocked.

20

A week later, on a Saturday afternoon, Florence hurried home from Odile's café after work. Her belly was rounded a little now – a few people looked at her with sidelong glances in the café, but she didn't care about what others thought. The news was out: the baby came first. Odile had taken being the perfect boss to another level, insisting Florence had lots of breaks to put her feet up, making sure she ate at lunchtime. Florence wished she had a pound for every time Odile said, 'How are you feeling right now, Florence? You need anything?'

In truth, she felt a bit tired. It was June already – the due date she'd been given of 3 October was rushing towards her like an express train. But at least she wasn't hiding the pregnancy and she wasn't ashamed. Why should she be? She was bringing a new life into the world, a new person to care for, and that feeling of being proud and protective would be with her for the rest of her days. Florence had so much love to give to her child.

She pushed open the front door: it was quiet inside the house – she expected to hear the hum of the television, but there was no sound. She called out, 'Dad?'

'Up here, princess,' came a muffled voice and Florence made her way upstairs, pushing open the door to the third bedroom, a small square room with one tiny window, the floors now covered with rumpled sheets. Dangerous Dave was wearing spattered overalls, balancing on the top of a stepladder, paintbrush in his hand, covering the green walls with pale-yellow paint. He smiled when he saw Florence. 'What do you think?'

Florence wasn't sure about the colour: it wasn't the vibrant sunshine yellow she'd hoped for in the nursery, but her father was doing his best. She beamed with positivity. 'If we get a pretty cot and have mobiles dangling from the ceiling...' In her imagination, she was already holding the baby in her arms, staring into his or her trusting eyes. 'And bookshelves, Dad – lots of things for the baby to look at, and a baby bouncer in the corner, toys...'

'This baby won't go without anything,' Dave said determinedly.

'We'll make sure of that,' Florence agreed. 'Thanks, Dad.'

Dangerous Dave applied a few more brush strokes to the top of the wall, leaning forward precariously as the ladder wobbled slightly. 'You don't think it's the colour of dog sick?'

'No...' It had been Florence's first thought. 'But we could always use this as a base coat and put something brighter on top.'

'We could.' Dave's face creased as he examined the colour and Florence knew that he wanted nothing but the best for her. Then there was a knock at the door downstairs.

'I'll see who that is, Dad – then I'll cook tea.'

'Oh, I thought I'd get us a takeaway tonight...'

'Great.' Florence was already on her way down the stairs and to the door. When she opened it, she caught her breath. 'Adam.'

Adam Johnson was in jeans and T-shirt, but he wore the smart jacket he used for work each day. His eyes were serious as ever beneath a thatch of twist curls. He wasn't smiling; he had something on his mind. 'Can I come in? Is there somewhere we can talk?'

'Of course.' Florence opened the door wide. 'Come into the kitchen – I'll get a coffee.'

He glanced at her middle. 'Are you drinking coffee?'

'I drink mostly sparkling water now – or orange juice. You know about the baby, then?'

Adam nodded. There was a look in his eyes that Florence understood to mean that everyone in the village was talking about it. He followed her into the kitchen, watching her as she put the kettle on.

'Decaf, no sugar?'

'You know me well,' Adam said. He leaned against the worktop, shifted position. 'So, how many months is it now?'

'Five, maybe. I'm due for my second scan next week.'

'Boy or girl?'

'Don't know – don't mind.' Florence busied herself with hot water and cups. 'How's Malia?'

'She's home at the weekend, finished uni for good. That's one of the two reasons I've come round, to tell you, although I imagine she's already messaged you.'

'She has.' Florence met his eyes. 'And the other reason?'

'I think you know.'

Florence sighed, passing him a mug of coffee, taking a glass to the fridge and filling it with cold water. 'Tell me anyway…' She took a sip.

'This baby…'

'My baby.'

'I wish we hadn't split up…'

'You know why we did, though, Adam,' Florence said sadly. 'I was twenty-one. You were so serious. I was too, but it was too early to be so settled, I wasn't ready for commitment. I thought we had more life to live…'

'I remember exactly what you said to me,' Adam murmured. 'You said, "We met too soon." And now…'

Florence exhaled. 'I know – now I'm pregnant.'

He reached out a hand to take her wrist, then thought better of it. 'I wish we'd stayed together.'

Florence almost nodded. 'But you're with someone else now.'

'I was, but we finished.'

'That didn't last long.'

Adam's eyes were round with regret. 'She wasn't you.'

'Oh, Adam…' Florence put a hand to her lips. 'I'm sorry.'

'Let me help you.'

'How can you help?'

'I can take you to the scan next week?'

Florence closed her eyes. 'I was going to ask Malia to come, now she'll be home. It's next Thursday.'

'But you know she doesn't drive. Why don't I take an hour or two off work and take you both?'

Florence slumped back against the kitchen worktop. 'Thanks.'

'I still love you.'

'Please don't...'

Adam gazed at the cup of coffee. He took his first sip. 'At least let me be a friend.'

Florence reached out a hand and touched his arm tenderly. 'I need a friend.'

There was a crash from upstairs, followed by a loud cry. Adam raised his eyebrows. 'Is Dave up there?'

'He's painting the nursery.' Florence put her glass down and followed Adam, who was already running up the stairs two at a time. He pushed open the door to the nursery where Dangerous Dave was lying on the floor, his legs stretched out, a pot of dull yellow paint upturned on his knee, leaking between his legs. The ladder was on its side. He raised an arm. 'I think I've sprained my thumb. Hello, Adam.'

'Are you all right?' Florence knelt by her father anxiously.

Dave tried to wriggle his thumb. 'It hurts.'

Adam stood behind Florence. 'Can you look after your dad while I start cleaning up in here?'

'Thanks, Adam – you're a good lad.' Dave laughed, making light of his fall. 'I'll just get these overalls off, love, we'll get everything straight in here and then I'll get a nice takeaway for the three of us. We could have a night in by the TV?' He shrugged and held up his sore thumb. 'I don't think I'll be painting again for a day or two.'

* * *

Minnie intended to see *Julius Caesar* at the Playhouse; there were tickets left for the matinee of the first performance, tomorrow, 17 June, so she bought one. Rehearsals would be in full swing now. It was warm outside;

she'd chosen to wear a bohemian dress, all yellow flowers, and a straw hat, red Doc Martens, and she set off on her bicycle towards the city centre at a fast pace, leaning over the handlebars excitedly.

Oxford was busy; it was Friday afternoon, with people bustling in the warm streets, shopping, leaving work, so Minnie weaved carefully through chugging traffic, down George Street, turning left. She gazed at the beautiful ancient buildings on each side, her mind forming the words of a travel brochure, imagining herself talking to her handsome American companion.

'Did you know, Jensen, that Oxford has the best-preserved university buildings in the world? A wealth of architectural gems with origins in the late Saxon period. We have it all here, timber frames, medieval masterpieces and the Ashmolean Museum is Oxford's finest neoclassical...' Minnie laughed out loud as she applied her brakes, clambered off her bike and locked it outside the Playhouse in Beaumont Street. She was already taking Jensen on a tour of the city and he hadn't asked her out yet.

To either side of the entrance doors, huge colourful posters advertised *Julius Caesar*, with photographs of the great Roman wearing a smart suit and red tie, and Mark Antony in a leather coat and another, in battle fatigues, snarling at a uniformed female Brutus. The red lettering was pierced with a dagger spattered with dripping blood. Minnie pushed the door and walked quietly inside. There was no one around but she knew her way into the theatre. No one noticed her sidle into the dark auditorium, past the rows of colourful seats. The stage was lit and an actor wearing a baseball cap stood in a spotlight, shouting out lines from the play towards a woman in an expensive dress.

'Cowards die many times before their deaths; the valiant never taste of death but once.' The actor paused, put hands to his head and tried again. 'Cowards die many times...' He shook his head. 'I can't get this right. I want to explain to Calpurnia what I mean, but I don't know how I'm supposed to be feeling right now.'

There was a silence in the darkness and Minnie watched with interest to see what would happen. Then an English female voice shouted, 'Jensen – can you help here, please?'

'Oh, sure.'

Minnie heard his voice, light and confident, then she saw him clamber onto the stage. Warmth exuded from his smile as he wrapped an arm around both actors.

'Okay, this isn't going to be difficult. Let's try some bravado, a bit of macho bluster from Julius.' Jensen grinned. 'So, what do we have happening right now? Calpurnia is fretful, she's had premonitions that her husband Caesar's life is in danger, but what if he thinks he knows better? She's wise, he's not. He thinks he's a hero, invincible, a god. But we're playing him as a foolish man in this interpretation. So, what he's saying here is, "This is me, dammit, I'm Julius Caesar – I'm the main guy and no one can hurt me – I ain't scared of nobody."'

A light chuckle came from the darkness below where directors and actors congregated, watching. Minnie smiled too.

'How do you suggest I say the lines?' the actor playing Caesar asked.

'Try it through in modern vernacular, just for fun...' Jensen shrugged. 'Okay, Calpurnia, what do you say to your husband in modern speak?'

The actor playing Calpurnia took a step back, put a hand to her head and was immediately in role. 'I don't want you going out there, Julius. Are you mad? I know what will happen – you'll go out and you won't ever come back and then what will happen to me?'

Jensen turned to her; he puffed out his chest like a cockerel; he was Caesar. 'Honey, you're worrying about nothing. Nobody can touch me out there. I'm Caesar, get it? I'm the big dude, the number one, and I'm sorry for all the losers, but my IQ is the highest in Rome – and y'all know it! Please don't feel stupid or insecure, it's not your fault.'

The actors and directors fell about laughing. Someone in the darkness screamed in mock-pain and laughed louder. Someone else shouted, 'Go, Jensen,' and there was a round of spontaneous applause. Jensen gave a small bow and then he turned to Caesar. 'Now try the lines...'

'I've got it now.' Caesar hugged him. 'Can we start from Calpurnia's lines again please, Tony?'

A male voice piped up, 'Okay, Calpurnia, "When beggars die, there are no comets seen..."'

Minnie turned away, moving silently towards the exit sign, a smile on her lips. She'd watched Jensen in action and she liked the way he thought about things, the easy way he expressed his ideas and how smartly they worked on the stage. The point was, there was so much she liked about him.

Out in the brightness of day again, Minnie unlocked her bicycle. It was early evening already. She had a ticket for the opening matinee tomorrow and she'd take in the whole play, then she'd give some serious thought to how she was going to engineer a meeting with Jensen.

She was almost ready.

21

It was Sunday, a warm evening around eight o'clock. Josie was immersed in a book, sitting in the bright conservatory filled with orange light from the sinking sun. She gazed out briefly into the garden, then back to the book on her knee, a new one that Minnie had given her at the picnic. It was a beautifully told tale of Circe the witch alone on an island. Josie would never have bought such a book for herself. She usually liked romances, sagas, historical stories. But books were such good company, especially nowadays. She raised her eyes from the page to glance around the conservatory; the photos on the window ledge told the story of her adult life. There were wedding photos, Josie in white lace, Harry gorgeous in a dark suit. Holiday photos: Spain, Greece, Croatia. She gazed at the most recent photo of her husband, taken months before he'd died. His handsome face filled the frame, his eyes twinkled: he looked the picture of health. She'd had no idea then that she was months away from losing him.

There was a photo he'd taken of her leaning against a Triumph Spitfire in a floppy hat and a maxi dress. It was in the 1970s. Neil had loved fixing up old cars, and in the early days, the four of them had been on several holidays to France, Neil and Lin driving the old Frog-Eyed Sprite, and Harry and herself in the Spitfire. None of them spoke French well, but they'd had great fun travelling around, sampling local wine, visiting markets and tourist attractions. She remembered once the car had broken down near Toulouse, steam hissing from the bonnet, and on Neil's suggestion, Harry had bought ground cinnamon to fix the radiator leak. Josie had such good memories of their holidays. Then heartbreak followed, as it always did: she had little left now except a few faded photos.

She read for a while longer, pausing to wonder how Lin was. They'd met earlier that day for coffee; Neil had gone for a walk and Lin had been a little tearful, wondering if her husband found her boring nowadays. Lin blamed her melancholy on the medication she took and Josie had asked if perhaps it was less about the medication and more about the debilitating effect of the arthritis itself. Lin admitted that it could be, and promised to mention it to Dr Müller next time she visited. Josie had wanted to tell Lin that she should make the most of her time with Neil, but she'd wisely said nothing – the remark would have hurt her feelings and, in truth, Josie's words were more about her own constant loneliness.

A shout made her look up from her book. She stared through the widow. In the front garden, a man was prancing barefoot on the grass, trainers in one hand, the other arm in the air waving a bottle. Josie recognised the song – 'The Wild Rover'. She leaned forward – it was Fergal Toomey, and he was drunk, dancing on her dahlias. She put the book down and sighed deeply, then she marched to the front of the house, opened the door and called, 'Fergal, stop it. You're ruining my borders.'

Fergal missed his footing and slipped, cannoning backwards, landing on his backside in a rose bush. He held up the bottle and the pain on his face changed to laughter. 'Josie – I brought a bottle of Irish slammer!' He scrambled to his feet, picked up his filthy trainers and staggered towards her. 'Do you want a dram of the Dublin drop?'

Josie put her hands to her hips. 'Do you have relatives in Dublin, Fergal?'

'My mother was a Dublin girl... my da came from Blanchardstown.' Fergal was inches away, his face creased with laughter. 'I haven't been to the place myself since I was a teenager...'

Josie could smell whisky on his breath. 'You can come inside, have a cup of coffee, then you go back to the barge, all right?'

'Ah, you're a good woman.' Fergal suddenly looked as if he might cry. 'I need a friendly shoulder. It would have been her birthday today, my Ros. I always have a drink or two on her birthday.'

Josie held the door wide. 'Come in, Fergal – we'll go into the kitchen, it's cosy there.'

She watched him sashay in front of her, noticing the soil and leaves clinging to the seat of his jeans, and she smiled sadly. They wandered into the kitchen and Fergal dropped down at the table, resting on his arms like a tired child. Josie busied herself with the kettle, clanking cups. 'I'll make you a strong coffee.'

'Make it sweet...' Fergal mumbled. 'Sweet as yourself, Josie.'

Josie rolled her eyes – she had no intention of putting up with Fergal's nonsense. She placed a mug in front of him and for a moment she felt the urge to ruffle his tousled hair. Instead, she said, 'Don't burn your mouth – it's hot.'

He turned grateful eyes towards her. 'It's a superstar that you are...' Josie noted that his accent was stronger now he was the worse for wear; his light Irish burr had been replaced by a stronger twang. She took a coffee and sat down opposite him.

'How are you feeling?'

He slurped from the cup. 'Not so good.'

'Have you drunk much today?'

'I started early – on an empty stomach.' Fergal winked. 'Never a clever idea, Josie.'

Josie sighed. 'You must miss Ros very much.'

Fergal beat a fist against his heart. 'There's a big hole here.' Tears filled his eyes. 'Ah, but hark at me, the miserable moaning one, when you've lost your own beloved Harry.'

Josie patted his hand once. 'It's always difficult, but I suppose there are times when it's even harder.'

Fergal put his head down on his hands for a while, breathing deeply. Then he looked up, his eyes intense. 'I came round here to kiss you.'

Josie moved back. 'I sincerely suggest you don't.'

He grinned. 'Ah, I'm a gentleman and that would be disrespectful. It's just the loneliness of it all. Don't you feel lonely?'

'I do. But I'd never want to replace Harry.'

'I don't want to replace my Ros. I'd never love another woman like I loved her.' Fergal's face had a kind of primitive fierceness around the mouth. 'But at times I wish someone would just hug me or hold me in their arms while I fall asleep at night. The loneliness is crippling, it's a kind of death in itself when you've lost someone you love, hanging in limbo with all these feelings and no one to give them to.'

'That's the whisky talking.'

'It's whisky talking sense – I'd never admit it sober. But I hate being like this, abandoned and still alive when she's gone, and there's no one to share a lonely hour.' He sipped coffee slowly. 'There should be a way for older people to get together and have some fun...'

'Do you mean like a care home or a pub?'

Fergal spluttered a laugh. 'Like neither – like being with friends who look out for one another. Like people who hug each other and clap each other on the back and laugh and cry together, human contact, sharing.'

Josie's face filled with sympathy. 'You have your boys.'

'They are young – they go out drinking, meeting friends. I'm alone on the barge at night and the silence is like an eternity.'

Josie sighed. 'Perhaps you need some friends too, Fergal?'

He gave a muffled sound of disbelief. 'I live on a barge, Josie. I've lived there since I was a kiddie. People in the village are nice enough, but I won't find myself invited to Bomber Harris's big house for a cup of tea, or sitting at the vicar's table slicing fruit cake. We're outsiders, we Toomeys – maybe it's not so bad for my lads, but for me and Ros, it was tough.'

'We'll have to change that.' Josie pushed the half-full mug of coffee away: it was almost bedtime and she didn't want to stay awake all night. A thought came to her. 'Next Sunday, why don't you come to dinner here?'

'Really? Me, Sunday dinner with you, in this nice house?'

'Of course.' Josie smiled. 'Do you like a roast? Chicken, maybe.'

'Do I like chicken? I certainly do.' Fergal licked his lips. 'And will there be dessert?'

'And wine.' Josie sat back in her seat, enjoying the delight on Fergal's face.

'Then it's a date.' Fergal folded his arms. 'Grand.'

'A meal shared between friends,' Josie warned, making her intentions clear. She was already thinking she might invite Lin and Neil, but that might seem like a foursome. Better a foursome than a date, she told herself.

'I'm looking forward to it already.' Fergal eased himself to his feet. 'Well, thanks a heap for the coffee, Josie. I'll be off home now to get my head down...' He paused and his expression was momentarily hopeful. 'Unless you'll let me sleep it off on your couch tonight?'

'The barge is ten minutes' walk away,' Josie told him sternly, then she smiled. 'It's good to talk, though, Fergal. Good to share things.'

'It is, though.' Fergal was already at the door. 'Night, Josie – and thanks again.'

Josie watched him wander down the path, a new spring in his step, mud clinging to the seat of his pants, and she smiled. She'd known Fergal Toomey since they were at school, but now he was widowed, perhaps she was getting to know another side of him. He was thoughtful, kind, good company. She liked him more than ever.

* * *

Lin sat in the back garden, gazing out over the ploughed field. The soil was rich red-brown and furrowed; Bobby Ledbury had been out planting something in the ground this week. George had been in his tractor too, driving up and down, Nadine at his side. Lin closed her eyes and felt the fading sun on her lids. She wrapped a cardigan closely around her, snuggling in the warmth. She could hear the Lovejoys' chickens clucking, a calming squawk as they bedded down in the coop. Then she felt an arm around her, and she leaned her head against Neil's shoulder as a light kiss landed on the top of her head.

'I brought you a glass of wine.' His voice was hushed. 'It's lovely out here at this time of night. So peaceful.'

Lin sat up and took the glass. 'You're so sweet.'

Neil shrugged. 'Well, you never complain – I'm sorry I was late home this afternoon – I lost track of the time, and you'd made that delicious egg salad...'

Lin gave an awkward laugh. 'I must be the only person in the world who can ruin boiled eggs and spoil a good lettuce.' She smiled, but there were tears in her eyes again. 'The ice cream we had afterwards was nice, though. I love salted caramel.'

Neil's arm tightened around her. 'Are you okay, Lindy?'

'Fine.' She swallowed wine, feeling the sudden sharp taste of lies on her tongue.

'I thought you seemed a bit down these last weeks.'

'Perhaps it's the arthritis.'

'Can you talk to Dr Müller?'

'I will.' They were quiet for a while. Lin usually found the times where neither of them spoke a safe and calm place. Now she was wondering if she just had nothing interesting to say.

Neil took her hand in his and pressed her fingers to his lips. 'It'll be our anniversary in October. I was wondering if you'd like to go somewhere – Wales perhaps?'

'Wales?' Lin marvelled at her unimaginative answer. 'Can we afford it?' Now she was being negative, penny-pinching.

Neil snuggled closer. 'We could manage a few nights somewhere nice.' He sighed. 'It won't be a Caribbean cruise but...'

'I wouldn't like all the heat...' Lin said.

'We should go somewhere, though, me and you, somewhere romantic. Leave it with me, eh? I'll sort something out. I'd like to....'

'All right, if you're sure... you decide.' Lin gazed out into the fields. Several crows were pecking in the ground. A pheasant was strutting close to a hedge, making a throaty squawk. Neil pulled her close to him, kissing her lips, and she felt the warmth of his arms.

'You know I love you, don't you, Lindy? There's nothing for you to worry about.'

She kissed him back, remembering sharply how much she adored her husband. She wasn't sure how to convey the depth of her feelings, so she said, 'You too, love.'

But almost instantly her mind bounced back to the fact that he had been away all day, that he'd been late home yet again, and his words came back again – 'There's nothing for you to worry about.'

Why would he tell her not to worry, unless the opposite was true?

Perhaps he had a secret: he was unwell, or he didn't love her any more. Or perhaps there was someone else – he was meeting another woman. Lin pulled herself together, reprimanding herself sharply. They would be all right – she was making up things to worry about.

But what if there was something wrong? What if she lost him?

Lin wrapped an arm around him, clinging tightly. She couldn't lose him, not after all the years they'd been together, not now.

22

Minnie left Middleton Ferris station behind her and strode past the village green towards Odile's café. It was a warm June day, and she was still thinking about the matinee she'd seen a week ago. It had been the most vibrant *Julius Caesar*, sharply political, modern, and the battle at the end had been all explosions and smoke. The direction reminded her of Jensen, vibrant, fresh, intelligent. She'd watched the play, sitting alone and undisturbed, her eyes fixed on the stage, analysing the meaning of every move. It helped her to know him better. At the end, as the exhilarated audience left the theatre, she considered going round the back to the stage door, finding Jensen, sharing a discussion. But it was still too early – she'd wait for the right moment.

As Minnie passed the rec, she gazed across the road and saw a familiar figure in the allotments, a hoe in her hand. She called out eagerly, 'Tina!'

Tina stood up slowly, her pale hair across her face. Minnie rushed across to the small gate that led to the separate patches of soil, weaving past flowers and newly sprouting vegetables to where Tina was standing, wearing overalls and wellington boots. She put a hand to her head. 'These bloody weeds won't get the better of me – I've been at it since seven this morning.'

Minnie surveyed the neat rows, the bright orange nasturtiums next to newly growing French beans and courgettes. 'It's all looking good.'

'So it should, the amount of time I spend here.' Tina wiped soil from her hands.

'I'm going to Odile's – come with me. I'm meeting Josie and Lin and Cecily.'

Tina pulled a face. 'Like this?'

'You live minutes away – we can pop to yours and you can change into shoes. You'll be fine.'

'It's not really my thing, all this Silver Ladies stuff...'

Minnie knew her sister of old: Tina didn't like the same things that Minnie did. She tried to find another way of reaching out to her. 'It'd be nice if we could spend some time together.'

'I like spending time with you, Minnie – don't get me wrong,' Tina started abruptly and Minnie took a breath: she knew there was a 'but' coming. 'But we're chalk and cheese.'

'That's no bad thing.'

'And I don't really get much from these social events with you and your friends. It was the same at the picnic you persuaded me to go to with Miss Hamilton, all books and chit-chat and singing songs. It's not really me,' Tina insisted, and her eyes flashed. 'It's all Dad's fault. He dictated which way my life would go when he let you go to the grammar school. You got a bunch of degrees and I got a CSE in Art. That was me finished for good.'

'But you've done so well.' Minnie was a little taken aback – she didn't know Tina had stored up so much anger. 'You've always been smart.'

'He stopped me doing things I'd like to have done, though.'

'What would you have liked to do, Tina?' Minnie settled herself down on the side of a row of potatoes. 'I mean, looking back...'

Tina sighed. 'I was reading the other day that you can do a degree in Organic and Sustainable Agriculture. You can find out all sorts of things about horticulture, soils, entomology. I'd have loved that but...' Her eyes blazed. 'I had to look up what entomology was.'

'The study of insects...' Minnie murmured without thinking.

'There's so much I'd have done with my life, given the chance...' Tina hit a weed hard with her hoe. 'I'd have been paid properly for doing what I love; I'd be independent like you are.' She met Minnie's eyes. 'Don't you go telling me I'm already independent and how well I've done for myself, because if you do, I might just bash you with this hoe.'

'I wouldn't be so patronising.' Minnie shook her head. 'I know it's not fair, Tina.'

'I felt sorry for you when we were kids...' Tina admitted. 'There was me and Mum and Dad living in the house and you'd gone to Oxford. We were left behind, the scruffy Moores, poor as church mice, but you didn't fit in with us any more, with your new airy-fairy posh ways.' She thought for a moment. 'Then Dad slapped you over the jam at breakfast...'

'...because I said "actually."'

'I burst into tears, Minnie, do you remember – not just because I was upset that he hit you – I *was* upset – but I realised at that point that you'd escaped, you had a new life, freedom, and I was stuck in Middleton Ferris for ever.'

'Tina, how come you've never told me this before?'

'I almost did, so many times.' Tina pushed a hand through her hair. 'When my marriage ended and Patrick left, I just concentrated on working hard. I shut everything else out. Then when I retired, I got the allotment here, and carried on slogging away.'

'I thought you enjoyed it.'

'I do – it keeps me alive – but it's all I know, hard work. Whenever I come to see you, Minnie, with your posh house and your clever friends, I don't fit in. Even here, at Odile's, you'll be talking about books and plays and bloody Latin. I don't get any of it.'

'But we're flesh and blood, Tina.'

'That's *all* we are, though.'

Minnie was silent: she had no answer. Then she said, 'I'm sorry.'

'It is what it is,' Tina said philosophically. She examined Minnie's face and saw the sadness there. 'When you're done lunching at Odile's, come back past here and I'll give you a few courgettes...' She tried a joke. 'You can make your clever friends some ratatouille.'

Minnie stood up and hugged her sister. She was thinner than when they'd last hugged. She was startled to realise that might have been ten years ago. 'I'd better go, Tina. Don't be a stranger.'

'I won't – you're all I've got. Pathetic really, isn't it?'

Minnie stared into Tina's eyes to see if there was any regret and found only determination. 'No, it's not pathetic. Our lives might be different, but we know each other. We've got that, at least.'

'We have.' Tina and Minnie looked at each other without emotion, recognising that they were the same, both stoical, tough women.

'I'll call in on the way back.' Minnie grinned. 'I'll bring you a bit of cake.'

'A cream horn might be nice.' Tina lifted her hoe and began to attack a dandelion. 'I'll see you later then.'

'Yes, okay,' Minnie replied. Tina was already busy hacking at the soil as she turned and wandered back towards the small gate.

Minnie hurried ahead to Odile's café where she met Josie, Lin and Cecily. The café was busy; Dangerous Dave was scoffing a fry-up, so were Jimmy Baker and Kenny Hooper. Linval and Rita Johnson were having lunch, and almost all the other tables in the little café were full. Florence arrived at the table with a tray, placing bowls of soup in front of the four women with a smile. 'Carrot and coriander, soup of the day – enjoy.'

Cecily glanced at Florence, trying hard not to look at the tightness of her apron around her waist. 'How are you, Florence? I hope you're not taking too much on.'

Florence smiled. 'I'm feeling quite good at the moment, lots of energy. I had my second scan and the baby is doing fine.'

'Do you know if it's a boy or girl yet?' Lin asked.

'I do, but I'm not saying.' Florence turned to go.

'You take good care,' Cecily called, watching her move towards the kitchen, through the colourful plastic strips, then she whispered across the table, 'I saw her in a car with her friend Malia. Adam was driving them back home... you don't think he's...?'

Lin glanced at Rita and Linval Johnson, who were oblivious, chatting. She lowered her voice. 'He might be – they used to be a couple...'

'I don't think we should speculate,' Josie suggested. 'We're bound to get it wrong.'

'It doesn't matter anyway,' Minnie added breezily. 'She's doing fine and that's all that counts.' She smiled. 'I went to see *Julius Caesar* recently at the

Playhouse. It was a wonderful production with a fascinating American co-director.'

'Oh?' Josie leaned forward, quick to pick up on Minnie's tone. 'Is this the new flame?'

'Another one to add to your list of adoring men?' Lin asked.

'It might be,' Minnie said coyly.

'And at our age – we're outrageous.' Josie grinned, then lowered her voice. 'I had a visit from Fergal Toomey last week. He's coming to Sunday lunch tomorrow—'

'Fergal?' Lin was shocked. 'Surely you and he aren't...?'

'He's lonely, poor man. He needs a friend and I'm happy to be one. So, on that note...' Josie was hopeful. 'I don't suppose any of you would like to join us for a roast lunch?'

'I'll be at home, I'm afraid,' Minnie said.

'Neil is busy with something tomorrow.'

'Come by yourself,' Josie insisted.

'I might.' Lin wasn't sure. 'Or I might just stay home and read in the garden...'

'I'll come.' Cecily folded her arms. 'You're not far from my place and besides, I have the scooter. I'll bring a bottle or two. What time?'

'Twelve.' Josie patted Lin's arm. 'You should come.'

Lin was suddenly tearful. She wasn't sure she wanted to go without Neil. She'd feel out of place, a spare part. She was annoyed with herself – Josie was her best friend. 'Can I think about it?'

'Of course.' Josie grinned. 'I thought about asking Tina – would she like to come?'

'I can ask...' Minnie thought about their conversation earlier. 'I'm not sure it's her thing.'

'I know what we should do...' Cecily gazed out of the window, the sun making roof tiles gleam. Gardens were in bloom, hanging baskets bursting with colour. 'Let's organise a big barbecue lunch and invite lots of people...'

'Tina might like that – cooking her veggies outdoors,' Minnie said thoughtfully.

'We could invite Bomber – and Fergal. All the people in the village who are in need of a lunch with friends,' Lin suggested.

'Yes, a barbecue might be perfect in the sunshine,' Josie muttered. 'I have plenty of space in the garden... I'll host it. It's my turn anyway.'

Linval had overheard; his voice floated from the adjacent table. 'I love a good barbecue. Fish on the grill...'

'Steak for me,' Dangerous Dave called out. 'I'll be the chef, if you like.'

'You'd set fire to the place,' Jimmy joked.

'Chicken.' Kenny examined a finger. 'With barbecue sauce.'

'Who's having a barbecue?' Odile chirped from Josie's elbow, where she was collecting empty glasses.

'I am, it seems, for the whole village.' Josie smiled. 'Remember what Miss Hamilton said? The Euripides thing about sharing lunch as friends?'

'I'll bring some sausages and we can do jerk chicken too,' Odile offered.

'I could bring a salad,' Lin said tentatively.

'I'll bring a dessert,' Minnie offered.

'Right, a Silver Ladies' barbecue lunch it is, for all our friends in Middleton Ferris.' Josie clapped her hands. 'How about we say at the beginning of July, the 1st or the 8th.'

'I'll check my diary...' Minnie smiled enigmatically and glanced at her phone. 'The 8th looks good.'

'You'll come, won't you?' Cecily called across to Florence, who was collecting plates at Dave's table. 'You're an honorary Silver Lady now.'

'I'd love to – but on one condition. I want to organise the next lunch after that.'

The doorbell tinkled and everyone stared as a young man burst in. He had tousled hair, a leather jacket, moody eyes. Bobby Ledbury had left his motorbike outside. Odile called as she walked back to the kitchen, 'Florence – can you see to it? I have eggs on the stove.'

'Of course,' Florence said professionally, then she turned to Bobby. 'Hello. What can I get you?'

'A strong coffee, please...' Bobby wriggled through the gaps between customers and plonked himself down by the far window, gazing out into the distance.

Lin whispered, 'He looks tired out – it must be hard work on the farm.'

Josie nodded. 'These youngsters can burn the candle at both ends – he gets up at the crack of dawn, Penny says.'

Lin mouthed, 'He stays out all night sometimes...'

Dangerous Dave called out, 'How are you, Bobby? How's George – and Nadine?'

Jimmy Baker snorted.

Bobby stretched out his long legs. 'I dunno... I haven't seen her since yesterday – or Grandad.'

'How's the Kawasaki going since I tuned it?' Dangerous Dave was determined to make conversation. 'I gave myself a nasty burn from the exhaust.'

'I don't know how that bike holds itself together,' Jimmy commented. 'On a wing and a prayer. It's past its prime, a bag of old nuts and bolts.'

'You'd know how that feels, I reckon, Jimmy,' Bobby smirked.

Jimmy laughed then stopped dead, realising what Bobby had said.

Kenny grunted. 'Not safe, those old bikes.'

Bobby spoke quietly. 'You sound like my Grandma Penny. She does nothing but whinge.'

Florence was by his side with a cup of coffee, placing milk and sugar on the table. She was about to leave when Bobby caught her wrist lightly. 'Florence...'

She hesitated as he met her eyes.

'I heard about the baby...' Bobby glanced at her expanding middle and the café was suddenly hushed. 'If there's anything you need...'

'I'm fine, thanks,' Florence said gently.

Bobby's tone was warm and well-meaning. 'A pram, baby clothes – I can get you a nice second-hand cot if you like.'

'That's kind,' Florence said. 'Thanks.'

'I'd be glad to help...' Bobby murmured.

'I know, Bobby.' Florence disappeared back into the kitchen and Bobby sipped his hot coffee, his face tired as he leaned his chin against his fist.

Cecily and Lin exchanged glances and Cecily whispered, 'You don't think he's the...?'

Lin shrugged. Josie was watching Dangerous Dave, who had stopped eating and was staring at Bobby Ledbury, his hands balled into fists, his brow creased as if an imminent thunderstorm was about to roll in. No one in the café moved. It was as if they were all holding their breath, looking at Bobby and thinking the same thing.

Minnie noticed too, and she waved a hand to distract everyone. 'Oh, here's a special announcement – just so you all know, there will be a barbecue lunch at Josie's on 8 July. You're all invited. Bring a contribution to the food and drink.' She smiled as Odile peered round from the kitchen, all interest.

'I love a barbecue. I'm up for the cooking,' she offered.

'Then that's decided.' Minnie looked around, delighted: the moment of tension had been dissolved. 'Let's have some fun, all our friends from the village together. And Odile, can you get me a cream horn please? I promised Tina I'd drop one in for her on the way back to the station.'

'I'll be there.' Bobby gave Florence a glance as he swallowed his coffee. Dangerous Dave watched him, fork in the air, leaning forward as if he was about to ask him a burning question. Cecily instinctively slipped back into teacher mode, lifting a commanding finger, her voice a practised classroom boom.

'Eat up, everyone – your food is going cold. And don't forget to put the barbecue at Josie's in your diaries. It's organised by the Silver Ladies. As the great civil rights activist Cesar Chavez said, "If you really want to make a friend, go to someone's house and eat with them... the people who give you their food give you their heart."'

23

On the morning of the barbecue, Josie stood in her garden, arms folded, staring at the neat rows of hollyhocks. The Toomey boys had made a good job of mowing the lawn and tidying the hedges: the garden was perfect for a party. Josie thought sadly that it would have been so useful to have Harry around. Holding a barbecue in the back garden by herself for half the village was no easy task. They had occasionally invited a few friends to dinner, but Josie had never done anything on this scale – the original idea of a Silver Ladies' lunch had expanded beyond her expectations. Penny Ledbury had invited everyone she knew, and Janice Lovejoy had done the same. Jack Lovejoy was providing music and Odile was planning on barbecuing up a storm. The garden would be packed with people. Josie's confidence was fading; an intimate gathering would have been easier. She'd have certainly felt calmer about it.

She thought back to the pleasant Sunday lunch she'd shared with Cecily and Fergal, and how grateful he'd been that she'd gone to so much trouble, although it had been no trouble at all. Cecily held forth with anecdotes from her years of teaching, recalling amusing stories from primary school that Josie had forgotten about. Dickie Edwards had put chewing gum in Sally Corbyn's hair and Fergal furiously forced him to eat dirt as a punishment. Kenny Hooper had smuggled a bottle of his father's medicinal whisky into the cloakroom, downed the lot at break time and spent the rest of the morning singing 'Puff the Magic Dragon' at the top of his voice. Cecily had to tuck him up in the Quiet Corner with a teddy bear while he slept it off for the afternoon.

Josie remembered Fergal's steady gaze as she passed him gravy, how he'd gripped the fork and chewed potatoes hungrily, how he'd been so thankful when she offered him seconds. He'd had a great time, drinking wine and listening to the chatter, laughing until his eyes watered.

Lin had stayed away; she'd spent a quiet afternoon in the garden reading, in case Neil came home early. He'd arrived an hour late. She told Josie later that she was furious with herself; she'd have enjoyed sharing lunch with her friends far more than staying at home watching the clock and fretting like a fool. She'd learned a lesson.

Josie hoped the barbecue would cheer Lin up. It was going to be a busy day, though – being a hostess meant continually topping up drinks, making sure everyone had food, someone to talk to: she wondered if she'd taken on too much.

A pleasant voice behind her disturbed her thoughts. 'I'm here, Josie, all ready to get a good fire going.'

Josie whirled round to find Fergal Toomey slouching, hands in pockets, a grin on his face. He waved an arm towards the garden. 'Where do you want me to set it up?'

'The barbecue's in the garage – I forgot to check it,' Josie said, remembering that it hadn't been moved since Harry got it out two years ago. It would be full of cobwebs. 'I've no idea what state it's in... it's an old gas thing – it's quite big, though.'

'Leave it with me – I'll spruce it up and give it a polish. It'll be right as rain for this afternoon.'

'Thanks, Fergal.'

'It's the least I can do after the lovely Sunday dinner you cooked.' He licked his lips. 'The lads will be here in a moment – they've got hold of some trestle tables from the pub, and a barrel of beer courtesy of Dickie Junior.'

'Oh dear,' Josie murmured. 'I hope there won't be too much drinking.'

'We'll keep an eye.' Fergal tapped the side of his nose. 'Everything will be dandy. In the garage is it, you say?'

'Yes, it's open...' Josie began, but he was already off towards the electric doors.

'I'm here,' a voice called from behind her, and Lin rounded the corner holding out two bowls. 'Neil made these – a coleslaw and a bean salad. Where shall I put them?'

Josie took them from her. 'I'll pop them in the kitchen for a while. Where's Neil?'

'Oh, he'll be joining us as soon as he's done a job on the Sharan – something to do with the timing belt.' Lin smiled. She looked relaxed in cropped jeans and a bright shirt. 'I'm looking forward to this afternoon.'

'Me too,' Josie said hopefully.

Devlin and Finn Toomey crossed the lawn, hauling a trestle table between them, shouting greetings, and Dickie Junior followed with Dickie Senior, carrying a barrel of beer. Then Minnie rounded the corner, Cecily on her arm, calling out, 'We're here, Josie. I've brought chocolate brownies. Tell us what we can do to help.'

'I've brought filled rolls,' Cecily added.

Then Jack Lovejoy was beside her. 'You should have brought a guitar – we could have jammed together.' He waved to Josie. 'Where shall I set up?'

'Set up?'

'I've brought an amp with me...' Jack replied cheerily. 'Just so that the sound carries.'

'It'll carry through the whole village,' Lin said anxiously, and Josie was suddenly worried. The barbecue lunch was already out of control: minibuses of flower-waving hippies might arrive at any moment, looking for a festival. She glanced nervously at Lin. 'Oh dear... I hope this is going to be all right.'

Several hours later, everything was ready, the food, drink, chairs, entertainment in place, and Josie's worries evaporated. The garden began to fill with guests, happy chatter and the rich aroma of smoky food. People tucked heartily into plates piled high, and glasses of beer or punch; when everyone was mingling cheerfully, Josie felt herself relax. Kenny Hooper and Jimmy Baker had already eaten most of Odile's sausages. Gerald

Harris was there, sporting a cream suit, chatting to Cecily; Josie heard him say something about old values being the best while Cecily argued furiously that as far as she remembered, those days weren't all they were cracked up to be.

The golden couple from the village, Darryl and Charlotte Featherstone, arrived, looking gorgeous. Darryl chatted animatedly to Dangerous Dave about the best place to service his newly acquired Porsche as Charlotte listened placidly. Odile cooked heaps of chicken wings doused in barbecue sauce and Janice and Geoff Lovejoy tucked in ravenously; Josie hoped Mrs B'Gurk and Susan were safely at home in the coop. Jack Lovejoy sang Ed Sheeran songs for all he was worth and Natalie Ledbury threw her arms around her fiancé Brandon, who looked awkward being smothered in a public smooch. Florence was talking to Malia and Adam. She was visibly pregnant now, oblivious to any sidelong glances or whispers about paternity. Dickies Junior and Senior served beer to an endless queue and the Toomey boys were the life and soul of the event, cracking jokes, helping Odile dish up extra food to anyone nearby. Fergal was talking quietly to Lin and Minnie as Josie watched, standing by herself, surveying her crowded garden. Then she felt a slight pressure on her elbow.

'Well, Josie, this is a wonderful turn-out.' The vicar smiled. 'Better than I get on a Sunday.'

'You should hold a barbecue in the vestibule, Andrew,' Josie joked.

Andrew nodded sagely. 'I was hoping to get the Featherstones to come along one Sunday. They are a charming couple. They might encourage more young people to attend.'

'They do seem nice,' Josie agreed.

'Darryl is a lawyer; he works in Charlbury now, it's much closer than London, where he worked originally, but he travels a lot. He was telling me he went to the US for three weeks recently, sorting out contracts between artists and an art gallery. What a fascinating life he must have.'

'Indeed.'

'His wife works in London sometimes – it's almost a two-hour commute. I wouldn't like to do all that travelling.'

'I think Charlotte works from home most of the time,' Josie replied.

'And...' Andrew gave a little cough and glanced at Florence. 'If I'm touting for business, I might mention that we do a good line in christenings...'

Josie smiled. 'I don't know what her plans are.'

'I might ask the father...' Andrew raised an eyebrow. 'It's young Adam Johnson she's with over there, isn't it? Although, I have to say, I heard on the village grapevine...' Andrew coughed confidentially, 'that Bobby Ledbury might be the father. Apparently, he was in the café offering to buy a pram...'

Josie said quietly, 'He was just being sweet.' She raised an eyebrow. 'Who told you that, Jimmy or Kenny?'

'Oh, Kenny's no gossip,' Andrew began, then his face flushed. 'Nor am I. Only, the villagers like to share news in order to – keep everyone under their wing. As it says in Ephesians, "Let no corrupting talk come out of your mouths, but only such as fits the occasion, that it may give grace to those who hear." So, if you'll excuse me, I might go and talk to Darryl and Charlotte about the joys of our Sunday service.'

Josie smiled. 'Please do.' She sidled over to Fergal, Lin and Minnie.

'It's going well.' Minnie raised her glass. 'Well done, Josie.'

Fergal nodded. 'Do you ladies need your glasses topping up? I'll get some more punch.'

'Thanks.' Lin moved closer to Josie. 'Everyone's talking about Bobby Ledbury being the father of Florence's baby.'

'I heard it. What rubbish.' Minnie shrugged. 'He might be or he might not, but people should mind their own business.'

'Adam's a nice young man...' Lin sighed.

Josie gazed across to where Andrew the vicar had joined Darryl and Charlotte; Dangerous Dave listened for a moment, then he moved away, bored. Josie watched as he mooched towards the barbecue, picking up a sausage, burning his fingers, then he tottered towards the trestle table that held the beer and refilled his glass. He drank it in one gulp and refilled his glass again before pausing to talk to Fergal. From where Josie was standing, she could hear him slurring his words. Lin had heard him too; she offered Josie a worried look.

Minnie simply said, 'Dangerous Dave is an accident waiting to happen.'

'He is,' Lin agreed, watching.

'Testosterone, a beautiful pregnant daughter, protective feelings. My dad wouldn't have cared less.' Minnie laughed once. 'He'd have shaken the man's hand and bought him a pint.'

Lin was immediately sympathetic. 'How's romance going in Oxford, Minnie? It's been very quiet recently since... who was the last one?'

'Frantic Felix?' Josie reminded her.

'Well, there is someone, as you know...' Minnie began. 'It's early days – in fact, we haven't dated yet, but we will...'

'The American director?' Lin asked, open mouthed. '*Julius Caesar*...'

'He won't be able to resist me,' Minnie said confidently.

'Then I can't wait for the next instalment,' Josie smiled.

Fergal was by her side with a tray of drinks. He muttered, 'Your man Dangerous Dave has had a few too many beers, I think.'

'Oh, I hope it's just catharsis.' Minnie accepted a glass. 'Relieving the pressure of mounting anxiety.'

Fergal looked anxious. 'It's a worry, for sure – he's asking all the men here if they are the baby's father.'

'Oh, surely not,' Josie said, gazing around.

Fergal sipped his beer, wiping froth from his lips. 'He just asked me about Finn, was he seeing any local girls, did he ever mention anything to me about Florence? I told him not to be so daft...'

'Oh, dear...' Lin pointed to where Devlin Toomey was chatting easily with Florence. He was laughing, patting her arm affectionately. They heard him say, 'It's no trouble at all, Florence – of course I'll do that for you.'

Dave stiffened, a pint in his hand. Then he called out, 'Hey, you.'

Minnie flashed her eyes. 'Here we go.'

Dangerous Dave staggered across to where Devlin was standing with Florence. Dave pushed between them, moving Florence gently to one side, and then he faced Devlin. 'What do you think you're laughing at?'

'Nothing at all.' Devlin laughed again, but this time it was awkward and defensive. 'You've nothing to take offence at here, Dangerous. Florence and I were just...'

'There is no Florence and you...' Dangerous Dave punched the air as Devlin ducked, stepping out of the way.

Florence called out, 'Dad!' as Dave staggered forward.

'I'd best step in and calm things down,' Fergal murmured, handing his pint to Josie and moving towards Dave, who was shouting now, his face creased in rage.

'You Toomey boys, running riot in the village, doing just as you want with who you want. She's my little girl, my princess...' Dave was close to tears and bubbling with rage. 'I'm asking you straight, Devlin, is it you? Are you the bastard who...?'

'Now, Dangerous, steady on there...' Devlin held up a hand in denial.

Florence gasped, 'Dad, you're making a show...'

'I asked you a question...'

Devlin took a step back. 'Look, there's no need to...'

Dangerous Dave took a swing at the air again as Devlin moved skilfully out of the way like a practised boxer. Dave raised both fists and roared like a lion. He charged towards Devlin just as Fergal stood in his path, grabbing him in both arms in a bear hug, muttering, 'Calm down, Dangerous – we don't want any trouble at Josie's house...'

Dangerous Dave tugged away, snorting through his nostrils, catching his breath. Then he hurled himself at Fergal, who remained fixed to the spot as the angry man cannoned backwards, arms in the air, out of control, falling against Odile who was busy frying more chicken. She tottered and a tray overturned as charred meat flew into the air.

Odile turned on him fiercely, waving a long fork. 'Get yourself outta my way, Dangerous, before you fall on my barbecue and burn your butt, or I do you some serious damage with this cooking prong.'

Dave sank to the floor in despair, and Fergal went to his side, picking him up gently. Florence rushed to her father, wrapping her arms around him.

Minnie murmured, 'He's just a good dad, looking out for his girl. Men like that are special – and rare.'

'Thank goodness for Fergal,' Lin said pointedly, then she glanced at her watch. 'Oh no, it's past four. Neil's taking a long time with the Sharan – he said he'd be here by two.'

Everyone was staring at Dave as Florence linked her arm through his. Josie asked, 'Florence, are you all right?'

'We're fine, Josie… I'll just take my dad home.'

'I'm sorry, Josie.' Dangerous Dave lurched close to her, his breath beery and sour. 'I didn't mean to ruin your barbecue, I didn't…'

'Don't worry,' Josie said soothingly. 'Just go home and sleep. You'll be all right.'

'I'll look after him,' Florence called, wrapping both arms around him.

Josie watched them go as Darryl and Charlotte Featherstone made their way over. Darryl kissed Josie's cheek, much to her surprise, and murmured, 'Thanks so much – we have to leave early, sadly – pressures of work…' Then he and Charlotte were on their way and everyone else returned to their conversation. Smoke billowed around Odile, who was cooking more chicken. Florence led Dave around the corner towards the front gate. Their heads were together, talking gently. The Toomey brothers were with Odile, picking up pieces of barbecued chicken from the grass, helping themselves to the food she was cooking. Josie hoped everyone wasn't too disappointed, or that they didn't think it was her fault.

'Mrs Sanderson…' A serious voice came from behind her shoulder. 'I'm so glad you invited me to your barbecue, because I really need to talk to you…'

Josie swivelled round. 'Gerald.' She met his eyes inquisitively: her instinct warned her that he had something to say that she wouldn't like. 'It was nice of you to come.'

'But I did say to you…' He lowered his voice. 'I really don't think you should spend so much time with Fergal Toomey. Trouble follows that family wherever they go, as you can see for yourself, with the dreadful brawl.'

'Brawl?' Minnie echoed. 'Hang on a minute, Gerald—'

'Please…' Josie took a deep breath. 'This isn't the best time…'

'I'm just thinking of your welfare.' Gerald placed a hand on her shoulder.

'Thank you, but I'm in no mood for...' Josie took a step back and shook her head as if bees were buzzing in front of her.

'He isn't your type, Toomey.'

'My type?' Josie was baffled. She felt Lin and Minnie close in protectively.

'You're a widow – you need someone to care for you properly. This afternoon shows that to be true, attempting to stage this barbecue by yourself with no partner to support you. Not really your wisest move, an older woman, alone.'

For a second, Josie was speechless. She knew Minnie was about to say something in sharp retort – she heard her inhale, but Josie beat her to it. 'Gerald. I'm fine as I am.'

'Clearly not.' Gerald coughed politely. 'The thing is, Mrs Sanderson, I might be of service...'

Josie was almost out of patience. 'What do you mean, service?'

'I wanted to ask you...'

'Ask me what?'

'I just wanted to say—'

Josie folded her arms and met his eyes. 'Then say it, for goodness' sake!'

'Mrs Sanderson, Josie – I wondered if I could – possibly – ask you – at some point in the future – when you are ready – and willing – to accompany me on a date?'

24

Cecily had left her mobility scooter in the car park. She sat on the high stool at the bar of The Sun Inn, waiting for her date. The stool was uncomfortable; her legs didn't quite reach the ground, and her back ached. She considered moving to a table with chairs, but there was something cool about being perched on a stool. Sitting alone at a table would make her look as if she'd been stood up when in fact she was just early: her 'date' wasn't expected until seven o'clock, another ten minutes. She gazed around. Kenny Hooper was sitting in the corner wearing his old grey jacket, talking to Jimmy Baker. The Toomey boys were chatting with a group of girls whom Cecily had never seen before. Linval and Rita Johnson were sharing a meal, their heads close. Cecily sipped her gin and tonic thoughtfully.

'Are you all by yourself?' Dickie Senior asked, drying glasses behind the bar.

'I'm waiting for someone...' Cecily smiled. 'I have a date.'

Dickie looked momentarily shocked. 'Can I get you anything else, Miss?' Cecily gazed at him for a moment; with his shiny head and hang-dog face, he looked almost as old as she was.

'No, thank you, Dickie,' she said kindly. 'What are you drinking? I'll buy you one.'

Dickie grinned. 'I'll help myself to a short and join you.'

Dickie moved to the optics and served himself a whisky. He returned to lean against the bar. 'I hear Josie's barbecue was quite a ding-dong.'

Cecily shook her head. 'It was a lovely afternoon. We all had a great time.' She frowned. 'You should have come.'

'I don't get out much.' Dickie scratched his scalp. 'The thing is, the wife's health isn't so good. She doesn't go out much either now. COPD, you know. And I'm not like I used to be – the diabetes holds me back and the hearing's not what it was, although the hearing aid helps.'

'Oh...' Cecily was full of sympathy. 'You'd have enjoyed the barbecue.'

'I'd have enjoyed seeing Dangerous Dave squaring up to the Toomeys.' His eyes moved to where Devlin and Finn were laughing with the village girls. 'Apparently, Dangerous thought Devlin's the father. I wouldn't be surprised if he was... We were talking about having a sweep on it in here – Bobby Ledbury's joint favourite with Devlin Toomey, Adam Johnson is evens...'

'That's enough, Dickie.' Cecily slammed a hand on the bar, making the ice jiggle in her glass. She gazed around; the Johnsons were sipping drinks, Linval laughing: they had not heard, and the Toomey boys were oblivious. Cecily was seething. 'When will people learn that a pregnant woman is not a target for gossip? It's a baby we're talking about here. Yes, there is a man to blame and he's got off scot-free while poor Florence deals with it all by herself, but it really is none of your business, Dickie Edwards.'

Dickie hung his head as he had done in class so often after being admonished by Cecily. 'I didn't mean...'

'Of course you didn't,' Cecily said soothingly. 'But rather than bet on the identity of the baby's father in the pub, wouldn't it be better to raise money for Florence to buy nappies?'

'That's a good plan, Miss...' Dickie began, then his eyes fell on Jack Lovejoy, who had just arrived and was standing next to Cecily. 'Good evening, young man – what will you be having?'

'I'll have a pint of Hooky.'

Cecily opened her purse. 'Thanks, Dickie – Jack's my guest tonight, so this one's on me. Jack, dear...' She eased herself down from the stool. 'Would you mind if we moved to a nice table? This stool is killing me.'

'Not at all, Cecily.' Jack adjusted the colourful cap on his head.

Dickie poured the pint and watched as Jack helped Cecily to a nearby table. He brought the drink across and moved back to the bar, turning his good ear towards them. He was fascinated to know why his old teacher was having a drink with a lad young enough to be her great-grandson.

Jack supped his pint. 'So, Cecily, what do you reckon I come round your house on Sunday evenings?'

'Maybe twice a week, three times if you have the time and the energy,' Cecily suggested. 'I could do Wednesdays and Fridays, if you're free.'

Dickie leaned forward, his eyes bulging, and gulped whisky: the conversation was becoming very interesting indeed.

'I'm up for it.' Jack nodded. 'I'm a novice compared to you, so I'm happy to put in all the extra hours. I need to get my technique as good as I can.'

Cecily agreed. 'And I have years of experience – I started in my early teens, you know, so I can share all I've learned. But you're bringing youth and energy to the table.'

'It's what I do,' Jack replied.

Dickie almost spat his whisky out. He leaned further across the bar. He couldn't believe his ears: Jack and Cecily were planning a fling together. He almost burst with the excitement of new lewd gossip.

'Shall I bring my equipment?' Jack asked.

Dickie held his breath, shocked, delighted.

'Oh, I think you should.' Cecily beamed. 'I don't know too much about these modern accessories, but I believe that they can improve things a great deal.'

'Oh, you'll be amazed at the difference they make,' Jack agreed.

'Well, I'm a bit rusty nowadays,' Cecily admitted. 'But I'm sure it will all come back to me.'

Dickie had a sudden coughing fit. Sex toys too, and at her age? He took his drink and shifted to where Jimmy Baker and Kenny Hooper were sitting. They'd be stunned when he told them. Dickie wouldn't have believed it himself had he not heard every word. He huddled at the table and leaned forward, whispering, intermittently staring over his shoulder towards Cecily.

Jimmy Baker's voice rang out. 'No... you're kidding. She must be ninety. Well, she always was a bit of a looker, though... I mean, I suppose once you have sex appeal, you don't ever lose it...'

'You're being disrespectful.' Kenny Hooper frowned. 'It ent right to talk about Miss Hamilton like that. You should both shut up.'

'But what if it's true?' Jimmy began. 'Just imagine...'

'You are being idiots.' Kenny sulked. 'It's wrong to listen and it's even wronger to turn it into dirty talk. I ent coming here to drink with you no more if you say rude things about Miss Hamilton...' He turned away, drinking his beer with his back to Jimmy.

'So, I'll bring an amp and the wah-wah pedal,' Jack said quietly. 'And an electric guitar and my acoustic.'

'I've always wanted to try a wah-wah.' Cecily smiled. 'We'll have to draw up a list of the songs we're practising. I used to play a lot of folk songs – Dylan, Joan Baez. But I liked Jimi Hendrix a lot too and of course Chuck Berry. He was so underrated.'

'Have you heard much Slash? Or Joe Satriani?' Jack asked.

'Oh, I have so much to learn.' Cecily rubbed her hands together. 'So, here's the plan. We duet together on the guitars...'

'And harmonies...' Jack added. 'I don't mind singing.'

'Oh, I can sing too...'

'Excellent,' Jack said.

'And we'll perform for the lunch Florence is planning, as a surprise – the Silver Ladies would like to make it a secret baby shower for her too.'

'So, when's the gig?'

'I'm not sure yet... all I know is that she asked Devlin Toomey if she could use the barge and the surrounding riverbank to put on a lunch.'

'So that's why there was the big kick-off at Josie's barbecue – Dangerous Dave thought they were talking about the baby together and he got a bit salty?'

'Exactly.' Cecily sipped beer. 'I spoke to Devlin and told him what my plan was after the barbecue. So you and I are going to turn it into a gig to remember... a baby shower, just for her.'

'Cool.' Jack reached for his pint. 'We'll be amazing. We'll have to think of a name for our band.'

'Not Jack and Cecily – or Lovejoy and Hamilton?'

'I'll give it some thought,' Jack smiled.

'You're such a nice young man.' Cecily reached over and patted his hand just as three pairs of ears from an adjacent table leaned towards the conversation, eyes wide.

Jack stretched his legs happily. 'You and me, Cecily, we're going to be amazing together.'

'It's my absolute pleasure.' Cecily raised her glass.

Dickie and Jimmy turned to each other in unison, their eyes popping. Jimmy muttered, 'Well, would you believe it – there's life in the old girl yet...'

'I told you not to say them disgusting things,' Kenny spluttered. 'Miss Hamilton's special.'

'She certainly is.' Dickie pressed a finger against his lips. 'You wait until I tell the whole village – nobody is going to believe it.'

* * *

It was late Sunday afternoon as Minnie strode through the Botanical Gardens, along the banks of the Cherwell. Clad in a fedora, a military jacket and black Doc Martens, she was strolling down to where the Cherwell met the Thames to watch the punts glide past. The Christ Church Meadow walk was one of her favourites; she'd often ambled along the riverbank over the years, dawdling with lovers or wandering alone, thinking about her studies. It was a calm place, passing the Jubilee bridge, the overhanging branches dipping leaves in the green river.

Minnie was still thinking about her conversation with Tina several days ago. It disturbed her, like an itch she couldn't reach. Minnie had reminded her they were flesh and blood, and Tina had replied, 'That's *all* we are, though.' It had taken her breath away.

She thought about the hug they'd exchanged on the allotments as they parted. Tina had felt vulnerable, fragile. Minnie had never imagined Tina as anything other than robust, healthy, but she was reminded now of her sister's mortality. Neither she nor Tina were young any more, and the thought made Minnie strangely melancholy.

She reached the boathouse; the river was beautiful and still. She loved the glassy smoothness of it, the way it reflected back the sky and the clouds, the foliage that hung over. There was a tranquil symmetry, a poetry; Minnie sat down on the bank where the students would often load themselves into boats and row away, arms pumping in unison. A starling landed in a small puddle and beat its wings, splashing in the water. From nowhere, one or two punters glided past, their poles digging deep as they called to each other cheerily. Then they were gone. There would be more boats soon; the river would be busy on a Sunday in summer.

Minnie looked deeply into the Thames, often called the Isis in Oxford, a place of stories and memories, and she loved the deep mystery of it. However hard you stared, you couldn't see the bottom. It was dangerous to swim in it, twenty metres deep, she'd heard, but the sight of the Thames twisting into the distance always thrilled her. Minnie liked unfathomable depths; it was like knowledge, it intrigued her, there was always more waiting to be plumbed, to be discovered beneath the smooth surface. Minnie smiled; her mood was lifting.

Then she heard footsteps behind her, followed by a warm New York accent. 'It's Minnie, isn't it?'

She whirled round. Jensen Callahan was smiling, wearing a blue jacket and neat jeans. She recognised the unruly white hair that stuck out from his head like a cloud, the gold-rimmed spectacles, the intelligent face.

'We met at a dinner party – Francine and Melvyn's...'

'We did – hello, Jensen.' Minnie had never been one to play games in relationships; other women might have paused, nonplussed, pretended they didn't remember him, but Minnie had always been direct when faced with an attractive man. She didn't believe in batting her eyelashes and playing coy.

'What are you doing down here?' he asked, interested.

'Walking – my Sunday constitutional,' she replied simply. 'And you?'

'The same...' He grinned. 'A night off from the theatre. The play's going well.'

'*Julius Caesar* – I know. It was excellent.' Minnie met his eyes.

Jensen grinned broadly. 'You've seen it?'

'I have – I went to the first matinee.'

'You should have come backstage. I'd have loved to hear what you thought of it.'

Minnie suppressed a smile as she recalled sneaking in to watch part of a rehearsal. She was direct as ever. 'I'll tell you now, if you like.'

'I'd like that very much,' Jensen said. 'Shall we get a coffee somewhere, maybe?'

'I don't think so.' Minnie shook her head, then a smile spread across her lips. 'Do you know what I'd really like to do now, Jensen? We should go for a punt on the river. Let's hire a boat. We can talk as we row.'

25

It was early Sunday morning. As Lin opened her eyes, the room was dim, but there was enough light from the crack in the curtains to see the wall clock. It was ten minutes to seven. She rolled over to gaze at Neil, who was facing her, his eyes closed. As she often did, she listened hard for his breathing – sometimes there was no sound at all, and nowadays it worried her. But then he gave a snuffle and Lin relaxed, taking in the crumpled face against the pillow, the serene smile that hinted of a sweet dream. She leaned forwards and pressed her lips lightly against his and he muttered something that sounded like 'Love you...'

She wondered whether to get up and make breakfast, to take it back to bed as a treat for him. She couldn't ruin orange juice, cereal. She ought to be able to heat up a croissant, although she'd left them in the oven once until the smell of scorching dough told her they were burned. Lin sidled out of bed and reached for her dressing gown. Slipping it on, she padded to the kitchen, thinking: her biggest problem was timing – she'd make the coffee and it would be going cold while the croissants heated. Or she'd forget about them while she busied herself with the orange juice and the plates on the tray. She'd put the kettle on first, get out two mugs – or should she use nice china and make a pot of tea? Lin put a hand to her head – it shouldn't be this complicated.

She felt arms wrap around her; Neil kissed the back of her neck and Lin immediately worried that she hadn't brushed her hair. She turned round, troubled. 'I was going to bring you breakfast in bed.'

'You're lovely.' He kissed her again. 'Look, Lindy – it's a beautiful morning.' Neil pointed to the window. Outside, the garden was already flooded with sunlight, a pink blush.

'It's very early,' Lin fretted.

'Then let's make the most of the day…' Neil said. 'Let's eat our breakfast out there. We'll listen to the dawn chorus and drink coffee – then we can go back to bed again.'

'But you're busy. You told me you had to complete – how many steps was it today? Seven thousand? Eight?'

Neil took her hands in his. 'We can step together.'

'Aren't you going for a long walk in Old Scratch's woods?'

'I've been neglecting you, Lindy.' Neil pressed his cheek against hers. 'Let's take the Sharan and go somewhere. We could go to Burford or Shipton under Wychwood, have lunch in a nice pub, go on a canal walk afterwards…'

Lin closed her eyes. 'I'd like that.'

'Right.' He began to bustle about. 'Croissants in the oven – kettle on – two nice mugs for coffee.' He opened the oven door, shoved in a tray. The kettle began to chug. Then he turned to Lin. Her face was covered with tears. 'What's the matter, love?'

She was in his arms. 'I thought you didn't love me…'

'Why on earth would you think that?'

Lin snuffled against his shoulder. 'I don't know.'

He hugged her closer and Lin felt the warmth of him through the dressing gown. She took a shuddering breath. 'I'm being silly.'

'No.' Neil held her away from him, looking at her face. 'It's me – I've been occupied with too many – other things – recently. I'm sorry. I need to make more of a fuss of you.'

'I shouldn't need fussing over – we've been married for forty-nine years.'

'Fifty soon,' Neil murmured into her hair.

'Am I just getting old and fretful?' Lin asked.

'No, you're adorable.' Neil smiled and she loved the way his eyes crinkled. 'I promise you – you have nothing to worry about.'

Lin nodded – there it was again, that line. Nothing to worry about. She took a deep breath and felt a shudder in her lungs.

Neil turned away; he was humming, pouring coffee, taking warm croissants from the oven, pouring juice, placing butter and jam and plates on a tray. She marvelled at his ease, the deft movements, the precision of his thoughts.

'Come on, Lindy, let's enjoy breakfast *al fresco*.'

Lin led the way to the garden, blinking in the bright glow of the sunlight, the twitter of birdsong in her ears.

Then she stopped and caught her breath. Neil was next to her, clutching the tray, not moving. At the end of the garden, where Neil had planted potatoes, the soil had been scattered, rough irregular trenches had been dug, and the remains of rooted plants were flung everywhere.

There in the middle of the vegetable patch, amongst the dirt and the newly dug holes, a black and white pig lay on her side, her small eyes squeezed shut. Nadine had gorged herself on the new potato plants and now she was fast asleep.

***

'Dammit!' Josie gritted her teeth as the rubbish spilled onto the kitchen floor. She was trying to tie the bin bag, which was bulging. She'd overfilled it. The bag had split and all sorts of smelly items tumbled onto the clean kitchen floor. 'Dammit,' she said again and was instantly surprised that a simple task such as putting the bins out made her so cross: she was usually so calm. She grasped the bag in two hands as if she would throttle it, and heaved it outside down the path to the wheelie bin, shoving the plastic down hard. She slammed the lid and tugged the bin to the edge of the drive, her teeth clamped as if she was dragging a naughty child to school. Then she paused by the gate and paused, exasperated. There was the recycling bin to do next, and the vegetable waste. She hated doing the bins – Harry had always put them out, never complaining, whistling that annoying tune,

'Don't Worry, Be Happy'. If only he was here now. She'd never grumble again.

Back in the kitchen, Josie contemplated her options. It was early afternoon now – she'd eaten a sandwich and she had nothing to do for the rest of the day. She could stay in and finish putting out the various bins for collection tomorrow, or she could make a cup of tea and drink it alone, or she could do something else, but she had no idea what. It was a Sunday; Odile's was closed. Lin was out with Neil – she'd texted earlier that she'd be gone all day. Josie was glad they were spending some quality time together. But the situation was the same for her – she was on her own.

She thought about popping down to the allotments for a chat with Tina Gilchrist, but Tina would be absorbed with weeding and tending her vegetables. Besides, what was worse, Josie would have to pass Chandos, and she didn't want to see Gerald Harris after he'd invited her for a date. She'd had no idea how to respond to his invitation – Minnie had bailed her out, suggesting that it was thoughtful of him, but Josie wasn't in need of someone to organise her life as if it was a military strategy, which was clearly Gerald's great strength. Minnie had been so sweet when she'd said it, Gerald had almost taken it as a compliment.

She reached for a light jacket, although she thought she'd probably end up carrying it. The air was warm outside, almost humid; she'd stroll towards St Peter and St Paul's church, down Tadderly Road and call in on Cecily. She'd take a packet of biscuits and stop for a cuppa. She needed company and Cecily probably did too.

Josie checked her phone. There was an email from *djellis*, and she read it quickly. David Ellis had adored her idea of creating a handsome love interest for his heroic inspector, Alain di Angelo. He wanted to thank her and to tell her that the novel was underway again; he'd completed 51,000 words. Alain, the protagonist, was currently fascinated by the dark mysterious stranger, Dario Elijah, although he wasn't sure yet if he was a friend or a suspect. Josie replied quickly – she was glad David was back on track with his opus and she wished him the best of luck.

She set off towards Nobb's End, where the big new-build houses were. She thought about Darryl and Charlotte Featherstone and decided she ought to get to know them better. She recalled that Florence had offered to organise the next lunch meeting, although Josie wasn't sure when it was, but she might ask her if Darryl and Charlotte could be invited. It would be a neighbourly thing to do.

Josie glanced across the village green, to the willow tree where Natalie Ledbury and her fiancé Brandon were sitting together. She paused and a little sigh escaped without her intending it to; at Natalie's age, she and Harry had cuddled beneath the same willow tree, holding hands. He'd proposed to her there. She'd said yes immediately – she'd known it was what she wanted for the rest of her life. She wondered if Natalie and Brandon would be standing where she was in fifty years' time, looking at another young couple all loved up beneath the willow. In her heart, she wished they wouldn't have to suffer what she was going through now.

Natalie stood up quickly, then Brandon was on his feet and Josie realised they were arguing. Natalie walked away and Brandon reached out and grabbed her arm to pull her back. Josie watched, wondering if it was just a tiff. Natalie shouted something angrily as she rushed down the road. Brandon chased after her, his voice distraught. Josie watched for a moment longer to make sure it was a lovers' spat, nothing more. Natalie wasn't being threatened – they were talking quietly now – so Josie turned away. She'd be at Cecily's in ten minutes.

Then she heard a familiar voice call her name and she swivelled round to see Fergal coming from the church. He caught up with her quickly. 'Hi, Josie – I've been in the graveyard talking to the dead again.'

Josie gave a weak smile. 'I took some flowers to Harry yesterday.'

Fergal shuffled his feet. 'And now I'm at a loose end.'

'Oh?'

'I don't suppose you fancy a swift one?'

'Pardon?' Josie asked.

Fergal took an awkward step back. 'In The Sun. A drink.' He shuffled his feet. 'I always feel like a glass of beer after I've been talking to Ros. I've been telling her about how the boys are, the malarkey that happened between Devlin and Dangerous at your barbecue.'

Josie remembered. 'The barbecue Gerald Harris says I shouldn't have had because a widowed woman can't cope by herself...'

'Ah, he's just sweet on you,' Fergal shrugged. 'So, will you take a glass of something with me?'

'Why not?' Josie smiled. A white wine in the pub beer garden might be nice – it might take the edge off the sour mood she'd been in earlier.

Fergal led the way into the bar; it was busy, as usual. Kenny Hooper and Jimmy Baker were sitting at a table with Dickie Senior and Dangerous Dave Dawson, who had his back to them as they walked in. Josie thought it might be better not to mention the barbecue, not yet, so she waved at Jimmy as she and Fergal stood at the bar, then they took their drinks outside to the pretty beer garden with a gazebo and colourful lights.

Fergal supped from his pint glass thirstily. 'So, Josie...'

'Fergal...'

'Bomber Harris – there's nothing between you and him?'

'There's nothing between me and anyone,' Josie said.

'Only...' Fergal took another slurp. 'Only, I was very grateful after you made the Sunday dinner for me... I really enjoyed myself.'

'I enjoyed it too,' Josie admitted.

'And the barbecue – I had a nice time there too... apart from the business with Dangerous Dave, and that was really to do with him having drunk too much beer and being protective of Florence.'

'The less said about that incident the better,' Josie agreed.

'So, I wondered whether you and I might go out somewhere one night, a dinner perhaps, or bring a takeaway on the barge.'

Josie sipped white wine as the sun sparkled through the glass and the drink was crisp and sharp on her tongue. 'Fergal, I'm not looking for romance.'

'Company, Josie, just company.'

'I don't know.'

'Think about it.'

'I will.'

There was a cough behind them and Josie glanced over her shoulder. Dangerous Dave was there, arms folded humbly, looking uncomfortable.

'Dangerous,' Fergal said by way of a greeting.

'Josie, Fergal – I'm glad I found you both together...' Dave began. 'I wanted to apologise for embarrassing myself at the barbecue.'

'Oh, there's no need...' Josie said kindly.

'There is,' Dave insisted. 'I was out of order. I drank too much Hooky and I saw your Devlin, Fergal, with my Florence and the red mist came down.'

Fergal frowned deeply. 'Devlin's not the father of Florence's baby, Dangerous – I asked him straight when I got home. He wouldn't lie to his da.'

'I know. Florence told me off too. She knows I'm only being caring – that girl is all I have.'

Josie patted his arm. 'Won't you come and join us?'

Dave nodded. 'I might – but I only came out for a swift half.'

'Me too – I was on my way to see Cecily,' Josie admitted. 'Then I bumped into Fergal.'

Dave's brow creased. 'I'm not sure you should go to see Cecily today, not after what I've just been told in the pub.'

'Gossip?' Fergal asked. 'I usually find it's best avoided.'

'No, it's something that Dickie and Jimmy overheard in the bar the other day. They were completely bowled over by it. I have to admit, I didn't believe it at first but – well!' Dangerous Dave shook his head. 'Incredible, really, but I suppose in this day and age, anything goes.'

'Is Cecily all right?' Josie was concerned. 'Why can't I go and see her?'

'Well, the thing is...' Dave sat down next to her, folding his arms, making himself comfortable. 'I'd say she won't want any visitors – she's too busy with other things...'

'What have you heard?' Josie asked.

'She has a lover.' Dave opened wide goggling eyes.

'That's daft.' Fergal reached for his pint.

'Cecily can do what she likes,' Josie retorted. 'She's her own woman, a free spirit.'

'Free spirit is completely right,' Dave chortled. 'Carrying on with a young man like that at her age. I still can't get my head around it.'

'Young man? What young man?' Fergal asked suspiciously.

'Well,' Dangerous Dave continued. 'Dickie and Jimmy saw them both in the pub together, drinking. They were talking openly about their love life, planning it – Dickie heard every word. Cecily is – get this – she's only having a bit of how's your father with young Jack Lovejoy.'

26

Florence was feeling just as she always had before she was pregnant – light, happy, carefree. She hurried through the front door with Malia behind her, Adam carrying a bag of takeaway Chinese food and, for a while, she forgot the weight of worry that bothered her constantly. For a fleeting moment, she was just having fun. They rushed into the kitchen and Malia reached for cutlery, Adam opened bottles of cola and sparkling water, while Florence emptied metal cartons, tipping noodles and tofu onto plates. They moved to the living room. Florence flopped on the sofa and Adam dropped down next to her, leaving the armchair for Malia, who flicked on the TV.

Malia's eyes were on the screen. 'Odile was great about our idea, wasn't she?'

'She was.' Florence nodded. 'Malia – I don't know what I'd do without you.'

'It's no sweat – I'm staying in Middleton Ferris until Christmas anyway so it's easy to share the work at the café until the baby is born. Then you can come back part-time when you're ready and I'll look for a job somewhere, to start after Christmas. It suits us both.'

'In London?' Adam asked, fork in the air.

'Definitely not here,' Malia sniffed.

'I like it here,' Adam retorted.

'You're just Dad's little mini-me...' Malia teased.

Adam glanced towards Florence. 'I'm happy where I am.'

Florence turned slowly. 'I'm so grateful to you both... People are being so kind.'

'That's because everyone likes you,' Adam murmured and Malia rolled her eyes.

Florence sat up. 'Have you seen the nursery now Dad's repainted it? The sunshine comes in and the room is so bright.'

'Have you bought anything for the baby yet?' Malia asked.

'Not yet, not really.'

'We'll have to go shopping together,' Malia said.

'I can help too – I'd like to,' Adam added.

'I'm organising a lunchtime picnic by the barge – Devlin said it would be okay.' Florence wiped her mouth on the back of her hand carelessly. 'For Josie, Lin and Cecily – Minnie too. They've been so supportive and sweet, and I want to say thanks. Will you both come?'

'Yes, I'll be there,' Adam replied without pausing.

'When is it?' Malia snuggled into the armchair.

'Next month – 12 August.' Florence's eyes were on the screen, oblivious as Adam stretched an arm across the back of the sofa behind her. She added, 'Devlin said he and Finn and Fergal would just go down the pub for a couple of hours and let me use the barge, but I asked them to come to lunch too.'

Malia smiled. 'It'll be fun – I like Finn and Devlin.'

'Most women do...' Florence muttered.

'Where's your dad now?' Adam asked, changing the subject.

'Down at The Sun, I think, with Jimmy Baker. They are a pair of old gossips when they get together,' Florence said affectionately. Then she exhaled. 'I don't know what I'd do without Dad – or you two.'

'You'll be fine, and so will the baby,' Adam promised.

Malia reached across and squeezed her hand. Florence closed her eyes, bathed in a feeling of warmth.

There was a sharp knock on the front door and Adam clambered to his feet. 'I'll get it.'

Florence's eyes were on the TV screen, but she was listening to the two male voices at the door, Adam's light one and a deeper, gruffer voice. Then she heard Adam say, 'You'd better come in.'

Florence turned to see Bobby Ledbury, who was carrying a white wooden cot with a floral mattress through the doorway. He put it on the carpet as Florence stood up, touching the rails with light fingers. Bobby shoved his hands in loose jeans pockets. 'It's got a washable mattress cover...'

'It's perfect.' Florence was already imagining the cot in the nursery with the baby in it, staring at her, reaching up a tiny fist.

'It's yours,' Bobby muttered, looking around the living room, his eyes moving to the TV screen. 'It's had about six months' use for two babies, but it's in good nick.'

'Thank you...' Florence smiled. 'Can I buy it from you?'

'No need,' Bobby shrugged. His eyes met Malia's then Adam's in a hesitant greeting.

'Do you want to stay for a coffee?' Florence asked.

'Nah, I don't have time.' Bobby shuffled his feet. 'Dad makes me work all hours so Grandad won't have to do so much, and in my free time I go to Tadderly to see Hayley.' He frowned, lost in thought for a moment. 'Her ex is a bit of a bastard, so I stay over sometimes. He's been round the house, making threats over the kids.'

'How old are they now, her little ones?' Malia asked.

'Alfie, the youngest, is one and a half, and Lily is nearly four.' Bobby sighed. 'They are lovely kids; I treat them just like they're my own. She wants me to move in but...'

'You haven't told your parents yet?' Florence said gently.

Bobby shook his head. 'They'd kick off, me being with a married woman in her thirties. Hayley and I have decided when her divorce is through, I'll break it to them and then we'll move in together.' He scratched his head. 'My mum will give me verbals and Grandma Penny is the worst of all – she moans about me being out all the time.'

Adam nodded sympathetically. 'It must be tough.'

Bobby forced a grin. 'Hayley says there are some baby clothes you can have too, in good condition – I mean, I know you'll want to buy new ones, but they'd be back-up – kids throw up a lot...'

'Thanks, Bobby.' Florence squeezed his arm. 'It all helps – tell Hayley that's really kind.'

'Anything else, let me know – she's got baby toys the kids don't use now they are bigger...' Bobby made his way towards the door.

'You're doing a great job with those kids,' Malia said and Bobby turned to go.

'I'll see you all around.'

'Bye, Bobby – and thanks,' Florence called as Adam followed him to the door.

'This is exciting, isn't it, your baby's cot... and it's in such good condition.' Malia's thumb traced the carved headboard. 'Shall we take it upstairs, see how it looks in the nursery?'

'We could.' Florence reached for her tumbler of water. 'It's all starting to feel very real...' She was thoughtful for a moment. 'Poor Bobby, having to keep his girlfriend and her family secret.'

'He does so much for her,' Malia agreed. 'He loves her to bits, and the kids.'

Adam came back into the room. 'Do you want me to take the cot up to the nursery, Florence?'

'Yes, let's do it. Oh—' Florence put a hand to her belly and smiled. 'The baby just kicked me.' Her voice became a whisper. 'You go to sleep, sweetie. We'll put your cot in the nursery, then Mummy's going to rest for an hour or two.' She glanced at Adam thoughtfully. 'I'm going to try to make the best of this time before the baby's born – after the birth, I'll be run off my feet for years...'

* * *

Minnie was sitting in The Old Bookbinders alehouse, eating crêpes with Jensen. She raised a glass of pale ale and smiled. 'What do you think to lunch in The Bookies?'

Jensen took in the dim lighting, the wooden fixtures, plush barstools, tiled floor. 'I love it.' He turned towards Minnie. 'It's good to have my own personal guide to Oxford. It's the coolest place. And the crêpes here are outstanding.'

'When you're not busy with *Julius Caesar*, what do you do with yourself?' Minnie asked, leaning forward. 'Do you spend a lot of time out with the cast?'

'I did the first week or two, and I was invited to that great dinner party with Melvyn and Francine.'

Minnie smiled. 'But do you get out into the town much?'

'I go to the Ashmolean Museum a lot – there's so much to see there. And when the show is over each night, I mostly just eat at home in my little room at the B & B. Mrs Tanner lets me use the TV room to chill out, so I tend to have a beer and watch something there or read a book before I turn in for the night.' He grinned. 'But now I've met you, I do exciting things – like punt down the Thames and eat out in cool bars.'

Minnie stretched out her legs, crossing her blue Doc Martens. 'We'll take another punt and see the backwaters next week, up the Cherwell to the Victoria Arms for a pint and a picnic. And I want to take you to Port Meadow, which is an ancient grassland, and I must take you to Evensong in Magdalen chapel.'

'Evensong? Are you religious, Minnie?'

'Oh, no.' She shook her head. 'But the atmosphere there is something quite special. Once the organ gets going and the voices soar, the hairs on your neck prickle. Trust me.'

'I do.' Jensen held her gaze. 'I'm beginning to love Oxford, almost as much as I love New York.'

'You're going back when – in September, did you say?' Minnie found herself reaching out to touch his hand and she pulled away, folding her arms to stop them from moving.

'October, when the run at the Playhouse finishes,' Jensen said quietly and Minnie tried to read his expression: she was sure there was an unwillingness to leave.

'Well, by then I'll have shown you some of the best things Oxford has to offer.'

Jensen smiled. 'I think I'm looking at one of them...'

Minnie burst out laughing. 'That's outrageous, Jensen.'

'I'm just being honest.' Jensen's smile disappeared and his face became serious. 'I love spending time with you. You're great company, you're clever and funny. I could get used to it.'

Minnie turned her attention to her glass of beer, hiding the sudden feeling of pleasure. 'Well, I thought tomorrow we'd go to Christ Church – the alumni list reads like a who's who of world leaders, writers and thinkers.'

'I'd like that a lot.'

She continued to talk; the strength of his gaze was becoming unnerving and talking gave her something to concentrate on. 'Christ Church has a connection to *Alice in Wonderland* – and *Harry Potter*. The Great Hall was supposed to be the inspiration for Lewis Carroll's rabbit hole – it has a hidden door used by the dean when he's late for dinner. Of course, the theory is quite wrong – the staircase wasn't actually built until 1908 and Carroll wrote *Alice* in 1865.'

'I'd love to see it.'

'Maybe afterwards we can go for dinner at La Casa or Za'atar Bake.'

Jensen's gaze was constant. 'I'd like that very much.'

Minnie turned back to her crêpe, cutting it in a business-like way, trying to arrange her thoughts: men always fell in love with her easily for some reason she didn't understand and here she was again, another man falling for her without her making any effort whatsoever. It had always been this way since she'd come to Oxford: besotted boyfriends had been drawn to her like magnets.

Minnie chewed thoughtfully as he smiled at her. She waited for the rush of ambivalence to hit her, the feeling of boredom that came with such an easy conquest. It wasn't there. Instead, she was fascinated by this captivating man. It was difficult to look away.

He finished his crêpe and reached across the table. 'We could get a dessert maybe? What's good here?'

'They do a delicious lemon cheesecake and really refreshing red tea.' Minnie deliberately left her hand beneath his. 'Then it's still early – we could go for a walk along the river.'

'That would be so good.'

'And perhaps afterwards...' Minnie took a breath, determined to find out what he would say if she made him an offer he couldn't refuse. 'Perhaps we could go back to my house and... discuss the Romans. I'm reading Pliny the Elder at the moment and I'd be intrigued to hear what you think about the legacy of his doctrine of signatures.'

'It would be a pleasure,' Jensen said eagerly. 'I have so much time for Pliny – I always thought that his belief in magic and superstition shaped so many scientific and medical theories.'

'Oh, I agree.' Minnie grasped his arm without thinking. Then Jensen smiled and she let his arm go as if it had burned her. She'd come to a decision. She'd take him home; they'd talk about Pliny and drink more wine. He'd stay late and they'd talk and talk some more.

Minnie knew that Jensen would still be sitting in her living room by the time the sun rose. They'd discuss the Romans, the Egyptians, Julius Caesar, Pliny the Elder, Pliny the Younger. And after that, she'd kiss him. Then she'd invite him to stay for breakfast.

27

'Eggs with soldiers are just about my favourite thing,' Lin said as she sat at the breakfast table watching yolk squelch over the side of the shell. She shoved a thin strip of toast in deep, before pushing it into her mouth. Neil watched her happily as he poured coffee.

'You're my favourite thing,' he replied gently and Lin felt filled with emotion; he was so sweet; he complimented her because he loved her, there was no hidden agenda.

She watched him tuck into his boiled egg with the same boyish enthusiasm, the same easy-going nature she'd always loved.

She reached for the mug of coffee. 'You are coming to the picnic by the barge today?'

'Oh?' Neil frowned. 'I thought it was next week.'

'No, today, 12 August.' Lin indicated the kitchen window as if it was proof. 'The weather's perfect – it's going to be glorious.'

Neil's face took on an expression of anguish. 'Lindy, I promised a man in Tadderly that I'd go and look at his car for him.'

'What man in Tadderly?' Lin was surprised by how irritated she sounded.

Neil's eyes were on the ceiling, then on his plate. 'You don't know him – a customer from when I had the garage.'

'Can't Dangerous Dave do it?'

Neil sighed. 'This customer asked for me – he's an older man, our age – he thinks Dangerous is a bit, you know, heavy handed...'

Lin pushed her plate away. 'So you can't make the barbecue?'

'I'm sure I can: if I set off now, maybe I'll be back by about two...' Neil looked around him shiftily. 'It depends how long the job takes.'

'All right.' Lin was visibly disappointed. 'It just seems that I'm on my own all the time now whenever we are invited anywhere. You keep making excuses and disappearing...'

Neil was shocked. 'I don't make excuses, love.'

'You do,' Lin countered. 'You're always helping someone or going walking or – all sorts of things, you'll do anything rather than be with me.'

'No, that's not true.'

'It is, Neil.' Lin pushed her chair back, making a harsh squeak, and rushed to the kitchen sink. 'If you're not doing one thing then it's another.'

'Don't be silly.'

'Silly?' Lin felt the tears spring to her eyes. 'You think I'm silly?'

'No, Lindy.' Neil was next to her, wrapping his arms around her. 'Of course I don't. I'm sorry, I just meant...'

She glared at him. 'What did you mean?'

'I'm just helping someone.'

'So you say.' Lin couldn't stop her words. 'You'll help anyone else but you don't care about me.'

'Please don't say that.' He looked hurt. 'I'll be with you as soon as I can. You're the most important thing in my life.' He kissed the top of her head. 'I promise you that.'

Lin blinked, staring at her husband through tears. 'You promise?'

'Of course.' He kissed her forehead. 'I'm sorry I forgot the date, but I won't be long. I'll be quick...' He kissed her nose. 'Look, I'll get going now, and I'll rush through the job. Is that all right? I mean, if you want, I'll stay with you and we'll go to the picnic – I don't have to help this man with his car...'

'No, you go, if you've promised,' Lin huffed.

'I'll be back in a jiffy.' Neil reached for his jacket, the smart one, then he changed his mind. 'It's warm outside – I'll be fine in a shirt.' He rushed back, kissing her again. 'I'll see you by the barge later. Trust me... there's nothing to worry about.'

He was gone, and Lin put her hands to her face. He'd said it again. A huge sigh shuddered in Lin's lungs.

She collected the two plates of broken eggshell, congealed yolk, the shattered remains. She felt the same as the shell, weak and crumbling. She depended on Neil too much – she should be stronger, like Josie. She took another deep breath – she'd put on her best summer dress and go to the picnic by the barge. She'd be carefree, cheerful and when anyone asked her where her husband was, she'd wave a hand and say breezily, 'Oh, Neil? He's off somewhere – doing his own thing. We don't live in each other's pockets, you know...'

Pockets...?

She glanced at Neil's jacket hanging on the back of the chair where he'd left it. Lin hesitated – she'd never gone through his pockets – she'd never considered it – until now. After all, they knew everything about each other, they had nothing to hide. Their marriage was based on trust.

Before she could think any more, she was by the chair, her hand delving deep into the pockets, bringing out an assortment of things that she deposited on the table. Some silver coins, a squashed piece of tissue, a small pencil – Lin knew he kept it for writing memos when he was working on cars – a key, some fluff and a piece of folded paper, the ends of which were curled. Lin smoothed out the paper and examined it – someone had written on it in biro in neat round handwriting, not Neil's scrawl.

Carole Frost. 1.30. The Sun Inn car park.

There was a mobile phone number written underneath.

Lin stared at it again and the writing blurred as her eyes filled with tears. Neil was meeting a woman called Carole Frost in the car park of The Sun Inn, in public in Middleton Ferris where everyone could see them. Lin felt suddenly foolish. Her husband was having an affair right under her nose: the scrap of paper in her hand was evidence. Lin wondered how many other people knew about it, laughing at her behind her back; she could imagine Jimmy Baker saying, 'Neil's a sly one – silly Lin Timms has no idea that he's been seeing another woman. Who'd blame him, though, eh?'

She leaned against the table for support as the truth fell on her like an avalanche. Her marriage was a lie – no wonder Neil was always off somewhere, out walking, helping Jimmy with his bike or an old customer in Tadderly with his car: it was all an excuse to meet Carole Frost.

Lin imagined what she was like: of course, she'd be young, attractive, much more fun than Lin was. No wonder he didn't want to accompany his ordinary boring wife to village events – it was the perfect opportunity to meet exciting Carole Frost instead. Lin was shaking; she couldn't believe it. Neil was always so nice to her, so attentive, and it was all lies, a cover so that she wouldn't suspect. He'd said that she had nothing to worry about and here was the evidence: Carole Frost.

Lin wanted to ring Josie, to tell her what had happened. Josie would understand. Lin wasn't sure what she wanted her friend to say – Josie would probably tell her that she was worrying about nothing, it would all be all right. But no, Lin thought – the evidence was in her hand: Neil was a cheat. They'd been married for almost fifty years and – she shuddered – perhaps Carole Frost wasn't the first woman. How many more had there been while he was sweetly smiling and kissing her cheek and telling her how much he loved her?

Lin felt utterly foolish. She wondered whether to ring him now, to tell him to come home because she knew the truth. Or should she pretend nothing had happened, then follow him at the first opportunity? She might even catch them together. She couldn't mention it to him until she had proof – she wasn't that sort of person. Her face would give her away; he'd know something was wrong. She had no idea what to do.

Then a screech from the back garden pulled her from her thoughts and she dashed outside. Janice Lovejoy was standing by the hedge, screaming like she had been bitten. Geoff and Jack had rushed out too, both looking horrified.

Lin gazed over the fence. 'What's the matter?'

Then she saw it: the hen house had been destroyed, the chicken wire pulled down, a post snapped. Janice was shrieking. 'They've gone – where are my hens?' She waved her arms. 'Susan? Mrs B'Gurk? Where are my babies? They've been eaten – look – feathers.'

'It's all right, Mum.' Jack picked up a speckled hen, handing it over gently. 'Susan's okay.'

'And there you are, Janice.' Geoff pointed to several chickens. 'There's Mrs B'Gurk – and look, here are the others – four, five – they're all fine.'

'Thank goodness.' Janice hugged the hen against her face. 'I couldn't bear it if anything happened to Susan.'

Geoff swept up another hen and stroked the fluffy feathers. 'Don't worry, love. You're all right now.' Lin wasn't sure if he was talking to the hen or to Janice.

Then Janice's face crumpled angrily. 'It's Nadine – George's pig. She'll have been here and knocked down the hen house – it's a wonder she didn't eat the chickens.'

'It's all cool, Mum...' Jack said calmly.

'No, your mother has a point,' Geoff snapped. 'That pig wanders everywhere. It needs to be kept under control.'

'Penny is always saying it should go to the abattoir,' Janice grunted. 'I'll tell her, I'm on her side. We'll get the village to sign a petition.' She rocked the chicken. 'Oh, Susan, that horrible pig might have killed you.'

'It was probably the wind blew the henhouse down...' Jack suggested.

'In August?' Geoff retorted. 'It will be that bloody pig. Your mum's right.'

Lin tried to look sympathetic, but her mind was elsewhere. Geoff was still ranting. 'I'm going to tell George exactly what I think of him and that animal, coming onto our land.'

'I agree.' Janice folded her arms. 'It ate Neil's potatoes, slept right there on the veg patch, didn't it, Lin? Right under your nose...'

'Right under my nose...' Lin agreed sadly.

'It shouldn't be allowed,' Geoff agreed.

'It shouldn't.' Janice turned to Lin. 'What do you think, Lin? That sort of behaviour is intolerable, running around the village, doing just as it pleases. The pig can't be trusted. It should be stopped.'

'It probably should,' Lin agreed, but her thoughts were not on Nadine, they were on the man she had loved for over fifty years. She rushed inside, so that her neighbours would not see her cry.

* * *

Josie stood on the Toomeys' red and white barge, a wide smile on her face; she'd just hidden the packages to be brought up later. She and Cecily had planned the baby shower, collecting many wonderful presents, clothes, a little hairbrush, nappies, a teddy bear, all wrapped in tissue. Florence would be delighted. Josie was looking forward to seeing her expression when she unwrapped the gifts. Right now, Florence was facing the other way, talking to Devlin Toomey, placing dishes on a small table helped by Adam and Malia. She moved slowly now, swaying as she turned.

Josie walked down to the riverbank, where Cecily was talking quietly with Jack Lovejoy, who carried a guitar case. She watched Jack and Finn Toomey setting up a cable and an amplifier. She'd heard the rumours that had been circulating; Jimmy Baker had told everyone in The Sun that the old lady was still full of beans and Jack was Jack the lad, all right. Most people had told him to shut up, especially Dickie Junior, but Dickie Senior had found it funny and Kenny Hooper had been visibly upset by it, repeating that if anyone hurt Miss Hamilton's feelings, he would give them a good hiding. Josie watched as Cecily laid a hand on Jack's arm and Jack grinned, his face warm with affection. The rumour was ridiculous; she watched Cecily and Jack begin to tune up, their heads close. Josie was looking forward to the music; it was going to be a lovely afternoon all round.

Fergal was boiling beans and sausages on the stove, and the trestle table on the riverbank was filled with food and drink. Josie gazed towards the village green. It was an idyllic setting, trees dipping their leaves in the water like lazy fingers, the river calm except for tiny ripples made by wriggling minnows. People had started to arrive in clusters; Jimmy Baker and Dickie Junior had brought fruit punch. They were talking to Brandon Dyer, his hands in his pockets, while Natalie chatted happily to Malia and Florence. Dangerous Dave was laughing with Jimmy Baker, eyeing Cecily and Jack. The Featherstones were there in pristine shorts and blazers;

Darryl Featherstone smiled and waved to Josie. She'd have found him attractive when she'd been young; he was good-looking and there was something about the intensity of his eyes that reminded her of Harry.

Josie wondered if Gerald Harris would arrive. He'd been invited, but he'd been a bit distant the last few times she'd passed Chandos. Josie knew why, of course; she'd refused him when he'd asked for a date. Some people found it hard to accept rejections, even polite ones.

Besides, she'd had a drink with Fergal a couple of times, and Gerald disapproved of Fergal. Josie watched him leaning over the stove, pushing sausages around with a fork. She liked him. The truth was, she understood his loneliness. They both understood how the other felt.

In the distance, Minnie and Lin were approaching across the village green. Josie waved a vigorous hand. She'd known them both for so long; they shared a special bond. Josie could tell that Minnie had some news she was eager to share by the energetic lope of her walk and the enthusiasm of her expression. Lin was taking smaller steps; her shoulders were hunched and she was smiling, trying to appear normal.

Josie knew by the exaggerated happiness of her grin that Lin was hiding a problem. She waved to Josie and called a chirpy 'Yoo-hoo!' in a tremulous, high voice. But her expression held a sadness. Something was very badly wrong.

28

'Hi, Lin, Minnie.' Josie hugged her friends. 'Florence's presents are hidden on the barge – Fergal showed me where to put them. We'll bring them out when the food's finished.'

'I'm starving.' Minnie grinned. 'Can we start on the picnic soon? I've brought a quiche – it's not home-made, I'm afraid, I haven't had time.'

Lin gave a heavy sigh. 'I brought a potato salad. Neil made it last night.'

'Where is Neil?' Josie asked, and wished she hadn't as soon as she saw Lin's eyes fill with tears. She added, 'Is he coming along later?'

Lin nodded. Minnie noticed her friend's crestfallen expression and took over. 'Tina's not coming. I called in to see her on the way here. I asked her to join us, but she said she'd rather spend the day on the allotment. She's becoming more and more antisocial.'

'I expect she feels a bit low on confidence in company...' Lin frowned. 'Didn't her husband cheat on her before he walked out?'

Minnie glanced towards Josie. 'I think so, yes. Patrick had another woman for a year or two. Tina came home early and found them together on the couch...'

'Oh...' Lin said. She wondered if she should make an excuse and go home. Perhaps Neil was there on the sofa, revving up with Carole Frost. She imagined the scene and was determined not to cry again.

Minnie wrapped an arm around her shoulder. 'Tina and Patrick had lived separate lives for years. She worked all hours; he did his own thing – they didn't see much of each other.' She hugged her friend. 'They didn't have a good marriage.'

Lin bit her lip. She'd hardly seen Neil these last few weeks: perhaps the truth was that she didn't have a good marriage either.

Josie took up position on Lin's other side. 'Come on, let's get some Pimm's and something to eat.' She guided Lin towards the table where the food was laid out and where Fergal was cooking sausages.

'I'll have some Pimm's,' Lin said boldly. 'It might cheer me up.'

Jack and Cecily struck up a few chords from their small stage and played their first song together. It was 'Que Sera, Sera', Cecily's voice plaintive and husky, Jack's stronger. Everyone turned from the picnic table, drinks in hand, and applauded at the end. Then Cecily muttered, 'I'd like to perform a song that was special to me many years ago...' She paused and her face took on a faraway expression. 'It was something I used to sing to someone who meant a lot to me...'

Cecily strummed a few notes, Jack accompanying her, then she began to sing 'Love Me Tender', her voice breathy. Lin listened, watching Cecily as she closed her eyes and sang every word as if it would break her heart. Lin knew at once; she'd loved someone too, and it had ended badly. She refilled her glass from the jug of Pimm's and drank the contents in two gulps.

Josie's eyes were on Lin, noticing how her hand trembled, then her attention moved to Cecily. When she and Lin had first been invited to the bungalow, she'd asked Cecily if she'd ever thought of getting married. 'Once,' Cecily had replied. Josie was sure from the sadness in her voice that Cecily's experience of love had changed the direction of her life.

It was Jack's turn to sing. 'Cecily and I have been practising hard so that we can bring you all the hot hits from the 1950s. And here we go with – "All Shook Up".' He gave his best impression of Elvis Presley, leaping up from the chair and twisting his hips while Cecily played enthusiastically. Jimmy and Dangerous Dave glanced at each other and stifled laughter; they'd realised at that moment that their gossip about Cecily and Jack had been completely foolish – they'd been simply talking about rehearsing together.

'All Shook Up' became 'Blue Suede Shoes' and 'Jailhouse Rock'. Josie dragged Lin and Minnie to their feet: these were the songs that Miss Hamilton sang with them at school and they owed it to her to dance to them with all the energy of their youth. Other people jumped up too. Dave was showing off his best moves, arms flying in all directions; the Featherstones were jiving together and Malia and Natalie were dancing too.

Florence put a hand on Adam's arm and they moved away to sit on the bank. She kicked off her shoes and dangled her feet in the river, enjoying the tingling cold sensation.

Adam sat close to her. 'It was a great idea to choose this setting for a picnic.'

'Devlin said it would be okay… we're using their generator for the music and Fergal wanted to make sausages and beans for everyone.' She glanced over her shoulder. 'Isn't it cool that everyone is dancing?'

'Do you want to dance?'

Florence wrinkled her nose. 'I'm a bit too big for that now.'

'You're looking good.'

'Blooming…' Florence said with a shrug. 'October's not far away.'

'Are you worried about it – the birth?' Adam asked.

'A bit, sometimes – I try not to think about it.' Florence rubbed the round bulge. 'The baby has to come out somehow.'

'I think you're amazing,' Adam muttered.

'I'm just me,' Florence grinned.

'As I said, amazing.' He took her hand. 'Would you like me to be there with you, when the baby comes?'

Florence closed her eyes. 'Dad has offered. I haven't made my mind up. My mother doesn't even know I'm pregnant, Dad said he'd talk to her, but he rang her number and it didn't work any more…'

'How does that make you feel?'

'I just don't think about it, to be honest.' Florence lifted her feet and swished water, watching little droplets glint in the sunshine. 'I suppose I ought to be upset about it – girls need their mothers at a time like this, but there are so many people who are being so kind to me.' She turned to Adam. 'You've been wonderful.'

Adam hesitated. 'I'd like to do more.' He chewed his lip. 'Florence, I just wondered if...'

She knew straight away. 'No, Adam, the baby's father hasn't offered to help.'

'People in the village think it's Bobby Ledbury. Some people think it's me,' Adam said. 'No one knows, though...'

'I'll tell you when I'm ready – but I'll only tell you.'

'Thanks, Florence.' Adam chose his words carefully. 'Do you... love him, the baby's dad?'

'No.' Florence watched the water ripple as she moved her toes. 'It was a one-off, a mistake.' She said nothing for a while, then she added, 'I don't know why, but I thought he liked me... I thought I liked him. I was stupid.'

Adam brought her hand to his lips tenderly. 'You're just human.' He took a breath. 'When I first heard you were pregnant, I was so angry at the idea that you could be with someone else. That was selfish of me.'

Florence met his eyes. 'I suppose that was human too. You and I were so special.'

'We still are...' Adam's voice trailed off. He leaned towards her, his eyes closing, about to kiss her. Florence moved back, but her face shone with affection.

'I'm not ready yet, Adam... maybe soon, but right now I'm not sure...'

'I'll wait,' Adam said. 'You know I love you.'

Florence glanced towards the barge, at the bank of grass where people were dancing. Jack and Cecily were singing 'Rock Around the Clock'. The Toomey boys were jiving furiously, kicking their legs out.

She smiled. 'Thanks, Adam...' Adam's arm was around her and she leaned her head against his shoulder. Everything would be all right.

* * *

Jack finished the song with a flourish and announced into the microphone that he and Cecily were going to play some modern rock songs they'd been practising. He launched into 'Seven Nation Army' on his electric guitar as Cecily accompanied him with a riff on her acoustic. Devlin, Finn, Natalie and Malia were swaying to the music, enjoying themselves. Lin dragged Josie and Minnie to the drinks table for a refill where Natalie's fiancé Brandon was engrossed in a conversation with Jimmy Baker, pints of beer clutched in their hands.

'I can't dance like I used to.' Josie waved a hand in front of her face to cool down.

'I can't do anything like I used to,' Lin added sadly, reaching for the Pimm's and overfilling her glass.

'Talking of which,' Minnie grinned. 'I have a lover.'

'A what?' Lin wasn't sure she'd heard properly over the music.

Minnie raised her voice. 'Jensen, from New York, the retired theatre director, over here as a consultant for the Playhouse. I mentioned him to you before. We're in love.'

Josie opened wide eyes. 'In love? That's not like you.'

'Well, it is now.' Minnie sipped her Pimm's.

Lin was puzzled. 'Does he live in Oxford?'

'Until October,' Minnie explained. 'Then he's back in New York.'

'Will you go there?' Josie asked.

'Oh, you can't leave us,' Lin exclaimed.

'Who knows?' Minnie's face was ambivalent. 'I'll deal with it when I have to.'

'Hello, ladies.' Dangerous Dave was next to them, helping himself to lemonade. 'I'm strictly off the sauce today.'

'I'm not.' Lin brought the glass to her lips.

'We have Florence's stuff for the baby shower on the barge,' Josie said. 'We ought to do the presentation soon.'

'I'm very grateful to you all.' Dangerous Dave's face creased with happiness. 'I just want the best for my princess.'

'We all do...' Lin agreed, raising her glass.

'Ah, Lin – where's Neil today?' Dave asked. 'I thought he was going to be here.'

'I expect he'll be along soon.' Lin tried to make her face cheerful. She swigged the drink desperately. 'He's helping a customer with a car... I can't remember where he's gone...'

'Oh, yes... I remember now.' Dangerous Dave's face lit up. 'He did tell me, a customer – in Charlbury, wasn't it?'

'Yes, no...' Lin felt blood rush to her face. 'I'm not sure.'

'Charlbury, definitely – he told me he was helping a young lad in Charlbury with his old banger – something about noisy tappets...'

'Yes, that was it,' Lin said miserably. Neil had told her he was going to Tadderly to help an older customer. Dave was blatantly covering for him. Lin swallowed more Pimm's, relishing the tang on her tongue and the blurring of her thoughts, thinking that her husband was a liar and a cheat who had got his friends to lie for him. She wondered who else knew about Carole Frost – Jimmy, probably, Dickie Senior, Dickie Junior. Everyone in The Sun. The whole of Middleton Ferris. They were probably all gossiping and laughing behind her back. Lin wondered if Josie and Minnie knew. She shook her head. The Pimm's was making her dizzy.

Jack and Cecily finished playing 'Monkey Wrench' as applause and cheers echoed from the crowd. Finn Toomey had his arms around Natalie and they were talking together while Darryl and Charlotte Featherstone were wrapped in a smooch.

'We should dance...' Lin lurched forward, wobbling on her feet. 'Jimmy Baker's here somewhere – he'll dance with me...' She giggled. 'He smells better than he did in primary school when no one would partner with him in country dancing... I'll dance with him...'

Josie looked at Lin, concerned: her friend was clearly tipsy. It might be an idea to take her home soon. She whispered to Minnie, 'Shall we get everyone together now and present Florence with her gifts?'

'We should,' Minnie said firmly with a glance at Lin.

Josie gave a sign to Jack and Cecily and Jack put his mouth close to the microphone. 'Right – we're going to make a special announcement. There's someone here today we want to make a fuss of, because we all care about her. And we have something special to say, some things we want to share...'

Cecily rose to her feet, smiling, watching as Josie scuttled onto the barge and disappeared below deck. 'Florence, you have a special place in our hearts. And we are all looking forward to the arrival of a new little one in October...'

'Hear, hear,' Dangerous Dave cheered. 'I'm going to be a grandad.'

'So, we have a few things we'd like to give you, with our warm wishes...' Cecily smiled as Adam led Florence to the front of the stage. 'I remember only too well when I was your age... no one gave baby showers...' Cecily took a deep breath, suddenly emotional. Josie was beside her, holding a cardboard box filled with the wrapped parcels. Minnie took up a position next to her, carrying another box.

'So, dear Florence...' Cecily began. 'Baby showers have become something of a tradition in this country. Of course, they never used to be in my day, but it's such a good idea, and we'd now like to present you with some goodies for you and the baby.'

'Thank you.' Florence reached out her arms for a hug as Josie passed her a present. With shaky fingers, she opened it and tugged out a cuddle pillow in the shape of a silver baby elephant. She handed it to Adam, excitedly unwrapping a bag of luxury baby toiletries.

'Thank you so much – oh, I didn't expect all this,' Florence gasped as Josie offered her the next package.

Lin turned and was surprised to see Neil standing next to her. He'd just arrived, offering an apologetic grin, placing his arm around her shoulders. He kissed her ear. 'I'm just in time. How are you, Lindy love?'

'I'm fine.' Lin turned away abruptly, just as Florence unwrapped the tiniest pair of baby socks embroidered with rabbits and held them up for the cheering crowd.

Brandon moved from the beer table to stand next to Natalie, a frown on his face and a beer glass in his hand. He stretched out to touch her as she edged closer to Finn Toomey. Natalie launched herself at Finn, kissing him as hard as she could. Then she turned to Brandon, her face furious. 'Just go away, Brandon.'

Brandon tried again. 'Natalie?'

'I told you. We're done.' She pulled the ring from her finger and pushed it into his hand. 'There. Now go away.'

'Wait...'

She ignored him, stood on tiptoes and snogged Finn once more.

Brandon glanced around to see who was looking. Those who had noticed shifted away and went back to their business. Brandon slunk off through the crowd. Finn extracted himself from the kiss, confused. All attention was on Josie now: she held out another present and the applause rang out as Florence unwrapped a musical mobile in a rainbow design.

Neil whispered into Lin's ear. 'I thought George's granddaughter was going to marry that bloke. Did they just split up?'

'I'm sure he deserved what he got.' Lin wrinkled her nose. She inhaled aftershave, not his usual brand, a new one. Neil smelled of something delicious that a man would wear when he wanted to impress a woman, a warm spicy scent that made Lin want to kiss him. She met his eyes and her own were small with contempt.

'I expect Brandon's been cheating,' she said simply. 'All men who cheat are pigs.' Then she turned on her heel and, without another word, she tottered away, heading towards the village green, hurrying home as fast as her wobbly legs would carry her.

She didn't want to talk to Neil now. She wasn't sure what to say. She had no idea how she'd ever be able to talk to him about the affair with Carole Frost.

Perhaps it was better just to say nothing at all right now. She'd go home, lie down, sober up and her head would clear. Then she'd know what to do. Lin was determined to find out the facts. She needed to be calm, lucid and assertive, to be sure about what was going on.

She'd ask straight questions, demand honest answers. And once she knew the truth, she'd tell her cheating husband of fifty years exactly what she thought of him.

29

September was the warmest month of the year, the sun beating down so hard in Middleton Ferris that only Tina Gilchrist stayed outside during the fierce noonday heat. She was working in her allotment, watering vegetables in the sweltering sunlight with a hose pipe while everyone else did their best to stay cool. The Toomeys lazed on their barge, Devlin and Finn swimming in the river, Fergal cooking Joe Grey on the stove or dozing below deck. Gerald Harris abandoned the weeds in his garden to watch cricket on TV. Dangerous Dave retreated to the cool interior of his garage; he was busier than ever, and the money would be useful for Florence and the soon-to-arrive baby.

It was as if Middleton Ferris was a melting oil painting in the sticky heat. Cecily sat in the garden drinking lemonade and playing guitar. She had developed an interest in the muddy guitar sound of Samantha Fish and coaxed Jack to help her find a cigar box guitar so that she could practise playing blues music. She was rehearsing daily, sitting by the open door, singing 'Bulletproof' until she got it perfect.

Bobby Ledbury worked long hours in the fields on the tractors and harvesters with his grandfather George, although George's pig Nadine would often be asleep in Lin's garden, rolling in the soil to keep cool. Lin didn't mind. She enjoyed the company. Neil was out every other day and

Lin was quietly angry. She was rehearsing what to say, waiting for the right moment to speak her mind. Neil looked sad, going about his business without a word, wondering why his wife was so distant and preoccupied.

Florence found she often needed to rest now. She did the occasional shift at Odile's café, although Malia cheerily took on most of the work while Florence relaxed on the sofa, dozing or listening to Natalie repeat that she was better off without a fiancé. Apparently, Brandon had called round again to beg her to accept his pathetic apologies, but she would never have him back as long as she lived. She had other fish to fry.

Josie spent a lot of time in the cemetery talking to Harry; it was cool there and afterwards she'd sit under the willow tree, thinking of the good times. Occasionally she'd meet Fergal and he'd persuade her to have a drink in the beer garden of The Sun.

Minnie was enjoying life despite the heatwave. She loved every moment from the second she woke in the morning, Jensen's arm across her body as he slumbered, and she sidled out of bed to take a cup of tea in the garden alone, to their evening together after he came back from the Playhouse. They'd drink beer and sit outside, breathing in night-scented stock and talking about the classics until the stars were high diamonds in the midnight sky.

Now they were sitting in the deer park in Magdalen College, surrounded by gold and russet trees. They had wandered through old cloisters, past the quadrangle bursting with the rising voices of new students, and he was excitedly pointing at the roe deer. Minnie smiled indulgently; she had seen it all before, although to her it was much more than a tourist attraction. Oxford was lodged deep in her heart; it had changed her life and she felt bound to it.

Jensen took her hand in his, almost speaking her thoughts aloud. 'The tranquillity, the beauty, Minnie – it's just breathtaking, the way this place exudes culture and tradition. It's almost impossible to think that it's normal for you to live in such an incredible place, and this is your home.'

'It is,' Minnie said. 'I love it.'

'You came to Magdalen as a student?' Minnie was impressed that he'd pronounced it correctly, *Mawdlin*.

'Oh, no – women weren't allowed here in those days. I was at St Hilda's.

I had a couple of boyfriends who were students here. I won't tell you their names. One's quite infamous, in the House of Lords now, I believe.'

Jensen smiled. 'You've lived an incredible life, Minnie.'

'I'm still living it...' Minnie gazed at a deer that had wandered from the group, moving towards them. 'There's so much more I want to do...'

'There is.' Jensen's eyes glowed behind the gold-rimmed glasses. 'You know, Minnie, I never thought I'd meet anyone I felt this way about.'

'After your wife?'

Jensen shook his head. 'Pamela and I were close, we had the kids, and now she's gone, I miss her. But you and I are different.'

'How different?'

'We connect completely.' Jensen ruffled his white hair. 'Mind, body and spirit – I mean, look at you. There's no one like you.'

Minnie gazed down at herself in the floral dress and green Doc Martens. It all seemed quite ordinary. She smiled. 'So, the day is entirely ours. What do you want to do?'

Jensen leaned forward eagerly. 'When can I meet your friends in the village – Josie and Lin and your sister Tina?'

'Why would you want to meet them?' Minnie was puzzled. 'Middleton Ferris is nothing like Oxford.'

Jensen laughed. 'These people are part of your life – I want to know all there is to know about you.'

'You're interested in my murky backstory in a small Oxfordshire village?' Minnie was amused. 'I can't imagine that you'd enjoy going there.'

'But you go there – you care about these people.'

'I do,' Minnie agreed. 'It's my past. But you're my present.'

'And future, I hope?' Jensen said hopefully.

'We should go...' Minnie stood up and brushed grass from her dress. 'Let's walk down to The Bookies – they do a good line in fish.'

Jensen stood up and took Minnie's hand. 'We should. We can discuss Plautus's plays.' He kissed her cheek. 'Then maybe we can get an early night and we can talk about us, and our great plans for the future...'

* * *

Lin wasn't sure about the future. Neil was trying his hardest, but whatever they did together, she always came back to the piece of paper she still kept in her handbag with Carole Frost's mobile number on it, showing the time and place of their date. Neil insisted on taking her for lunch in The Sun, but she'd been uncomfortable the whole time. She felt others' eyes on her: she was sure Jimmy knew; Dickie Junior knew. He insisted on taking her for trips out in the Sharan for picnics, shopping, drives in the countryside. He held her hand, asked her what was bothering her, but she offered the same blank expression and said that she was fine. A voice inside her head told her she should talk to her husband; perhaps he'd put her mind at rest. But a second voice asked: why give him the opportunity to lie again? No, she knew he'd slip up soon, she'd catch him red-handed, and then he wouldn't be able to weasel his way out of it. The truth would be out.

Then, one morning after breakfast, Neil kissed her cheek and pulled on his best jacket, asking her if she'd mind if he took a walk through the woods and called into The Sun afterwards to see Jimmy and Kenny for a pint. Lin watched him go, clenching her fists in frustration. Familiar tears filled her eyes and she wondered momentarily if she was depressed.

She rushed to her handbag and pulled out the piece of paper, staring at the number. Perhaps Carole Frost wasn't a person – perhaps it was the name of a shop or a café. Lin knew she was clutching at straws, but she was suddenly filled with determination: she would ring the phone number and find out once and for all. Her hand shook as she picked up her mobile, pressed the buttons and listened to the ringing in her ear. Then a woman answered. 'Hello, this is Carole.'

Lin froze. She had no idea what to say.

'Hello?' The voice became louder. 'Hello...?'

'Sorry – wrong number,' Lin garbled and ended the call. She was immediately relieved that she hadn't just cut herself off – Carole Frost might have phoned her back. At least she'd said 'wrong number' – Carole wouldn't think of her again.

Lin's heart was thumping; she was shaking with fear and her mind raced. She had been brave, she'd phoned. Now she knew that Carole was real, she had spoken to Neil's mistress and she was so close to accusing him face to face.

Lin reached for her bag and door keys. She'd go and see Josie. She needed her friend's advice and she'd held back too long, not wanting to upset anyone. By saying nothing, Lin had hoped it might not be real, but Carole Frost was a real person on the phone, she had a strong, confident voice. Lin wanted to tell Josie straight away, she'd know what to do.

It was almost eleven o'clock and the air was sticky as Lin rushed past the allotments. Tina was too busy to notice her wave. There was a woman walking a dog on the rec, another with a child on the swings, but no one saw her pass by. Gerald wasn't in his garden, which Lin thought was unusual. She rushed past Chandos, rounded the corner to Charlbury Street and on to The Willows. Her heart was bumping as she knocked on Josie's door, already formulating what she'd say – 'Josie, I need your help. Neil is having an affair... I just spoke to her... she's as real as you and me...'

Lin knocked again, but there was no reply. Josie was out. Lin wondered where she could be: she might have gone to Odile's, or she might be in the Co-op. Lin stood on the doorstep, flustered. Then it came to her. She'd go to Cecily's. She had so much wisdom, so much experience. She'd know what to do.

Lin was very warm as she rushed along the road in the beating sun. As she passed the village green, she was perspiring. She saw herself as others might see her, a woman in her seventies, past her prime. She felt no longer elegant or attractive or interesting: Lin wondered what she was achieving in her life. She couldn't think of a good reason to keep going, she felt unwanted. Even Debbie rarely had time for her – they'd spoken a fortnight ago on the phone, and Lin had asked how the grandchildren were, but Debbie explained that they were always so busy. She thought about her friends: Josie, widowed and alone, Minnie, single and always active, and it was easy to compare herself with them unfavourably. They were strong, independent, fun. Lin felt shabby and boring.

She stepped off the kerb, intending to cross the road to Cecily's bungalow, tears blinding her vision, and almost walked into a silver car as it sped by. It was a Porsche Boxster, Darryl Featherstone at the wheel. She recognised him but not the passenger with him. Lin caught her breath; she could have been knocked down, killed. That would have ended it all. She shuddered with the horror of the thought.

Then common sense came flooding back and she pulled herself together. Life was precious. She was precious. Lin looked both ways and crossed the road, walking briskly to Cecily's door, knocking twice. She listened, wondering if Cecily was inside, playing the guitar, but there was no sound so she knocked again and waited.

A moment later, the door opened and Cecily stood facing her, wearing red lipstick and light loose clothes, waving a hand in front of her face to cool herself down. She took in Lin's flushed face and smiled.

'It's good to see you, Lin. I've been in the garden, watering my tomatoes. It's so hot. Come in – let's have a glass of cool lemonade and sit outside under a shady tree.'

30

Lin and Cecily sat in the garden drinking pink lemonade, gazing at the flowers. Lin wasn't ready to say what was on her mind, so she said, 'The clematis looks lovely.'

'It does, doesn't it?' Cecily turned to her with keen eyes: her instincts were sharp as ever. 'I've been wanting to talk to you, Lin. Since the picnic.'

'Oh...' Lin examined her fingers and brightened deliberately. 'Florence loved the baby shower. And your singing with Jack was so much fun.'

'It was a wonderful day.' Cecily smiled. 'But you appeared to be having too much fun, or perhaps not enough...' She leaned forward and pressed Lin's hand. 'Tell me, is everything all right?'

'Oh, it's all fine,' Lin said. Cecily looked at her levelly, then Lin's face fell. 'No, it's not. I think Neil's having an affair.'

Cecily raised her eyebrows. 'Really? You've been married for fifty years.'

'Almost.' The words fell from Lin's lips. 'I found a piece of paper in his pocket. It was a woman's name, Carole, and her phone number.'

'There may be a completely innocent explanation.'

'But he's always going out, Cecily. He wears his best jacket. He's bought new aftershave.'

Cecily shook her head. 'I bought myself perfume last week but I'm not seeing a new beau...'

Lin sighed, a shudder that went through her whole body. 'I don't know what to do.'

'Yes, you do,' Cecily said firmly.

'You're right,' Lin agreed. 'I need to talk to him.'

'Exactly.'

'But I'm afraid what I'll find out.'

Cecily made a muffled sound. 'Sometimes the truth hurts. But it's best that you know it and then you can deal with it.'

'Yes.' Lin raised her chin. 'And I will.'

'Believe me. I'm sure everything will be fine. But in the unlikely event that it isn't, I promise you, it may hurt at first, but you'll grow stronger.'

'You sound like you've been in that place yourself.'

'I have.'

Lin waited and Cecily said nothing, so she added, 'Is that why you never married?'

'I know how it feels to be second best – oh, I know it well. I lived in Sussex when I was younger. My mother abandoned me when I was a child.'

'Why?'

'She didn't marry my father and I have no idea who he was. She never spoke about him and I always felt unwanted.'

Lin frowned. 'Surely she loved you more than anything in the world... just like I love Debbie, like Florence will love her baby.'

'She resented me – then she left me when she found a new man. I was three years old. I hardly remember her, but I remember how her rejection felt.' Cecily's voice was a whisper.

'What happened to you then?' Lin asked.

'My grandmother brought me up and she was my role model: strong, intelligent, independent. She gave me feelings of self-worth and I realised just how important it is to believe in yourself. I determined that no one would ever take that away from me.'

'You're so strong.' Lin's eyes shone with admiration.

'Sometimes being strong means going through heartbreak first...'

Cecily took a breath. 'When I was twenty-two, I met a wonderful man, Eddie Blake. He was my whole world – we loved each other with a passion.' Cecily paused, remembering. 'In many ways, he was like your Neil. I could depend on him completely. I thought I could...'

'Did he let you down?'

'He let himself down, just once,' Cecily muttered. 'Once was enough to change our lives forever.'

'What did he do?'

Cecily shrugged. It was a long time ago, but it felt recent. The emotions were still raw. 'We were engaged to be married. In those days – it was the 1950s – I wanted to wait until my wedding night before we...'

'Slept together?' Lin finished her sentence.

'Don't get me wrong, I loved him and it was hard to say no – he was so passionate and we adored each other – but Eddie respected that. I know it's not that way now, times have changed, but for me then, it was important to do things properly.'

'I see.'

'We were due to be married in July. It was February,' Cecily said, her voice a whisper. 'And Eddie made a mistake I couldn't forgive.'

'What did he do?'

'I had a friend, Joyce, she was my closest friend, like you are with Josie. We went everywhere together. She was very glamorous. When I first met Eddie, she was dating his brother, Albert. Eddie always said both he and Albert fought over me first. Albert and Joyce didn't last long, but Eddie and I were made for each other. Keepers, that's the word they use nowadays.'

'So what happened?'

'Joyce happened. She drank too much one evening when Eddie and I and she were out together. He took me home first – he had a car – then he arranged to see her safely home, to make sure she was all right.'

'And?'

Cecily's face was etched with sadness. 'Eddie told me Joyce seduced him – she took off her clothes and he couldn't help himself. Of course, that's complete nonsense. If he'd loved me, he'd have kept his hands off her.'

'How did you find out?'

Cecily's voice was quivering. 'Joyce was pregnant and she told everyone that the baby was Eddie's. Eddie had been a fool, but he was honest. He admitted it – they had slept together once, and that was it.'

'So, what did you do?'

'In those days, there was only one thing a man could do when he got a woman in the family way,' Cecily said. 'He did the decent thing and married her.'

'Oh, Cecily.'

'I told him to – I insisted on it.' Cecily spoke firmly. 'It was his duty. I gave Eddie his ring back and he and Joyce married in May.'

'That must have been hard for you.'

'I went to the church service.' Cecily's eyes glistened. 'It broke my heart. But he was the baby's father.'

Lin nodded slowly. 'Then what happened?'

'Joyce had a baby girl. She called her Elizabeth Cecily and asked me to be the godmother. Of course, I refused. It wouldn't have been appropriate.'

'So, what did you do?'

'Lin, I saw them together all the time and I couldn't bear the way he still looked at me. I knew he still had strong feelings – I did too. He was a good man, despite everything. Eddie and I had always talked of having a child – it was heart-breaking to see the three of them, the little girl in his arms, the way Joyce looked at him as if he was her world.'

'And you still loved him?'

'Absolutely. I wanted to take him back in an instant. But I had to be strong.' Cecily put a shaky finger to the corner of her eye. 'So I made a decision and left. I couldn't stay – Joyce was a happy mum, oblivious, and Eddie's eyes were full of sadness every time he saw me. I wanted nothing more than to break all the rules and throw myself into his arms. I knew he wanted the same thing. I had to go.'

'And you became a teacher?'

'I couldn't settle for anyone else, not after Eddie. He was my one true love. But...' Cecily gazed into her empty glass. 'I loved teaching; I loved my pupils and I dedicated my life to them. I'm not sorry I made that choice.'

'It seems such a shame.'

'It was,' Cecily agreed. 'Eddie didn't love Joyce. He'd have been a good father to Elizabeth. But we'd have been good parents together.' She sighed again. 'It was a pity, but there you are.'

Lin stared at her hands again; the fingers tingled. Cecily patted her shoulder. 'Go home, Lin. Talk to that wonderful husband of yours. Hopefully, it's easily explained. You love each other – this is just a difficult patch. Sort it all out, laugh about it – you have a good marriage to save.'

'I hope you're right.' Lin stood up slowly. 'Whatever happens, I'm ready now. Thanks, Cecily – you've made me feel stronger. I'm really glad I came.'

'I'm glad too.' Cecily hugged her. 'We'll catch up at Odile's soon. Text me. I'll drive up on the mobility scooter and we'll have a cup of tea. Bring Josie.'

'Definitely. The Silver Ladies, supporting each other...' Lin's face shone with gratitude. 'Thanks so much.'

Lin strode towards the village green, her heart and her step lighter. Things weren't so bad; Cecily was right. She'd go home via Odile's and buy two cream cakes. When Neil came back, they'd take them into the garden with a cup of tea in the sunshine. Then she'd explain what she'd found, the name on the scrap of paper, they'd talk it all through and everything would be fine. And, if Neil admitted the truth, if he and Carole were an item, she'd deal with it firmly, as Cecily did with Eddie. She was strong too. The truth was awful but it was better than constant worry.

As she approached The Sun Inn, she saw a familiar figure leaving, shambling out in his old jacket. It was Kenny Hooper. Lin waved a hand. 'Hello, Kenny.'

He saw her and she noticed his face change; he'd recognised her and then he turned to lope away. She called after him. 'Kenny, wait.' He hesitated and she walked briskly over to him. He'd been the same at primary school, a little unpredictable. She put a hand on his shoulder. 'Are you all right, Kenny?'

'I ent telling you nothing,' he replied and Lin frowned. She had no idea what he meant.

She offered him a kind smile. 'Have you been in the pub for a pint?' She remembered Neil had intended to call in for a half. 'Is Neil there?'

'I ent telling you.' Kenny's face clouded. 'It ent right.'

'What isn't right?' Lin was puzzled. 'Are you okay, Kenny?'

'It ent right, Neil and that blonde woman in the car park, and him giving her lots of money. But I ent telling you about it,' Kenny added, then he chewed his fingers. 'It ent my business and I don't want to say nothing, do I?'

Lin took a step back and suddenly she felt dizzy. 'Blonde woman?'

'I ent told you nothing.' Kenny began to walk away, shaking his head.

'Kenny?' Lin called.

'I ent saying nothing to nobody,' Kenny repeated, breaking into a run.

Then Lin heard the sound of the intermittent wail of a siren in the distance. She stood frozen as an ambulance sped past her along Tadderly Road, screeching around the corner to Orchard Way. Kenny was watching and pointing, shouting, 'It's an ambulance. Somebody has got killed.'

People appeared from nowhere; Dickie Junior hurried from the pub and stood watching, hands in his pockets. Three Toomeys emerged from the barge and walked across the village green. Josie appeared from the church yard, calling to Lin who was next to Kenny, her hand on his arm to calm him.

Then Josie was by her side. 'That was an ambulance I heard, wasn't it? Where did it go?'

'I saw it...' Kenny flapped his elbows nervously. 'It went past the rec.'

Lin's mind flashed to people she was concerned about: Gerald Harris, Tina Gilchrist, George Ledbury on the farm, or Penny. She hoped they were all right. She turned to Josie. 'Should we go and find out what's happened?'

'We might be able to help,' Josie agreed.

They hurried forwards, past Chandos and the allotments. Then they saw the ambulance with its doors open not far from Odile's café. Lin panted. 'It wouldn't be Odile? She's as fit as a fiddle – oh, I hope she hasn't hurt herself...'

'No, they are parked on the other side, next to the garage...' Josie gasped.

'Look, there's Neil outside, standing by the ambulance.' Lin pointed, her face anxious. 'I thought he was in The Sun.'

Lin and Josie reached the garage where Neil loitered nervously in dirty overalls, his hands covered in oil. He turned to Lin. 'There's been an accident…' His eyes were wide and his breathing was shallow. 'I saw it happen but I couldn't do much to help.'

Two paramedics emerged wheeling a trolley. Dangerous Dave was lying on it, his face contorted in agony. He was wearing an oxygen mask, groaning loudly, and one of his legs was covered in blood, the knee of his overalls torn and the blue material blotchy and dark as if it was soaked in beetroot juice. Lin grasped Neil's arm. 'What happened?'

'I popped in to see Dangerous… he needed a helping hand.' Neil gestured towards his overalls. 'He was moving a heavy gearbox from a Peugeot. He put it on a stand, but he hadn't got hold of it properly. He was chatting to me, talking about Florence and the baby, what names she might choose, and he slipped on some oil and the gearbox fell and crushed his knee.' He took Lin's hand. 'He was in agony, blood everywhere – a hell of a mess, so I called the ambulance as quickly as I could.'

A paramedic had appeared, an efficient woman with a ponytail. She spoke to Neil. 'We're taking him to the General in Tadderly.'

'He has a daughter,' Josie said quickly. 'Shall we arrange for her to come in to be with him?'

'Of course.' The paramedic was calm, as if it was just routine. 'Best to ring the hospital ahead to find out where he is.'

'Will he be all right?' Neil asked.

The paramedic gave a half smile. 'He'll be seen quickly once he arrives.' She turned to go. 'You should get yourself a cup of sweet tea,' she suggested. 'You had quite a shock.'

'It was horrible…' Neil shuddered. He forced himself to think straight. 'I'll make sure the garage is locked up – Dave's keys are inside, and his wallet, and I'll take them all down to Florence.'

'You get off home,' Josie offered. 'Lin will make you a cuppa. I'll go and see Florence.'

'Right. Wait there.' Neil disappeared inside the garage and rushed out with a set of keys and Dangerous Dave's jacket. Josie and Lin watched as he locked the doors and handed the keys and Dave's belongings to Josie. 'Thanks. Poor Florence.' He was concerned. 'It'll worry her…'

'Leave it with me, Neil,' Josie said soothingly. 'You need to go home and sit down.' She turned to Lin, still clutching Dangerous Dave's jacket. 'Text me later – we'll work out the best way to support Florence. Maybe Adam can give her a lift into Tadderly – I'll call in on Linval and Rita.'

'Right.' Lin watched as Josie made her way towards Newlands, the housing estate where Florence lived. She shook her head. 'It's a good job you were there.'

'It is.' Neil was still breathing heavily; he was clearly shaken. 'I popped in to see how he was and he was struggling with the gearbox.' He indicated the oil on his hands. 'It weighed a ton.'

Lin stared at him. He had oil on his face. He was trembling. She spoke gently. 'Come on. Let's get you into a hot bath and make a nice cup of sweet tea, just like the paramedic said.'

'Thanks, Lindy.' Neil allowed her to take his arm, to shepherd him home towards Barn Park. He muttered, 'I can't bear to think what might have happened if Dangerous had been on his own. He couldn't move – and he was in agony all the time.'

'Let's go home.' Lin was mystified as to why Neil had been in the garage helping Dangerous Dave when he'd said he would take a walk before going to The Sun. She wondered where Carole Frost fitted in. Lin assumed she was the blonde woman that Kenny had referred to. She glanced at Neil, feeling his weight as he leaned against her. She'd get him home, make him tea, look after him. That came first.

Later, when he was calm, she'd ask him all the questions that were bubbling inside her head. There had to be a simple answer, one she hadn't thought of yet.

Or perhaps it was the one she feared most: he was in love with someone else. And if that was the case, Lin was ready.

31

Three days later, in the early evening, Florence and Adam helped Dangerous Dave, who was on crutches, into the hospital lift at Tadderly General. No bones were broken and the wound was healing; he was cracking jokes and in good spirits. He'd have to stay at home for a while, but he didn't mind – Florence was just a few weeks away from her due date, so they could keep each other company in front of the TV. He grinned happily as the automatic doors swung open and they walked towards the car park. A silver Porsche Boxster slowed down in front of them and a pretty nurse slid out, waving as the car sped away. Florence shepherded her father towards Adam's old banger. Dangerous Dave eased himself into the front seat and Adam helped Florence to wriggle into the back, adjusting her seat belt, making sure she could stretch her legs comfortably.

Once they were back home, Adam put the kettle on and rang the take-away to order a delivery, bringing in a tray of tea before settling down on the sofa next to Florence. Dave closed his eyes, relaxing in the armchair with his bandaged leg sticking out.

Adam rested an arm on the back of the sofa behind Florence. 'Are we all going to the Autumn Festival?'

'I'm not going to be much good at the bun throwing,' Dave said with a laugh and pointed towards Florence. 'Nor are you, princess.'

Adam glanced at Florence protectively. 'I thought we could wander down to the village green and enjoy the stalls.'

'When is it?' Florence asked. 'I'll go as long as I feel up to it.'

'Next Saturday, the 30th.' Adam passed Florence's tea to her, watching her cup her hands around the mug. 'We could all go.'

'I'd like that.' Florence nodded and her eyes travelled to the TV screen as Dave switched on the set. 'Last year there was a woman who did reflexology – I could do with someone massaging my feet.'

There was a sharp knock at the door and Adam stood up. 'That'll be the food.'

Dangerous Dave watched as he left the room, listening as he opened the front door and chatted to the delivery driver. Then he winked at Florence. 'He's a keeper, Adam.'

'I know, Dad.'

'There aren't many young men who'd take on a...'

'I know, Dad.'

'I'm just saying – you could do worse.'

'Dad...' Florence grinned as Adam came back in the room, carrying bags of Chinese food. Florence eased herself upright. 'I'm starving.'

Adam adjusted a cushion behind her back, dragging a stool towards the sofa so she could put up her feet. Florence gave him a look of pure affection as he sat down beside her.

'What about me?' Dave grumbled as he unwrapped his takeaway. 'Don't I get the special cushion treatment?'

'Only if you're pregnant, Dad,' Florence quipped and Dave patted his belly.

'Four months gone, I'd say,' he chuckled. Then he turned his attention to the TV.

Florence closed her eyes, rested her head on Adam's shoulder and felt the baby wriggle. An elbow stuck out and she rubbed it gently and smiled. Everything was falling into place.

* * *

Lin was eating macaroni cheese that Neil had made from scratch. She had opened a bottle of white wine and they sat across the table from each other, munching quietly. He met her eyes and smiled. 'How's the food?'

'It's good.'

'We can have some fresh fruit for pudding.' Neil topped up Lin's glass. 'I thought we could go to the Autumn Festival at the weekend. The weather forecast is looking promising.'

Lin lifted her fork. 'As long as you're not too busy.'

Neil looked piqued. 'No...'

Lin examined his tone for signs of guilt, the rising note at the end of the word – *nooooo*. It sounded like he was protesting too much. She wondered what to say, then she muttered, 'I just thought that – you've been so busy lately, walking and... things.'

He winked. 'Oh, I'll be done with all that soon.'

Lin wondered what he meant, what the wink signified. She forced herself to ask a question. 'Do you mean you'll be done with walking?'

'Well...' Neil waved his fork. 'It's autumn and the weather won't be so good – it'll be damp outside and cold.'

'Oh?'

'I like autumn and winter – we get to cosy up by the fire together.' He reached across the table and touched her fingers. 'I know I've been neglecting you a bit this summer. But I'll make it up to you.'

Lin stopped eating. 'Neglecting me?'

'I've been out a lot...'

'Ah... you have.' She frowned, her face cross. 'I had noticed...'

Neil met her eyes. 'What's worrying you, Lindy?'

She felt a burst of strength from somewhere – she didn't realise she had it in her, but it was out of her mouth before she could stop it. 'Are you seeing another woman?'

Neil was shocked but Lin couldn't tell if it was surprise or guilt. Then his face softened. 'There couldn't ever be anyone else for me. Only you.'

She forced herself to go on and was surprised that there were no tears. She heard the toughness in her voice. 'Only Kenny said he saw you with a blonde.'

'Not me,' Neil said with excessive certainty. 'You know what Kenny's like...'

'So...' Lin blurted it out. 'Who is Carole Frost?'

'I've no idea,' Neil said simply and Lin thought he looked like a rabbit in the headlights. 'I don't know a Carole Frost...'

'Only I found her phone number in your jacket pocket...'

'My pocket?' Neil was horrified.

'Yes, a piece of paper with her name on it and her number and it mentioned the car park of The Sun.'

'It must be some mix-up – I must have picked someone else's rubbish up and stuffed it in my pocket, you know, to throw away later...' Neil gazed down at his hands, then he looked up at Lin. 'I promise you, there's no other woman but you. You have to believe me, Lindy. I promise you, on my life.'

Lin was puzzled – someone else's rubbish? It was a strange excuse, and not very believable. 'You promise?'

'I love you – I always have.' Neil seemed troubled. 'I'd never do anything to hurt you, or our marriage. Please believe me.'

Lin wasn't sure what to say, so she murmured, 'All right.'

Neil's face flooded with relief. He indicated the plate. 'How's the macaroni cheese?'

'It's fine,' Lin said flatly as she forked another mouthful.

'That's good.' Neil resumed his meal as if their previous conversation had been normal. It was as if he wanted to forget what they had just spoken about, as if it didn't matter.

Lin watched him, her body tense and cold as ice. He'd lied to her again. She should have asked him straight out, but his ability to deceive had shocked her into silence.

The paper in her handbag with the name *Carole Frost* was no piece of litter. The man she loved and trusted was a liar, but he wasn't very good at it. She knew something was wrong. Lin narrowed her eyes; she'd await her chance. There would be more evidence – or she'd catch him in the act. She'd watch him like a hawk and he'd make a mistake. Then Neil would get his final comeuppance.

* * *

Josie read the email from *djellis* eagerly. David Ellis had finished his book about the detective in St Lucia and was pleased with it. He wasn't sure if anyone else would enjoy it, but it was a heartfelt tribute to Alan, the man he loved, and his central protagonist Alain di Angelo had solved the crime and fallen into the arms of the suave mysterious stranger, Dario Elijah, who turned out to work for the FBI. It would be a marriage made in heaven. Josie replied, encouraging David to contact a publisher, to believe in himself. She said she'd look forward to reading it on her Kindle.

Then Josie glanced at the clock; it was almost eight in the evening and she'd forgotten to eat. A message buzzed and she picked up her phone. There was a text from Minnie saying that she was coming to Middleton Ferris for the Autumn Festival at the weekend. Her new man, Jensen, wanted to come too but Minnie preferred to spend quality time with her friends. Besides, Tina was exhibiting lots of her organic vegetables in the fruit and vegetable competition, and Minnie intended to support her. It promised to be a great weekend and Josie replied quickly that she was looking forward to it too.

She wandered into the kitchen, looking for something to eat. It didn't seem worth cooking anything, not for one. She didn't fancy a sandwich. Nothing appealed, really – she had no appetite. She'd just have a cup of tea. If Harry had been alive, she'd have cooked something for them both. Harry liked salmon and new potatoes, or a nice pasta salad. He'd always eaten sensibly; he was fit, slim. It really wasn't fair.

There was a knock at the front door. Josie sighed: she wasn't in the mood to talk to anyone. She could see the tall shadow of someone behind the glass and hear a light whistling. The tune was one she recognised: it was '(Sittin' On) The Dock of the Bay'. She tugged the door open to see Fergal Toomey leaning against the door post, his face cheerful. Josie wasn't sure she wanted to be greeted by a chirpy person; she wasn't in the mood. She tried hard to sound positive. 'Fergal.'

He grinned. 'Can I come in?'

Josie thought about it. Once he was in, he'd want a cup of tea and a chat. She mightn't get rid of him for hours. She wasn't in the mood for it – she felt too low.

'I'm busy.'

'Oh, that's a shame.' Fergal's positivity wasn't affected by her glum face. 'I've come over because I need a bit of company. I thought maybe we could go out...'

Josie shook her head. 'I'm not in the mood for going out, Fergal.'

'So, what will you do with yourself instead on this fine night?'

'I'll go to bed.' Josie folded her arms.

Fergal offered a cheeky grin and winked mischievously. 'I'm fine with that – we can take it from there...'

'That's not funny...' Josie's frown deepened. 'I'm really not feeling sociable.'

'Harry, is it?' Fergal came straight out with it – he knew. 'I've been sitting in the barge, feeling sorry for myself as well.'

'I'm not feeling sorry for myself.'

'Ah, Josie...' Fergal sighed. 'The boys are out. They are both in Charlbury. Finn's with a new girl, Natalie Ledbury, the farmer's daughter. She's packed the fiancé in – apparently, he was too controlling.' He laughed once. 'She'll be all right with Finn; he's not controlling at all. Anything goes with that boy, Devlin too.'

Josie nodded, pressing her lips together. She wasn't going to let Fergal draw her into a conversation.

He wasn't deterred. 'So, I was sitting there alone, feeling sorry for myself, thinking what I'd be doing now if Ros was with me. She'd cook us some food and we'd take a walk by the riverbank under the starlight, hold hands and talk about what we'd do tomorrow.' He shrugged sadly. 'There's no tomorrow for me and Ros now. Only yesterday.'

'I know...' Josie nodded. 'I'm not really feeling like being in company.'

'Then I'm your man,' Fergal insisted. 'Let's go down to The Sun and sit at a nice table by the log fire. We can have a drink and buy fish and chips and share a pudding and feel sorry for ourselves together.' He watched for a reaction. 'It's better than sitting at home alone.'

Josie shook her head. 'I don't know.'

'I know, only too well.' Fergal wasn't going to give up. 'And perhaps we'll smile and chat. We might even have a nice time. You can tell me about Harry and I'll talk about Ros. Then we can have a walk down to the Cherwell together, sit on the barge and drink coffee and brandy, and we can talk about them some more.'

'I'm not so sure.'

'I'm positive about it,' Fergal persisted. 'I'm not being rude, but you have a face on you like a slapped bum.' He grinned. 'And you've such a pretty face.' Josie glared at him and he made a cheeky expression. 'Aw, come on, Josie – come out with me. We'll have a much better time down the pub with friends than sitting indoors all alone feeling the weight of the world on our shoulders.' He sensed her weakening. 'Am I not right?'

She met his eyes and there was the beginning of a smile on her face.

'Come out with me, if only to get me off your doorstep.' His eyes sparkled. 'People will start to talk if I keep standing here, and there's too much gossip in this village already.'

'All right...' Josie sighed deeply; he had won. Fergal had a point; the apathy would only disappear if she made an effort. She'd enjoy his company: he was a nice man, cheerful, positive. 'I'll get my jacket,' she said without much enthusiasm.

Fergal waited for her to come back, then they closed the door behind them and set off, listening to the sound of their feet crunching on the gravel. The sky was dark now, the last traces of orange splashed on the horizon. Josie rounded the corner, Fergal at her side, and she could see the glimmering lights of The Sun Inn in the distance. She could almost feel the warm glow of laughter and good company inside the pub. She was glad she'd agreed to go out. They'd have a pleasant evening together: she might even order the salmon and new potatoes, Harry's favourite, and drink a glass of wine and toast Harry, reminisce about the past.

But this was the present now, Josie thought, and she owed it to herself to make the best of it.

32

Minnie sat on the train, thinking. Jensen was back in Oxford, in her house, browsing through her books, relaxing in her garden while she took off to Middleton Ferris to the Autumn Festival to be with her friends. She hadn't wanted him to accompany her, and she was trying to puzzle out why she felt happier leaving him behind. He'd been disappointed not to come along, but Minnie was firm. She wanted to be with her friends and with Tina – she valued their private time. It was precious and she didn't want to spoil it by having to introduce Jensen and to have to work at incorporating him into her group. Being with her friends was special.

Besides, Minnie liked to compartmentalise her life. Work, home, love, study, Oxford friends, childhood friends, family. Jensen fitted into the *love* category. Minnie sighed; if she was being selfish, well, it was unavoidable but that was how she was. At her time of life, she wasn't about to adapt simply because she'd met the man of her dreams.

She left the train and the railway station behind her, walking up Nobb's End towards the village green where the festival was being held. The sky was cloudy, but the air was sweetly warm, and the aroma of barbecued food drifted from the distance. She could hear music buzzing in her ears already; a folk band was playing, a violin and accordion. Minnie paused as she glanced towards one of the big modern houses. A

Porsche Boxster whizzed from a gravel drive across her path with a loud crunching sound and a cloud of dust. A woman with a ponytail rushed out onto the pavement, shouting after the car as she stood gulping air and shaking. Minnie approached Charlotte Featherstone, her face filled with concern. 'Hello. It's Charlotte, isn't it?'

Charlotte wiped her cheeks with the edge of her sleeve. Her eyes were wild and her mouth opened but no words came out. Minnie tried again. 'Are you all right?'

'Yes – no… I don't know.' Charlotte was breathing heavily.

Minnie knew she'd been through some sort of trauma. 'Do you want to go inside? I can make you a cup of tea…'

'No.' Charlotte stared at her for a moment. 'I'm not sure I want to go in that house ever again.'

Minnie rested a gentle hand on her shoulder. 'Do you need to talk?'

'It's Darryl. We just had the most terrible row…'

'Was that him I saw speeding away?'

Charlotte nodded.

'Is it just a tiff? Maybe he'll be back soon and you can talk about it?'

'No.' Charlotte shook her head vigorously: she was too furious to speak. She brought her hands to cover her face and sniffed loudly.

'Can I help?' Minnie asked.

There was more vigorous shaking of her head and then Charlotte removed her hands. She was flushed, clearly angry. 'Why are we so stupid?'

'We?'

'Women, wives?'

'Ah…' Minnie said.

'Darryl's been sleeping with someone else.'

'I'm sorry to hear that,' Minnie replied.

'She stayed overnight in our bed…'

'Oh,' Minnie said quietly.

'I go to London from time to time, for work. I usually stay over with friends there. Darryl seems to have made the most of my absence.'

'Are you sure?' Minnie asked. 'There's no mistake?'

Charlotte shook her head. 'The first time he cheated on me was when we were engaged. He promised me faithfully that it was a one-off, he was drunk, he was sorry…'

'That old excuse…'

'But he brought this woman back while I was away. He didn't try to deny it. In fact, he was quite smug.'

'That's horrible,' Minnie agreed.

'He's very persuasive, very charming. He's like it with all women. She's probably not the first – I've had my suspicions for a while.'

'Why would he be so stupid?' Minnie asked simply.

'He's arrogant, narcissistic… I can give you a long list.'

'I see.' Minnie took a breath. 'Why did you marry him?'

'I love him. He promised to change for me. I believed he would.'

'Oh.' Minnie shrugged. 'He's clearly a rat. And you trusted him?'

'Not any more.' Charlotte took a shuddering breath. She waved towards the house. 'It was our home. We picked the furniture together; we planned a future. I don't want to go in there ever again. She's been there, the woman he's been with, sleeping in my bed – not just sleeping – I bet they were both laughing at me.'

Minnie wrapped an arm around Charlotte. 'He doesn't deserve you.'

'That's where he's gone now, to her, I'm sure of it. I'm finished with him.' Charlotte wiped her face again. 'He didn't even deny it. Do you know what he said to me?' She shook with anger. 'He said, "You're my wife, you're the one I'm with all the time. I don't love her. It's just a bit of fun." As if I should be grateful.'

'That's awful,' Minnie muttered.

'We've only been married for a year.' Charlotte shrugged. 'I've been a fool. He married me because I work hard, I'm professional. I suit his image. Meanwhile, he thinks he can behave how he likes.'

'What are you going to do now?' Minnie prompted.

Charlotte looked sad. 'I've no idea.'

Minnie took a breath. 'You need the company of women.'

'What do you mean?' Charlotte frowned.

'Go indoors, grab your handbag and come to the autumn festival with me. My friends are all there and we're going to enjoy our day. You don't want to be alone inside the house, thinking about Darryl. Forget him for a while. Give yourself some time.'

Charlotte seemed unsure.

'Come on.' Minnie took her arm. 'There will be lots going on at the festival – we'll take your mind off your ridiculous little husband and his ridiculous little womb weevil.'

Charlotte almost laughed. Then she nodded. 'Thank you. You're right. I do need company, strong women, people who will talk some sense...' She took a breath and glanced back at the house. 'I'll just get my bag...'

* * *

People swarmed across the village green between bright stalls and flapping bunting. Minnie recognised Jack Lovejoy with his guitar waiting next to the stage, where several musicians were already playing folksy tunes. Penny Ledbury was busy selling jam; Jimmy Baker and Kenny Hooper were chatting near the beer tent. Then Tina rushed over and grabbed her sister's arm, speaking in a breathless rush. 'They're doing the judging now... I have put some pumpkins in, some carrots and onions and peppers. And I've done a flower basket.' Tina's face was flushed with excitement and Minnie smiled to see her sister so thrilled.

'Tina, I'm sure you'll win them all.'

'Oh, I don't know. Penny's done a flower basket too and so has Bomber Harris. I think Josie's done one... Janice Lovejoy too, and she's entered her eggs.'

'Are there lots of competitions?' Charlotte made an effort to look interested, although her mind was elsewhere.

'Oh, yes.' Tina was animated. 'There's even a Best Pet Friend competition. George Ledbury has entered his pig – it's lined up next to all the dogs, cats, rabbits and gerbils.'

'Nadine?' Minnie laughed.

Tina's eyes were wide. 'Oh, George is fussing around her like a proud dad. He's even brushed her hair. I swear he's painted her toenails too.'

Charlotte almost laughed. Minnie turned to Tina. 'I hope you'll win...' Tina nodded nervously and Minnie crossed both sets of fingers and held her breath. The Toomey boys disappeared into the refreshment tent. Close by, Cecily was chatting to Josie, who was standing with Fergal, Lin and Neil. Lin waved.

Minnie waved back. 'Let me get us all a drink and something to eat.' She wrapped a protective arm around Charlotte and Tina. 'I think we need some sustenance. Then we'll check out how many competitions my brilliant sister has won.'

* * *

Florence was seated carefully on a blanket, rubbing the round of her belly. Her protruding navel was visible beneath her T-shirt and she smiled at the thought that the birth was only days away now. She felt ready: she was looking forward to meeting her baby. Her back ached constantly and she shifted position to become more comfortable. Nowadays, that was almost impossible.

Malia and Natalie sprawled next to her, looking at their phones. Then Malia said, 'My dad keeps asking me all sorts of questions about Devlin. He thinks I'm going out with him.'

Natalie laughed. 'My mum did the same about Finn and us all being out together, saying the Toomeys were a bad lot, then my grandad got cross and said that he'd been friends with Finn's dad since primary school and they were a great family.'

'And are you – going out with Devlin and Finn?' Florence asked, only half-interested. Her mind was elsewhere nowadays.

'We just hang out and have fun.' Malia shrugged. 'I'll be off to London after Christmas – I'm not in the market for a proper relationship.'

'Nor me, not after Brandon.' Natalie rolled her eyes. 'I'm so glad I saw the light.'

'You were so wrapped up in him,' Malia said gently.

Natalie agreed. 'I was – but I think I was more wrapped up in the idea of the beautiful dress and the big wedding. I'd have woken up the next day and wondered what I was going to do with the rest of my life.'

'What made you change your mind?' Malia asked.

'It was his attitude to you two that put the nail in the coffin,' Natalie scoffed. 'He didn't like it when I spent time with my friends. It was always like, "You're my girlfriend, you should be at my side." At first, I thought it was because he couldn't bear to be away from me – I thought it was cute. But no, he just wanted to control who I spoke to. When we were with his friends, they'd all laugh and joke and I'd just be sitting there like a spare part, but he hated it when I was with you two and not him.'

'You'll find someone who deserves you. You're worth so much more.' Florence massaged her belly where the baby had thrust out a foot. She smiled. 'It's not far off now.'

'Do you want us to be there with you?' Malia asked. 'Have you made your mind up about who you're going to have as your birth partner?'

'Adam keeps asking me that.' Florence gazed into the distance. 'Dad too. I said I'll know when the time comes.'

Natalie shook her head. 'Aren't you scared of the pain?'

'Not now.' Florence smiled. 'I've done everything right through the pregnancy and I'm ready to meet this little one. I even have a name...'

'I bet you won't tell us...' Malia pouted.

'You'll have to wait until the baby's born.' Florence smiled.

Malia and Natalie took her hands. 'We're there for you, Florence.'

Florence sighed. 'I know. You're just like sisters.' She picked a daisy from the nearby grass and held it to her nose 'You'll be Auntie Malia and Auntie Nat... It doesn't matter that my own mother has no idea she's about to be a grandma. I've got Dad and you two and Adam looking out for me. And Bobby keeps bringing gorgeous baby clothes from his girlfriend. I'm really looking forward to being a mum now. This baby will be so loved.'

* * *

'Your veggies are the best, Tina – you'll win everything,' Minnie promised. She was sitting around a table with the large group, eating cake and drinking tea. Fergal had disappeared to the bar, leaving Neil looking uncomfortable as the six women chatted amongst themselves.

Tina was biting her nails. 'I don't know what I want most... I really want to win the best vegetable prize and the best flower basket this year… but no one ever wins two things.' She met Minnie's gaze nervously. 'And if my pumpkins don't win – what has the whole year been about?'

Josie grinned. 'My basket is pretty average. I won't be any competition.'

Tina wasn't convinced. 'Penny has gorgeous fuchsias…'

Minnie winked in Charlotte's direction. 'Let's finish our coffee and cake and we'll go to the tent and see what you've won. The vicar's guest must have finished judging by now.'

'It's the judge who worries me,' Tina said anxiously. 'She's a local councillor, Margaret Fennimore, a member of the bridge club in Charlbury. Gerald Harris knows her – I've heard she's really sour and very hard to please.'

Neil gazed around, a little distracted, then he said, 'There's a display of classic cars on the rec. I might go and look at them. Then I'm going to call in on Dangerous – I think he's in the pub… his leg's still not right…' He pecked Lin's cheek. 'If you don't mind, Lindy.'

Lin reached for the slice of cake on her plate. 'Do what you want. I'll meet you at home for tea later.'

Neil stood up, looking grateful. He waved in Fergal's direction, then sauntered away.

Lin watched him go, then she smiled to cover her feelings. 'I don't think he was getting much from the festival.'

Cecily raised her eyebrows. 'So, you sorted out the problem over the woman you thought he was having an affair with?'

Minnie felt Charlotte stiffen next to her. Josie turned to Lin, her face astonished. 'Neil, having an affair? Never.'

Lin noticed all eyes on her. She was surprised that she didn't feel embarrassed; instead, she felt empowered. The secret was out and she'd make sure her friends knew everything. She could count on their support. 'I found a woman's name and phone number in his jacket pocket, a meeting place and time…'

'No!' Tina exclaimed. 'Neil?'

'What did you do?' Charlotte held her breath.

'I asked him straight out about her – eventually.' Lin shrugged.

'And what did he say?' Josie asked.

'That it wasn't his piece of paper – he'd picked up someone's rubbish, to throw away later.'

'And you believe that?' Charlotte asked, horrified.

'I can't understand it.' Cecily frowned. 'Neil isn't that type.'

'They are all that type,' Charlotte said bitterly. 'I can't be dealing with all that "Stand By Your Man" stuff. A cheat is always a cheat, in my opinion.'

'It's hard to believe he'd do that to me after all these years...' Lin began. 'We've been married for...'

'Oh, time's no barrier to cheating,' Charlotte grunted and Josie was amazed by the younger woman's bitterness.

Lin opened her mouth but Minnie raised a hand. 'I should explain... I hope it's okay to tell everyone?'

Charlotte nodded and Minnie said, 'Charlotte's husband has been playing away.'

'Oh, no...' Lin gasped. 'I didn't know.'

'I'm so sorry,' Josie added.

Cecily folded her arms. 'How did you find out?'

Charlotte took a breath. 'I was in London for two days, working. When I came home, the stuff in my bedroom on the dressing table had been moved around – perfume bottles, that kind of thing. I asked Darryl and he couldn't deny that he'd had his floozy to stay in our bed. In fact, he was quite proud of himself.'

'I hope you threw him out on the street – that's the place for him,' Cecily retorted.

'I'm moving out – he's welcome to his little love nest,' Charlotte said, realising that she had made a decision. She'd go to London and stay with friends. She'd be happier there, surrounded by people she trusted.

Lin swallowed, feeling suddenly sad. 'You're young – you'll find someone else, someone better...'

'You don't need to find anyone at all,' Minnie said determinedly.

'You must do as you please...' Josie suggested.

'Put yourself first for a change,' Tina added.

'You're the important one,' Cecily concluded. 'Take time, heal, think of yourself.'

Charlotte took a deep breath. 'I think he's been cheating on me since we first got married. Do you know, I found an earring in my bed, one time after Christmas? I'd been away for several days working in London – I'd gone to a party with friends. I showed the earring to Darryl and he said it must be one of mine. It looked similar but I knew it wasn't.'

'He's not to be trusted,' Cecily grimaced.

'You'd be wise to move on,' Lin said.

'I don't think I'll trust a man again…' Charlotte muttered. 'Daryl's shattered any faith I had.'

'I know exactly what you mean,' Lin added. 'Believe me.'

'Let's not even give him the time of day. You're too good for him,' Tina muttered grimly. She was thoughtful for a moment, then she added, 'In my experience, you're better off spending time growing vegetables than wasting it on a useless man.'

'Yes, I agree,' Lin said, her mouth set firmly.

She gazed in the direction where Neil had gone. She imagined he'd be in The Sun Inn, meeting Carole Frost. But Lin was like Charlotte; she had her friends, good advice, support. She wouldn't break, not now.

33

The huge crowd muttered amongst themselves in the judging tent as Minnie eased Tina forward to hear the announcement. Her entire year's work in the allotments was going to be proved worthwhile or not in a single moment. Cecily placed herself next to the elbow of a woman in a white suit and a broad-brimmed hat whom she presumed was the judge, Margaret Fennimore. Cecily offered her a sweet smile and said loudly, so that Charlotte could hear, 'We were just comparing vegetables to men. I hope you've gone for substance rather than veneer.'

The judge pretended she hadn't understood. Lin stood closer to Charlotte: she felt really sorry for her. Darryl Featherstone was handsome, charming, just as Neil was. And they were both cheats and liars. Lin peeked at Charlotte's face and noted the signs of tiredness and stress. She had been through the wringer. It was so unfair. Lin determined she'd be just as strong when she found out the truth. It couldn't come soon enough now.

Andrew the vicar gave his familiar little cough that meant that he was about to speak. Penny Ledbury sidled up to Tina and dug her in the ribs with a sharp elbow. She whispered, 'I'm sure my fuchsias will win. Your basket is a close second, though, Tina.'

Tina ignored her and concentrated on the vicar's mouth; she was so nervous, she could hardly hear his words.

'This year, the standard was very high… flower baskets… very pretty indeed… our judge was impressed… unusual to have a male winner…'

Tina screwed up her eyes, hoping she'd hear better. 'The first prize for the flower basket goes to Gerald Harris…'

Gerald pushed to the front and waved triumphantly. Margaret Fennimore was beaming, grabbing his hand and not letting go, simpering as he simpered back. The moment lengthened into a gushing conversation between Gerald and the judge, sharing words of mutual appreciation. They posed, faces close, as someone from the press took a photo.

Penny whispered, 'They play bridge together. It's favouritism.'

Cecily caught her breath. 'Really?'

'Oh, they are great friends,' Penny insisted. 'In fact, I rather think she has a soft spot for him. Look – she's all over him like eczema.'

'That's not very fair…' Lin whispered.

Gerald brandished the envelope he'd been given with the words *First Prize* on the front, containing his winnings, and kissed Margaret's cheek again, leaving her blushing as he moved to the back of the crowd, glaring at Josie as he went. Minnie felt Tina shaking next to her. Andrew muttered, 'The prize-winning vegetable competition… so many close contenders… such a high standard this year…'

'Oh, get on with it, please – I'm dying of nerves here,' Tina muttered beneath her breath.

'The runner-up prize goes to – Tina Gilchrist for her pumpkin.'

Tina's shoulders rose awkwardly as she shoved her way forwards and took the second prize envelope, her face crumpled with disappointment.

Andrew was still smiling. 'And first prize again goes to Gerald Harris for his onions.'

'Two prizes?' Tina was amazed.

Minnie pointed to the table of vegetables. Next to Tina's bright shiny pumpkin were two small onions. She laughed. 'Look at those shrivelled little things. They're nothing special at all.'

Gerald was a few feet away, shaking hands with Margaret Fennimore again who kissed his cheek, leaving a lipstick print. He turned to the crowd angrily. 'Did someone say something about my onions?'

'I merely pointed out that they are hardly prize winners,' Minnie spoke up clearly. 'Tina's pumpkin is perfect. I'm just suggesting that perhaps the judge's decision is a little clouded – her eyesight too.'

Josie muttered, 'There are tiny black spots on these onions.'

'That's the beginning of mould,' Tina gasped.

'That's true.' Cecily was shocked. 'Those onions are going bad...'

Gerald's face flushed crimson. 'I won the competition fair and square.'

'In fact,' Minnie was on her high horse now, '...the onions are rotten and so is the competition. It appears that you've won because you have friends in influential places.'

Margaret Fennimore placed her hands on her hips. 'The fact that Gerald and I are bridge partners has nothing to do with it...' she said fiercely. 'The fact that we had dinner together last night is irrelevant...'

'Dinner?' Cecily smiled.

'Is that what they call it nowadays?' Penny barked a laugh.

'I call it cheating,' Josie said quietly.

Gerald was furious. 'My onions...'

'Your unimpressive onions...' Cecily suggested.

Gerald snarled. 'I won the prize for best vegetables because they are superior to the pumpkin...'

'I thought the pumpkin looked rather nice...' Andrew admitted. 'And the onions are perhaps past their best.'

'It really doesn't matter now,' Tina said, admitting defeat.

'It does,' Minnie called out. 'It's about fairness, Andrew, and I suggest that there's a degree of favouritism going on here.'

'Hear, hear,' Penny shouted.

Gerald turned angrily to Minnie. 'You're Tina's sister – that's nepotism.'

'Not at all,' Minnie replied smartly. 'I'm simply stating things as they are. Everyone can see your dwindling little onions are hardly in the prize-winning department.'

'How dare you, you – you... old crone,' Gerald gasped.

'Crone again? I clearly need to launch another curse,' Minnie replied smugly. 'So – *Lupus non timet canem latrantem*. Or, if you prefer, *a wolf is not afraid of a barking dog*.'

'You're not a wolf, you're a... bitch!' Margaret Fennimore clasped Gerald to her in a protective hug.

Minnie smirked. 'I rather think of myself as a *malus asinae*,' she laughed. 'That's a bad ass, if you need a translation.' She turned to the vicar. 'Well, Andrew, I hope you'll be a little more circumspect about who you choose as a judge next year. Try to pick someone impartial. Really, things haven't improved much since Julius Caesar was stabbed in the back.' She wrapped a protective arm around Tina. 'Come on, Tina, let's go and get a drink. Onwards and upwards or, as the Romans would say, *ad meliora*.'

'Bravo.' Cecily clapped her hands.

Minnie was thankful she hadn't brought Jensen with her: he'd never seen that side of her and she wasn't sure how he'd have reacted. But Tina was her sister and Minnie couldn't abide injustice.

Then someone shouted, 'You're a cheat and that ent right and proper, Mrs Fennimore.' Kenny Hooper picked up a potato from the vegetable table and hurled it. It landed with a thud against Margaret's wide-brimmed hat, knocking it to the floor. Gerald bent to pick it up and another potato hit him on the backside. Another flew over his head; another missed the vicar by inches.

Then there was a cry from outside the tent and George Ledbury rushed in, his expression aghast. 'Nadine... Nadine...'

Everyone turned to look at him. Penny Ledbury called out, 'I've always said he thinks too much of that pig.'

'She won first prize in the Best Pet group.' Andrew the vicar beamed happily. 'I just pinned the rosette on her.'

'She's gone...' George gasped. 'I went to the tent to collect my prize and Nadine's disappeared.'

'With a bit of luck, she's roasting on the barbecue,' Penny smirked cruelly, but there was a glint of concern in her eye.

'She's not in the tent, where I left her...' George cried again.

'She won't be far away,' Cecily said kindly.

'We should go and find her,' Josie suggested.

'She's probably digging up someone's flower bed,' Gerald grunted. Margaret arranged her face to look shocked.

'Someone please give me a hand.' Cecily grasped the arm Lin offered gratefully. 'We'll all go together and search. Don't worry, George – we'll find Nadine. She can't have gone far...'

The search party wandered around, past the drinks tent and the fortune teller, the stalls selling pies and cakes and jams, the craft stands, the New Age jewellery. George and Penny Ledbury tagged behind, talking animatedly about the pig, and with them Jimmy and Kenny, keeping their eyes peeled. They followed each other into the churchyard, where the birds tweeted, breaking the heavy silence. Josie passed Harry's grave and pressed her fingers to her lips. The graveyard was quiet, a stillness hanging over it, as if filled with unspoken thoughts. There was no sign of Nadine.

Josie led the way as they passed the willow tree. Jack Loveday was sitting there, strumming his guitar, singing to himself. Cecily paused. 'Hello, Jack. I thought you were performing at the festival?'

'I've done my set...' He beamed. 'I'm practising some folk songs. I've got to learn "Scarborough Fair", "The Cuckoo's Nest" and "Matty Groves" by the weekend. I was chatting to a couple of the guys in Glyndŵr, the folk band that played this afternoon. Their guitarist is leaving and they asked me to join. They have gigs everywhere, all over the country.' He met her eyes. 'I'm just so pleased – it's what I want.'

'And it's richly deserved – I'm delighted.' Cecily smiled, then she remembered. 'I don't suppose you've seen George's pig?'

'Nadine? Not recently.' Jack returned to playing chords, then he looked up again and sniffed the air. 'But I can smell meat cooking.'

'I told you she'd end up on a hog roast,' Penny gasped. 'Oh, I hope not.' She was concerned now and George's face was distraught.

'I can smell it too...' George pointed towards the riverbank. 'Over by the Cherwell.'

The party scurried forward as one before Lin stopped suddenly. 'It's coming from the Toomeys' barge, and it's definitely roasting pork.'

'Surely they wouldn't hurt Nadine,' Josie said.

Jimmy chuckled. 'The Toomeys kill rabbits and pheasants and fish to eat on their barge. Why not a pig?'

'That pig's a lot of bacon...' Kenny protested. 'You're all being silly. They'd never turn a pig into rashers so quickly – I don't know what the fuss is all about...'

Josie and Minnie led the way, Cecily on Lin's arm, Charlotte next to George and Penny. She surged forward and clutched her husband's arm, feeling suddenly troubled; losing the pig would break George's heart and she was filled with an unspoken fondness for the animal that she hadn't realised she had before. Nadine gave her something to grumble about and she enjoyed the banter that ensued between them. George gazed down towards her anxiously, looking for support. 'Penny, you don't think...'

'No, George, surely not...' She took his hand.

As they approached the Toomeys' barge, smoke funnelled from the deck, and the smell of searing meat and fat. George gazed around, troubled. 'They wouldn't do that to Nadine.'

Devlin Toomey was sitting on the deck watching Finn splashing his feet in the river, forking a rasher into his mouth. Fergal held a large frying pan over the stove. He called out cheerily. 'Anyone fancy a bacon roll?'

Everyone stared for a moment, then Josie called, 'Fergal – have you seen Nadine?'

'Ah, yes...' He waved his fork. 'Come aboard.'

Penny squeezed her husband's hand: George looked as if he would cry.

Devlin was on his feet. 'Are you looking for the pig? We've got her here. She came down an hour ago.'

Finn licked his lips. 'Come and join us. There's nothing like bacon, the way my da cooks it, with plenty of fat and a bit of ketchup.'

'Nadine!' George groaned, putting his hand to his face. Penny wrapped an arm around him to comfort him.

'Fergal...' Josie put her hands on her hips. 'Where is Nadine exactly?'

'Follow me...' Fergal winked. 'It's not a pretty sight, though...'

'Oh, George,' Penny moaned. Fergal led Josie down the steps as George and Penny followed, their faces nervous, searching for a glimpse of the pig, or what was left of her.

Below, the accommodation was divided into sections, two bedrooms, three beds, a galley kitchen, a table, chairs. Fergal pointed to the smaller bedroom, where a double bed was pushed against a wall, wooden panels below, yellow paintwork above. On the bed was a grey duvet and lying on the duvet, snorting softly through a pink snout, was Nadine, her eyes closed, pointed ears and pale lashes, trotters sticking out and a smile curving her face.

'She's asleep.' George gasped and ran to the pig, stroking the rough hair of the skin. 'Nadine – oh, Nadine, you're all right.'

'She's better than all right.' Fergal laughed. 'She came down here, ate half a box of cornflakes and got herself onto my bed and now she's away with the fairies. I didn't have the heart to wake her.'

'I thought she was...' George faltered, rolling his eyes upwards to indicate heaven or the upper deck, sniffing the cooking food dramatically through flared nostrils.

'We thought you were frying her in the pan...' Penny explained, tucking an arm through George's protectively.

'Ah, we wouldn't do that to Nadine,' Fergal said cheerfully. 'She's part of the village community now.'

Finn appeared with cans of beer which he'd found in a kitchen cupboard, handing them round with a grin. 'Get your mouths around a lager each. And then come upstairs – Devlin's shovelling bacon into butties for you all.'

'If you wouldn't mind...' George said quietly. 'I'll just have a beer – unless you have anything vegetarian I can put in a bread roll.'

34

Florence shifted uncomfortably in bed. Her back ached badly and she twisted from one side to the other, but she couldn't relax. It was past midnight – she could hear Dangerous Dave snoring in the next room like a busy buzz saw. She clambered out slowly, easing herself upright; she'd go down to the kitchen for another cup of water. She padded onto the landing, then a pain made her double over and grasp the vertical rails of the staircase. She stayed where she was, recovering for a few minutes, then a second twinge took the air from her lungs and she opened her eyes wide, surprised at the intensity. She breathed deeply and tried to stand upright but another ache, even stronger than the first two, held her so tightly that she couldn't think beyond that moment. She glanced at her hands, gripping the wooden banister with twisted fingers. She stayed still for a while, trying to regain her composure and to work out what to do. Florence realised she was shivering; her shoulders were shaking and her body ached with the violence of the spasm that tightened in her abdomen. She found her voice and called weakly, 'Dad...?'

Florence sank onto the top step and listened to the continued snoring. Dave was fast asleep. She thought for a moment; his leg wasn't properly recovered, so driving might be difficult. Florence knew there was only one person she wanted with her now. She moved slowly back to her bedroom and perched on the end of her bed, reaching for the phone and pressing a button. A voice spoke to her almost immediately, and she whispered, 'Adam. It's started. The baby's coming.'

'How often are the contractions?' Adam was calm, his tone steady.

'I don't know. But they are coming fast.'

'I'm on my way.'

'My bag's packed in the hall, I'm ready to go.'

'This is it, then,' Adam murmured. 'I'll be with you in minutes.'

'Thanks...' Florence said, then another wave of pain came and she groaned. She closed her eyes: this was it. Her baby would be in her arms soon. Florence was cold, her skin prickled but she felt something akin to relief and resignation.

An hour later, Florence leaned against Adam in a small room in the hospital as the contractions came and went. A cheery midwife stood next to them, smiling confidently, hands on her hips. 'Right, Florence – all is going just as it should. Baby's heartbeat is good – you're not fully dilated yet, so I'll be back in a while to see how your labour is progressing. We've some time to go yet, but you're doing really well. Walk about if you can, or find a comfortable position on the bed.'

'What about pain relief?' Adam asked anxiously as Florence gripped his sweatshirt in her fist, twisting the material.

'I'm all right for now...' Florence muttered.

'We'll keep an eye on it.' The midwife winked. 'Don't worry, Dad – Mum's doing fine.'

Adam watched the midwife leave. 'She thinks I'm the baby's father...'

'I wish you were...' Florence blurted without thinking. 'It makes me so cross...' She leaned against Adam and they moved to sit at the edge of the bed.

'What makes you cross?'

'Fatherhood. Mothers have all the stress. The man who made me pregnant – his contribution was so short...' Florence groaned again and Adam put a hand to her brow to soothe her.

'Do you want to lie down?'

'I'll try; I'll see how I feel,' Florence panted, rolling onto the bed, curling on her side. 'I want to tell you what happened...'

Adam took her hand. 'Only if you feel all right about it.'

Florence frowned. 'I was stupid. I can't believe how stupid I was.'

Adam sighed. 'Everyone makes mistakes.'

Florence groaned and shifted uncomfortably. 'But my mistake will be with me for the rest of my life. I don't mean the baby – I'm so pleased that I'm going to be a mum – but the shame of it. I won't name the father on the birth certificate – he doesn't deserve it. He doesn't deserve anything.'

Adam squeezed her hand. 'He doesn't matter.'

Florence wriggled again. 'He came into Odile's when I was working one afternoon. I thought he was good-looking and he was so nice. I brought a coffee to the table and he touched my wrist really gently. He kept looking at me and his eyes were full of something – I don't know what it was – I couldn't help noticing – as if he really liked me, as if he thought I was special.'

Adam placed a hand on Florence's back. 'You are special.'

Florence paused, catching her breath a moment, then she continued. 'He was waiting for me when I left work. I was surprised to see him there, outside Odile's. I suppose I was a bit flattered. He's very sophisticated, well dressed, really attentive. He told me he couldn't resist me; he couldn't help how he felt; he said we should have dinner together. I thought he was taking me out somewhere nice, but we went to his house.' Florence waited while another spasm came, then she said, 'I saw photos, him and his wife, their wedding framed on the wall, and he told me they'd split up and he didn't love her. Then he started to kiss me.'

Adam's eyes were tender with love. 'Florence...'

'He fooled me, Adam. The only person I'd slept with before was you. We went upstairs to his bedroom – it was beautiful in there, it smelled lovely, everything was so cool, yet a voice in my head kept telling me I was making a mistake. But he was sweet, he said lovely things; he pretended he was falling in love with me.'

Adam's eyes flashed. 'He lied.'

Florence groaned and the pain held her still for a moment. She squirmed, trying to find a comfortable position. 'I thought I'd stay the night with him, sleep in his arms, but I didn't even stay to dinner. After we'd – made love – he was really cold, as if I was nothing. He went to the shower and when he came back, he was surprised I was still there, in his bed. I didn't know what to say.'

Adam wrapped her in his arms. 'He's not important now.'

'No, he's not.' Florence took a light breath, then another. 'I wasn't in his house for more than two hours. I was such a fool...' She groaned again, grasping Adam's hand. 'That was his only contribution to the baby. I didn't know what to say to him afterwards. I was embarrassed. He acted like I should have known it was just a quick fling. He even said...' Florence held her breath as another wave of pain came, then she made a low noise. 'He even said that the women he slept with always knew the score, and that I was naïve if I expected anything more. His exact words were, "Both you and I knew we were just playing games. I wouldn't leave my wife for a quick shag with some local girl." Then he told me to leave. I felt so cheap, Adam.'

'What a bastard.'

'I got out of his house as quickly as I could. I felt stupid. Then I noticed his business cards in a holder on the hall table and I took one – I don't know why. It had his phone number on it and his name, Darryl Featherstone.' Florence twisted towards the edge of the bed. 'Adam, I want to move around again...'

'All right.' Adam held out a hand. He felt helpless, but he was determined to be there for her. The story of her seduction had made him feel even more protective, and he knew he would do all he could for her and the baby. He'd make things right.

Florence took a breath. 'I phoned Darryl when I knew about the baby, although I had no idea what I expected him to do,' Florence muttered. 'He wouldn't answer. I don't even know if he's aware the baby's his. That's why...' She paused, panting lightly. 'That's why I don't really want to tell anyone his name. He's not a proper father, like my dad is. He's just a man I made a mistake with...' Florence turned to Adam. 'The baby is mine.' She met Adam's eyes. 'He doesn't deserve the title of father. But...' Florence's voice was a whisper, '...you can be the baby's father, if you want to... I'd like it to be you.'

'I'd like that too.' Adam kissed her lightly on her forehead. It was damp. 'I love you, Florence, you know I do. I'll take care of you both.'

Florence rested her head on his shoulder as the midwife breezed in. She grinned broadly. 'Oh, it's nice to see a young couple so in love.' She checked her watch. 'It's past six o'clock already – we're getting there.' Then she indicated the bed. 'Okay, Florence, let's check your progress.' She beamed at Adam. 'This lucky baby is going to be part of the sweetest family – I can see you can't wait to be a daddy. Right, let's see how baby's doing.'

* * *

Dawn was breaking over Middleton Ferris as Bobby Ledbury sped along the Tadderly Road on his motorbike. Behind St Peter and St Paul's church, the sky had turned a melting orange. Hayley was back in Tadderly, still asleep, and Bobby was thinking about how they had taken the children to the park the evening before, how Lily had laughed when he'd pushed her on the swing, how Alfie had chuckled as he'd been lifted into the air. He thought of Hayley, how she'd snuggled close and they'd whispered about having another child, how her divorce would be through soon and then they'd get married. Bobby turned the corner. He knew he ought to tell his parents about his new family, but he couldn't – he'd do the same as he always did. He'd arrive home, listen to the grumbles from his mother and his grandmother about the hours he kept, their suspicion that he was out causing trouble, probably taking drugs. He'd pay them no attention – he'd be thinking of Hayley – then he'd tuck into a hearty breakfast and go straight out to work on the tractor.

Bobby accelerated along Orchard Way towards the rec. He hated this charade. Perhaps today would be the day he'd come clean. They ought to know. He was proud of Hayley, the love they shared and their little family. But once he'd mentioned her, there would be all the questions about her past, about the children, about the father who had been in prison, who had come out to find his wife in love with a man who treated her right. It wasn't worth the hassle, Bobby decided. Then he saw something strange from the corner of his eye and he slowed down. A figure was leaning against the gates of the allotment, slumped forwards, not moving.

Bobby stopped the bike, swinging his leg off. He tugged off his helmet and rushed over to where Tina Gilchrist flopped against the gate. He put a hand to her shoulder. 'Tina – Tina, are you all right?'

She tried to speak, but her speech was slurred and one side of her mouth drooped down. Bobby wondered if she was drunk, but it was only eight o'clock in the morning. She attempted to raise an arm to say something, but her coordination was all over the place. She was trying to explain something to him, clearly confused. Then it occurred to him what was happening. He tugged his mobile phone from his pocket quickly and dialled. A voice crackled in his ear straight away.

'Hello. Ambulance, please – I'm at Middleton Ferris – by the allotments on Orchard Way. There's a woman here who I think has had a stroke. She can't speak properly and her face has fallen on one side. Yes – my name is Bobby Ledbury – she's called Tina – yes, thank you.'

Bobby turned to Tina, not sure what to say. He put out a hand and touched her arm as she leaned against the gate. 'Tina – it's Bobby Ledbury. You'll be all right. The ambulance is on its way.' He thought for a moment. 'You used to be an ambulance driver, didn't you, Tina? Well, you know how good they are. They'll be here any minute. Hang on in there. It's going to be fine. You'll be in safe hands.'

35

It was almost eleven o'clock. The October sun was streaming like honey as Dangerous Dave wriggled out of Neil's car, a bunch of flowers crumpled in his hand and a wide smile on his face. Josie, Lin and Neil followed him through the hospital doors; he was moving remarkably quickly for a man recovering from a leg injury. Despite the stick he used to help him limp along, he blustered towards the packed lift and squirmed his way in, announcing, 'I'm a grandad,' to the six people in there, who nodded politely and muttered congratulations.

They arrived at the ward and Josie hesitated in the corridor. 'You go in. We'll wait out here. It's best not to start off with too many people in there – it might be too much for the baby.'

'All right.' Dangerous Dave couldn't keep the grin from his face. 'Adam's taken the day off to be with her – I expect he's exhausted. He made all the phone calls once the baby was born...'

Lin tried to cover her smile. 'Florence did the real hard work, though.'

Josie took a seat. 'Go on, Grandad – in you go.'

Dave nodded, still beaming, and barged through the doors. Josie could hear him saying, 'I've come to see Florence Dawson. I'm her dad. I'm a grandad now, you know...'

As he limped to the ward, he made a beeline for Florence, who was sitting up in bed, holding a tiny bundle swaddled in a yellow blanket. He noticed the bundle had a puckered face, eyes blissfully closed. Florence grinned. 'Hi, Dad.'

'Florence, how are you, princess?' He offered her the flowers but her hands were full, so Adam took them.

'I'm fine.' Florence winced as she shifted position.

'She was amazing.' Adam felt tears come again. He was still exhausted but so happy; he couldn't contain the emotions that kept coming back, so much love and admiration for Florence, and a strange disbelief at the new baby. She had arrived into the world with a struggle and a cry, then he was holding her in his arms, stifling a sob, his face wet.

'So, how's my other princess?' Dangerous Dave asked nervously.

'Elsie Louise Dawson is six and a half pounds, and she's doing great.' Florence glanced at her father. 'Do you want to hold her?'

Dave shook his head, his eyes shining, full of emotion. 'She's so small – I can't...' He peered into the bundle. 'She looks just like you did, Florence, when you were first born.'

Adam murmured, 'She's beautiful.'

Florence's face was flushed with pride. 'She's perfect.' She glanced up at Adam. 'I don't know how I'd have managed without Adam. Or you, Dad. When we bring Elsie home, Adam will be spending most of his time at ours. We're...'

Adam looked tired. 'We're together.'

Dave exhaled, sinking down in a nearby chair. 'I'm a bit overcome with it all – a baby – I'm a grandad,' he muttered, then he burst into tears.

Josie, Lin and Neil had made their way to the ward, and were standing at a distance, clutching gifts, gazing at Florence with affection. Josie said, 'We've brought some things for the baby.'

'She's called Elsie Louise.' Florence was still smiling.

'For you too,' Lin added. 'And there's something here from Cecily. She sends her love – she's looking forward to seeing the baby.'

'Odile's coming in later,' Neil said. 'She's bringing cake.'

'And Malia, and Natalie, and Mum and Dad will be in this evening.' Adam's voice was still full of emotion.

'We'll have to have a party, to celebrate the baby...' Josie said.

'Oh, I know – isn't it my turn to organise a Silver Ladies' lunch?' Lin asked. 'I'll do something special.'

'And it's our fiftieth anniversary soon...' Neil blurted. 'October will be full of celebrations.'

'We haven't arranged anything,' Lin replied bluntly.

'Oh, I promised - leave it with me,' Neil stammered. 'I'll – take you out to lunch or... something.'

'I don't really care.' Lin seemed bitter for a moment, then she smiled. 'I'm here to see this beautiful new baby.'

Josie's phone pinged and she examined the message. 'Oh – that's strange.'

'What is?' Lin asked. Florence wasn't listening – the baby was yawning, a small round mouth, then she gave a sleepy snuffle. Adam and Dangerous Dave leaned over the baby in perfect unison, their eyes fixed on her every move.

Josie frowned. 'Minnie's here, in the hospital.'

'Is she coming up to see the baby?' Lin asked.

'No – she's here to see Tina. Apparently, she's been taken to Juniper ward...'

* * *

Minnie hurried up the stairs as fast as her Doc Martens would carry her. She'd received the message from the hospital just after nine o'clock, thanks to Bobby naming her as next of kin; Minnie's number had been on Tina's phone in her pocket. She'd been having breakfast with Jensen, talking about the plays of Aristophanes and how he should direct *Lysistrata* once he was back in New York. She'd teased that she'd even go with him as his classics advisor. Then her phone rang, and she'd taken the first train to Tadderly. Jensen had wanted to come with her, but Minnie intended to deal with the situation herself.

She arrived at Juniper ward and took a deep breath as she walked through the swing doors. She had no idea what to expect. The person who'd called her from the hospital had simply said that Tina had suffered a stroke and Minnie had promised to be there as soon as she could. She gazed around as a nurse approached her and asked, 'May I help you?'

'I'm Dr Moore – I'm here to see my sister, Tina... Albertina Gilchrist.'

'Oh, of course.' The nurse took in the army coat and black beret, the St Hilda's scarf. 'Just a moment – I'll just give Dr Podichetti a call.'

'Can I see Tina now?'

'I'll ask the doctor first.'

The nurse walked away. Minnie's heart was bumping hard. She had an image in her mind of her sister lying in bed, unconscious, on a drip, or paralysed and unable to speak. She'd get the best treatment for Tina, whatever it took. Minnie would make sure of it.

There were footsteps behind her and Minnie turned to see a doctor in a white coat, abundant dark hair in a plait down her back. Her name badge said that she was called Devika Podichetti. She met Minnie's eyes. 'Hello. Have you come to see Albertina?'

'Tina's my sister,' Minnie said quickly. 'How is she?'

A frown creased the doctor's smooth brow. 'She's suffered a transient ischaemic attack. She's comfortable. We've given her an IV injection of recombinant tissue plasminogen activator. She's stable now and we'll start working on her rehabilitation straight away.'

'What does that mean in terms of her recovery?' Minnie gazed into the doctor's eyes for signs of how severe Tina's illness was; she found none. 'Is she going to get well again? How bad was the stroke?'

The doctor chose her words carefully. 'Fortunately, the young man who called the ambulance was on the scene quickly – your sister has the best possible chance of a good recovery. She's sleeping now, but we'll start immediately to analyse any physical or cognitive impairments and begin work on them.'

Minnie felt her heart lurch. 'Will Tina recover?'

'We'll monitor her over the next week or so in hospital, but her chances are good. It's early days, but during the first three months, we should see notable improvements. The brain is still in a state of heightened plasticity, which means that rehabilitation will have a bigger effect during this time.'

'So she'll be able to come home soon?'

'Of course. Once we've assessed her needs, we'll be able to give you a clearer picture of what will happen and a timescale.' The doctor smiled. 'Does she have someone at home who can look after her?'

'No...' Minnie began.

'Only we'd expect her to continue recovery both on her own at home and in outpatient therapy.'

'Then I'll look after her,' Minnie said quickly.

'It's likely she'll need physical therapy, occupational therapy and speech therapy to regain lost skills. But every stroke is different and therefore every recovery will be different.'

'Right,' Minnie nodded. 'But it would be better for Tina if she came home with me, rather than being on her own.'

'It would, yes,' the doctor said. 'As long as you can accommodate her needs.'

'I can,' Minnie replied determinedly. 'We're flesh and blood – what else would I do?'

* * *

That evening, Lin and Neil sat in front of the television. Lin was wondering how to express the jumbled thoughts in her mind, how to broach the subject of Carole Frost again. They were clutching mugs of coffee and there was a packet of chocolate biscuits on the table. Neil said, 'It's properly autumn now – the nights are becoming chilly.'

'They are.'

'Summer is over.'

'It is...' Lin continued to stare at the TV screen. 'It's been a strange summer.' She glanced at Neil. 'You were out a lot.'

He patted her hand. 'I'm home now.'

'You are...' Lin gazed into her coffee mug. 'Florence's baby is gorgeous, isn't she?'

'Oh, yes.' Neil reached for the biscuits and offered one to Lin first. 'I remember when Debbie was a baby. I loved being a new dad.'

'We haven't heard from Debbie in ages.'

'I spoke to her a few days ago.'

'Did you?' Lin sat up. 'You never said. Where was I?'

'I thought I'd mentioned it?' Neil stammered, looking a little guilty. 'You were probably at the Co-op.'

'Oh?' Lin nibbled a biscuit, wondering if it was yet another lie. 'Penny told me she'd heard that Charlotte has left Darryl Featherstone for good now. She's gone back to live in London.'

'He's not a very nice man by all accounts,' Neil muttered. 'Not if what you told me about him playing away with other women is true. A man shouldn't do that to his wife.'

'He shouldn't. Men who cheat on their wives are disgusting.' Lin shot her husband a sidelong glance. She thought he looked decidedly uncomfortable. 'So, what about our fiftieth wedding anniversary? It's next week.'

'It is.' Neil seemed to have no idea what to say. 'Leave it with me – I promised you I'd take care of it.'

Lin wrinkled her nose. 'I don't like surprises – especially unpleasant ones.'

'I'll take you for a meal in The Sun, then.'

'For our fiftieth? Really? I hoped I was worth more than that...'

'You are. I'll sort something out. I will...' He kissed her cheek. 'Trust me.'

Lin looked away. She used to trust him. But he'd just suggested condensing fifty years' celebration to an ordinary pub meal. She was silently furious. She sipped her coffee and changed the subject, just to show him that she didn't care. 'So – onto important things – I need to organise a lunch for the ladies. It's my turn.'

Neil gave her his full attention. 'You could all go to Odile's.'

'We always go to Odile's. I want to do something special. Special is important sometimes, Neil. I like to make a fuss of people who are important to me,' she said pointedly. 'Florence organised the food by the barge, Minnie took us to Stratford, Josie held a barbecue, Cecily had a picnic in the woods. I want to do something nice too.'

'You could cook them all a meal round here.'

'Me, cook?' Lin was astonished. 'Are you joking? You know I can't cook for toffees.'

Neil smiled. 'I'll help you.' He reached for another biscuit. 'Let's just watch the end of *The Green Planet*, then I'll help you *plan-et* all out.' He grinned at his own joke. 'What do you think, Lindy? It might be fun...'

Lin turned away, avoiding his eyes. She wondered what sort of deceit he was working on now. Perhaps he'd leave her cooking with her friends in the kitchen and sneak out to meet Carole Frost again. It wouldn't surprise her at all. She'd watch him like a hawk; she was ready for his next move.

She kept her voice light. 'I don't know yet. I'll decide what I want to do. I'll give it some thought and let you know...'

* * *

Minnie rested her head against the window, watching the scenery flash past as the train rattled along. The lurch and rumble of the carriage was helping her to think; she had to get her thoughts in order before she reached Oxford. Jensen had texted that he'd be waiting for her when she arrived. He was worried about her and wanted to know how her sister was, how he could help.

Minnie was wrestling with a problem. Jensen was a lovely man and that was making the decision all the more difficult. Minnie was in love with him. She wasn't sure how she could bring Tina back to her home in Oxford, look after her, and keep the blossoming relationship with Jensen going. He'd be returning to New York soon. She'd liked the idea of going with him, at least for a few weeks. She knew she wanted to be with him and she knew he loved her to distraction. But Tina came first. They'd know soon the extent of the damage the stroke had done, and Minnie would have to prioritise her sister's recovery.

It occurred to her that she'd have to let Jensen go, and the thought of saying goodbye to him brought a lump to her throat. She'd never been in love before, not really, not completely. Jensen was her equal and now she'd found him, she'd have to set him free.

The conversation she'd had with her sister came floating back to her through the rumbling rhythm of the train's wheels.

'But we're flesh and blood, Tina.'

'That's *all* we are, though.'

Minnie thought about it carefully. When she'd left Middleton Ferris all those years ago, she couldn't wait to escape. Oxford had saved her life; she'd metamorphosed, become a new person. And now she'd met Jensen, her soulmate. Her life was complete.

But she was still the same Minnie Moore who'd sat at the desk in Miss Hamilton's class, piles of books in front of her, desperate to learn. She was the same Minnie who punched Dickie Edwards and knocked his front tooth out in the rec when he'd tried to bully her sister. She was the same bright young thing who'd said, 'I don't like jam, actually,' and her father had slapped her as she sat at the breakfast table, whack! Out of nowhere. She was still Tina's sister and Tina would come first every time.

Minnie stared through the window as hedges and fields and pylons slipped by, as she tried to plan how she would tell Jensen that it was over.

36

Lin woke up on the morning of their fiftieth wedding anniversary in an empty bed. She'd been waiting for days for Neil to discuss the plans with her, to say something like 'Why don't we book a long weekend in Wales?' or 'Let's get off in the Sharan to Cornwall – what about a spa hotel?' But as time ran out, he had carried on as usual, looking pleased with himself, as if it was another ordinary day, or he'd been secretive. She'd tried to talk to him about it, but he'd change the subject – he was shiftier than ever now. Lin told herself that this might be the last anniversary of her marriage. She'd expect nothing.

She'd bought him a photograph of them together in a personalised gilt frame and a T-shirt that said *Fifty Years of Awesomeness*. It was her way of giving him the benefit of the doubt, although there was little doubt left in her mind. She'd hoped to go somewhere special, to have discussed it together, shared the cost, a fitting gift to each other, and she was filled with bitter disappointment. The presents were wrapped in shiny paper beneath the bed. It felt strange, offering tokens of love to a man who probably loved someone else. But today was the day. She'd find out the truth for certain, and she'd deal with the consequences.

She could smell coffee brewing; Neil was in the kitchen making breakfast. Lin slipped on a dressing gown and slippers, swept up the two presents from beneath the bed and padded downstairs. She wasn't quite sure how she would greet him: *Happy anniversary, love* felt false. She was almost in the kitchen when she heard him talking on the phone. His back was turned to her and she stopped to listen, unseen.

'Right, I'll see you there then. Don't be late. You know where we're meeting, yes?' He listened to a voice chattering for a while and she heard him chuckle. 'No, of course she doesn't know – she doesn't suspect a thing.'

Lin held her breath and waited for him to finish the call. He said, 'I'm looking forward to it – I haven't been this excited in ages.' Then she stepped into the kitchen as he hid the phone in his pocket.

Lin kept her voice steady. 'Who was that?'

Neil wore the guilty look she'd seen so often recently. 'Oh, nobody. No one at all...'

'Who *was* it?'

Neil took a breath. It was clear he didn't know what to say. He looked around for an excuse and found none, so instead he said, 'Happy anniversary, Lindy love.' He saw the presents. 'Are these for me?'

Lin nodded. She wasn't sure how to react. He had lied to her and he was behaving as if nothing was wrong. She changed the conversation. 'So – what are we doing today? Shall I pick somewhere to go, a last-minute thing? Or is there going to be a big surprise?'

'Not really...' Neil looked relieved to be asked a simple question that he could answer easily. He pulled out a chair. 'I'm just going to spoil you rotten. Sit down.'

Lin sat reluctantly. He placed a dish of croissants in front of her and began to pour coffee. He smiled, full of himself. 'I want you to enjoy breakfast and then – I bought you some nice bubble bath. I put it in the bathroom with a scented candle, and I want you to have a long soak then put your glad rags on and we'll be off down The Sun for lunch.'

Lin bit her lip: toiletries and a pub lunch after fifty years were disappointing to say the least. She was still thinking about the phone call she'd overheard, and the fact that he'd lied to her yet again. 'So, who were you speaking to when I came in?'

'Erm – Dangerous Dave.' Neil gave a wobbly grin that made Lin's heart sink. 'I was asking him about the baby. He wanted to know if I could just... slip out this morning and help him with some adjustments – to the pram.'

Lin frowned. 'The pram?'

'The – back wheel is loose. I'll only be half an hour.' Neil beamed. 'Oh, I love this T-shirt.' He had unwrapped the first present and was struggling into it, pulling the material down and smiling. 'And can I open this one later, this evening?'

Lin gritted her teeth. He could do whatever he wanted; she didn't care any more. It wasn't going to be the special day she'd hoped for, and he was telling her blatant lies. But it was her anniversary and she'd do just as she pleased. Today was the day she'd know for sure. She'd find out where he was going: she was positive it wasn't Dangerous Dave's house. She turned away abruptly. 'All right... I'll have a long soak in the bath...'

Neil gulped his coffee, his face relaxed now. 'That's great, Lindy. And I promise, I won't be long at Dave's.' He reached for a croissant. 'I'll be back before you know I'm gone...'

Lin finished her croissant too quickly and slipped up the stairs, calling, 'I'll see you...' She lowered her voice, '...sooner than you think.'

She heard him call from below. 'Right, love.'

In the bathroom, the scented candle gave off the aroma of cinnamon and honey; Lin turned on the taps as if she was filling the bath, rushed to the bedroom, her fingers sore and shaking as she pulled on a hoody and tracksuit bottoms. They were a rose-pink colour, not the black anonymous clothes she needed, but they'd have to do. Back in the bathroom, she twisted the taps to stop the flow of water, blew out the candle and exhaled. She checked everything: trainers, front door key, sunglasses. This was it. She didn't like what she was doing; she was terrified of the consequences, but it had to be done. She paused, took a breath, willed back the tears that brimmed in her eyes. She couldn't turn back now.

As she closed the front door behind her, Lin could see Neil in the distance, heading into Harvest Road. As she had done for the last fifty years, she felt her heart expand with love at the sight of him. But she was determined, following him like a spy, the hood pulled over her head, her hair tucked in, dark glasses in place. She loitered a moment, watching him stride past Jimmy's house. He carried on towards Orchard Way. If he'd been going to Dangerous Dave's, he'd have taken the road to Newlands, to the right. Lin guessed he was going to meet Carole Frost. She took a deep breath, then another. Her palms were damp. She'd find out what was going on, then she'd confront them both. It would break her heart but at least she'd know for certain.

She followed him, blood pumping faster than it should as she ducked behind hedges, dodging into gateways, crouching low so that she wouldn't be seen. It occurred to her that if anyone was watching her, they'd think she'd lost the plot, rushing around, snooping like Miss Marple. Neil was almost level with Odile's café and Lin was worried she'd lose sight of him, so she broke into a run. It had been years since she'd actually tried to run anywhere and she was quickly out of breath. Then she saw him disappear into Dangerous Dave's garage.

She paused for a moment, thinking: perhaps Dangerous Dave was there, perhaps he'd brought the baby's pram for Neil to fix. There was only one way to find out. She was moments from the truth and she had never been more scared in her life.

She slunk towards the garage, sidling towards the door, her back against the wall, edging towards the sound of voices. She listened carefully, panting audibly, shivering, shaking with fear. She could make out Neil's cheery chatter and a woman's high tinkle. Lin was filled with new dread. It must be Carole Frost: she'd lost her husband forever. For a moment, her legs were weak beneath her and her courage almost failed. There was another voice, a man's rumble. It sounded like Dangerous Dave.

She heard someone mention her name. 'Where's Lin now?'

Neil replied carelessly, 'In the bath, I hope.'

Then she heard a laugh. It was Josie's voice; she was sure of it. 'You did well, Neil. She has no idea, does she? I'm so glad you rang me this morning...'

Lin was momentarily shocked. So it was Josie he'd phoned at breakfast time and they'd held a secret conversation. She didn't understand. She took a deep breath: it was now or never. She leaped forward into the garage, arms wide, her face flushed. Her voice trembled as she shouted bravely, 'I'm not in the bath, Neil – I'm here.'

There was a stunned silence. So many pairs of eyes were staring at her as she stood in the garage entrance, gazing back, frowning behind the sunglasses, completely puzzled. She took in every face in turn: Neil, Josie, Cecily, Fergal, the Toomey boys. Dangerous Dave was there, Florence and baby Elsie. Adam, Linval and Rita Johnson, Malia, Natalie. George and Penny Ledbury were standing next to them, smiling. She looked at Jimmy Baker, Kenny Hooper, Geoff and Janice Lovejoy and Jack. She saw Minnie and someone she didn't recognise, a tall man with gold-rimmed spectacles and a halo of white hair. Then she caught her breath. Debbie was smiling, standing next to her husband Jon and their children. Melissa and Louis were big now, all grown up. Lin held the moment in her eyes while the assembled group gaped at the small, puzzled woman in a pink hoody and sunglasses, then Neil spoke up.

'You're a bit early, love. You weren't supposed to be here until I fetched you. I just came to check that everything was ready, then I was going to come back and surprise you.'

'I don't understand,' Lin stammered. 'You were going to fix the pram...'

'I fibbed.' Neil grinned and the group parted, moving to both sides of the garage to reveal a broad brown tarpaulin covering a sleek shape. Neil shrugged shyly and said, 'Happy fiftieth anniversary, Lindy.' He whisked off the cover to reveal a gleaming green Frog-Eyed Sprite sports car.

'I'm confused.' Lin shook her head and she heard a champagne bottle pop. Josie was beside her, handing her a flute of fizzing bubbly. Debbie hugged her.

'It's been too long, Mum. I'm sorry we've been so busy – but we couldn't miss your special day.'

'It's your fiftieth anniversary car, love.' Neil took her in his arms and kissed her. He took a deep breath. 'I've been hiding it here, working on it for months. It was a bit of a wreck when I bought it, but it's good as new now. It's just like the one we used to have when we first got married. We can go away in it together – all over the country. In fact, I've booked us a long weekend in a manor house in Dorset, just me and you.'

'You renovated a Sprite – in secret – for me?' Lin felt the tears come. It wasn't the arthritis or the tablets. It was relief, guilt, happiness, embarrassment. And more than anything, it was love.

'I bought it from a woman called Carole Frost – she advertised it online,' Neil admitted. 'I was really worried when you found her phone number in my pocket. I'm such a terrible liar. I thought you'd really think I was seeing another woman.'

'As if...' Dangerous Dave barked a laugh.

Lin kissed her husband again. She met Josie's eye and noticed the complicit wink.

Dave piped up, 'I knew about it, and Jimmy, and Dickie Senior. No one else had a clue most of the time. It wasn't easy covering up Neil's tracks while he was sneaking off here to do the car up.'

'A long weekend in a manor house in Dorset,' Lin said dreamily and sipped a mouthful of champagne. 'Can I sit in the car?'

'Of course you can.' Neil walked over to the shining Sprite and opened the driver's door as Lin clambered in. All their friends burst into a spontaneous cheer and raised glasses.

'I've been so stupid.' Lin was overcome with emotion. 'I can't believe it...'

Neil leaped into the passenger seat and threw an arm around her as Debbie took a photo, then he said, 'Do you want to go home and change into something nice, love? Dickie's booked The Sun for lunch, the whole pub. Everyone will be there... all our friends.' He indicated the group, who were refilling champagne flutes. 'It was meant to be a surprise.'

Lin threw her arms around Neil and kissed him for all she was worth. When she pulled away, he was blinking, his face flushed. 'Happy anniversary, Lindy,' he grinned, and their friends cheered again.

* * *

Everyone was inside the pub, chatting noisily, drinking champagne. Minnie tugged Jensen outside, holding his hand. She led him across the road and they sat on the seat beneath the weeping willow on the village green. Jensen looked around. 'What a quaint little place. And what great friends you have, Minnie. It was so good to meet them.'

'And they all like you too.' Minnie smiled. 'They are lovely people.'

'They sure are.'

'Jensen,' Minnie began, and she stared at his hand clasped around hers. 'Tina is coming out of hospital next week.'

'I'm glad. She's making good progress.'

'She is,' Minnie said. 'And I'm bringing her to my house to start her rehabilitation straight away.'

'That's good,' Jensen agreed. 'I hope she'll make a full recovery.'

'I'll make sure of that...' Minnie sighed. 'And you're going home to New York in a week's time.'

'You said you'd come visit.'

'I did.' Minnie shrugged. 'I can't deny how I feel about you, Jensen. But I'm staying here for Tina. It won't work between us long distance.'

Jensen frowned. 'I don't agree, Minnie. There has to be a way.'

'There isn't.'

'I'm a patient man.'

'And I'm a determined woman. Tina will get well. I'll be with her every step.'

'I know.' Jensen held her hand to his lips. 'It's one of the many things I admire about you.'

She looked at him, her eyes shining. 'And your ability to understand me completely is one of the many things I admire about you.'

'You're asking me to back off?'

'For now, at least...' Minnie said.

'And when Tina recovers?'

'I'll let you know.'

Jensen took a deep breath; he was quiet for a while before he said, 'All right. I'll give you the space you need, you and Tina.'

Minnie leaned forward and kissed his lips. 'I won't forget you.'

'And I'll never forget you, Araminta Moore. The love of my life.'

Minnie stood up to go. 'It's best you catch the train back alone.'

'It is.' He still held onto her hand. 'I'll get my things from the house and be out of your hair.'

'You're a good man.' Minnie smiled and began to walk back to The Sun. 'I'll miss you.'

He watched her for a moment, his gaze level. Then he waved a hand. 'I won't give up on you, though, Minnie. I'll be in touch. We'll meet again, you'll see.'

'Maybe we will,' Minnie called over her shoulder.

'I'm sure of it.' Jensen's voice was just audible.

Minnie fixed her eyes on the pub door. She'd go in, sit with her friends and order another drink for herself. She wouldn't look back. Tina was her priority now.

37

October 28th was a windy Saturday, a bright cloudless morning. Lin gazed through the kitchen window: it was almost 8.30. Neil had taken himself off to see Dangerous Dave – Lin didn't need him under her feet, not today. In the field beyond the garden, George Ledbury was perched on his tractor, driving through the thick soil, Nadine in the cab by his side. The leaves on the trees were starting to fall now, twirling on the breeze, tumbling to the ground in mounds of gold and amber.

Lin was looking forward to the lunch she would be cooking for everyone today, but she was still anxious. She'd burn something, drop something on the floor, she'd leave out an important ingredient or put too much salt or sugar in, and the dishes would taste awful. She gazed at the recipe book Josie had bought her, *Tastes of the Caribbean*, and took a deep breath. She was making rum punch, chicken stew, a rice dish called a pelau, a pulled pork dish substituting jackfruit for the meat, a vegetable curry, and a rum cake. It was going to be tough, but she'd do it. Her fingers ached a bit, the arthritis wasn't so bad, though, now she had new medication. She massaged them gently: today she'd make a delicious lunch for all her friends that they'd remember for ever. She'd be fine. There was a sharp knock at the door, and Lin rushed into the hall eagerly. Odile was there, holding out an apron, smiling broadly. She stepped inside. 'You ready, Lin?'

Lin steeled herself. 'I'm ready.'

'Then let's hit the kitchen and cook up a storm.'

* * *

Josie locked the front door behind her; she was running late. She'd said she'd be at Lin's house in Barn Park for half past eight. At the gate she met the postman who offered her a cheery grin and a small package wrapped in brown paper. She pushed it into her capacious bag, which contained an apron and several ingredients including a bottle of rum, and hurried on her way. As she passed the village green, she heard a voice calling her name. She turned to see Fergal rushing towards her and she waited for him to catch up.

He grinned. 'I thought I'd come with you.'

'To Lin's?'

'I'm a dab hand at the cooking nowadays.'

'We're making Caribbean lunch for twenty people.'

'I can roast a goat.'

'There won't be a goat.'

'Then I'll make a pan of Joe Grey and add rum to it.' Fergal brandished a tin of beans. 'I've brought some of the ingredients.'

Josie started to walk along Orchard Way and Fergal kept pace with her. 'The thing is, Josie, I've been wanting to talk to you...'

'Oh?'

'There's something I need to say... I've been practising so that I can say it right...'

Josie was intrigued. 'Oh, well, go on then.'

They had reached Chandos. Gerald Harris was in the garden, sweeping leaves. Josie called out, 'Good morning, Gerald. You're up early.'

Gerald waved a hand. 'Up with the lark, Mrs Sanderson. Good morning, Mr Toomey.'

'Morning, Bomb – er... Gerald,' Fergal said.

Gerald leaned on his rake. 'All these leaves – I have to keep the place looking nice.'

'Indeed he does.' A crisp voice came from the doorway and Margaret Fennimore emerged from the house in a fluffy cream onesie.

Josie noticed that Fergal was staring in disbelief, and she elbowed him gently. He closed his mouth and she smiled. 'Margaret, Gerald, we're making lunch at Lin's for one. You'd be welcome to join us. It's a buffet...'

'A luncheon club!' Margaret was delighted. 'Oh, I think I'm going to enjoy living in Middleton Ferris, Gerald.'

'I do hope so, my dear,' Gerald beamed and went back to raking up leaves.

'So...' Josie asked as she and Fergal walked on. 'You were saying something.'

'Was I?'

'Something you've been practising.'

'Oh, so I was.' Fergal stuffed his hands in his pockets. 'The thing is, Josie, I mean, I want to say it straight and clear, that...' He paused and pointed to the allotments. 'Oh, there they are, my boys, working on Tina's allotment, keeping it nice for when she's back.'

Josie waved a hand. 'Morning Devlin, Finn.'

Devlin and Finn looked up from where they were digging and waved a hand. Fergal smiled proudly. 'They are taking pumpkins to Rita Johnson, so she can use them in the primary school with the kiddies for Halloween on Monday morning. They're making lanterns with the outsides and cooking soup with the rest of it.'

'That's good,' Josie remarked as they walked on.

'So, how's Tina doing?'

'She's making good progress.' Josie shrugged. 'Minnie will tell you all about it later – she'll be here soon. She's dropping Tina off at physiotherapy and then she'll come straight to Lin's and go back after a couple of hours in time for Tina to finish.'

'Minnie's looking after her well.'

'She is. She's devoting almost all of her time to Tina now.'

'That's love for you,' Fergal commented, and his eyes strayed to Josie.

'So, you were saying...'

'Was I?' Fergal shook his head to remember. 'Oh, yes...'

'You've been practising...'

'I have,' Fergal agreed. 'So, Josie...'

'Fergal.'

'I've been thinking...'

'That's good...'

Fergal took a breath. 'The thing is, see, I was hoping you'd go out with me, make it a regular thing.'

Josie frowned. 'I've explained already – I'm not looking for—'

'Hear me out, Josie.' They had reached Dangerous Dave's garage. The door was open and two figures could be seen in the darkness, talking, laughing, hands in pockets. It was Dangerous Dave and Neil. Fergal called out, 'Morning, lads.'

There was a reply, a guffaw, then Josie and Fergal were on their way. Odile's café was closed for the day. A sign in felt pen in the window said, 'Sorry for inconvenience – training day.'

Josie and Fergal walked on, and Fergal was about to speak when there was the sound of a loud klaxon behind them. They turned quickly and a mobility scooter sailed past them, a woman in a faux fur coat and hat.

Josie called after her. 'Cecily...'

'I'll see you at Lin's – I'm running late.' Cecily's voice faded as she sped forward towards Harvest Road.

'So...' Fergal began.

Josie turned to Fergal. 'I'm not looking to replace Harry, Fergal.'

He stopped and took both her hands. 'And I don't want to replace my Ros. I don't want kissing or love or sex or to set up home with you, Josie. I want someone to share dinner down the pub, a hug when I'm feeling a bit low, lots of laughter. We get on, you and me.' His eyes were intense. 'Why can't we be together as friends?'

Josie thought for a moment. 'Was that the speech you practised?'

'It was.'

'It's a good one.' Josie smiled.

'So, what do you think?'

Josie sighed. 'It makes sense. We do get on.'

'We're close friends,' Fergal agreed. 'I need someone and you're the best someone I know.'

'Harry liked you, Fergal. And we have known each other since school. Miss Hamilton's class, remember – she got you attending regularly.'

'She did,' Fergal said. 'And Ros liked you. She said you were a good sort.'

Josie smiled, then she threaded an arm through the crook of Fergal's elbow. 'Well, friends it is – now we understand each other.'

'Good friends,' Fergal beamed.

'People in the village will talk when they see us together,' Josie suggested.

'Ah, let them.' Fergal grinned as they walked along. 'They need something new now they've stopped talking about Florence's baby or the Featherstones' failed marriage.'

Josie knew what he meant. 'It's all Bobby Ledbury at the moment. Penny was saying in the Co-op that he has a girlfriend with two children in Tadderly and they're getting married in the spring. George has given them one of the cottages at the farm. The kids will go to the primary school.'

'That's nice,' Fergal muttered. 'And Adam Johnson is saving up for a place in Tadderly for himself and Florence and the baby.' He pulled a face. 'At least Dangerous will get a good night's sleep.'

They turned the corner to Barn Park. Behind them, clouds gathered over Old Scratch's woods and Fergal sniffed the air. 'It will rain this afternoon, at around three.'

Josie hugged his arm. 'Dinner tonight at my place then – I have a nice piece of fish and it's too much for one.'

'Right you are,' Fergal said cheerily. 'The boys will be out – so I'll bring us a bottle of wine. And we'll watch something on the TV perhaps?'

'Have you seen the latest in the *Happy Valley* series?'

'I haven't...'

'Oh, I think you'll like it, Fergal...'

'*Happy Valley* it is, then.'

* * *

Three hours later, the table was covered with steaming dishes of rice, stew and curry. There were flatbreads, cake and rum punch. Lin shook her head in disbelief. 'Did I make all this?'

'You did brilliantly,' Odile said proudly.

'With a little help from your friends,' Cecily added, then she burst into a Beatles song.

'It's amazing what a group of people can do together.' Josie rearranged plates, placing a cake and cream on the table.

'I'll put out some glasses for the rum punch,' Fergal offered. 'I'll just try it and see if it needs...' He ladled some amber liquid into a glass. 'A little more rum, I think – and a bit of ginger.'

Lin caught her breath as she surveyed her handiwork. 'I really enjoyed cooking with everyone's help. I think I might be able to do it by myself one day... I mean, once I stopped worrying, it was much easier than I thought.'

'Isn't life always that way?' Cecily said, hugging her.

Minnie arrived in her army coat, beret and purple Doc Martens boots, carrying cheese and biscuits, protesting that she could only stop for an hour. Her handbag was stuffed full of books wrapped in tissue for Cecily, Josie, Lin, Florence and one for baby Elsie. Neil bustled into the room with a hungry Dangerous Dave, looking for food, sniffing greedily, then there was a steady stream of people through the front door. Jimmy Baker and Kenny Hooper had brought Dickie Senior and his wife with them. Rita and Linval Johnson were quickly followed by Jack Lovejoy, Janice and Geoff from next door with a plate of meringues from Susan and Mrs B'Gurk's eggs. Lin was the perfect host, serving everyone with rum punch that Linval swore was exactly as his mother had made it years ago.

The conversation subsided as everyone started to eat; chatter was replaced with sounds of pleasure, compliments to Lin and Odile and the other cooks on the delicious dishes they'd made. Gerald and Margaret arrived, eagerly sampling the Caribbean fare and exclaiming that they enjoyed it so much, they'd make it themselves at home.

'Margaret's marvellous in the kitchen too,' Gerald beamed and Josie was sure she saw him pinch her bottom before she glowed with delight.

Neil moved to Lin and kissed her, whispering in her ear, 'I married the most gorgeous person in the world – and a wonderful cook.'

Lin kissed him back. 'So did I.'

Minnie stood by herself sipping rum punch when Cecily touched her elbow and whispered, 'How's Tina doing?'

'She's making progress. A taxi is picking her up from physio later. I'll have to be back in Oxford to meet her at the house. She's very positive and chirpy.'

'And what about you?' Cecily's eyes were full of concern. 'Are you managing all the extra work?'

'I'm doing all right.'

'You gave up that wonderful man we met at Lin's anniversary lunch.'

'I did.' Minnie clamped her lips together. 'But I have Tina, my home, my friends, and my books. I'll be just fine.' She sipped from a tall glass. 'Besides, Jensen calls me from time to time. We're still in touch. Who knows which way it will go?'

'Oh...' Cecily's eyes filled with tears. 'I'm just so proud of everybody. You, Lin, Josie, Fergal – you've turned out so well.' She waved a hand around the room. 'Look at you all here – and Neil and Jimmy, Kenny, Dickie. I'm so glad I was your teacher. It was just the best job in the world...'

Minnie wrapped an arm around her, then everyone turned in unison as Florence came in, holding baby Elsie. Adam was a step behind her, smiling, carrying a bag stuffed with nappies and spare clothes. Florence was surrounded by cooing voices and she looked happy and relaxed. Then Odile called, 'Anyone for Jamaican rum cake?' and there was a clamour of eager voices.

Florence turned to Lin as the baby wriggled in her arms. 'Can I just pop upstairs? Elsie needs a feed.'

'Use our bedroom.' Lin suddenly recalled the warm maternal feelings she'd had with Debbie. They'd spoken on the phone earlier – Debbie had promised to ring at least once a week. 'Top of the stairs, go left.'

'Thanks, Lin.'

Adam was by her side. 'Shall I come with you?'

'No, you stay, have some cake... I'll be down soon.' Florence heaved the bag onto her shoulder, adjusting the baby's position to make her more comfortable.

She'd almost reached the bottom of the stairs when someone appeared at the front door – Lin had left it open for guests. Florence stopped, clutching Elsie, as Charlotte Featherstone faced her in the hall. Florence's first thought was to ignore her, but she took a breath and said, 'Hello.'

'Hello,' Charlotte replied uncomfortably. 'I heard you'd had the baby.'

'Yes.' Florence was unsure how to reply.

'She's beautiful,' Charlotte murmured and both women stared awkwardly at each other.

They spoke at the same time: 'I was just going up to feed her…'

'I wanted to talk to you, Florence…' There was another silence, then Charlotte said, 'I'm living in London now with some friends. I just came back to the house to pick up a few things. I heard there was a party and I wanted to say goodbye.'

Florence nodded. 'Good luck in London – I hope it works out.'

'I wanted to give you this…' Charlotte rummaged in her pocket and held out the silver hoop earring. Her eyes were on the one that matched it, still in Florence's ear.

'You knew?' Florence put down the baby bag and took the earring. 'Thank you.' She gave a deep sigh. 'I'm so sorry…'

'Don't be.' Charlotte shook her head vigorously. 'Darryl did the dirty on us both.'

'He did.' Florence kissed the top of Elsie's head. 'But I have my baby. He doesn't matter.'

'And I have my freedom and a whole lot of experience that I'll learn from – mistakes I won't make again.' Charlotte said. 'And you're right, Darryl doesn't matter. Not now.' She forced a smile. 'I'm not thinking about him.'

'Nor am I.' Florence said. 'It's Adam and Elsie and me and my dad… that's my family.'

'I have my job and good friends…' Charlotte was thoughtful. 'I'm a more confident person without him. I'm happier.'

'I'm glad for you, I really am.' Florence glanced at Elsie, who had started to open her mouth and turn her small head. 'She's getting hungry…'

'I won't keep you.' Charlotte smiled. 'I'm pleased I've seen you, though – I'll just pop in and say thanks to Cecily and Josie and Lin, then I'll be off...' She put out a finger and touched the baby's cheek. 'Good luck.'

'You too,' Florence said, picking up the bag and moving upstairs, feeling suddenly light and happy.

Inside the kitchen, Odile was handing everyone cake and rum punch. Josie moved to Lin and wrapped an arm around her. 'The girl did good.'

'She did.' Lin gazed around, taking in the food and her guests. 'We did well, Josie.'

'We're a team, we have been for so many years.' Josie grinned.

'The Silver Ladies,' Lin suggested.

'The whole village are Silver Ladies now.' Josie hugged Lin closer. 'One big family. "Friends show their love in times of trouble, so we share lunch as friends." Remember?'

'We've come a long way since Miss Hamilton's class.' Lin smiled at the memory. 'It seems a lifetime ago.'

'And yet it has passed in the blink of an eye...' Josie replied. 'Oh – I forgot...' She leaned over to the chair where she'd left her bag. 'The postman gave me a package earlier. I ought to open it.'

She pulled out the small brown paper parcel and Lin said, 'It's a book.'

'It must be,' Josie agreed. It was the right size and shape. She unwrapped it with deft fingers and held out a paperback. The book had a bright cover, with turquoise sea and sky and a golden sun, and a dapper man in a smart suit with a red dicky bow standing on a beach holding a small gun. The title was in bold letters: *The St Lucia Sleuth* by David J. Ellis.

Josie was delighted. 'Oh, he's done it – he's written the whole book and had it published.'

'The man you met on the cruise last spring?' Lin asked.

'Yes, I'm so pleased for him.' Josie opened the first page, touching the creamy white paper. Then she glanced at the dedication:

For Alan, the man I love, and for Josie, who saved my life.

Josie and Lin turned to each other. 'That's so nice,' Lin whispered.

'I'll treasure this,' Josie said, feeling suddenly emotional. 'Like I'll treasure the Silver Ladies' lunches, and every precious moment we have together.'

Lin wrapped her friend in a hug and saw tears glisten in Josie's eyes. She waited for her own to fill up, and was surprised when they didn't. But Lin was calm now; she was in control. She turned to the guests and raised her voice.

'More cake everyone? Rum punch? There's plenty where that came from... just help yourselves.' She whispered to Josie, 'It's like Miss Hamilton used to say – good friends are like four-leafed clovers. But here in Middleton Ferris, we have a whole field of them...'

ACKNOWLEDGMENTS

Thanks always to my agent, Kiran Kataria, for her wisdom, professionalism and integrity. Huge thanks to Sarah Ritherdon who is the smartest, most encouraging editor anyone could wish for.

Thanks to Amanda Ridout, Nia Beynon, Claire Fenby, Jenna Houston, Rachel Gilbey and to the generous, supportive family of Boldwood Books. I have so much appreciation for everyone who has worked to make this book happen: designers, editors, technicians, magicians, voice actors, bloggers, fellow writers – thanks to you all.

As always, thanks to beloved friends who continue to support me with kind words, hugs and wine. Thanks to Jan, Rog, Jan M, Helen, Ken, Trish, Lexy, Shaz, Gracie, Mya, Frank, Erika, Rich, Susie, Ian, Chrissie, Kathy N, Julie, Martin, Steve, Rose, Steve's Mum, Nik R, Pete O', Martin, Cath, Dawn, Slawka, Katie H, Jonno, Norman, Angela.

So much thanks to Peter, Avril and the Solitary Writers, my writing buddies.

Love to my awesome neighbours and to the local Somerset community, especially Jenny, Claire, Paul, Gary and Sophie and everyone at Bookshop by the Blackdowns.

Much thanks to the talented Ivor Abiks at Deep Studios.

Thanks to cousins Ellen from Florida and Jo from Taunton, to Robin and Edward from Colorado, and to teachers everywhere.

Love to my mum, who showed me the joy of reading, and to my dad, who proudly never read a thing. Special love to our Tony and Kim.

Love always to Liam, Maddie, Cait, and most of all, to my soulmate, Big G.

Warmest thanks to my readers, wherever you are. You make this journey incredible.

MORE FROM JUDY LEIGH

We hope you enjoyed reading *The Silver Ladies Do Lunch*. If you did, please leave a review.

If you'd like to gift a copy, this book is also available as an ebook, paperback, large print, digital audio download and audiobook CD.

Sign up to Judy Leigh's mailing list for news, competitions and updates on future books:

http://bit.ly/JudyLeighNewsletter

Explore more fun, uplifting reads from Judy Leigh:

FIVE FRENCH HENS
JUDY LEIGH
THE OLD GIRLS' NETWORK
JUDY LEIGH
HEADING OVER THE HILL
JUDY LEIGH
CHASING THE SUN
JUDY LEIGH
LIL'S BUS TRIP
JUDY LEIGH
THE GOLDEN GIRLS' GETAWAY
JUDY LEIGH
A YEAR OF MY MAYBES
JUDY LEIGH
THE HIGHLAND HENS
JUDY LEIGH
THE GOLDEN OLDIES' BOOK CLUB
JUDY LEIGH
THE SILVER LADIES DO LUNCH
JUDY LEIGH

ABOUT THE AUTHOR

Judy Leigh is the bestselling author of *A Grand Old Time* and *Five French Hens* and the doyenne of the 'it's never too late' genre of women's fiction. She has lived all over the UK from Liverpool to Cornwall, but currently resides in Somerset.

Visit Judy's website: https://judyleigh.com

Follow Judy on social media:

facebook.com/judyleighuk
twitter.com/judyleighwriter
instagram.com/judyrleigh
bookbub.com/authors/judy-leigh

Printed in the USA
CPSIA information can be obtained
at www.ICGtesting.com
LVHW031050190124
769407LV00009B/69